Mrs. Shumak's Boarding House

by Marty Kam

with Nick Reiff

MKO
PRESS

Mrs Shumak's Boarding House

Copyright © 2006 Martin E. Kam

ISBN 13: 978-09786823-0-9
ISBN 10: 0-9786823-0-0

Second Edition

For information contact MKO Press

www.mkopress.com

In memory of Susie

Acknowledgements

I would like to thank Grace Barker, Nick Kam, Thia Rogan, Rachael Coleman, Jonathan Gullery and Alan Salabert for their help with this book.

"You know…sometimes…you just never know…you know?"
—Bert Wodehouse

"Some coffee? I roast my own beans. They're shade grown, from Guatemala."

Masters raised his eyebrows with amusement. "Interesting. Thank you, then, I think I *will* have a coffee."

Inside, the breakfast table was in the midst of being abandoned; Mrs. Noonan and Mr. Manicotti remained at opposite ends of the table, and Claude was pensively inspecting a halved grapefruit. Alan Berman was in the living room, down the hall, watching TV (as always); the Johnsons were gone.

No sign of the deranged brother, Masters observed.

"Have a seat," Mary instructed. "Billy, bring the gentleman a cup and saucer." She cast a glance at Collin and caught him staring, but he didn't avert his eyes; he had a look of absolute confidence and gravity, as if a hurricane couldn't move him. His face, his hands, his crossed legs and Gucci shoes—all seemed perfectly composed, planned, rock solid. His eyes twinkled at her.

"Who are all these people?" Masters asked. "Your family?"

"They're boarders," Mary answered, as Billy arrived with the cup and saucer. "Billy, say hi."

"Hello," Billy said sourly. "Can I go now?"

"Billy, is it?" Masters asked with a paternal smile.

"You can call me *William*." He didn't smile back.

"You're excused, William," Mary said, shrugging and pouring out a cup of coffee.

"Boarders, eh?" Collin mused.

"They all get a check every month—disability or Social Security or something. I make meals and take care of the little things. Some of them need help."

"Are you a nurse?"

"No," Mary said with a shadow in her voice. "Just getting by, and helping people as I can."

"That's wonderful. Really. So tell me about the house. How old is it?"

"Records say 1762, built by the Von Haagen family. Germans, obviously. How's the coffee?"

"Lovely. Really delicious. Have you lived here long?"

"It belongs to my husband's family. I moved in sixteen years ago. So, a while."

"So it belongs to your husband?"

Mary cleared her throat.

"I guess I should have been clearer. Brian's dead. My husband... died six years ago." She rubbed the back of her neck, and cleared her throat again.

Brian's dead.

That never, ever sounded right.

"I'm very sorry, Mary. Terribly sorry." He pursed his lips somberly for a moment. "So," he said at last. "You now own the house?"

"Yes. It's mine. I'm going to pass it along to Billy and Sarah. It's their legacy."

Collin nodded thoughtfully.

"Really, really fine coffee, Mary." He clapped his hands together. "You think I could have a look around?"

The two of them toured the first floor, with its cavernous, antique rooms of twelve to fifteen-foot ceilings, corroded moldings, oak furniture, and *clutter*. It was as if the detritus of two hundred years of escalating consumerism had built up without abatement, leaving a stupendous, dusty flotsam of junk—bald eagle commemorative plates and porcelain unicorn statuettes, cat-themed tissue box holders, cherub figurines, chipped lighthouse models, stacks of Life and Time and National Geographics that seemed to date back to the Monroe Administration.

Mary wasn't much for cleaning, Collin gathered, stepping over some debilitated Barbies and GI Joes that were strewn in the middle of the hallway. Then again, how could one person ever hope to keep up with a house this huge?

The basement was full of cardboard boxes—more clutter, except contained and hidden. Decorated pinecones and broken model airplane wings emerged, coated in cobwebs, from the gloom. The place smelled dank, like dry rot and water damage and seeping brownness; the stench, Masters thought, of fermenting teddy bears.

"Brian's family had difficulty throwing anything away," Mary explained. "And I just don't have time. I guess one day I'll get around to chucking all this junk." Masters nodded, walking carefully so as not to get any cobwebs or dirt on his suit.

They emerged back upstairs and Collin took a seat at the dining room table. The TV was blaring reruns of Sanford and Son down the hall, where Alan sat, clipboard in hand, recording information about today's episode in clear, minuscule handwriting.

"Mrs. Shumak," Collin said, popping open his attaché case. "It occurs to me that a house like this could be quite a burden for one person to handle. I mean, the upkeep alone is overwhelming. I can see that. Not to *mention* the property taxes." He looked Mary in the eye. "I love this house. It's fantastic. Which is why I'd like to buy it from you."

Mary blanched. She suddenly remembered what Ned had said over breakfast, and suddenly the suit and the Escalade made more sense.

"I'm sorry, Mr. Masters," she said. "It's not for sale."

"Look, I know the house has a great deal of significance to you. You want to leave your children with a good legacy. But this house is *not* a good legacy. It's beautiful and historic, but in its current state it's already depreciating fast and it's a fire hazard. Surely you can see that. The repairs you'd need to make to bring this place up to code would be *very* expensive."

"Up to code for what?" Mary said, a slow chill filling her chest. Something like a threat seemed to be forming before her very eyes, right where a pleasant architectural historian had sat a few minutes before.

"For having boarders. Especially boarders with mental deficiencies. Frankly, some people in the county government might think—if they saw the condition of the house—that those boarders of yours are at risk."

"They're not at risk," Mary told him sharply. "This is their *home.*"

"That may be. But let's look at the facts, Mary. You've got mold. You've got infestations. You've got a shifting, cracked foundation. Maybe even some lead-based paint. Your roof is leaking."

Mary was getting flushed. Masters pointed a finger at her.

"Any inspector is going to see all that in a second. Hell, they might even order the place demolished. I don't want that to happen. You don't want that to happen. It's home, but home is where the heart is, right?"

"Oh please, Mr. Masters," Mary said bitterly.

"I'm offering you a very, very generous sum," Masters said, taking a cashier's check from his briefcase and sliding it across the table. Mary looked at it without picking it up.

It was for $250,000. It seemed like a small sum for such a large house and all that land.

"Invest that money and you and your kids will have a nest egg for college. For expenses. For a down payment on a nice new house. One without the kind of structural problems this one has."

A real estate contract had appeared on the table.

"No," Mary said. "No, I'm not selling. I'll never sell it."

"I won't make this offer again. It's very generous and you know it."

"Mr. Masters, you should go now."

"Life will become very difficult if county inspectors come over and see what I've seen."

"Get out," Mary said hotly. "*Now.*"

Masters looked at her with his blank, chubby face, sighed a bit ruefully, and put the contract back in his briefcase. He shut it deliberately, with a crisp snap.

"I gave you a chance, Mrs. Shumak," Masters said, rising from the table. "Everything that happens here on out is your own fault. Thank you for the coffee. Don't bother rising. I can find my own way out."

Mary stayed at the table, stewing until Masters was gone; once she heard the screen door slap shut, she got up and hurried into the front hall. In the corridor she nearly collided with Bert. She got one good look at his face and knew immediately that he had been listening.

"Were you *eavesdropping*, Bert?" she snapped, cornering him between the doorway and the wall.

"I was looking for something," he said, looking a bit wild. "I thought I'd left a pen by the phone..."

"You were *eavesdropping*."

"Okay, alright, fine," Bert said, rolling his eyes, "So I happened to hear a bit of your conversation. Is that so wrong? I wanted to know what was going on in there. You know? I'm just looking out for you, sis. That's *all*."

"Well, I hope you had fun," Mary said tensely, moving towards the door to watch the Cadillac pulling back down the drive.

Bert fidgeted for a moment, and then blurted out, "I met him yesterday. On the road. He was looking at the house with a pair of binoculars. He gave me his card."

"Where is it?"

"I threw it away. But he's not an architectural historian at all, Mary. He's a developer. Ned was right."

"A developer," Mary said quietly. "Yeah. I guess that makes sense." She turned back to Bert, and managed a smile. "Well, I'm sure it's nothing." After a thoughtful pause, she pointed a finger at Bert, and said with mock seriousness, "But I don't want you sneaking around here any more, you hear? Not even with the best motives."

Bert winked at her, and smiled. "I'll do what I can, but I've gotta warn you, sis– a leopard can't change his spots."

4

After breakfast the next morning—a Saturday—Mary decided to run a few errands in town. Sarah came with her; Billy was much too busy in his room to be bothered with a trip into Lewiston. They walked to the garage where the '85 Caprice was parked. It was a dull brown color, certainly not winning any beauty contests with its bondoed doors and fenders. Still, it ran all right and it was built like a tank; it was a car that refused to roll quietly into the night.

The engine started with a solid rumble and they pulled down the drive, Sarah scrolling through country western stations and NPR and static and evangelists with a tremor of sweaty fanaticism in their voices. Mary was trying to remind herself about the various things she had to do in town; food supplies for the coming week, a package to be picked up at the post office, a new bottle of Clorox bleach.

Her thoughts simply wouldn't stay on any of *that*, however; they kept returning to the man who had been in her house the day before—and the threats he had made. Collin Masters was exactly the kind of man she had always loathed, more for the system he represented than for his moral deficiencies, since it seemed to Mary that people would be more moral, more human, if the system itself weren't so greedy, so cutthroat, so Darwinian. Who knows, in a different world a greedy son of a bitch like Collin Masters might be a decent person, somebody you'd invite over for coffee or see at church.

Why on earth did he want the house so badly? His card said *developer*. His brother: also a developer. The conclusion seemed painfully, unpleasantly clear. She no longer believed that he had the slightest interest in Greek Revival architecture, or the history of the House on the Bend, or really anything having to do with the house at all. During his tour, she thought, he'd examined the place as you would knowing that it would soon be gone.

Looking at it in the past tense.

Damn him.

It's our home.

Lewiston appeared gradually, first clusters of trailer parks and a few sleazy motels, followed by streets of frame houses with plywood porches and peeling vinyl siding and crabgrass lawns. Turning onto main street, there were the former mansions of the captains of Lewiston industry: the Furtzwater Mansion, the Peabody house, mostly carved up into cramped tenements for migrant Mexican workers, or else boarded up and blackened with streaks of fire damage. Homeless people pushed shopping carts overflowing with wadded up clothes and boxes and plastic implements, pausing to pick through overflowing trashcans. There were water-damaged couches on lawns. Rusty refrigerators. Lawn chairs reduced to aluminum skeletons. Battered maroon Oldsmobiles parked in broken glass sprays in the humid air.

And then suddenly at 15th Street it turned on a dime, the mansions had big new windows and giant signs announcing the sale of new condominium units that featured granite counter-tops and hardwood floors; Land Rovers were parked curbside, "Historic Lewiston" signs hung on Victorian-style lampposts. Residences gave way to commercial buildings at 4th.

The last graffiti was disappearing as facades were repainted bright reds and blues and canary yellows. Everywhere was the sound of sawing and hammering and renewal. On the right was Al's Diner. Mary slowed down to look inside. To her annoyance it looked pretty busy. A cute antique store had opened next door.

The neighborhood looked very different back when the Pax Café had been there; it had been bounded on one side by a pawnshop and on the other by an abandoned building. In those days, Lewiston was engaged in a downward slide that showed no signs of slowing, with layoffs every day and shops closing up all along Main Street, a steady procession of going out of business sales and last minute clearances as the lifeblood drained out of the city. In the midst of that climate of heartbreak and despair came young Mary Shumak, straight out of the University of Pittsburgh's philosophy program. She'd grown up in Lewiston, down on Temple Street in a frame house that later was torn down for parking lot space; she left town just as things were going from bad to worse and then reluctantly came back, abandoning a stint in the Peace Corps to care for her ailing father.

Her first job on returning to Lewiston was at a corner diner that had occupied the first floor of the brick Fullerton Building since 1921, one of the old style lunch counters that already, in the early 80s, were an endangered species. She poured weak coffee and served omelets and patty melts all day for meager tips—*really* miserable ones, even by rural Pennsylvania standards, usually just a few coppers, a bit of silver, and a good helping of pocket lint. The first winter she was concerned with her father, who got steadily worse in his tiny apartment, coughing and shivering under a blanket, refusing to see some "quack doctor," complaining of a giant weight on his head that pressed and pressed and pressed—

And then, mercifully, in early February, John Wodehouse had a heart attack and died. Bert was nowhere to be found— later she discovered that he was trying to sell swampland to retirees in Florida at the time—so it was up to her to cover the funeral expenses. When the day came it was an inauspicious occasion featuring a pine box and an icy ceremony attended by a few drinking buddies of John's, and Mary's Aunt Ethel.

Her father's will left Mary a surprisingly good amount of money remaining from his pension, as he had subsisted on ramen noodles and peanut butter sandwiches; John Wodehouse had been a fanatic spendthrift who had derived an almost erotic pleasure from pinching a penny where he could. Mary decided that she'd better put the money to use before Bert swung into town with some bizarre scheme that needed financing—a new orange sun block he was working on, say, or an investment in a Chinese fireworks factory.

She'd noticed that, despite a dearth of jobs or money in Lewiston, everybody still managed to scrape together enough change for a morning cup of coffee. She'd been a great devotee of coffee houses in Pittsburgh—she loved open mic nights at Hemmingway's, or the cozy yellow closeness of the 61C in winter. A coffeehouse was more than just coffee: it was nourishment for the soul, a nexus of ideas, a place to challenge and soothe. She called up a friend in Pittsburgh who had a hookup with a Guatemalan coffee cooperative. She researched coffee roasters and shopped around at Goodwill and Salvation Army for secondhand furniture that was shabby enough to be cool, but not so shabby as to be junk. She got a hold of every local artist she could think of and asked them for paintings and photographs. She joined BMG music club and put together an eclectic collection of music, ranging from the Ramones to Deep Forest. She bought a Panini machine.

In late September, she opened the Pax Café.

Opening day was a smash. The place was full of people eating free muffins and enjoying the rotating music acts, mostly folk, with a bit of poetry thrown in for good measure. Business didn't drop off much after that. Immediately there was a legion of die hard regulars who came every day, sometimes twice; there were morning regulars and there were evening ones.

Mary used the café as a platform for raising awareness about a number of important issues: the repression of the people of Tibet, the massive death toll in Angola's civil war, the civil wars in Central America. She invited speakers and gave pride of place to local artists who tackled these issues, or at least gave it a shot.

She got to be on a first name basis with almost all of her customers, with the mod artists and the hipster writers and the slouching jean-jacket ex-factory workers. And so when a young, good-looking guy in a blue dress shirt and a big belt buckle showed up one day, looking amused and inquisitive, she had to scout him out.

Although Brian Shumak was very handsome, he was not immediately attractive to Mary. He'd been a Lewiston resident all his life but lately he'd been traveling around the northeast selling cutlery. And not just any cutlery, he told her without the faintest hint of irony, but possibly the *best cutlery the world has ever seen.* The handles were made of bowling ball material; the rivets were nickel; the tang (the piece of metal that extends into the handle) was full, meaning that it went all the way in, not just half way like a lot of inferior knives. The steel was the star of the show. This wasn't your average steel: this was surgical steel of the highest possible grade. A good set of knives wasn't just a purchase. It was an investment.

This could, very possibly, be the last set of knives you will ever buy.

Mary started laughing.

"Why are you laughing?" he asked her.

"It's all so ridiculous. I mean, come on. Really."

At twenty dollars for a paring knife—it went up from there—Brian Shumak did very well for himself on commissions. He had an intensity to the way he spoke, a way of making you feel very important and interesting and privileged that he felt so benevolently towards you.

"I'm not following," Brian said, looking slightly vexed.

"Frankly, I think it's all a bunch of crap," Mary said.

"What is?"

"You know, buying and selling and wanting stuff all the time."

"It's what makes the world go round, Mary."

"It's killing the world. We should be concentrating on love, not what things we're going to hoard next."

"That's all fine for a bunch of hippies, but let's be honest. Would the Roman Empire have existed but for greed? Huh? What about this country? The United States of America? All our bridges and skyscrapers and highways—it's all because we wanted *more*."

"*More* leads to children being soldiers. And if greed built this country, then it's killing it too. Lewiston is dying because everybody started craving something else, and nobody gives a damn about the people who got left behind."

"Survival of the fittest, my dear."

"That's a horrible way to look at things."

"Fortune favors the bold."

"What about 'the meek shall inherit the earth'?"

"I'm pretty sure He was speaking metaphorically. Look, I'm not saying that we've got to go around clubbing each other. I'm just saying that we do great things because we're driven to by competition, by the fire of desire, sorry for rhyming."

"But that leads to so much misery!"

"Gotta break a few eggs..."

Their first conversation left Mary angry and Brian irritated. But despite that they never missed a chance to spar on Saturday afternoons. If Mary thought religion was dead, Brian thought it was stronger than ever. If Mary thought Art was the key to the human condition, Brian thought it was a complete waste of time. Imperialism in the Third World was horrible; no, it was modernizing! Modernization was robbing cultures of their distinctiveness; who cared, it they got medicines and education! Who cared about a bunch of shrunken-head shaman mumbo jumbo anyhow?

Mary vs. Brian.

Finally, one night they ended up having dinner at a burger joint nearby, splitting a bottle of cheap Chianti out behind his huge family house just outside of town, and somewhere along the way they ended up kissing and then suddenly making love in the grass under the trees.

They made love as an extension of their arguments, and the same frustration that made Mary red-faced and stuck a barb into Brian's cool façade turned their dalliances into some kind of competitive sport. The battle was played out in the back of Brian's car, in the café after the lights were turned out, in the woods by Brian's house and on Mary's kitchen table. They went at it like wrestlers, until one tapped out. They played it out three times a day, until they were too sore to do it again.

Mary was pregnant four months later. They got married soon after that.

They were friends, which helped matters a bit. But the truth was that they wouldn't have gotten married except for Billy, and they both knew it. Brian was busy with work and they made love a lot less and argued about new things, like money and chores and who did what around the house, arguments that didn't thrill, only angered. The Tibetans never seemed to come up any more.

Mary managed to hang onto the Café until Sarah was born. Then, realizing that her life as she'd known it had changed beyond all recognition, she sold the café and said goodbye to the person she thought she was going to be.

Now she was Mom.

The horrible thing about life and love, Mary thought, is that you *always* take it for granted.

Day in and day out, a routine goes on. The squabbles and the "I'm mad" vs. "you can't be mad because I am," the push and pull and getting on with life, negotiations that weave from one day into the next, and all the while Mary wondering where she'd gone astray, why despite every intention to the contrary she'd ended up just like her mother—

And then, one day, she got a phone call.

Brian Shumak had flipped his car on the Pennsylvania turnpike. He wasn't wearing his seatbelt and he'd been thrown through the windshield as the Ford Taurus did cartwheels, shedding hubcaps and bits of fiberglass. He sailed through the air, landed, and continued the cartwheeling motion, except in miniature. When he stopped finally he was broken in a hundred pieces and dead.

When her mother died, Mary had been in high school. She had largely ignored the problem of her dead mother by concentrating on piano class and painting, and she succeeded, mostly, in compressing that vast chill into a little place somewhere inside. Her mother *was*; then she *wasn't*. Life goes on.

When her father died, she did the same thing. She distracted herself with affairs of the estate and figuring out a way to invest the money. She told herself that a heart attack was merciful. She put that abrupt awfulness away, on the shelf next to her mother.

Now Brian was dead. Her children had a lot of difficulty understanding what was happening, Sarah especially. She played with her dolls obliviously as Mary and Billy sat in terrible silence in the vast emptiness of the Shumak house.

At first Mary was furious, because her reaction to anything bad was to get angry. She was furious that Brian hadn't worn his seatbelt, furious that she was on her own now with two kids and no job, furious that she was in this position at all, when this wasn't the life she'd wanted in the first place.

Then she realized something.

It's not all about you.

Brian was her partner in this giant compromise. She's stopped seeing him at all, really, as anything except a lump in the bed next to her and a man at the breakfast table, but the fact was they were partners, and that he'd given up just as much as she had.

She felt the seals against all the grief she'd saved up beginning to burst.

She'd neglected Brian, because she'd seen him as the door barring her path. Now she saw that she'd done both of them a terrible disservice: she'd squandered a chance to know him, to have had a marriage that was more than just a financial arrangement. All the ingredients were there.

But she'd been too damned selfish.

That was how the House came to be her new love, her posthumous promise to Brian, her last chance to make something beautiful out of what she'd wasted.

Collin Masters didn't know about any of this, and he didn't care.

He wanted to take the last thing that was of her husband and tear it down.

The question was why.

Mary pulled into the parking lot of the Wal-Mart Superstore that dominated the eastern edge of downtown, a great behemoth of cheerful blue and gray that was parked up to the hilt with Saturday shoppers, shopping carts left abandoned and rolling wistfully in the breeze. Sarah was immediately excited to be here. There was some strange, dark magic about Wal-Mart that excited people, and it wasn't just children. The people heading into Wal-Mart seemed to share a look of happiness and expectation, as if something wonderful was awaiting them inside.

Within, it was madness: a sea of jostling NASCAR hats and gray pony tails, ratty children in stretched-out Pooh t-shirts, Mexican families of diminutive stature moving about in herd-like formation.

"Mommy, *can* we?" Sarah said, pointing at a large display of cheap plastic jewelry by the entrance. "Can we *please?*"

"Get a cart, honey."

Sarah got a cart. This was pure excitement. After a week of being cooped up at the house all day, with just Billy and Uncle Bert and Alan Berman for company, a trip to Wal-Mart was something transporting, not unlike a visit to the circus. Behold, the endless rows of shiny plastic and inexpensive foods, the smell of nacho cheese, the blaring of announcements on the PA and the excitement of never knowing what loot she might score this time. Then there was the added thrill of handling the cart, of maneuvering it skillfully through the isles, around stationary carts and old women considering different skin creams, then blasting, free and clear, onto the fluorescent boulevard—and then down the next canyon, onto the next obstacle. When she was younger she'd always loved riding on the bottom rack, until one time she'd unwisely stuck her finger into the wheel and gotten a chunk of skin ripped off; after that, actually *piloting* the cart seemed far more sensible.

They were in the food section. Mary had to buy everything in bulk, and she was busy stacking crates of eggs in the cart when Tom Johnson, Ned and Vera's son, walked by, holding a basket full of frozen Pillsbury biscuits.

"Mary! Sarah!" He smiled. He had Ned's smile, but he was lean and tough looking, without the thoughtful drawl of his father. "Stocking up for the week, huh?"

Mary put the last eggs in the cart.

"How's business?" she asked him. She studied his thick arms and shoulders. He was a contractor and looked hardened.

"Good, real good. You know. There's a lot happening. I've got a couple projects over on Central. Remodeling. You know." He smiled at her, cleared his throat, and smiled a different smile at Sarah. "School starting pretty soon, huh?"

"Yes," Sarah confirmed unhappily.

"Junior High," Mary said. "Baby's growing up."

"*Mom.*"

"So everything's good over at the house?" Tom asked, shifting feet.

"Everything's great." Mary paused for a moment, and licked her lips. "Actually, there *was* something. Do you know a guy named Collin Masters?"

"Oh, yeah," Tom said vigorously. "Victor Masters' brother. Between the two of them they own half-a downtown. Victor's the big guy. Collin's the hatchet man."

"You ever work for them?"

"Naw," Tom said, making a face. "He always works with Jim Primanti. Some kinda *special* deal."

"Uh-huh."

"Why?"

"Collin Masters came over yesterday. Wanted to buy the house."

Tom snorted. "You told him to go to hell, right?"

"I sure did."

"That's good. People like them Masters, they think *everything's* got a price tag."

The PA suddenly demanded a cleanup in the men's bathroom.

"Why do you think he'd want to buy my house, Tom?"

"It's pretty far from town. I don't know. Must be some reason, though."

"Yeah, right." Mary shrugged quickly, and let her hands slap her thighs. "Oh well."

"I'll see you around, Mary." Tom squeezed Mary's arm and smiled.

"Come out to the house sometime," she said. "I'm sure Ned and Vera would like to see you."

Tom made an uncomfortable face. "Soon as I can."

Next up was the pancake mix, and maple syrup, and coffee filters. Sarah's Wal-Mart enchantment was beginning to wear off. She was no longer zooming around with the cart. This, too, was part of the Wal-Mart experience. First, came elation. Then followed over-saturation and exhaustion. At checkout you found blank-faced, conquered parents battling their shrill children, everyone ill from an overdose of sugary *more*.

They were in line. Sarah was champing at the impulse buy racks, her fingers tracing gum and Snickers bars and Slim Jims. A heavy, red faced woman was loudly complaining that a Daffy Duck sweatshirt had been clearly marked on the rack to be $6.99, yet the computer, brazenly, insisted on $13.99. The call for a price check went out. A tide of exhaustion, like a psychic groan, moved through the line.

Next to the impulse buy racks were the magazines and newspapers, among them the dreadful, comic book-thin Lewiston Observer.

Front page: "Casino Rights for Second Riverboat go to Master Developments."

Below: "Several Sites for new Riverboat dock considered, but mum's the word."

"Mum's the word": normally its use in a front-page headline would have riled Mary, but she was too busy looking at the photo to notice.

White suit, shaking hands with a member of the Lewiston chamber of commerce, looking like an older version of the chubby worm tongue who had visited her house the day before.

Victor Masters.

A casino boat.

Son of a bitch.

She picked up the newspaper and added it to the cart.

5

Although he did very little during the week, Saturday morning still had a special significance to Bert. He didn't have breakfast with the others; instead he took a box of Lucky Charms and a half-gallon of 2% and sat—in his underwear and a pitted-out T-shirt—in front of the TV, channel surfing through the offerings of cartoons, news shows, and evangelist telethons. Whereas weekday mornings the TV was mired in a dully predictable sludge of smarmy announcers and cute banter—which the average day worker took some demented comfort in, he supposed—weekend TV had an unpredictable aspect to it. You never knew quite what you would end up watching.

Mid-morning he had finished with his Lucky Charms binge, the coffee table a crime scene spattered with milk and sugary marshmallows, and was reclining in a most unflattering pose, legs splayed, when Alan Berman and Claude came in. Alan had his clipboard, which could only mean one thing: he meant to wrest control of the TV away from Bert.

"Why don't you go outside for a change?" Bert suggested preemptively.

"It's hot and sticky out there," Alan said matter-of-factly. "Anyways, I have some work to do." He reached for the remote.

"*Excuse* me, I happen to be watching this."

"You're not even paying attention."

"Sure I am."

"I can see it in your eyes, Mr. Wodehouse."

Claude shook his head either with vexation or disapproval.

"I happen to be enjoying this..." Bert paused, to glance at the TV—"Documentary about the Battle of Stalingrad."

"You just scroll from one program to the next," Alan complained. "You never really watch anything."

"That's because it's mostly crap."

Alan snatched away the remote.

"If you have that attitude then you won't mind watching Magnum, PI." He switched the channel to 49. The credits were rolling: Magnum, grinning in the cockpit of the Ferrari; TC, in his Island Hopper helicopter. Alan sat down with the clipboard, and clicked his pen into readiness. They watched the show in silence for a little while. It was one of the Vietnam episodes, dealing with Magnum's wife. Bert had never liked these episodes: he respected the show for tackling Vietnam and all, but come on. Let's get back to Rick getting punched in the nose and Higgins building his model bridge.

Alan was feverishly making notes.

"What are you writing?" Bert asked.

"Character information."

"About Magnum?"

"Please. You're distracting me."

At the ad break, Alan sat back with a sigh and stretched his hand. He was left-handed, so there was smeared ink all over his palm.

"What's after Magnum?" Bert asked. "Airwolf is on after that, right?"

"No, then I switch over to Batman: The Animated Series on the WB. They show the new, inferior episodes early; the episodes from the Emmy-winning first run are on at 11:00."

"Emmy winning, huh?"

"There was a double length episode about the creation of Two-Face. Bruce Wayne struggles with despair as his best friend, Harvey Dent, goes mad and becomes a super villain. It sounds campy, but it's not at all. It's heartbreaking."

"Adam West never won an Emmy."

"His show was very different. A big difference—the key to it all, I think—is Chief O'Hara."

"Chief O'Hara?"

"The Irish Chief of Police who hangs around with Commissioner Gordon in the Adam West series."

Bert had watched the Adam West series maybe ten times.

"Oh?"

"O'Hara—who dates from the Silver Age comics—doesn't appear in the Animated Series (itself inspired by Tim Burton's movie and Frank Miller's comic The Dark Knight Returns) because he is Camp Personified. He's a walking stereotype, the essence of Adam West's acting, the color scheme of the Batcave, the wackiness of Joker's plots. By contrast, in the Animated Series, O'Hara has been replaced with gritty Detective Bullock, an overweight, toothpick-chewing, hardnosed cop."

"Another stereotype."

"Yes, but a very different kind of stereotype. Bullock is a dark character; O'Hara is comic. They are, oddly, a miniature version of the attitude of the shows."

"What about in the new episodes? The ones earlier Saturday?"

"The update? Crap, pure crap. No Bullock *or* Chief O'Hara. They made it for kids. No respect for the source material. They take the poetry out of Batman."

Suddenly Magnum returned.

Mrs. Noonan joined them. She whistled to herself, quietly, asking, "Who's the man in the moustache?" or "What's happening?" every three or four minutes. Bert watched Alan grow agitated, but he wasn't letting up on the note taking.

Another ad break.

"How do you decide what to watch?" Bert asked him.

"I have a method."

"What is it?"

"I'd rather not discuss it, actually."

"*THAT'S A PICKLE!*" declared Claude.

"Oh yes, oh my," Mrs. Noonan said agreeably.

There was a newsbreak from WGNN Lewiston. John Hernandez and Ellie Hong appeared on a faded set after a burst of dynamic music.

"Coming up on the news at 11:00—local mega-developer Victor Masters wins the contract for a *second* casino riverboat, though he hasn't disclosed the site of the development. Supporters say 'the more the merrier' for the economy, but opponents are crying foul, with accusations of back room dealing."

Victor Masters appeared, looking puffy faced and out of breath at a news conference. His brother Collin was standing next to him.

"We are considering several sites for the new riverboat casino. We're currently in talks with a number of local landowners. We're going to put Lewiston squarely back on the map in Eastern Pennsylvania. We expect a huge upsurge in casino tourism with the opening of the second boat: Bluebeard's Pirate Clipper!"

The shot cut back to the anchors.

"Representatives from Master Developments have said that the new boat will be much larger and more theme-oriented than the Master Plays casino riverboat on Lewiston's waterfront."

"Cadillac Man, Cadillac Man," Bert said, whistling. "You want to park that big bastard right here, don't you?"

"Shhh!" Alan hissed. "Magnum's coming back!"

Suddenly Bert was too agitated to sit still any more. He got up and left the room.

Alan was glad. Bert was intrusive, and worse still he fell into the class of people who Didn't Take TV Seriously. They were the channel surfers, the talk-during-the-show-ers, the people who thought nothing of zoning out to MTV2 or the Shopping Channel. As people went, Bert wasn't bad. But he liked Claude better. When Claude wasn't sweeping the house, he just sat there with a benevolent look on his face—occasionally fogged with a hint of inexplicable worry. He never said anything except his tag line, which he uttered whenever things were heating up. Alan didn't know anything about Claude. He hadn't *heard* anything about Claude, either. Claude had just shown up one day with a State disability check and a little leather suitcase.

Another thing Alan didn't like about Bert was how *messy* he was. His clothes were always wrinkled, often soiled, and never matched; his shoes smelled. He had a very bad haircut and his teeth had never been touched by an orthodontist. His attitude slouched as much as he did. Bert was a perfect example of the sweating, misshapen, restless human animal.

Finding out things about people was invariably upsetting. Behind every façade were grief and tears and family muck. It made him feel the viscosity of humanness just to think of it.

People are dirty.

TV was not.

On TV things had symmetry, and things were clean and orderly and ended at the top of the hour. Yet that didn't mean that the world of TV wasn't complex. On the contrary, to really think about TV was a daunting task. Alan would lie awake at night trying to plan his TV watching for the next day. The urgency of it made him sweat. He'd toss and turn. The vast wall of TV programming, past and present, from the Brady Bunch to Lonesome Dove to Charles in Charge to Arrested Development, it was thrilling and awful at the same time. He knew with a certainty that he could never hope to see every episode of every show; even seeing a representative of every show was probably impossible, because every year there were new ones and sometimes good TV programs overlapped each other.

And there was the problem of Alan's age. He was only 23; it would be extremely difficult to catch up on all those years of TV greatness that he'd missed by virtue of not being alive yet. The Andy Griffith Show! Lassie! Dallas! The original Battlestar Gallactica! Thank God for reruns; they were the great equalizer of the TV world.

How he envied and pitied the channel flippers! They knew not what they missed, and so they were spared the agony of knowing all they could not hope to see. Seinfeld, for instance, he'd watched in syndication for several years, yet while he'd seen certain episodes again and again, there were so many clever details to the show that had yet eluded him. He'd only seen the Bubble Boy episode three times. That alone was almost enough to drive him to tears.

Alan kept his notes in plastic filing cases in his room. What had begun as a casual attempt to remember the names of characters on Dark Shadows had grown to include a catalogue of the cases on Law and Order. That had gotten wildly out of hand; the endlessness of the task had led him to the realization that he could spend forever just on Law and Order, all the while missing out on the brilliance of Babylon 5, the cleverness of M.A.S.H., the raw fun of the Dukes of Hazzard.

Too many shows. Too many characters.

So he began making catalogues of them all—plot points, character names and traits, notable guest appearances. He would look at the TV guide with the eye of a general preparing for battle, organizing a strategy for the week that would allow him:

1) Maximum exposure to each show of merit
2) Exposure to the maximum number of shows of merit
3) Exposure to shows that *could* be of merit but were so far unknown.

This last one sometimes ended fruitlessly: for instance, Alan's bad date with Elimidate or brief flirtation with Sex in the City—which he hated passionately.

Alan's Aunt Beth, with whom he'd lived after his mom went to rehab, had preferred daytime talk during the day and the shopping channel at night. She loved Montel and Geraldo and Jerry Springer. She watched "her stories" on the old Sony Trinitron that sat on her living room floor. It was missing quite a few buttons, probably consumed by her vile dog Fluffy, a dreadful, vicious, petty creature that was given unfettered rights of vandalism in the moldy, ranch-style Brownsville, PA home; it frequently urinated on the couch and shat on the floor, upon which Aunt Beth would pile newspapers. The dog shed, leaving caked hair on every surface, in every crevice and in the drinking glasses—hair even appeared in his morning bowl of Cheerios. Aunt Beth was a fat, red faced, asthmatic woman who smelled like early rot and queasy halitosis; her arms, big like cured hams, were blotchy with rashes. She breathed hard all the time, even when she was sitting still. She fried up Chef Boyardee and Spam for dinner five nights a week, and made a frozen pizza on the other two.

She let the toilets overflow and then blamed it on Alan. She let the dishes pile up until fat centipedes could be seen within, slinking about without fear; she shouted at Alan for letting things get so far. When he did try to wash a dish or unplug the toilet he'd hear her noisy breathing right behind him, monitoring him, finally seizing the dish in question and barking,

"Such a *dumb* kid, I swear to Christ." The effort of the exclamation made her gasp.

When Alan complained that the dog had pissed on his bed, she said that he was lucky to have a bed at all. He wasn't allowed to leave the house alone, nor was there a washing machine on the premises, so he slept on the floor for a month, until finally some canine feces appeared on the blanket and Aunt Beth was forced to change it at last. Alan developed asthma as well; he, too, started getting rashes on his arms.

One day when Alan was 17, Aunt Beth went out for the afternoon. Alan was left at home to watch TV. Sitting in the midst of that dog-piss-smelling living room, seeing Norm and Carla bantering was like a glass of cold water in the desert. It was one of three channels the damaged TV could pick up, but it was better than nothing.

Aunt Beth came home late in the afternoon and screamed. She had discovered that Fluffy was dead on the back porch. She wept and wept until her face sagged like a shriveled wet red balloon. Alan went out and looked at Fluffy's stiff body. The dog had actually gotten quite bald in its later years; there were great pink spots all over its belly.

Then, suddenly, Aunt Beth erupted into a volcanic rage, accusing Alan of killing her dog, telling him in a voice quite transformed and not unlike nails on a blackboard, that he had been jealous of Fluffy since day one, she'd seen it in his eyes, she knew that he'd been plotting to kill the dog for years, he'd probably been feeding Fluffy poison for weeks now, or maybe just a big dose of Clorox bleach the moment she left the house—

A second later and Aunt Beth was wielding a hammer, and with ponderous difficulty was trying to chase Alan around the house. He hadn't done anything to Fluffy. *Surely* she must know that. Alan was crying even though he hated Aunt Beth, hated Fluffy even more, and knew that Aunt Beth couldn't hit him with that hammer, not in a million years. He was crying because all at once he had the crashing knowledge that this was his life and there was no getting away from it.

Except there *was* getting away from it: Aunt Beth threw him right out onto the street. He had an old Steelers jacket and some beat up Wranglers and a unicorn T-shirt and that was it. He didn't have any money and he didn't know how to get any. He was hungry. He stood outside of the house, hoping she'd let him back in. She screamed that she'd have him arrested for murdering her dog. He really didn't want to go to jail, so he wandered off without any idea about where he might be going.

Finally the police did get Alan, while he was trying to steal a candy bar from 7-11. He was shaking from hunger. After talking with him, they took him home and then had a very stern chat with Aunt Beth, who feigned shock and told them that Alan was a "special" boy who'd left school on account of his "specialness;" he'd blamed himself for the death of the dog, it was awful, just awful, that he'd thought she was actually *angry* at him.

The police suggested she call the local Department of Human Services and they gave her the card of a social worker. Soon after the police were gone, Aunt Beth held up the card and hissed, "You're going to the nuthouse."

Alan wanted to watch TV that night, but Aunt Betty locked him in his room. He lay on his bed, rigid and furious, listening to the din of Aunt Betty's "stories" down in the living room.

He felt totally alone.

But it all turned out okay: in a couple of months he started getting an SSI check and he was packed off to Mrs. Shumak's house. After that, life improved greatly.

And now, best of *all*—Batman was on next.

A casino. As if one wasn't enough in Lewiston, now they wanted to build another.

Bert was on the porch in his boxers, blinking in the hot sun. He felt somehow responsible for all this, as if his chance meeting with Masters the Lesser on the road had set all this in motion. It was odd, feeling responsible for something, especially when he knew he wasn't.

If it wasn't for the free food, man, forget it, Bert thought.

I'd be *outta* here.

Mr. Manicotti appeared on the porch and produced a silver cigarette case.

"When're you gonna stop smoking, Giuseppe?" Bert asked, leaning on a peeling column.

"When I die," Mr. Manicotti answered with a smile as he lit a cigarette.

"Huh," Bert said with a little laugh. "I'll bet if the Masters brothers tried something like this with *your* house back in the day you'd have just had him whacked, right?"

"What you say?"

"Oh, nothin'" Bert said, folding his arms across his chest. "I'm just sayin', if somebody tried to muscle in on your territory back then... well, you know."

"I was a tailor," Manicotti answered in his thick Sicilian brogue. "I made a-suits."

"Concrete galoshes, more like it. Come on, Giuseppe, you can tell me. Come on. Capone? Right? You were a hit man?"

"I'm-a no hit," Mr. Manicotti insisted. He looked away, then glanced back, and saw Bert's eyebrows raised in expectation. "*What?* I once a-made a suit for Al's a-brother, Ralph." He paused in reflection. "He was a very big tipper."

"C'mon. Tool of choice: Tommy gun? Or piano wire?"

"You think a-Mr. Capone was a bad a-man? When I was in the Old a-Country, we had a-worse. And-a besides, Mr. Capone was from a-Chicago. I lived in Philly. How could I have a-worked for him?"

"But didn't you get your start in Chicago?" Bert prodded.

Mr. Manicotti paused uncomfortably. "I'm-a too old to remember."

Bert winked and cleared his throat. "Well, if you ever feel like talking—secret's safe with me."

Mr. Manicotti took a drag on his pall mall.

"I was a tailor." He winked back at Bert, and donning his panama hat, strolled down the verandah.

An engine was growling up the drive, and the Caprice appeared, loaded with groceries. Mary parked the car out front.

"Billy!" she called. "Get out here and help with the groceries!" She looked up at Bert, who was still leaning on a column, watching Sarah take the bags out of the trunk.

"Bert!" she said. "What're you doing half-naked on my porch?"

"Thinking," he answered. "Clothes just get in the way."

"Well, give us a hand."

Bert made a helpless face. "I'm in the middle of something important, Mary. Sorry. I really am."

"Sarah, honey, your Uncle Bert'll take that in," Mary said, relieving Sarah of some gallon jugs of orange juice. "Here."

Bert reluctantly descended from the porch and grabbed the orange juice.

"I saw that Masters guy on the news," he said. "His big brother's building a casino."

"Some kind of pirate boat," Mary said.

"Oh, you saw it too?"

"Bought the paper."

Bert nodded.

"Billy!" Mary shouted. "Sarah, go and get your brother."

"Canna I help?" Mr. Manicotti called from the verandah.

"You stay right where you are, Mr. Manicotti!" Mary told him. "But thank you just the same!"

"Why don't you let him carry something?" Bert suggested. "He asked if he could help, right?"

Mary gave him a dirty look.

"Well?" Bert said with a shrug. "Right? Didn't he?" They climbed the front steps. "So what do you think he's gonna do? Masters, I mean?"

"They said he was considering a couple spots," Mary said, pausing by the front door. "Maybe he'll just forget about us."

"Yeah," Bert said. "Maybe."

"I don't know," Mary said with a sigh. "Maybe I should have sold."

Bert made a face.

"Come on," he said. "You don't mean that."

"You're right."

"He can't have the house, Mary."

"No, he can't. We're keeping it."

"That's right. We are," Bert said.

"We're *keeping* it, and that's all there is to it," Mary insisted.

"And besides," Bert said with a laugh. "What's he gonna do? Send hit men?"

6

On Monday afternoon, at about three, Mrs. Noonan was preparing her usual afternoon tea. This consisted of a pot of rather weak Lipton English Breakfast, and scones and dainty finger sandwiches, usually devilled ham or tuna on Wonderbread with the crusts cut off. Mary kept a supply of paper doilies in the house for use in this daily ritual, to be placed under the pot on the old pewter tray.

"Just like Beaumont," Mrs. Noonan said as she brought out the tea to Ned, Vera, Mary, and Mr. Manicotti. Bert was inside watching TV with Alan, Claude was sweeping the upstairs, and the kids were out. Mrs. Noonan walked slowly, so slowly that Mary always worried that her arms would tire and the trembling platter would come tumbling to the ground; yet Mrs. Noonan stolidly refused help.

"I like to do it mah-self," she said when someone came to her aid. "Just like in Beaumont."

The people gathered at the porch table watched with great patience and some concern as Mrs. Noonan inched her way along, her feet encountering the door frame and hesitating, finding a way over the top while the pot trembled and clattered, her lips forming an "o" as she whistled a soft, nonsensical tune.

"You don't need help, Mrs. Noonan?" Ned blurted out, unable to contain himself.

"I like to do it mah-self."

Just like in Beaumont, it was a hot day full of cicadas and crickets and noisy birdsong.

And then there was the sound of an engine, coming up the drive. A white Ford Explorer appeared and cautiously approached the front of the house. It crawled to a stop. All eyes at the table were on the SUV, except for Mrs. Noonan, still intent on her glacial progression towards the table.

"Who do you suppose that is?" Ned wondered.

"I've got an idea," Mary answered darkly, jumping to her feet. "Everybody go on and enjoy the tea."

Mary came down from the porch and walked towards the Explorer, where two men in white short-sleeved button-downs and ties were getting out, squinting in the sun. One was bald and athletic; the other was curly haired and stocky. The stocky one saw Mary coming, and arranged his face into a blatantly ingenuous smile, all compressed lips and rosy cheeks.

"Mrs. Shumak?" he greeted with an extended hand that Mary ignored.

"Can I help you gentlemen?"

"We're Inspectors for the Pawnee County Department of Safety," the bald man announced in a threatening baritone. "We were informed that your house is in unsuitable condition for the boarding operation you're running here. We need to check it out."

"This is private property," Mary said firmly.

"We have a court order to inspect the premises," the squat inspector said apologetically, handing Mary a folded document on thick bond paper. "It would be best for everyone involved it you just let us do our job."

"You don't want to interfere with a court order, Mrs. Shumak," the bald man intoned.

Bert appeared on the verandah with a banging of the screen door. He paused for a moment, then jogged out to join them.

"Ask to see their ID," Bert said. "Let's see your IDs, fellas."

The men cleared their throats, and produced county-issued ID cards in leather holders. Bert took both IDs out of their holders and held them up to the sun, turning them this way and that, making noises of comprehension.

"Nice try, guys," Bert said at last, handing the IDs back to the puzzled building inspectors with a slow shake of the head. "No hologram. You think you can trick us? You think we're just bumpkin country folk?"

"The IDs don't *come* with holograms, sir. None of them do," the bald inspector boomed, the tendons in his neck flexing. "We have a court order and that's real enough. If you want, just go ahead and try to stop us. We can have the Sheriff over here in an hour."

"Don't make trouble, please," the squat man begged. "Just let us do our jobs."

"Bert," Mary said with a wave of her hand, "Forget it, okay? I can handle this." She stared grimly at the two inspectors. "Well? You just gonna stand there all day?"

"Let's do this," the bald man growled enthusiastically, slapping a cloth case down on the hood of the Explorer and unzipping it. Inside were two clipboards. He handed one to his partner, and they promptly split up, the bald man heading inside and the squat man circling around outside. Bert and Mary stood there in the sun, watching them go.

"This is no good," Mary said direly. "Masters said we've got all kinds of structural problems."

"What structural problems?" Bert said. "Overflowing gutters? A cracked back window? A couple mice? Big deal. I'll tell you what's going on here. He's trying to scare you. That's it, plain and simple. He wants to force you to sell."

Mary's lips pressed into an angry, thin line.

"They've got a court order, Bert," Mary said. "You saw it."

"What, are you an expert on what court orders look like? I'll bet you Masters printed it up on his home computer."

"Look, I'm gonna go talk with them," Mary told him. "Could you just go watch TV or drink some tea? Please? They're all having tea on the porch. *Go.*"

"Come *on*, Mary," Bert called after his sister as she jogged across the lawn. "I'm trying to help, here!"

Mary didn't answer. Bert watched as she caught up with the squat inspector. He was looking up at the roof.

"What's the damage?" Mary asked as nicely as she could.

The inspector made an apologetic face.

"You know, it's an *old* house, Mrs. Shumak," he said, jotting some notes on a form he had on the clipboard. "It's old and it hasn't had any repairs in a long, long time. In the biz it's what we call 'deferred maintenance.'"

"Everyone who lives here has everything they need," Mary pleaded.

"For *now*, maybe," the inspector interjected. "But all it takes is a bit of faulty wiring, a defective gas line, a few years of airborne asbestos."

"There's no asbestos in this house. All the insulation's fiberglass."

"Okay. Maybe you're right. Or maybe you're mistaken. See, right now I can see just by looking at the outside, that you need a new roof on this eastern part of the house." He noted it in his report. "And over here." He pointed at a dead spot in the grass. "I'm going to have to recommend that PEPA tests for leakage from a septic tank or other underground storage tank. It looks like there might be some seepage."

"We don't have a septic tank," Mary insisted. Her voice was getting edgy. "We don't have any tanks at all."

"Previous owners may have made certain improvements unbeknownst to you."

"It's been in my family for one hundred and fifty years, Mr—I don't even know your name—believe me, I know what is and what is not in my ground."

The inspector jotted something down.

"I'm sorry, Mrs. Shumak. I've got to report it just the same."

Inside, meanwhile, Bert had caught up with the bald inspector, who was in the attic, inspecting the insulation and crawl spaces. He was furiously making notes.

"Boy, you've sure got a lot to put in your report," Bert said, standing nearby and bouncing a rubber ball of the pine-plank floor.

Thud.

Thud.

Thud.

"You like what you do?"

"Stop distracting me, sir."

"Come on, you're gonna come over here and make things up about this house, you might as well be friendly," Bert scolded. "So. Do you?"

"Do I what?" the inspector asked without pausing in what he was doing.

"Like your job?"

"Yes."

Thud.

Thud.

Thud.

"Love it?"

"*Please* stop talking, sir," the inspector said, rubbing his eyes. "You're making it difficult to concentrate."

"Does your 'court order' forbid me from talking?"

"Maybe I'll go back and get one that does."

"Yeah, go back to Judge Judy or whatever scam court you're paying off and get a gag order. I dare you." The inspector made a mistake and scratched it out with a grimace.

"I'll bet you're not even a real inspector. Or maybe you're a poultry inspector."

They descended to the second floor. Claude was down the hall, sweeping, as he did most afternoons once TV ceased to interest him.

"You have mold," the inspector announced. "And water damage. And termites. And a rodent infestation. This roof is buckling. Several supports are painted with lead-based paint." He angrily scratched each announcement into the report.

"And you're a fake inspector."

The inspector turned furiously and looked at him, his jaw flexing. "You saw my license, you little shit," he barked suddenly. "I've had just about enough. This isn't just the county, okay, buddy boy? Do you know who we represent?"

Bert smirked.

"The lollypop guild?"

"Now with gay jokes!"

"Gay jokes... haven't you ever watched—"

"One more word out of you and I'll have the Sheriff over here to fine you for interfering with my inspection. And let's just say that we can make things very hard for you in ways that are *way* beyond the Sheriff. Do I make myself clear?"

"That's a pickle!" Claude cried from the end of the hall. He looked very upset by all the noise.

"Maybe I would have gone easy on this old heap, but now—" the bald man laughed bitterly. "You've gone and pissed me off."

"Hey, now, come on," Bert said, beginning to sweat, as he suddenly, crashingly, began to suspect that he'd crossed the line. "I'm just joking around,"

"Too late for that. *Way* to late."

Bert shrugged at Claude.

"Well, then," Bert said, rubbing the back of his neck, "I guess I'll be having tea, if you need me."

After half an hour the two inspectors met up again. The bald man's mood had gone from bad to worse. The clipboards went back into the cloth zippered case.

"Look, at least tell me the truth," Mary said as the inspectors scrolled through their digital camera files to make sure they hadn't missed anything. "Is Victor Masters behind this?"

"Nobody's *behind* this," the stocky inspector said with a rueful face. "This house is dangerous. We're looking out for the welfare of the people living here. That's it. That's all there is to it."

"What's going to happen?"

"We're going to file our report and the county will send you a list of modifications you need to make."

"Or else?"

"Or else we bulldoze the place," the bald man growled. "And seize the land."

"You can't do that!" Mary cried. "There's no way!"

"We're just the messengers," the squat one said, holding up his hands defensively. "Don't worry, they'll pay you for the land."

"A little," the bald man added.

"What is *wrong* with you?" Mary hissed at the bald inspector. "This is my home!"

"Maybe you ought to keep a tighter leash on your brother," answered the bald man.

She felt a quick, awful, plunging feeling in her chest as the two men—without another word to her—got into their car and pulled back down the drive.

Then it was sticky and hot again, quiet but for the opera of crickets in the tall grass.

The screen door banged.

Bert approached cautiously. "So... what happened?"

Mary turned and walked by him without looking at him.

"I asked you... to *stay inside*."

"I *did* stay inside."

The phone started ringing.

"I don't want to talk to you right now, Bert."

The phone rang and rang.

Mary got up onto the porch as the machine in the front hall picked up.

"*Mrs. Shumak, this is Collin Masters,*" came a scratchy electronic voice. "*I hope you're well. I'm still interested in your house, but I'm afraid that I will have to offer you fifteen percent less than I did last time; I've learned that there are some building violations that I didn't know about. It's still a good offer. Don't pass it up. Remember, we'll get the house one way or another. My patience is waning, Mrs. Shumak. I know you're there—*"

Mary ripped the answering machine out of the wall and with a mighty swing, heaved it—trailing a castrated power cord—across the lawn and towards the river.

Mary watched it land and scatter into cheap plastic debris.

"No sale," she said quietly, and stepped back inside.

7

Collin Masters lived in a large house in Brownsville, not far from the mansion of his brother, Victor Masters. Collin's was a Spanish-style construction, all white plaster and striking, stark lines topped with honey colored terra-cotta tiles. It sat behind a set of wrought iron gates, and the drive went past the two-car garage where he parked his Cadillac Escalade (for business) and his Dodge Viper (for fun). In the back there was a twenty foot in-ground pool and a mosaic deck with a stainless steel barbeque. From his lawn he could see the Versailles-style façade of Chateau Victor, reputed to be the largest single residence in Pennsylvania.

Collin Masters did most of his work at home. He had a giant white office decorated sparsely with black Bauhaus furniture and a few modernist paintings; in the hallways there were low end tables, maybe a slim black vase filled with dry baby's breath. The living area featured a Japanese sand garden and polished black pebbles in bowls, banks of giant plasma TVs, and long, angular leather couches that looked too uncomfortable for anything short of laying out a corpse.

The odd thing that visitors to the house noticed was that there were very few objects of a personal nature. There were no family photographs, no personal mementos, and no books except of the coffee table variety. On the desk in his office sat a single laptop and a fountain pen reposing in a felt-lined box; that was all. The only distinctive object that could be seen in the house by the various contractors and local officials that visited on business was a giant painted portrait of Victor Masters that hung over the fireplace in the Great Room. Rumor had it that the house had been deeded to Collin on the condition that the painting always remain there.

Late Monday afternoon, the two inspectors from the Health Department—Henderson and Vallone—stopped by after their visit to the House on the Bend, as they had been instructed to do. A buzzer at the front door admitted them into the front hall, where an attendant, dressed all in black, showed them down a white corridor to Masters' study.

Collin Masters was sitting at his desk, apparently either in the process of deep reflection or of doing absolutely nothing. As was his habit, he was wearing a white dress shirt and black suspenders, his tie loosened slightly. He looked up as they came in, and sighed as if he had been waiting all afternoon.

"Have a seat," he said, gesturing to two white modernist chairs next to his desk. "What did you find?"

"That house is a mess, Mr. Masters," said Vallone, the squat inspector. "Buckled east roof, termites and dry rot throughout, outdated wiring, what looks like mold in the attic and basement; here, take a look for yourself." He handed his report to Masters.

"Did you file with the county yet?"

"You asked us to check with you first."

"Right you are," Masters said, tapping his temple with two fingers. He exhaled through his nose and leafed through the report, nodding and pursing his lips. "Yeah. Okay. What can we do with this?"

"The Shumak woman is running a business," boomed Henderson. "So we can treat it as a commercial property. Pawnee County statutes give us the right to shut her down if she doesn't fix the problems within a court ordered period."

"I'll give Judge Randall a call. Can we do 30 days?"

"Maybe" Henderson intoned doubtfully.

"You shake her up like I asked?" Masters said.

The two men made uncomfortable faces.

"You know…" Vallone said slowly, "Maybe you should send over leg breakers if you want to intimidate a single mother. We're inspectors, not thugs."

Masters nodded, and leaned forward.

"Listen to me," he said coolly. "You are whatever I tell you to be. Do you understand?"

Vallone looked away nervously.

Henderson was studying his hands.

Masters pounded the table with his fist. "*DO YOU?*"

"Yeah."

"Yes, Mr. Masters."

Masters inspected his fingernails. "You like the bonuses, the cash rewards. You like all that, don't you?"

The inspectors nodded.

"What we give, we can take away." He pointed a stern finger at them. "Don't forget it." He waved them away. "Get out of here. File that report before you go home for the day."

The inspectors got up and walked out quickly, bumping into each other in the doorway in their haste to get out.

After they were gone, Masters folded his hands and rested them on the table. A moment later he massaged his forehead. Pressure was massing behind his eyes.

His intercom beeped.

"Yes?" he said without looking up.

"Bill Muldoon is here to discuss the 14th Street development," his attendant told him over the speaker.

"Later. Tomorrow. I'm finished for the day."

He was angry with himself for yelling at the inspectors. Counter-productive. The *opposite* of persuasion is anger. Anger builds walls, persuasion brings them down.

"Anger builds walls, persuasion brings them down," he said out loud. His voice sounded small in the big room.

His breathing was getting heavier.

Something bad was stirring.

No. No.

NO.

Masters yanked violently on his tie and pulled it down halfway.

Getting hot in here.

"Anger builds walls. Persuasion brings them down."

Breathe. Easy.

He shook his head.

"Need to work out," he declared to the giant room.

Collin Masters had a gym in his house, in a room directly adjacent to his office. Like his office it was a very large, impersonal space, in the midst of which was a cluster of sleek black weight machines, a few racks of rubber-coated free weights, a stationary bike, and a treadmill. There were no mirrors. On the far wall was another oversized portrait of his brother, Victor Masters.

He took off his tie, turned on the TV, and got on the bicycle machine. He kept a half-smoked cigar in the drink holder of the bike, and now he lit it up and pedaled and watched Moneyline on CNN. He felt things begin to slow down in his head as he worked up a bit of a sweat and the nicotine rushed in and made him buzz.

Some key stocks were up. The Dow was up. Okay, okay. Things are okay.

After three minutes or so, the PA system for the gym crackled on.

"Mr. Masters. Your brother is on line one."

Collin went to the phone on the wall and picked up the receiver.

"How's your workout coming along?" Masters the Greater inquired from the other end.

Collin looked up at the portrait.

"Fine."

"Any word on the house?'

"Report is in the works."

"I just got turned down on my bid for eminent domain. Seems a casino isn't in the public's best interest."

"Oh."

"That means it's up to you."

"Okay."

"Don't mess this up, Collin."

"I won't."

"If you mess this up I'll throw you back out there. I will."

"I know."

"You don't want that, do you?"

"No. No, I sure don't."

Collin looked up at the portrait.

"I love you, Collin," said Victor. "You know that."

"Yeah."

"But business is business. I'm placing a big bet on you here." Victor paused for a moment, to let it sink in. "I know you'll come through."

8

The following week grew hotter by the day. It was nearly September, and the season seemed desperate in its late intensity. The trees and bushes, the pansies and the rosebushes by the verandah, all seemed to pale in the sun, which in its ferocity had overpowered everything green.

All was not all right in the world. A horrible civil war had broken out in Togo. The Kingdom of Nepal shrank farther and farther away from democratic freedoms. 150 people died in car bomb explosions in Iraq. And yes, the Tibetans were *still* oppressed.

Mary Shumak had said almost nothing to Bert for several days. Bert tried a chipper hello at breakfast; she answered him coldly, with downcast eyes. He tried to strike up a conversation while she and Billy did the dishes; he and Billy ended up talking about how cool the new GT Mustang was, but Mary never contributed anything. He tried to invite her on a bike ride; no, too busy. A game of scrabble? Ditto. A round of boggle? *No.*

There was no way around it: Mary was bothered by something.

Bert let himself imagine for a day or two that *possibly* it had to do with the particularly gruesome car bombing of an elementary school in Mosul, or the assassination of a prominent human rights activist in Burma. At least, those were things that *once* had preoccupied his sister.

But even when she had been most passionate about such things, (which, now that he thought about it, was many years ago), she'd never acted this way. So he had to finally conclude that it was about the house, and it was about him.

The more he thought about it, the gloomier he got. He shuffled around the house, feeling, for the first time in a great while, kind of useless. Thursday afternoon was the sort of day that invited melancholy: hazy, oppressive, hot beyond reason or fairness and with a sense of claustrophobia hanging over everything like an ill-mannered guest. It was the sort of day that made everything sticky and itchy, irritating, the sense of time as boxed in as the sky, the malignance of a long afternoon that stubbornly refuses to pass as afternoons should. Bert was hungry; he'd made a grilled cheese for lunch, but that was an hour ago.

He felt like pizza. He took the cordless out onto the porch; here he found Ned, Vera, Billy and Claude. Vera was crocheting and Ned was telling Billy about a serial killer who stalked truckers at rest stops round about the time when he was doing runs up through that part of New Hampshire. Billy was listening with rapt attention: trucks *and* serial killers! Vera had molded her face into an expression of disdain for the subject, but Bert could tell, by the way her face wasn't moving at all, that she was listening with just as much interest as anybody else. Claude just sat and stared.

"Who wants pizza?" Bert asked.

"Me," Billy answered, half-raising his hand.

"Ned?" Bert checked. "Vera? A little Papa Joe's?"

Vera shook her head and let out a disapproving "Mmm-*mmm*," as if ordering pizza at two in the afternoon was something terrible to do.

"More for us, right Billy?"

"Yeah. Right," He turned back to Ned. "So, what about that guy? Did they catch him?"

"It wasn't a him. It was a *her*," Bert blurted out.

"Uncle Bert!" Billy cried.

"Naw, it wasn't," Ned said, laughing. "He's thinkin' o' that movie Monster."

Bert shrugged and dialed Pappa Joe's. After he'd ordered a large with extra sausage, he looked at Claude for a long moment, smiled deviously, and then said, "Wait right there."

A few minutes later Bert was back on the porch with a pair of scissors, some gauze bandages, and a small container of red paint, lifted from Sarah's art supplies. He sat down next to Claude, and, biting his lip, began to wind the strip of gauze around Claude's bald head.

The conversation on the porch stopped.

"Bert," Vera asked with obvious displeasure, "What in *heaven's* name are you doing to poor Claude?"

"Hold on, hold on," Bert said, holding up a hand to beg quiet. "You're witnessing greatness here, folks." After two lengths of gauze were wrapped firmly on Claude's head, Bert opened the miniature pot of red paint and dabbed a small amount on his forehead, a thick little gob that glistened and started to drip downwards. Bert quickly wrapped the next layer of gauze on top—the red paint bled through. Then another layer; the paint soaked through again, but less this time; and so on until the red paint was only dimly visible through the outer weave of the bandages.

"Okay, Bert," Ned said at last. "What's this all about?"

Bert set down the remaining length of bandage and red paint, and folded his arms with satisfaction. "Looks real, don't it? Looks like something happened to poor Claude's head, right?"

"It looks totally fake, Uncle Bert," Billy said.

"Well, from a distance it'll look right." Bert pulled his chair in a bit, leaned towards the others conspiratorially, and said in a low voice, "Here's the thing—Papa Joe's Pizza has a thirty minutes or it's free policy. Right? So. I got this great idea just now—Claude here is gonna go lie down in the drive, real close to the main road. When the pizza guy comes along, he'll see poor little Claude lying there and stop to help. He'll ask Claude, 'Dude, what's wrong?' but Claude won't answer, except for maybe his old pickle thing. Point is, even if he says that, pizza guy's not gonna know what's wrong with Claude. Did he fall over? Get hit by a car? Was he trying to escape? He'll probably be stoned or something, and get all crazy trying to figure out what to do. Meanwhile, the clock's ticking. By the time he puts Claude into his car and comes up the drive to deliver the pizza, it'll be over thirty minutes, and voila! Free pizza!" He threw his hands into the air and stomped his foot. "Pretty cool, huh?"

"Bert Wodehouse," Vera said with a stern, apocalyptic shake of the head, "That is the meanest, dumbest, just plain *nonsense* thing I ever heard. First of all, you're tricking the poor driver—second, if he *does* stop to pick up Claude, then he's a good man and shouldn't be *punished* for doing just what our lord Jesus would've done!"

"Not to mention." Billy pointed out, "What if he takes Claude to the hospital? Then we'll have to go over there to get him *and* you'll never get your free pizza, or if you do, it'll be all cold and nasty."

"Plus," Ned added, "They're gonna take off his bandage and see it's a fake; then they'll know what you were up to."

"Guys, guys," Bert cried, "Have some faith. I've thought it out to the last *detail*. It's fool-proof! The perfect plan! I'm tellin' you!"

"Telling them what?" Mary said as she came out onto the porch with her purse in hand, ready to run some errands.

"Mary, you won't believe what this boy is cooking up," Vera thundered, shaking her head and making 'tsk' sounds. "Just about the biggest load of pig slop I ever heard."

"He's gonna put Claude in the middle of the road, Mom," Billy said. "To distract the pizza driver so he can get his pizza for free."

Mary rubbed her eyes and began to unwind the bandage. "Bert, what if the driver hit Claude?" she asked.

"*Hit* him?" Bert repeated.

"Yes. As he was driving along. With Claude sitting in the middle of the road."

"Well, we'd put him in clear view—"

The bandage was off—a bit of red paint had bled through and stuck to Claude's dome. Mary gently wiped it off, and opened her purse. She got out twenty dollars and pressed it into Bert's hand.

"How nice to have three children," she said. "Here, just ask for the money next time, will you?" She snapped her purse shut. "I'm going into town. Vera, don't let him get into any more mischief, will you?"

"I'll keep my *eye* on him, Mary," Vera boomed.

"I know you will." Mary looked at Bert for a moment, laughed, and shaking her head in disbelief, marched down the side porch steps and across the yard to her car.

"Bunch of spoil sports anyhow," Bert said with a snigger, and went in, towards the kitchen.

While in the hall, he heard footsteps on the front verandah. Through the living room window, Bert could see Gertrude, the Pennsylvania Dutch mail carrier, busy stuffing the mail box with letters. He waited until she was gone so he could avoid chatting, then grabbed the letters and continued on his way to the kitchen.

Bert absolutely loved getting mail.

He poured himself a tall glass of lemonade, dropped in a couple ice cubes, and sat down at the kitchen table. He used his index finger to rip voluptuously into each letter. There were credit card applications (for Mary, of course), a Publisher's Clearinghouse sweepstakes package that disgorged a wad of coupons and promotions; there was a bill from the electric company. There were also a couple catalogues, one from LL Bean and another from Land's End.

And there was an envelope from the Pawnee County Department of Safety.

Bert stopped what he was doing and regarded the letter for a moment. This was already a sensitive issue, after all, the whole production with the inspectors and Collin Masters; it might be best to simply leave it to Mary to open later on.

He did actually hold out for several minutes, but the thought of that letter, a veritable Pandora's box sitting ever so innocently next to the other, totally innocuous mail, it was tempting—oh, ever so tempting.

This letter was *not* innocuous.

It was a bringer of bad tidings.

Bert knew that he could not simply allow the letter to remain there unmolested. He would need to either throw it in the garbage or open it at once.

Compulsively, he seized the envelope and tore it open. Within was a folded packet of information, written in minute, thick black court font, looking dense and difficult to understand.

"...within thirty days to make necessary certifiable modifications to the structure at 431 Riverbend Road, failing which will follow automatic revocation of the applicable permit to operate a—"

Bert had the gist of it, but his eyes were bouncing around the page, his fingers flipping the pages impatiently.

"Item 1: Infestation by wood-boring insects in the wall paneling of all upper quarters of the house, specifically—"

Eyes jumped down.

"Item 6: Probable lead based paint use on pipes, supports, and joists in upper level and basement level. Recommend encapsulation and certification by licensed lead-based paint inspector—"

"Item 11: Buckled east roof. Further water damage probable, subsidence and collapse likely within—"

Uh-oh.

He flipped on two or three pages.

Remember, he thought, Baldy was writing up a storm before you got up there. It's *not your fault.*

But Mary might think it is.

And the fact was, Bert did not have a very good track record with Mary. He was AWOL when their father died; AWOL when Brian died; sarcastic and unhelpful when their mother died. He had borrowed close to $15,000 and had not paid back a single red cent of it. He had, so far, contributed nothing to the house except one more mouth to feed, because he didn't pay for his own food, either.

Not that he minded being a leech, so long as he could be amusing; but now he'd failed in that as well and it was clear that he would be perceived not only as useless, but now actually as *detrimental.*

Bert made a split second decision.

He was going to do something right.

He was going to fix this problem.

Hey, why not? He saw Ty Pennington and Bob Villa renovate houses on TV all the time. There was even an episode on the Apprentice where the contestants (who, it might be noted, had no construction experience either) fixed up houses and resold them for a profit. The point was that the job didn't need to be perfect: only competent. He just had to fix the stupid problems they'd cited in the stupid report, get another inspection done, and *voila*! Problem solved, and Bert Wodehouse would be hailed as a hero, buying him enough good karma credit with Mary to coast along on for quite some time—maybe even forever.

The first problem was that there was quite a bit that he didn't understand about the letter: a lot of terms and wording that might as well have been in Chinese. Problem #2: He didn't know how to do anything. He could hammer a nail, he was pretty sure. He'd learned that while building birdhouses in the Boy Scouts years ago. However, clearly, this would be a job that would require greater skill than the simple insertion of nails into wood. Problems #3 and #4: He couldn't do it all himself, and he couldn't afford it all himself.

And the last problem, the biggest and most crucial: for it to be a successful surprise, Mary couldn't know a thing about it.

Bert finished his lemonade and got out a yellow pad of paper.

He was going to need to enlist allies.

The pizza came with seven minutes to spare and Bert paid for it, reluctantly, out of the twenty that Mary had given him; he pocketed all the change for himself, and shut the door in the driver's face when he looked like he was about to ask about a tip. Bert took the food out onto the porch where Billy and the Johnsons were sitting. Mr. Manicotti had joined them; within an hour, Mrs. Noonan would have tea ready, and Mary never missed tea if she could help it. He had to be quick.

After everybody who wanted to eat was finished, Bert cleared his throat.

"Hey, Vera," he said. "Mrs. Noonan was looking for you."

"Oh?"

"Yeah. She needs some help making tea."

"Oh, well then..." Vera got up and went looking for Mrs. Noonan. As soon as she was gone, Bert took out his yellow note pad, where he'd recorded the list of modifications in nearly illegible scrawl.

"Listen up, guys," he said quickly, leaning forward and looking over his shoulder to make sure Vera was gone. "We got a letter today from the Department of Safety. They want to shut us down, if we don't fix some stuff around the house."

"What?" Billy exclaimed.

"Naw, come on," Ned said slowly. "Come on, they can't do that."

Bert made a face. "Well, *yeah* they can, because they're the Department of Safety. So, here's the plan—I want to fix the house before Mary finds out about this, you know, as a surprise. I need your help, though. You with me?"

"I don't know," Ned said doubtfully. "I don't know anything about fixing houses. Just driving truck, that's all I know."

"Yeah, Uncle Bert, what do you know about fixing houses?" Billy asked.

"Look, you ever been to Home Depot?"

"I guess so," Billy said.

"They've got books and guys who know the books back to front. Ask any questions, believe me, they know the answer. So we just take this list down there tomorrow and they'll tell us how to do everything."

"I just don't know," Ned repeated.

"What about you, Mr. Manicotti?" Bert asked the Sicilian.

Mr. Manicotti tipped his panama hat, and winked.

"I-ma at your service," he said, lighting a cigarette with his silver Zippo.

Bert dramatically put one stroke next to the "helpers" bar at the top of the pad.

"Come on, fellas. Don't let me down."

"All right," Ned said finally.

"Billy?"

"Yeah, whatever, sure."

"That's it. You're good at building stuff, Billy. We need you, kid." Two more strokes. "We can count on Alan." Another. "Claude..."

"Better leave Claude out of it," Billy warned him.

"No, we need somebody to clean up," Bert said. "He's perfect."

"You ever try to tell him *where* to sweep?" Billy asked.

Bert added another stroke anyway.

"Mrs. Noonan!" thundered Vera from somewhere far off.

"The jig's just about up," Bert said. "Next thing, materials. I don't know quite what we need, but I'm guessing we'll need paint, drywall, and a bunch of wood and crap for a new roof."

"A new *roof?*" Billy said nervously.

"Not the whole thing, just part of it."

"There's paint in the coach house," Ned told him.

"Yeah, it's all lead paint. That's half the problem. We gotta get rid of that stuff. Oh, and insecticide. And mousetraps or rat poison. I think we need about five hundred dollars. I've got three hundred, so you guys need to pony up the rest. Alan hasn't got anything."

"Vera has all the money," Ned told them sadly.

"Mom gives me fifteen dollars a week," Billy said.

"Didn't you win two hundred at Bingo just last week?" Ned asked.

"Yeah. That's part of the three hundred."

"All you've got besides that is a hundred dollars? Come on, son."

"Come on, pops," Bert snapped back. "You gonna let the ol' battleaxe squeeze you for every penny?"

"*No.*"

"Well, looks like she is."

"I have a hundred a-dollars," Mr. Manicotti said.

"Great! One hundred, Ned. Come on."

"Mrs. Noonan don't need help!" roared Vera from inside the house.

"Ned! I need a one hundred dollar commitment here!"

"Fine, fine, I'll get it somehow," Ned said quickly. "Shhh! Here she comes!"

Vera came back.

"You hear, me, Bert? She *don't need help.*"

Bert shrugged. "Huh. Thought she did."

Vera shook her head, and went back to crocheting. Bert rubbed his hands together, and snatched up another slice of pizza.

"So Ned," he said, his mouth full, "Can you drive me into town tomorrow?"

9

Bert Wodehouse had one philosophy in life: it's too short as it is, so lap it up and don't bother wasting time with work. The way he saw it, every hour spent laboring was an hour lost forever: you'd never get back that lovely afternoon you just wasted behind the fryer at Burger King. His mother had worked very hard, and Bert always blamed her untimely death on the stress of her job as a maid. Right before she died, somebody at one of the houses she cleaned had accused her of stealing something, a pair of earrings, he seemed to remember it being. Joanna Wodehouse was scrupulously ethical—that's why she and Dad had gotten along so well—so the accusation seemed patently ridiculous to anybody who knew her. Still, she was devastated. The very notion that someone would *suspect* her was enough to send her into a deep despair. She went about her work listlessly, stopped smiling, got sleepy all the time. Her cooking suffered: the chicken was leather, the meatloaf a parched log; the casserole had a black shell on the bottom. Then she got a cold that turned to pneumonia. But, well, she had to work, didn't she? Work, work, work. She only stopped going to work when, one morning, she simply couldn't get out of bed. She died three days later.

Bert thought about her sometimes. At that age—he'd been 19 at the time—he'd felt monumentally awful that she was missing from the world and for a long while he couldn't see straight from the pain of it. He made jokes about the whole thing to take the edge off. Mary hated him for that; she wanted to see him cry and roll around on the floor, or maybe tear his hair out or something. Well, that just wasn't his way. Sorry. To admit his grief to her—not to mention his father—would have only acknowledged the fact that his mother had died, that this permanent fixture really *had* been ripped violently out of the fabric of the family. And that would have been intolerable.

Soon after, things started falling apart. Dad, with his job at the milk company, just couldn't pay the mortgage *and* all the rest of the bills, though he made a damned good show of trying, whistling just like he always did, asking after everybody's day at the dinner table, intercepting the mail every afternoon so nobody would see the letters from the debt collectors and the mortgage company. He walked with the same swagger, swinging his keys in a jaunty circular motion. But there were changes. First off, he never stood quite as straight again. He stopped going for a beer after work. He would spend an hour after dinner *holding* the newspaper, like he always did, only now he wasn't reading it, just staring at it with big saucer eyes. His hair turned grey in a year. His skin turned ashy. Despite his manly smiling you could see his insides were being eaten away by grief and guilt.

He'd told her to keep on working. "It's just a cold," he'd said. "Tough it out." *He* did, after all.

But now she was dead.

So it occurred to Bert right around this time, when the TV was pawned and the car got sold and the repo man came and took the couch, that his mother had really, totally wasted her life. She'd done everything in her power to get *stuff,* to make enough money to get this little house and then enough clutter to make it seem like home. She's spent years denying herself the things she liked: chocolate, jewelry, a nice pair of shoes. She never went to the ballet, which she loved, and she never went to the movies. All so that there could be some stuff in a little house, and they could call it *theirs.*

Only now it wasn't. With every piece of furniture and every appliance that vanished, he saw clearly just how futile her life had been. She'd worked all those years for absolutely nothing. They were taking it all back anyhow.

Before they could take the house, Dad sold it. It was just a few days before the court ordered sale and he sold it for three quarters of its true value to a snaky local real estate investor who promptly bulldozed it and put in parking spaces for a forthcoming shopping center. The shopping center never materialized: the investor later went bankrupt and the county seized the parking lot. Weeds came up in cracks. Soon it was an abandoned lot like any other, home to a discarded sneaker, a few crushed Busch Light cans, and a forgotten shopping cart.

Dad took that money and sent Mary to college.

"Son," he told Bert one night as they sat in the new apartment, wrapped in blankets and watching their breath fog the air. "We both know she's the best hope we've got. She'll do great things. We're men: we can take this life. We've got grit. We're built to take it. Now we've got to stand strong. We need to be... strong shoulders for her to stand on."

Bert often wondered if Dad had rehearsed that. Anyhow, he gave it a little thought. He'd always tended towards goofing off: he was not programmed with the kind of Soviet work ethic his father had. That particular evening, by the light of one naked soft-watt light bulb, he was presented with a stark choice: be a good person and work and save and do his part, or... not.

At first the choice seemed clear. Stiff upper lip. Request more hours at Burger King. Take a second job, at Convenient, maybe. The milk company was full up, but what about the bakery down the street?

Wait a second.

What the *hell* are you thinking?

It dawned on him, in one radiant moment, that simply by having the courage to *blow this joint*, he could do what so few people ever managed to do—enjoy life. Sure, he had no skills and no money, but what did that matter? A future of infinite choice, no matter how bereft, was always better than a lifetime of overtime at Burger King.

Two days later, Bert quit his job, packed a bag, and said goodbye to Lewiston, and to Eastern Pennsylvania. He headed south.

He didn't say goodbye to his father—just left him a note on the coffee table saying that he was going on a trip.

He never saw the old man again.

Over the years Bert got darned good at goofing off and spending very little money doing it. He was perpetually strapped for cash, so he developed, out of necessity, a host of tricks to save it. He liked coffee, so he would save his paper Starbucks cup for days on end, and go in at busy times to ask for the fifty-five cent refill. He would buy boxes of Little Debbie oatmeal pies for a dollar and nine cents, and eat that together with ramen noodles (the ten cent ones, not the fifteen cent ones). He slept in parks and shelters, wore out his welcome on the couches of friends, and skipped out on his motel bill when he felt like something fancy. He stole handfuls of crackers from Wendy's; he took a dollar or two from the counter tip jar at taco joints when nobody was looking. He visited bakeries right at closing time and ate day-old bagels for weeks, until they were so hard you could practically hammer a nail with them. If he wanted a beer, he'd go find a high school or college keg party and sneak in the back way. Once inside, surrounded by the all these bumping and grinding young people, he was free to drink to his heart's content; sure, he was the creepy guy nobody knew, but as long as the buzz was real, who cared, right?

All in all, his expenses for the week, generally, amounted to about thirty-five dollars. No doubt about it: he was poor. His clothes were way beyond second hand—they were actually disintegrating, with his skin visible through the brittle fabric. His tennis shoes would not have looked out of place hanging from a power line after a storm; his wallet was taped together with duct tape to keep its meager contents from falling out.

Sometimes he was reduced to begging at the side of the road with a sign that said, "will work for whatever you've got" by thruway overpasses, smiling at each car as it veered off the highway. He was the guy outside the Piggely Wiggley asking for a quarter. He was the guy holding the 7-11 door for a tip. He stole newspapers and resold them on the roadside. These were less dignified moments, relieved by periods when he took some sort of job that fit his description of acceptable: that is, no punch-in, punch out, no drudgery, nothing hateful. He sold jewelry for a Senegalese guy in Atlanta at street fairs; he passed out fliers for clubs in Miami. He collected for very dubious charities.

Bert spent a good deal of the past twenty-five years being the dingy, suspicious guy people don't like to make eye contact with, somebody who regular folks looked at with a mixture of pity and disgust as they drove their Ford Broncos toward nine hours at the Ralston Purina plant, or eight hours at the accountant's office, or a nice back-breaking swing shift with the

DPW. Then they'd go home to their ranch-style house and lock the door (so that people like Bert couldn't break in) and turn on their big screen TV and enjoy the four hours that remained of their day. They pitied him, then forgot him.

The thing they didn't know about Bert was that he was probably happier and more fulfilled than they would ever be. He could dimly remember a time when owning a nice stereo system or a good pair of shoes had been important; but now that's all it was, a dim memory. He was one of the blessed few who knew nothing of *modern want*. Wanting a hot cup of coffee or a sandwich was good because you ended up cherishing it when you got it; wanting a new car/TV/lawnmower only led to further wanting, a cycle of Get Get Get that never let up, never, and never brought satisfaction.

A hippy girl on Miami Beach once told him that he was a Buddhist and, like, didn't even know it. He read up about it next time he was at the public library, and liked what he'd read. Free yourself from desire.

Right on.

You might call it laziness or sloth, he thought, but Bert called it bliss.

"Idle hands are the devil's playground," the saying went. Whoever said that had never really known what it was to be content. Because for every time he had to beg for a quarter or snatch a half-eaten steak off a plate at a restaurant, there was an afternoon of pure bliss, relaxing on the beach in the sun, or a nap on a park bench in the dappled light, the church bells ringing across the green, the breeze hissing in the leaves, whispering of the endless, lovely afternoons that awaited him in this perfect life of his.

Yeah, he had it good. No doubt about it.

But then he found out that Mary's Brian had died. Over the years he'd made a point of calling his sister (collect) every so often to see how she was—and, occasionally, to ask for a bit of cash—but he had not seen her in some time. Visiting Lewiston was offensive to him; there, the scorn of the eyes on the street stung, because they might very well remember who he was, and his was a lifestyle that required anonymity to be a comfortable one.

Bert was in New Orleans, scamming tourists with a shell game on Bourbon Street (he'd been taught by a master shell game artist from Baton Rouge), when he learned of Brian's death during one of his calls home. He was caught off guard. He felt miserable. Dad, everybody knew was going to go, but Brian wasn't supposed to die. Bad things like that weren't supposed to happen to Bert's little sister. He stayed on in New Orleans for another week, going on about his business in the sweaty press of the French Quarter, drinking whiskey out of a paper bag in Lafayette Park with Skooch and Lamar and his other con artist friends, but he couldn't get the thought of Mary being all alone out of his head. He loved the Big Easy, but this tragedy up north had brought a chill that had muffled the sweet lament of the blues, dried up the elixir of the Technicolor night. He had to go.

His last night in New Orleans, he took everything he owned to a pawn shop, got one hundred and fifty dollars in return, and jumped on a Greyhound to Philly.

Like so, he turned the page on his Southern Adventures, and went to Lewiston on a mission to be there for the one person in the world to whom he could make a damned bit of difference.

And *that* was the biggest high of all.

10

After breakfast the next morning, as the dishes were being cleared away, Bert waylaid Mary in the kitchen.

"So... ah, what's going on today?"

"I'm taking Sarah to look at violins."

"Violins?"

"She wants to take violin in orchestra this year."

Mary made a thin-lipped expression that said 'so what do you care?' and started scraping plates into the garbage.

"Just wondering," Bert said. Then, after an awkward pause, "When do you expect to be back?"

"I don't know—two? We'll have lunch in town. Why? What's going on?"

"Just wondering. Just, you know, taking an interest in the family."

"Uh-huh. If you're *that* interested, you could always do these dishes while I go make some phone calls."

Great. *Just* great.

"Yeah. I'd love to. Hand it over! Go have fun!"

"Sure. Making dentist appointments is *loads* of fun." She rewarded Bert with a little smile. "Thanks."

Bert spent a half hour elbow deep in suds and sticky maple syrup residue, loathing every second of it: he thought of enlisting Sarah's help, but then he decided that this might be one to take for the team. After he was done, his hands pruney and the front of his shirt soaking wet, he went surreptitiously to Mr. Manicotti's second floor room. He found the aged Sicilian listening to an old vinyl recording on his gramophone, smoking a cigarette by the window with his legs crossed. His room was decorated with a baffling stratum of photographs: photographs of baseball heroes, mobsters, politicians, centerfolds, boxers, family portraits from the Old World, pictures of Mr. Manicotti in his Army uniform, looking fresh faced and optimistic. Aside from the photographic chaos on the walls, the room was the model of perfect order: shaving kit arranged on his oak desk, a few books, his record collection neatly stacked by the window by his marble ashtray, his shoes paired and polished, lined up by the wall as if in a military review.

"Psst!" Bert aid, poking his head in the door. "Hey! You got the money?"

Mr. Manicotti nodded slowly, and put out his Pall Mall with great care. He went into the closet and took out an old Beech Nut coffee tin. From inside he produced a small roll of hundreds, presumably his entire savings, since he made no secret of his mistrust of banks. As he gingerly peeled off a single Benjamin, Bert tried to sneak a peek inside the closet. Within, cloaked in shadows, he could just make out the black curve of a guitar case.

Mr. Manicotti replaced the coffee tin, and shut the closet door.

"Much appreciated," Bert said, folding the hundred in two and putting it in his pocket along with three hundred of his own, taken from the fireproof metal lock box in his room where he collected his riches (he, too, mistrusted the bank, but he was also wary of house fires).

Mr. Manicotti lit up a second cigarette after he had resumed his pose by the window.

"Mr. Wodehouse," he said with a little smile. "I'm a-too old to move now. Too old to start in a new place. *Capisce?*"

"Yeah. Capisce."

"I don't want to move. I'm a-finished moving," Mr. Manicotti told him, his face kind but resolute.

Bert nodded, and then seeing that the Sicilian tailor was finished talking, he went downstairs.

He waited around in the living room, half-watching the Odd Couple with Alan and Mrs. Noonan until he heard Mary and Sarah go out, and then a few minutes later, the extended crunching sound of tires on gravel as the Caprice pulled down the driveway.

As soon as the car was out of earshot, Bert jumped off of the couch.

The clock was ticking.

He went and got Ned, who was outside by the coach house, washing his Chevy Suburban. He was wearing a blue Agway t-shirt that was tight on his belly and around his thick arms, which still looked strong. He saw Bert and took off his Mack truck hat to wipe the sweat off his forehead.

"Ready?" Ned said nervously.

"Yeah," Bert said. "Let's do this."

They both jumped in the truck, revved the engine, and took off down the driveway, leaving the sudsy water bucket and sponges where they lay.

"What about Vera?" Bert asked.

"She watches her soap at one," Ned told him. "She won't come out of her room while The Days of Our Lives is on. But she's gonna wonder why I'm gone so long."

"We already discussed this. You'll tell her that I needed to stop in a couple places—the library and the bike shop. I need a new chain for my bike. That's why I can't go into town myself. Because my bike needs fixing."

"Vera can always smell a lie," Ned said, his eyes wide with fear. "She'll pick me apart in a second."

"Look—just remember, it's not like we're doing anything wrong. Right? This is for everybody's good. For Mary. Vera likes Mary. And look—the only reason she knows you're lying is because you've got that raccoon-caught-in-the-garbage-can look on your face."

"Raccoon, huh?"

"You know what I mean."

Ned knew what Bert meant. After years of withering a constant bombardment from Vera—he didn't do the wash right, should wash his feet more often, shouldn't waste so much time reading the sports section, screwed up this, messed up that—he had found himself trapped in a veritable minefield that he tiptoed around every day. Every action performed in the course of the day, from how he dressed in the morning to whether he flossed before bed, was subject to her scrutiny, and thus he went about his life in a perpetual state of suspense, like a cringing dog, never quite knowing how he would upset her next. The only certainty was that he *would* eventually upset her—and she would unleash her scorn. After thirty-eight years of marriage she knew what buttons to push. She knew that she could berate his manhood and wound him as deeply as ever, and that there wasn't a damned thing he could do but take it. To fight back only made it worse. Besides, how could he argue that he'd paired the socks correctly when he really wasn't sure if he had? How could he be sure about anything in the face of Vera's blistering certainty?

It hadn't always been like that. Once, long ago, Vera was deeply in love with him and proudly referred to him as "her man." She fell asleep in his strong arms every night, melting into him, telling him that he was a "good man" and a "strong man" and a "quiet man, but a lion underneath."

God, how he missed that. He hadn't heard it in so many years.

If only he hadn't messed up.

Why are men so weak?

One transgression was all it took, a nice dose of the clap from a roadhouse in Kansas.

Only did it once. Honestly.

You can't explain away the clap.

Not when your wife gets it from you.

Just like that, pride was replaced by contempt. Love with scorn. Never again did Ned's words mean anything, His promises held no weight.

To have and to hold, till death do us part.

Vera was a good church-going woman, and so she took that vow very, very seriously.

So she held on, and ate him bit by bit.

He'd done wrong by Vera that night back in Kansas, a blurry night of tequila shots and Budweiser long necks and a pretty white girl in tight jeans and a flannel shirt unbuttoned to show off her assets. They'd gone at it for maybe three minutes and then he finished abruptly and she was demanding twenty-five dollars, and he realized suddenly what an *idiot* he'd been, how *stupid* he'd been to be flattered, what a *mistake* he'd made.

He prayed that night, prayed and cried his eyes out.

Please, Lord, forgive me my sins.

I've done wrong by my woman.

I'll do my penance. I'll swallow my guilt.

A month later, about when the guilt was just a sodden, sick feeling in the back of his skull, the shadow of a skeleton left back in Kansas, he started feeling a burning sensation when he pissed.

It got worse and worse.

The Lord was going to punish him. And had been ever since.

So when Vera told him to be a man and fix the dryer, he knew what she was really talking about. The fact that he was rotten and worthless hung over everything like an indelible fog.

That was a door, when you stepped through it you could never go back.

"Hey!" Bert exclaimed. "Wake up! Home Depot, hard right!"

Ned veered into the parking lot and found a space not far from the front door. The place was parked up with the usual assortment of Ford pickups and Chevy vans and populated with men in paint-spattered Harley t-shirts, stonewashed jeans, and steel-toed boots. Home Depot had always seemed profoundly mysterious to Bert, and to Ned as well—an enormous place full of hardware, materials, and tools that neither man had any idea of how to use, and full of guys who browsed the place like kids in a toy store, guys who could install a sink or rewire a house like you might start a load of dishes in the dishwasher.

The two of them wandered around the aisles, looking at door handles and radial saws and high and medium gloss paint, nodding and making little "hmm" sounds as they looked at sheets of drywall and power drills.

"Okay," Bert said at last. "Just checking here—you have *any idea* what you're looking at?"

"No. Do you?"

"No way."

A young guy in a back brace with a nametag identifying him as "Tim" was walking by; Bert waylaid him by thrusting the list sent by the county into his path.

"Can I—help you?" Tim asked, taking the sheet out of reflex.

"Yeah. Take a gander at that list there," Bert said. "Tell us what you think."

A loud whine started up at the woodshop nearby. The thud thud thud of the paint mixer.

"Uh, you need to hire a professional," Tim said at last. "Wow. That's a lot of stuff."

"No can do," Bert said. "Look—this isn't impossible for us to do, right?"

"Well, no, it's not impossible."

"So, why don't you give us a little Home Depot advice on how to proceed, okay?"

Tim directed them to the how-to book shelf, and stacked up a bunch of volumes on roofing and pest control and painting technique, to name a few.

Bert checked his watch. It was 12:30. They had an hour and half.

"We need to speed things up. Okay, Tim. Materials. Let's get materials."

Ned and Bert each wheeled a shopping cart that they filled up with tools and material. Bert ordered a bunch of 2x4s and had them taken out to the truck and bungeed onto the roof. Ned paged through the how-to books.

"I hope you're better at this than I am," he said doubtfully.

"It isn't rocket science," Bert said with a shrug.

"If you don't do it right the first time, it could end up being even more costly than if you'd just hired a contractor in the first place," Tim advised them.

"Hey Ned," Bert said, pointing a thumb at Tim. "Did we ask Tim's opinion?"

"I don't think so," Ned said meekly. "Did we?"

"Nope. Don't recall it being so. Thanks anyways Tim."

12:55.

They had the stuff bought and crammed inside the Suburban. Total cost: $420. They still had eighty dollars—Bert had hoped to get some subs with anything they had left over, but they'd barely have time to get back as it was.

"Punch it!" Bert shouted as Ned peeled out and expertly maneuvered into traffic. He was smiling ear to ear.

Bert was white knuckling the oh-shit bar.

"Careful... *careful...* look out! Watch that... *shit.*"

"Relax, Bert," Ned said, as they weaved through traffic, the old Suburban shuddering and gorging on gas as the engine roared. The 2x4s on the roof swayed and bounced. "This is what I do."

They got back to the house in record time.

It was now 1:05. Vera would be into her soap.

"Pull around to the coach house!" Bert cried out, his voice sounding almost hysterical with tension. "Hurry!"

"We've still got fifty-five minutes," Ned told him.

"Unless you hadn't noticed," Bert said, leaping out and swinging the garage doors open, "There's a lot of crap in the back and we don't have the Tool Squad to help us this time."

Next to the wall, behind an old, partially dismantled tractor, they piled the supplies: buckets of paint, several cases of shingles, boxes of rat poison, cans of termite killing insecticide fog, hammers and saws and plastic goggles.

An engine suddenly was rumbling up the drive.

"Back early!" Bert exclaimed in a harsh whisper. "Ned! Grab the tarp. *Grab the tarp!*"

Ned grabbed a big blue tarp and unfurled it—it got twisted and snagged, and when they first tried to untwist it they ended up winding it tighter still.

"Grab—wait, no, grab *this*—pull it—"

The sound of car doors slamming.

"Good enough!" Bert choked out, pushing Ned out outside and pulling the doors closed.

Mary and Sarah came around the side of the carriage house. Sarah was smiling and holding a violin case.

"Uncle Bert! I got a violin!"

"It's a rental," Mary said. "We'll buy you one if you end up really liking it."

"Great," Bert said.

"Fantastic," Ned seconded. They were leaning on the door.

"What're you two doing out here, anyways?" Mary said, narrowing her eyes.

"We were washing the car," Ned told her.

"Weren't you washing it when I left?'

"We took a long break," Bert told her. "Just about done now, though, right Ned? Shall we get back to work?"

"Yeah, Bert," Ned said, stifling a laugh. "I guess we've been relaxing long enough."

11

Gilliam's Steakhouse was one of the great institutions of the Lewiston-Brownsville area. It had been passed down from generation to generation since 1842, when it was founded as Gilliam's Tavern of Brownsville. At that time it was a rough and ready stagecoach stop between Philadelphia and Harrisburg, in the days when Brownsville was just one street and a few thatch-roofed inns.

Since that time, both Brownsville and the fortunes of the Gilliam family had matured like a good Bordeaux. Brownsville, home to a small theological college, came to be endowed with a great number of stately row houses and modest churches, pleasant parks and squares, and an unhurried gentility that was sharply at odds with neighboring Lewiston. When Lewiston boomed and mansions sprouted like mushrooms along its new boulevards, Brownsville remained quiet and learned, a place where motorcars were slow to arrive and everybody knew everybody's name. And when Lewiston's factories closed and the great blight turned its grandeur to squalor, Brownsville, as it always had, remained the same.

Gilliam's was part of this timelessness, a permanent fixture on Main Street, across from the park. By 1880 it was no longer a stagecoach tavern: now it was Gilliam's Steakhouse, known far and wide for having the best hand-trimmed, impeccably aged Porterhouse in the state and a wine cellar that was a veritable library of Bordeaux and Riesling and everything in between. Like Antoine's in the Big Easy, this was the kind of place where rich folk willed reserved tables from generation to generation, so that on a Friday night the maitre'd would smile knowingly and with a deft sweep of the hand, say,

"Your table is ready, sir. I will dispatch the sommelier immediately."

The Masters family was one such family. Archibald Masters came to Brownsville at the tender age of sixteen as a simple laborer—by the time he breathed his last he'd started a paper mill and a foundry in Lewiston, but kept his riches in Brownsville in a nice French style villa. He willed the table at Gilliam's to his son Brigham, who expanded the family fortune by manufacturing weapons in WWII. He ate at Gilliam's every Friday night, and when his boys were old enough, he introduced them to "the best damn steak this side of Omaha."

Victor, a shy boy who disliked smoke and backslapping, never took to the place; Collin on the other hand relished in the attention from the Brownsville-Lewiston good old boys, the jet set of small-town Pennsylvania Industry. He got drunk on Château Margeaux, slugging it down like wine cooler, and snapped his fingers when he wanted something.

"Yes, Mr. Masters. Of course, sir."

Was he unruly? Yes. Needlessly condescending to professional waiters of thirty years? Of course. But he was a *Masters*. After dinner, while his father was drinking brandy and enjoying a Cuban, he'd slip out, slapping the Maitre'd on the back and giving the doorman a half-joking jab to the kidney en route to a night of wild vandalism.

Years later, Collin Masters returned after a long stint in business school, looking much paunchier and balder than before. But it wasn't just his hairline and belt size that had changed, the waiters remarked among one another.

The Maitre'd braced for a backslapping but one did not come.

"A Bottle of the Chateau Lafitte Rothschild '64," Collin said instead, adjusting his Armani tie. "And a decanter, if you please."

A wild animal had become a sophisticate.

Roger Gilliam, for one, said he'd expected it all along.

"He's a Masters, and they all go through it. But then they come around."

No mention was made of Victor, who never came in except rarely with a state senator or a Supreme Court judge; that he had amassed a fortune ten times greater than his ancestors and bought most of Brownsville's housing stock was not disputed, but he had never been considered, among the good-old-boys of Gilliam's, to be a real Masters.

Now that Collin was back, the old Masters table was once again full every Friday night. Masters would appear with one or another local beauty, but never the same one twice; or else a banker or investor from New York or Philly. He ordered the Porterhouse rare, as his father did; his taste in wine ran to the expensive end of Bordeaux. As his father had, he ordered the Oysters Rockefeller. As his father had he draped his napkin over one knee.

And as his father had he used Gilliam's as a staging ground for his business strategies, and conspiratorial meetings.

So there was nothing at all unusual about this particular Friday night, when the Mayor of Brownsville, a State

Representative, local uber-contractor Jim Primanti, and two financiers from Philly sat down with Collin Masters over dinner to discuss the House on the Bend and the role it would play in the greatest casino ever seen this side of Atlantic City.

They sat around the big table swathed in curlicues of smoke from their cigarettes, drinking a Lafitte-Rothschild and nibbling on paté and caviar. Everybody at the table knew everybody except for the two financiers, both Italian-looking gentlemen in flashy suits and slicked back hair who apparently were big money from the big city.

The Pirate's Clipper was the talk of the evening. Jim Primanti told the men about the plans he'd reviewed, sent over from Masters Architecture, the design firm Victor had founded. He described, with blunt excitement, how incredibly cool it was going to be. Master Plays was the Casino Royale of Lewiston—debonnaire, very James Bond. Pirate's Clipper was a whole different animal.

"Okay, get this," he said, holding out his thick sausage hands to better kindle their imaginations. "Three floors of play area, two theaters, a buffet seating three hundred, a fine dining place with a view over the river."

"We're talking with Roberto Ruez in LA about a concept," Masters told them. "We want elegant but huge."

"Never heard of him," said one of the money men.

"Pick up a Bon Apetit some time. He's white hot. He's got a fusion restaurant in LA and another one in Vegas."

"What kind of food?" money man pursued.

"He does a Latin-Hunanese fusion at one; the other's Moroccan-Hmong," Collin told him with enormous gravity. "*White* hot."

"Right, right," Primanti said impatiently. "The best part is the hull decoration. We've got a twenty-foot naked girl on the front, and all kinds of gothic shit on the sides. Masts that fire laser beams straight up into the sky. You'll be able to see this thing for a hundred miles at night."

Mayor Burnside smiled.

"This is going to be huge," he said with relish.

"Bigger than huge," Collin assured him seriously. "On shore, the mooring facility will be distinctive as well, right Jim?"

"This mooring facility will have another restaurant, a miniature golf, and a kid's play land."

"Plus a children's museum, with pirate-themed exhibits of a very high standard," Collin said. "We've got a design firm in Hong Kong working something up."

"Hong Kong?" Money Man 2 asked.

"Victor's idea. He's got a guy there."

"The building'll be built to look like a Spanish fort," Primanti told them. "We plan to have battle reenactments, complete with costumed extras, on special promotions nights involving both facilities at once."

"The Chinese in on that too?" Money Man 1 asked.

"Yes. There's some complicated laser light and pyrotechnics that we've farmed out to them," Collin told him. "It'll be unlike anything you've ever seen, period. People will be saying, 'forget Disney World, let's go up to Lewiston.' " He pressed his hands flat on the table. "This is going to be the biggest tourist draw in the Northeast. This buzz is going to be massive. The revenue this will bring Lewiston and Brownsville will be staggering."

Everybody was nodding with excitement.

"But you haven't broken ground yet," Representative Craig Horrowitz pointed out. "Have you?"

"No," Collin said, clearing his throat and glancing at Jim Primanti. "There's just one *little* snag."

The Mayor made an "I'm afraid so" face to Horrowitz and the two money men.

"It's like this," Primanti said. "The design for the casino will only fit in one place on the river here in Pawnee County. Most places the river's not very wide or deep."

"And *that* piece of land is held by a local landowner who is playing hardball."

"Hardball?" Horrowitz said.

"She won't sell."

"What'd you offer her?" money man 2 asked.

"Something generous," Collin assured him. "It's been in her family for a hundred years. She has unconditionally refused to sell,"

"What are we doing to fix this problem?" Money Man 1 asked with a threatening edge in his voice.

"We've slapped a bunch of building violations on them," the Mayor assured him. "She hasn't got much money. She runs a boarding house. Once that boarding house gets shut down next month, it's only a matter of time."

"That sounds like uncertainty," Money Man 2 said.

"The *problem*," Collin said, "Is that even if we shut her down, there is no guarantee that she will sell the house even then—or that she will agree to sell it to us."

"We've tried going the Eminent Domain route," the Mayor lamented, appealing to Horrowitz. "But the courts turned us down."

"What does that leave us?" Money Man 2 asked.

"What we want to do," Primanti said, "is condemn the house. We need to present the case before the County Circuit Court. We'll portray the house as a danger, a *menace*."

"This sounds dubious," Horrowitz said.

"That's why we're informing you right now," Masters told him. "We need everybody on the same page here. We all need to be firing on all cylinders. This needs to go through."

"If it hits the press that we're trying to squeeze this woman for her house, there'll be a shit storm," Horrowitz said. "For all of us."

"That's why we need you running interference," Masters said. "With cooperation between the Mayor's office, the State Legislature, and the County Government, we can apply enough pressure to make this happen. Call in favors. Bend a couple rules. Get your PR departments to jump on any negative press."

"So we need a judge to rule that the house is unfit for habitation to condemn it," Money Man 2 reiterated.

"The Department of Safety will certify it unfit for habitation; the judge will rule on the seizure," Masters said. "She's got kids. We can use that. We also need to demonstrate that the house is presenting some kind of environmental hazard. Then, the judge rules a county seizure of the property and sells it at a court ordered sale, and bingo."

"Pirate's Clipper," Jim Primanti said, frothing with excitement.

"What's the odds this'll work?" Horrowitz asked. "I mean, just how bad is the house?"

"The house isn't the issue. It's the judge. It depends on the judge," Masters said.

"If it goes to Randall, we're fine," the Mayor pronounced. "But if it goes to McHenry…

"I say we arrange something else," Money Man 1 suggested, sniffing with vigor. "Something permanent."

"I didn't hear that," the Mayor said.

"What are you saying?" asked Horrowitz.

"Mr. Vecchio's got a peculiar sense of humor," Masters said with a calm smile. "Moving right along."

Afterwards conversation shifted to tax revenues, and Vecchio excused himself to see the score in the Pirates game over at the bar. Masters went and joined him. The bar was loud and smoky and their voices were drowned out by excited baseball talk.

"I'd prefer you not speak that way in front of the others," Masters said.

"About what?"

"You know about what."

"Look, Mr. Bertolucci expects this to happen. We're frontin' a lot of money. We *expect* it to *happen*."

"It *will* happen. Legitimately."

"You comin' up with lawyer tricks to steal her house is the same thing as burnin' it down."

Masters pointed a finger at him.

"Remember our agreement. You let *me* call the shots."

"Mr. Bertolucci calls the goddamn shots, Masters."

"I've got money coming from twenty places," Masters said. "We don't need your money."

"I'd like to see you try and refuse it," Vecchio said with a dangerous chuckle. "*That*, I'd like to see. It's a little late in the day to be changing the rules."

"We're gonna do it straight," Masters reiterated, as if he hadn't heard Vecchio.

"And if that doesn't work... *then* we'll try other alternatives."

"Great," Vecchio said. "Now shut up. I'm tryin' to watch the game."

12

Billy Shumak woke up Saturday morning with the crushing realization that school was only two days away. It hit him suddenly: one moment he was lying on his back, peering through sleepy eyes at the room, basking in the diagonal light of morning, so full of possibility and summer; and the next he was crushed under the semi-truck weight of the imminence of the tenth grade.

TWO DAYS AWAY.

Two days was far enough off to feel grateful that it was not upon him yet, but close enough to make his stomach turn. *Tenth grade.*

He rolled over and buried his face in the pillow.

"Ah, crap," he said into the bed.

How exactly did it happen? The school year finally dwindled and ran out, hot days in classrooms gave way to finals in the gymnasium, and then freedom. The first afternoon after the school year ended was the sweetest thing in the world. One morning he was in class; and then he was free, with the months stretching out before him, months of freedom from hall passes and geology and the malignant, aggressive buzz of high school society. The trees hummed with green, the sky was dazzlingly blue. Time slowed down. Walking down the school drive, Billy would cast a final glance over his shoulder, say "So long!" and plunge, headlong, into summer.

Now, mysteriously, it was two days before the new school year. Like an army poised for battle, nine and half months of school loomed over him threateningly.

Where did all of that time go?

Like sand through his fingers, it had escaped in the blink of an eye.

Billy hated everything about high school. He hated his classmates, first and foremost: the preppy kids with their Hollister and Abercrombie and cologne and well toned physiques and in-jokes and casual cruelty, their women who'd just as soon spit on Billy as look at him (and looked at him with a lip curl of disgust). He hated the gangsta kids from the projects and the slums of Lewiston, with their hand signals and slouching walk and "what you looking at *punk*" attitudes; he hated the kids from the trailer parks and the farms, who were likely dropping out soon if they hadn't already, smelly, badly dressed kids who loved hunting deer and pounding fags. He hated the nerds, the art kids, the band kids, the jocks. He hated those three guys who weren't part of any group and thought they were James Dean and wore leather jackets, but being three, were numerous enough to constitute a group. He hated all those people because somewhere along the line—seventh grade, he reckoned—political boundaries had been drawn up, alliances formed, rivalries hardened, the caste of who could date who and who could be seen with who, who beat up who, and so on—the whole thing was carved up like so and somehow he'd slipped through the cracks and ended up outside it all.

He ate lunch with John Fitzgerald, a kid who could draw very well, Adam Cho, a Chinese kid with no distinguishing attributes, and Chrissy Stelmach, a gangly girl with straight dark hair and a plain, oval face. They weren't a group, just scraps left over after the dividing up that happened to be swept together during the lunch hour. They never said much; everybody just ate and watched John draw his latest warlock or ogre. Billy sat there in the roar of the cafeteria and let his eyes wander around. Hot girl table. Jock table, full of broad shoulders and short haircuts. A black gangsta table, glaring at a Mexican gangsta table. If he was lucky there might be a fight.

It was strange to feel so alone in the midst of so many people. It burned him to watch any show or movie set in a high school, which inevitably involved a cast of fresh faced, bright-eyed, well adjusted kids who hung out with friends and spoke in well-lubricated, rapid fire banter.

It annoyed him because he knew that he'd never know what that was like. All around him at lunch he could catch snippets of it—Vince messed around with Linda, Ron got totally drunk at Mitch's house. There was a world of clandestine, teenaged fun that everyone in that room seemed to be invited to—except him. He'd never even kissed a girl before. That was very upsetting. It was more than upsetting: it was monumentally unfair.

It seemed like a cosmic mistake that things had ended up the way they had: he was good looking, not insufferably dorky, and dressed like anybody else. There were gawkier, uglier, weirder kids, who belonged somewhere, who had people to talk to and places to go. But not Billy. Something had misfired at a crucial point in his social development, at that moment when he and his peers made the jump from kids to teens, and he'd been ejected into social purgatory. He ought to have had a girlfriend by now. He ought to at least have had *friends*.

But he didn't.

High school.

Two days away.

Somebody was knocking, very quietly, on the door.

"Pssst!'

Knocking. And knocking.

"Hey!"

Uncle Bert.

"What?" Billy groaned.

"You up yet?"

"Yeah."

Bert came in and opened the drapes as wide as they would go, letting in a broad swath of sunlight.

"Hey," Bert said. "Remember what today is."

"What's today?"

"Vera and your Mom just left for the Lewiston Jewelry Expo," Bert said. "Which means the coast is clear. Get up. We've got work to do."

Every year, Vera and Mary went to the Jewelry Expo in Lewiston, where they spent most of the day browsing the long rows of jewelers who had converged from all over the tri-county area to sell their wares, a blinding array of bangles, necklaces, and rings ranging in style from Lil' John to Sitting Bull. On that particular morning, so as not to miss the best deals or the few early hours when the Lewiston Convention Center was not insufferably crowded, the two women departed at the crack of dawn, leaving a breakfast buffet of cereal, juice, donuts and coffee on the dining room table. This was one of the few occasions when Sarah and Billy had a chance to sleep in—Mary did the whole set up, leaving them responsible solely for cleaning the mess, such as it was, that was left in the end.

This year, Bert had other ideas.

With the utmost secrecy, Bert had spoken with each of his allies throughout the week, giving each person a how-to book and instructing him or her to study up on their area of responsibility, so that everyone would be ready to spring into action when the day came.

Bert and Billy had taken on one of the bigger jobs: the dry rot in the attic and basement needed to be removed and replaced, Bert postulated, with dry wall. He also had spackle, which he planned to use in filling in any holes that might remain. Alan was in charge of pest extermination: spraying termite nests with insecticide and laying out rat traps. Ned was doing the repainting—nobody was sure what was lead-based paint and what wasn't, but the book on lead-based paint hazards recommended painting over it with a coat of non-lead-based paint to seal it in (they said it needed to be done by a licensed professional, but come on—paint's paint). Mr. Manicotti was assigned to roof detail—the Sicilian had often commented that he was impervious to heights, so it was logical that he should go up there and start removing shingles. Sarah and Claude were the clean-up crew—there was definitely going to be a huge mess. Mrs. Noonan would handle refreshments. The plan was, after other people finished their jobs, they'd go up to the roof and help Mr. Manicotti with the roofing job, which was arguably the biggest job and would take the longest. Bert would remain on the ground and direct the operation from there.

After he'd given each team member a how-to book and his instructions, he left them with the final word that he would summon them at the appropriate time on Saturday morning by blasting an old air horn; then they would assemble on the verandah to commence the operation,

Saturday morning was here at last. At 8:30 sharp, the air horn blew. Alan reluctantly turned off the television; Ned put down the shoe he was polishing. Mr. Manicotti stubbed out his cigarette and donned his panama hat. One by one, each at his own pace, Bert's crew assembled in the morning heat on the verandah. Bert, with Billy at his side, tried to look steely faced and resolute, gazing at the sun through narrowed eyes. Under one arm he held his yellow pad: the battle plan. When everyone was amassed, shuffling around and whispering amongst one another, Bert finally turned about and addressed them.

"You all know why you're here," Bert said. He looked at each of them in turn. He held Claude's vacant gaze. "We're gonna save this house."

He let it sink in for dramatic effect.

"As you all know, the county wants to take this house and turn it into a casino. Now, this place means a lot to my sister. It means a lot to me. It means a lot to everyone here, right?"

Nodding and "mmm-hmmm" sounds.

Bert whipped out the letter from the county, which now was wrinkled and coffee stained and ten other kinds of dog-eared from a lengthy tenancy in Bert's pocket.

"They sent us this list," he said with a dramatic flourish. "A challenge to—"

"Bert," Ned interrupted. "Can I say something?"

Bert gritted his teeth, irritated at being interrupted.

"Yes, Ned?"

"You told us about this before. Remember? When you gave us the self-help books?"

"Yes," Mr. Manicotti agreed. "We already a-know about the letter."

"It's called an *inspirational speech*," Bert said. "Unless you hadn't noticed, I was trying to fire up the troops here. Provide some *motivation.*"

"I'm motivated right now," Billy said, raising his hand.

"Me too," Ned said.

"I'm motivated to get this over with," Alan piped up. "I feel like Al Borlan on the set of Tool Time."

"You're nothing like Al Borlan," Bert said.

"Well, you're no Tim Taylor," Alan shot back. "And he wasn't even a very good handyman."

"He was a fine handyman," Ned said. "Just a little clumsy."

"Oh, my," Mrs. Noonan said.

"We're getting *way* off topic," Bert said.

"Can we *please* just get to work," Billy sighed.

"I'm bored," Sarah said. "Can I go play?"

"What's going on?" Mrs. Noonan asked.

"Star Trek: Voyager," Alan said with a shake of the head. "Now there was a boring show. At least the first two seasons were. Then they encountered the Borg…"

Bert clapped his hands, whistled, and finally blew the air horn.

"So in summation and conclusion!" he declared. "Let's get to work!"

13

First of all, Bert had to get all his people into place. Bert had designed a rudimentary pulley system from some bits and pieces he'd found in the garage. He climbed out of the attic window and attached it, along with forty feet of nylon rope, to the apex of the roof, tying it into place using a second length of rope and a chimney. During the week, it had occurred to him that Mr. Manicotti, being 96, was a bit too fragile and certainly not of sufficient strength to hoist himself onto the roof from the attic window; hence the pulley. Once he had the pulley tied in place, he gave it a mighty tug and put his whole weight on it. The rope slipped a tiny bit but then held fast.

"Okay!" he shouted down, his head swimming with vertigo. The ground below swelled nauseatingly. He suddenly realized that he'd have to climb back down into the window—a horrifying thought that he pushed into the back of his head as the pulley began to turn, the nylon rope went taught, and Mr. Manicotti appeared below in the window, fastened into a harness which was in turn attached to the nylon rope. Once Mr. Manicotti—

hat in hand—was out of the window, his feet dangling in midair and a sheer drop below him into the rhododendrons, the situation became more complicated. The pulley suddenly refused to budge any further—when it did, the rope, which was caught on the edge of the roof, made a dangerous sawing sound as it dragged along the asphalt tiles. The violence of the rope's struggle did not move Mr. Manicotti upwards—he dangled there, swinging to and fro with increasing vigor.

"It's not moving!" Billy's voice came from inside.

"I see that!" Bert shouted back. "Don't worry, Mr. Manicotti. We'll get you up here!"

Mr. Manicotti did not seem disturbed. He was dapperly dressed as usual, though the harness had caused his suit to bunch up unflatteringly and his pant legs to ride up nearly to his knees, revealing his socks and thin calves.

The rope was making ever more hellish noises.

"Ho hey hey!" Bert shouted down. "Not to alarm anybody, but that rope is getting chewed up somethin' fierce. Hold on a sec!"

Bert spit on his hands and grabbed hold of the rope. Mr. Manicotti, ancient and shriveled as he was, surely couldn't weigh very much.

He gave it a tug, but it wouldn't budge and it pinched and burned his fingers and pinned them on the roof tiles. Bert hissed and shook his hand in the air. Rope burn. Just great.

"Teamwork, Billy!" he cried. "Need a little teamwork here!"

"You told me to hold on a sec!" Billy answered from below.

"Okay! Count of three! I'll pull and you pull at the same time!" Bert flexed his injured hands and laid hold of the rope again. "One! Two!"

On three he pulled, and Billy pulled, and the rope did finally move. Mr. Manicotti began to inch his way upwards.

"Keep pulling! *Keep pulling!*" Bert screamed desperately, the rope burning his hands like a hot iron. The rope stopped again. Mr. Manicotti was now jammed against the eave.

"Mr. Manicotti!" Bert shouted. "Grab on to the roof. That's it! Grab on! Just like that!"

The Sicilian had placed two limp paws on the edge of the roof.

"Now! Haul yourself up!"

Bert knew this was an impossibility even as he said it. Nevertheless, he watched with a crazy optimism. Mr. Manicotti's hat sailed downwards in a spiral and landed in the grass. His body shook for a moment, but he didn't budge.

"Oh, shit," Bert hissed. His fingers were slipping. If he let go, Mr. Manicotti would drop suddenly; Billy, surprised, would lose his grip on the rope; and Mr. Manicotti would fall to his doom.

"Can… you…make it?" Bert gasped to the Sicilian, hopeful to the last.

"I droppa my hat," Mr. Manicotti answered amiably.

"We've got the rope!" Ned shouted up.

Thank the Lord. Ned had joined them.

"Grab him! Pull him up!" Billy said.

Bert seized Mr. Manicotti's hands and pulled, grasped, yanked, and rolled, until they were both on the roof, Mr. Manicotti folded over him and Bert heaving for breath.

"Got… him!" Bert announced, slowly getting to his feet, forgetting that he was on a slope, and nearly losing his balance.

"Oh my god," he breathed wildly. "I gotta get off here. Go to town, Mr. Manicotti. Get those tiles!"

Mr. Manicotti, slightly disoriented from the ordeal, pulled out his hammer and nodded.

Bert looked over the edge and blanched.

"I have no idea how to get down." Then, louder, "Hey, Mr. Manicotti, just for a minute—" he said, licking his lips. "Lend me your harness."

Meanwhile, Alan was in the basement with an armload of insecticide products. It was 9:15—at that very moment he could be watching Hunter on channel 13 or 21 Jump Street on 32. Instead, now he was creeping around in the dark, cavernous recesses of the basement, brushing aside cobwebs, searching for the very vermin that people usually try to avoid. The basement was a distressingly filthy place. It had not been given a good scrubbing in ages, *centuries* it seemed: to everything there was a patina of age and scum, dust balls and dark patches where mold had flourished despite past attempts to wipe it out with a lick of paint.

There were old boxes filled with moldering god knows what, dust, rusty sinks, pipes hung thickly with cobwebs like Spanish moss. The concrete floor was strewn with grit and mouse droppings.

The rodents were certainly a prime source of concern. Alan set out some rat poison baits around the perimeter of each room, spacing them evenly. Next he took out several packages of mousetraps from the paper bag where he was keeping his supplies. He unwrapped them and clicked on the overhead light so he could get a better look at how they operated. He pulled on the spring-loaded wire and felt its grim resistance. He pulled it to halfway, panicked, and eased it back to its starting position. He tried it again. No way. The threat of getting his finger snapped off was immediate and terrifying. He stared, frustrated, at the offending mousetrap.

There was no way he could load up these fiendish devices and bait them with the Jiffy peanut butter he'd brought along. It was odd, this encounter with an object so familiar from TV and yet so alien in the real world. He realized that although he had seen many mousetraps on TV—on Tom and Jerry cartoons mostly—he had never handled one before this moment. This was another important separation between TV and the real world—the fact that on TV nobody had problems doing simple things, nobody got scared at awkward moments. He had been working on this project for—he checked his watch—an hour, and all he'd accomplished was laying out a few rat poison traps.

There were insects to kill as well.

Termites. He remembered Bert saying that there were termites that needed killing. Termites lived in wood, but the basement was predominantly concrete and cinder block. Termites weren't in residence here. He needed to move upstairs.

Alan climbed out of the gloom of the basement into the light of the first floor.

Am I done killing rodents already? Alan wondered darkly. I am responsible for killing all rodents in the house. Each person has a responsibility and that one's mine. Before I move on to termites I need to make sure I'm through with rodents.

He couldn't be sure. The answer wouldn't arrive by the top of the hour. It was very hard to say whether the traps would do the job, entirely or even in part.

Termites. Moving right along.

Alan tapped on the wall in the dining room and pressed his ear to it. He imagined that if the wall was full of crawling insects, he should be able to hear their scratching and millings, the throb and scuttle of large scale insect industry.

Tap tap.

It sounded hollow but he didn't hear any insects. He went into the hallway and tapped on that wall. Also hollow sounding, beneath the yellowing wallpaper. Still no insect noise.

Could a man really hear a bug through a wall? Suddenly that idea didn't seem to hold much water. One could hear insects on TV because the producers used powerful microphones. Of course! Stupid! How could the naked human ear ever hope to detect the footfalls of a termite? Which meant, of course, that there was only one way to get to the bottom of this.

From This Old House he'd learned that there are places in the wall where there are joists and places where there aren't—between the joists was the place to look for bugs. Alan carefully took a chisel and hammer, and placing the tip of the chisel on the wall in a spot unimpeded by a joist, he gave it a tap. The tip drove into the soft wall. He pulled it out, causing a small cascade of dry wallpaper flakes and wood chips. The hole was very small, smaller than a dime in diameter. Alan peered into it, but it was hopelessly dark in there. He would need to make a bigger opening.

He replaced the chisel next to the hole and gave it a second tap. He repeated this several more times. The last time, a violent foot-long split appeared and ran downwards in the wallboard. The hole was now a gaping, ragged wound.

Alan looked at the mess he'd made, but reasoned that this was really the only way to determine if there were termites in the wall. He peered into the hole. *Still* too dark. He gave the lower portion a little tug, hoping to bend it and admit some light. With a loud crack the wallboard sheared off a large brittle triangle.

Cockroaches appeared—three of them, clinging on the broken wallboard, bewildered and trying to escape back into the shadows. Each was half an inch long and reddish brown. Alan recoiled in horror. In the light shed on the wall's innards, Alan could see that although there were no termites in evidence, there were hundreds of cockroaches. They squirmed around, waving their tentacles at the light as if in mild irritation.

"My God," Alan said aloud with a shudder. "My *God.*"

He seized his can of Raid and began spraying. He sprayed and sprayed until the air tasted bitter and he could feel certain that this area of the wall had been bug-bombed into the Stone Age.

Bu he could *not* say the same for the rest of the house.

This one, small area was crawling with roaches like an exhibit at the Science Museum. Just imagine what the rest of the house was hiding. Millions. No, *billions* more.

He took his hammer, went into the TV room, and knocked out a big segment of the wall. There were fewer roaches here, but now there were termites as well, little white soldiers that seemed to be living amiably in cockroach society.

Alan sprayed and sprayed. Then he sprayed some more.

His hands were shaking and he had a headache, equal parts bug-fear and Raid-buzz. He swung the hammer into the parlor wall. Then, two kitchen walls. He returned to the hallway and knocked out a new section there. Each demolition revealed a new glimpse into a hidden world, an empire of crawling things and moldy darkness.

His job was to exterminate all of them.

He could not fail

He wound up and swung again.

In the attic Ned was stirring paint and Billy was helping Bert strip away wall paneling. Underneath they could see that everything was badly decayed—the wall posts were softening and splintering, the wall board itself was rotten, the insulation was fragmenting and full of mouse droppings and cockroaches. From overhead they could hear the steady click-*click* click-*click* of Mr. Manicotti peeling off the roof tiles. It was getting very hot in the closed space of the attic.

Sarah appeared at the stairs.

"Uncle Bert!" she cried out. "Alan's destroying the whole house!"

"Whadya mean?" Bert asked as he inspected the rot and tried to decide what to do.

Click-*click*. Click-*click*.

"Oh, dammit, I just spilled paint everywhere," Ned lamented. "Oh, I should have put down some newspapers."

"He's knocking holes in all the walls, looking for bugs. He's going crazy. He's making a huge mess."

"What's Claude doing?"

"Sweeping."

"The mess?"

"No. He's out front sweeping the walk."

"Did you tell him to clean up the mess?"

"Yeah, but he wants to sweep the walk."

From downstairs there came a loud crash.

"See?" Sarah said.

"Let me go and check it out," Bert said. "Hold on a second."

Bert descended from the attic. The sounds of destruction grew louder and louder. Then he saw the damage. There were holes in the walls up and down the hallway. There were piles of rubble. There were countless dead cockroach carcasses.

He found Alan in the dining room, knocking out a big part of the wall. He looked half-deranged, sweating hard, with plaster dust all over his windbreaker.

"Hey! Ho! Alan!" Bert shouted. "Buddy! *What* are you *doing?*"

"Mr. Wodehouse," Alan said, turning to address Bert with a curt salute and a slight tremor in his voice. "This house is far more infested than we knew. It is an empire of insects. There are termites, yes. But there are also legions of cockroaches, and spiders, and ants, and centipedes. I don't even want to comment on the rodent situation. Although I haven't actually seen a rat, there is ample evidence that they have been running wild. The situation is dire, but I am taking steps to bring it under control."

"By knocking out every wall in the house? " Bert whined.

"How else are we going to get at the infestation?"

Bert looked around, at the bugs dropping off the walls and lying, half-dead, in drifts on the floor. Alan's policy did, indeed, seem to be working—and besides, he did a nice salute.

"See," Bert said with a big smile. "I knew I put you in charge of this for a reason. Keep up the good work. We'll patch it up later."

There came the clinking of ice in glass from nearby. Bert caught sight of Mrs. Noonan with a tray of lemonade and glasses, inching from the kitchen towards the stairs.

"Mrs. Noonan?" Bert called out. "Where are you going?"

"Upstairs," she answered, "With some lemonade for y'all."

"Why don't I take that for you," he suggested, leaving Alan to his devices as he crashed thought another wall.

"I like to do it mah-self," Mrs. Noonan said. "Just like back in Beaumont. Oh, we did love lemonade. Real lemonade, that is, with real lemons. Yes, yes, very nice."

From the next room came a violent popping sound and then a whiff of smoke.

"You OK in there, Alan?" Bert called.

"I just hit an electrical thing!"

"You alright?"

"The light blew out but I'm fine."

"We'll fix it later," Bert said, watching Mrs. Noonan as she resumed her long journey to the attic. She might as well have been scaling Mt. Kailash. By the time she'd get up to the attic there they'd be done with the repairs. "Get Claude to help you clean up. I've gotta go back upstairs."

Back in the attic Bert found Sarah and Ned trying to mop up the paint he'd spilled—there were wadded up paper towels everywhere and paint smeared and streaked all over the floor. Billy had gotten some on his sneakers and had tracked it all over.

Click *click*. Click *click*. Mr. Manicotti was working steady as a metronome.

"Eh, doesn't need to be pretty," Bert said. "Don't worry about it. We aren't trying to make the cover of *Old House Journal*."

Bert and Billy stacked up the old wallboard and got out the drywall. Billy made measurements to attach it to the gaping holes in the walls.

"OK," Bert said, putting on some goggles. "Take the pick-axe and start digging out all that rot. I'll cut the drywall."

Billy regarded the pickaxe doubtfully.

"I'm not sure…"

"Come on, Billy, this is no time for screwin' around. Jump to it!"

Billy hesitated for a moment longer, then shrugged and gave the pickaxe a swing into the rotten wall joist.

Wham.

Billy tripped backwards, shook his head, dislodged the pickaxe, and swung it again.

Wham.

Bert set the drywall on the two wooden hobbyhorses. Then he plugged in the radial saw that he'd found in the coach house.

Wham.

Click *click*.

"Cover your ears everybody. This might be a bit loud."

He switched on the saw. The high whine of the blade filled the attic. Ned, tracking paint far and wide, was slapping thick acrylic paint on the pipes overhead. Bert brought the saw to bear on the drywall. The blade bit in and released a dense white cloud of dust into the air.

Bert started coughing but kept at it, cutting deep into the wallboard. The air filled with ever-denser plumes of drywall dust. Pretty soon everybody was coughing, rubbing their eyes and covered with white powder. It looked like a volcano had erupted nearby.

"Take five!" Bert gasped between violent coughs. "Break!"

Billy let loose one last swing of the pickaxe.

Wham.

The last impact was followed by a slow peal of shuddering wood, splitting load-bearing beams, and rapidly sagging roof supports. The roof shuddered and dropped an inch. A massive, dangerous split had appeared.

Everybody froze.

The sound of the hammer from above had stopped.

Ned coughed.

Bert coughed.

"Mr. Manicotti!" Billy shouted. "You still up there?"

"Yes!" the Sicilian answered. "Whatsa happened?"

"Little problem!" Bert answered, his face caked in white drywall dust. "Just a little, ah, *don't move!* Okay?"

The roof was making little groaning sounds. Then it stopped, and everything was silent.

From far off came a familiar cry.

"That's a pickle!"

It was followed by another familiar cry.

"BERT!"

Bert swallowed and looked at Billy, Ned, and Sarah.

"NED!" came a different, equally volcanic scream. Ned swallowed and sighed heavily.

"Oh man am I gonna get it."

Vera and Mary were standing in the front hall. Mary was literally red in the face, blinking with rage. She was holding the hammer that she'd snatched from Alan's hand.

Bert, Alan, Ned, and the rest of them—except Mrs. Noonan, who was MIA with her lemonade—were lined up in the front hall, covered from head to toe in dust, or in Alan's case, bits of wood and cobweb. Behind them, three giant holes were visible in the hallway walls. There were wood shards and bits of wallpaper littering the ground. The place smelled poisonously of Raid.

"Okay," Mary said in a trembling voice. "Somebody *please* explain what is going on here."

Bert sheepishly produced the wadded up letter from the county and handed it to Mary.

"They said we'd get shut down unless we fixed that stuff," Bert said meekly. "I thought we could get the place fixed up for you."

"By knocking holes in the walls?" Mary shouted. "By grinding up drywall? By destroying the attic?"

"By putting Mr. Manicotti on the roof?" Vera chimed in. "Somebody's gotta get him offa there. *Now.*"

"Mr. Manicotti was doing a great job up there," Bert protested.

"The man's 97 years old!" Vera cried. "If he falls off the roof he'll break every bone in his body!"

"Whoa!" Bert said, holding up a hand in protest. "First of all, he *wanted* to help. How do you think he'd feel if we left him out? And news flash: he's 96, not 97. If you're gonna start screamin' your head off, at least get your facts straight." Bert smirked at her.

"What's it matter if he's 96 or 97 if every bone in his body's broke!" Vera thundered, planting her fist in her side and leaning in towards Bert.

"Hasn't happened yet!" Bert answered. "Unless you forgot to tell me that you got your fortune teller's license!"

"Don't you talk back to me, I'll take my *shoe* off!"

Ned flinched instinctively.

"That's a pickle!" Claude announced.

Bert swallowed and held out both hands.

"Okay, okay, easy Vera. Easy now."

"That's enough, both of you!" Mary shouted. She looked like she was close to tears as she stared at the letter. "*Please*, Bert, get Mr. Manicotti off the roof. And *be careful.* The rest of you, clean this place up." She made a tight, pained face. "I need to do some thinking."

Mary was sitting in her room an hour later, her face in her hands, when Vera came in. The letter sat next to her. Vera closed the door quietly and sat down next to Mary on the bed. Gently, she put her arm around Mary's slight shoulder.

"Come on, dear," Vera said. "Come on, now."

Mary raised her head. Her eyes were red but she wasn't crying.

"Why is he such an *idiot?*" she said in a thin, furious voice, through clenched teeth.

"Who?"

"Bert!"

Vera shook her head.

"God made some men with more sense than others. Some men got tonsa sense and others got none. That's how it is. Bert got no sense, dear. Ned ain't got no sense neither."

"Oh, Vera," Mary sighed. "Ned's such a good man. He loves you so much."

Vera made a sad face.

"I know he's a good man." She swallowed, then said louder, "But so's your brother. That boy's as dumb as an old mutt but he wants to make you happy like an old mutt, too. He looks at you like you was the sun. You see that, don't you, dear?"

"He hid this letter. For a *week*. We've lost a whole week. And now he trashed my house."

"Dear, this place was already hurtin' Bert only helped it along. But I'm telling you, in his way, mind you I ain't saying it's right what he done, but *in his way* this is how he says he loves you."

Mary smiled despite herself and shook her head. She wiped away a tear.

"I know it, Vera. He just makes me so mad."

"That's how it is with the ones you love."

Mary nodded, then looked at the letter. She smoothed it out, looking at it sadly.

"I honestly don't know what to do," Mary said. "I can't afford to hire somebody to fix all this stuff."

Vera saw something in the window.

It was Mr. Manicotti, swaying in the breeze, smoking a cigarette and being lowered, bit by jerking bit, down to the ground.

Vera hugged Mary until Mr. Manicotti was past.

"I'm gonna call Tom," Vera decided.

"Vera, I don't want to make you do anything you don't want to do."

"He done Ned wrong and he done me wrong," Vera said bitterly. "He's been a *bad* boy, disrespectin' his father the way he did." She smiled at Mary. "But we do need some help, don't we?" She started laughing despite herself.

"Yeah," Mary said, laughing too. "It looks like we do."

14

Tom Johnson loved houses, and because of this, odd as it was to say so, he considered himself extremely lucky to be living in Lewiston. Lewiston was struggling: its jobless rate had improved in recent years but was still in the toilet. Drugs were dealt openly in some quarters of the city, and rusty cars lay abandoned on the yards of crackhouses, with weeds growing lush around softened tires as a testament to the machine's permanence there. There was graffiti; there were gang bangers in long white t-shirts and cornrows down on 15th Street; and there was an awful lot of plywood around instead of glass.

The Puerto Ricans sat in their windows—they kicked out their screens—and in crowds on porches, their canary yellow Caddies parked on front lawns; the Mexicans hung big Mexican flags from their sagging balconies and cruised down the streets in their pimped Mitsubishis, blaring ranchero music and looking to fight the Puerto Ricans. The whites sat out on ancient lawn chairs in wifebeaters, beer in hand, their kids playing in a half-deflated kiddy pool, wife pregnant and cooking up some hot dogs, their clapboard-tarpaper house falling down behind them. Yes, Lewiston was very poor.

But God, what houses there were.

Growing up in Lewiston, back when the place was in slightly better shape, Tom had no interest in architecture. He came from a very modest, blue-collar home; Dad a truck driver, Mom a part time secretary at the trucking company, house ranch-style in the worst sense of the word. Growing up they spent summers at the municipal pool or else at Pawnee State Park, grilling polish sausage, Dad in his Mack Truck hat and agricultural or industrial themed t-shirt, Mom in jeans and tucked in tank top, the both of them sweating and bickering like crazy. They drove a '76 Oldsmobile station wagon, a big thing with fake-looking wood paneling and cracked red vinyl seats. Dad was away much of the time on runs cross-country. Mom did her best to keep things together: the house, her marriage, her job, her son.

But it was only years later, after the economy had tanked and Lewiston had gone from blue collar to no-collar that Tom started noticing just how *rich* the city actually was.

It happened one day in the late 90s, walking down a stretch of Main Street to a job site where he was building a porch. At that time, most of Main Street was boarded up or burned out, looking like a scene from Bosnia. Around where he lived at that time, in a white part of town, a neighborhood of modest bungalows and trailer parks, he was looked at with suspicion when he walked to the store or went for a bike ride; it was disconcerting that only on Main Street, and the avenues thereabouts, neighborhoods of "his people" where handguns outnumbered books and crack *was* the economy—only here could he walk around and not attract "the hell *you* up to?" glares.

While he was considering this—and he considered it quite often—he happened to gaze up at the Wilber T. Bludhaven house, a greystone hulk from 1884, built to resemble a Bavarian castle, complete with turret and medieval iconography. At that time he didn't know the name of the house, or its date of construction or what iconography was—only that it was achingly beautiful. He stopped and stared. And stared. Two black guys were on the porch, smoking a joint.

"The fuck you lookin' at?" one asked.

"Your house!" Tom said. "You got a beautiful house, you know that?"

"Fuck you talkin' about, Negro?" the other inquired.

Tom shrugged and started on towards the job site. He looked at one house, and then another. He'd lived in Lewiston his entire life—twenty five years, at that point—and he'd never noticed it: Main Street was a *museum*.

Over the next few weeks he started walking around town, up and down the streets, gawking at these treasures, made all the more precious in their late decrepitude. There were Victorians, Queen Annes, Greystones, Brownstones, Colonial Revivals and Second Empires. On the side streets there were two-story row houses still sporting traces of their original cheerful colors. There were stained glass windows, cherubs, and angels realized in stone, wrought iron fences and grilles fit for a street in Paris. There were murals and Art Deco mosaics downtown in Central Square. It filled him with a raw excitement as he realized that he might very well be the only person in the city who realized that Lewiston, for all its decay, was astoundingly beautiful.

He spent evenings after work at the library, reading books on architecture, about styles and architects and the philosophy that guided his craft. He'd spent the past seven years learning how to wire a house, how to put up a frame, how to lay brick. He was well on his way to being a master craftsman, but until now it had been simply because the pay was good and the work was steady and it was something more worthwhile than what his father did. But now he understood that he was party to something far greater than simple bricks and mortar, nails and wood: he was an agent of visual poetry.

Tom had not been to college. He got his high school diploma and started working full time. He'd always felt too proud to ask his parents for anything, and thanks to the problems that had led to his abrupt departure from home, he couldn't live there any longer even if he wanted to. Anyhow, it was exciting in those early days to be living on his own, making his own money doing roofing and construction, partying in his apartment at night, blowing all his money on enough beer and whiskey to keep his place popular with the ladies. There were lots of girls around. Sometimes he and his buddies picked them up at local bars and brought them back to Tom's apartment. The next morning was always like an Easter egg hunt, looking for a missing bra, discovering used condoms or a pile of vomit instead.

More than all that, being on his own was an assertion that he was a man.

A real man.

From very early on, Ned had wanted his son to follow in his footsteps. Since Ned was a truck driver and Vera worked in the same company, it made perfect sense that in time Tom, also, should work there—that is, get his commercial license and start making long hauls as well. Ned had long dreamed of sharing a cold beer on the porch with Tom, swapping stories of the road. Tom would understand and respect his father for being the greater truck driver at first, and learn the tricks of the trade in a kind of apprenticeship. Eventually, when Tom was the best damned driver the Company had ever seen, and exceeded even Ned, Ned would retire gracefully and a dynasty of truck drivers would be established. This had been his dream since Tom was a little boy.

At first, Tom was mad about cars and trucks, as all small boys are, and when he wasn't playing with a toy semi he was running around making dramatic engine sounds, swinging his arm in a circular motion that was meant to imitate a steering wheel. He would sit in the cab of Ned's rig and look with devotional wonder at the instruments, the gear shift and the rubber accordion that enclosed its base, and thrill to the sound of the mighty engine starting up.

But as he got older, his interest waned. This, again, was typical, but whereas most parents paid it no mind, Ned was hurt that Tom suddenly was interested in baseball and dinosaurs instead of trucks. For a while, Tom reluctantly played with his truck toy at Ned's prodding; out of habit he sat in the cab of the rig and tried to seem interested. But nuance is not a strong suit of little boys, and he just couldn't stop thinking about his baseball card collection, or how cool Tyrannosaurus rex was. So one day when Ned saw Tom reading a dinosaur book and suggested that he and Tom go and hang out at the truck garage, Tom, impatiently, blurted out,

"*Dad*, I don't want to see any stupid trucks!"

Ned knew that the words of a ten-year-old ought not carry much weight. After all, children are fleeting in their attention and he was too young to understand the outstanding benefits of driving truck: the insurance, the good pay, the retirement package. None-the-less, Ned was devastated. There was something thrilling and childlike about Ned's love of trucks, a kind of love that he could only share with a child. His co-workers didn't get it, and even if they did, how would it seem for two grown men to enthuse about tractor-trailers in such a way?

But now he saw that door slam shut. He realized that he'd seen it coming, but had turned a blind eye to the warning signs: Tom never played with his trucks any more; he never asked questions about the rig or how it worked; he never talked about what he wanted to be when he grew up any more—at least, not around Ned. In company of friends, Tom liked to say "Paleontologist" or "Major League Pitcher" and realized guiltily that if he added "truck driver" at all, it was only out of some sad nostalgia. Finally he'd blurted out his disinterest, and after that, he didn't bother hiding it anymore.

Still, Ned would needle Tom about it from time to time, realizing that while Tom might not be crazy about trucks now, he, as the father, ought to at least steer his son in the right direction: to remind young Tom about the steady work that awaited him as a driver for the Company.

Somewhere along the line, however, Tom's disinterest in truck driving turned to disdain. Several years later, Ned came back from a long haul out to Seattle and recounted the story to Tom on the back porch. Rather than faking interest, Tom yawned and rolled his eyes.

"Don't you make that face, boy!" Ned commanded. "You hear me?"

"Why not? It's *boring*."

"You won't think it's boring when you've got a wife of your own and you make lots of money and get to see the world!" Ned countered hopefully, his insides seething with resentment.

"Yes I will," Tom said. "The kids at school say truck driving's for hicks and it gives you hemorrhoids."

The Kids At School.

How Ned hated them. To him they were not real people, but rather some malignant force that stole a bit more of his son each school year. *The Kids At School* taught him to swear. They taught him to talk "black." They taught him that he should smoke weed and have sex and "be cool."

"Don't you listen to them, now," Ned said, as calmly as he could. "How can your dad be a hick if he's black? White folks are hicks. Not black folk."

"It's still stupid and boring," Tom said, kicking his feet impatiently.

It was like talking to a brick wall. Ned had never laid a hand on Tom, but by God, he wanted to shake that boy, just *shake 'im* until some sense crept in or all that nonsense fell out, whichever came first.

"What do you want to do when you grow up, then?" Ned said, asking that question he used to relish and now regretted, even as he said it.

"I think I want to be either a boxer or a soldier," Tom said.

"But you just hurt people in those jobs. And get hurt."

"Yeah, but it's cool. Oh, or maybe a pro-wrestler. Like Mr. T."

Mr. T. It made Ned literally sick to his stomach.

"Ned!" Vera shouted from the kitchen. "Get in here!"

Ned obeyed and met Vera in the kitchen. She was wearing big hoop earrings that swayed, very distractingly, when she talked.

"Ned Johnson, where is your sense?" she whispered angrily. "He's twelve years old! Stop bullying him!"

Ned made a face and looked at his son.

"Has be been getting' in fights?" When she didn't answer, Ned glared at Vera, something he almost never dared to do. "Answer me, woman. Has that boy been gettin' in fights?"

"Now and again," Vera admitted at last. "But he always wins."

"He always—" Ned squeezed his eyes shut, trying to push the rage inside. He desperately wanted not to start shouting. "What have I *always* said about fighting, Vera?"

"You want our boy to grow up into some kinda wimp? Some kinda momma's boy?"

"*You're* the momma!" Ned cried. "*You're* supposed to want that!"

"I want a *man* as a son," Vera boomed, banging her fist on the counter. "Somebody I can count on!"

"Don't you bring *that* into this!" Ned screamed, sweat glistening on his forehead. "We're trying to raise a good boy here! This ain't the place for your complain' and troubles with me!"

"*We're* trying to raise a good boy?" Vera said with a laugh. "Funny you say *we*, when alls I ever see is one parent round here, and that's me! I gotta be momma *and* daddy, Ned! You talk to him like he's some kinda little boy, but he ain't. You know he's got a girlfriend? Do you?"

Ned felt like somebody had just blindsided his truck.

"No," he said quietly. "Vera, he's too *young* for that..."

"You think so 'cause you think he's still eight! How old is our son, Ned?"

"Who puts this roof over our head?" Ned shouted, retreating to safe ground. "We all have to make sacrifices. You think I *like* being on the road all the time?"

"Do you?" Vera boomed. "'You tell me, Ned Johnson. 'Cause I get to wondrin' how you'd find time for all yo' women if you had to stay round here all day long!"

"Dammit!" Ned wailed. "Why you gotta bring that up!" He looked to the doorway. Tom was standing there, eyes wide, listening.

He's not eight.

He's twelve.

He *understands*.

Ned raised his hand to Vera in his sudden fury. He felt a tear running down his cheek.

My son knows.

My son knows.

Tom stepped into the room and gave Ned a hard jab in the kidney. Ned felt the strength leave him, and he staggered into the fridge. Magnets and report cards fell to the ground.

It hurt. It was a strong punch, for a twelve year old. A kid who knew how to fight.

But it wasn't the punch that shut him down.

The hurt went so much deeper than that.

Ned reared up and smacked Tom much, much harder than he'd expected to. Tom stumbled backwards and fell to the ground. He immediately burst into tears, his eyes wide with the dawning of a new understanding of things. Ned immediately felt awful.

But it was far too late.

"Ned Johnson you horrible man you get outta this house right now!" Vera roared in a voice so full of molten rage that he was actually frightened that she might grab a cleaver and come at him.

Tom was crying in gasping sobs. His eye was getting puffy. There was a broken bit of skin on his temple where Ned's wedding ring had bitten in.

"No son of mine is going to hit people!" Ned shouted, realizing the folly of his declaration even as he said it. Vera was holding Tom, making "shhh" sounds and rocking them back and forth. "He hit me, Vera!"

"You was gonna hit *me!*" Vera hissed. "He's just defendin' his momma, same as any good boy's gonna do!"

"I was not going to hit you, Vera, I swear to Lord Jesus!" Ned pleaded.

"You were gonna hit momma!" Tom shouted, his voice thin and sharp as a blade. "I saw it!"

"I've never hit you, Vera, *never*. And I never hit you, Tom, not until—"

"Just…" Vera said in a voice that was suddenly many decibels lower and quivering with restraint, "*Leave.*"

Some doors, when you went through them, there was no going back.

That night Ned made an attempt at sleep in the cab of his truck, tossing and turning and crying, wondering at how incredibly wrong things had gone in just ten minutes.

How, in ten short minutes time, an entire world was torn down.

In the morning he went back home. Vera let him come in without argument. He made some coffee, poured some orange juice. Tom sat at the breakfast table eating Frosted Flakes from a big yellow bowl, his eye swollen. Nobody said anything.

"Drink your orange juice, dear," Vera said sweetly to Tom, *extra* sweetly in fact, so that Ned would know that he was now, and would be forever, on the outside looking in.

Ned, for the tenth time in twelve hours, started crying. Great sobs started to shake his big, muscular frame. He held his spoon, full of limp, wet cereal, and let it rain milk back into the bowl as he shook.

Nobody looked at him.

"I gotta go to school, Momma," Tom said, getting up, kissing Vera on the cheek, and heading out the door without a glance at his weeping father. As if he were invisible, or a ghost, Vera brusquely cleaned up the table, and went into the kitchen.

"Vera?" Ned called miserably.

She did not answer. The sink came on in a loud rush.

He was alone.

15

Tom couldn't exactly say that he stopped loving his father that day; perhaps that was the problem. In his mind things were still the way they should be—a quiet, happy home, made brighter when Dad was around, a place full of hugs and kitchen smells that offered some kind of shelter from the increasingly rough world that he ventured out into each day. But then he would come home and remember, yet again, that the old way was broken forever, and it would make him sore with loneliness and hot with rage. He was furious that his father had turned out to be such a little person. Even at twelve, he was not without the understanding that a grown man was pathetic for hitting a woman or a young boy. It would have been easier to simply hate him; the hard thing was to hold his beloved father in newfound *contempt*.

The world outside did get rougher. At twelve it was baseball and shoving matches; at age thirteen it was marijuana and full on brawls; by fifteen Tom was having unprotected sex with three different girls—two of them best friends—and selling dime bags on the side with a switchblade for protection. He spent a lot of time in basements of various run down houses around town, in a haze of pot and bourbon, his vision in multiples of three. There were a dozen guys who didn't want to just kick his ass—they wanted to murder him.

He was away from home for days, and when he came back Vera would be waiting up, grateful that he had come back at all, that he was alive, that he hugged her and asked for a meal.

"You been goin' to school?"

"Nah."

"Why not?"

"I got ma'own business now, Momma."

Vera knew what this business most likely was, and it horrified her; but she was alone in this fight now and she was scared that if she tried to lay down the line, Tom would just walk away from her the way he'd walked away from Ned. She knew that she was the only one holding this whole fragmenting mess together.

I can't lose Tom, she thought. If I lose Tom I'm finished at everything. I've failed at life.

Then, one day, Tom came home and stayed home. He started going to school again, and came home late at night covered in sawdust, his hands cracked and bleeding but with a new light in his eyes. Something had changed.

It happened like this: Tom's friend Zack was murdered two months before his sixteenth birthday with a 9mm gunshot wound to the head. Tom's other friends suddenly became consumed with the mission of finding Zack's killer and killing *him*, along with his friends and maybe his momma, too. For Tom this was too much. He had always liked fighting but he never liked really *hurting* anyone. Knocking out somebody's front tooth was bad enough, but *killing* someone? No way.

But his friends were insistent: night after night they cruised around the *barrio* at Richmond street, looking for the Puerto Ricans who had killed Zack. They had three revolvers and a shotgun. They got a lot of stares, a carload of black kids in Lewiston's Puerto Rican hood. Everybody knew what they were up to. Low-riders would cruise up, bass rippling the air, and curses would fly back and forth.

Tom knew it was only a matter of time before something *really* bad happened.

About that same time, another friend of his, an Italian kid named Nick, ran into him on the street dressed in brand new clothes and a gold chain around his neck. Nick's family was dirt poor—alcoholic father, methadone junkie mother.

"Been dealin'?" Tom asked.

"Nah, man," Nick said. "Roofing, man. There's so much work it's ridiculous. Come over to Primanti's. I'll hook you up."

Tom did just that. Within a week he was back in school and working every afternoon, plus all weekend. He made eight dollars an hour starting. It was hard work, hot and painful, but the money was good, the guys were fun to hang out with, and best of all—he was just *never* available to go cruising around, looking for Zack's killers. The longer he spent away from his old friends, the better he liked it. When they asked him where he'd been, why he didn't come around any more, he just told them,

"Man, I gotta help my momma. She needs me to work. I gots to, you know."

It was tough to argue with that.

Within a year, two more of Tom's friends were dead, another was in the hospital from an overdose, and a fourth was serving hard time in Freemont Penitentiary for Second Degree Murder. Meanwhile, Tom was getting very handy at bricklaying. He was well known and well respected as being a hard working kid anybody could count on.

"Don't worry, Tom can handle it."

"Johnson, that kid'll get 'er done on time."

"I want Johnson to do that. We need it done *right*."

Hearing those words made him swell up inside. It gave him a feeling he'd been missing for years.

Graduation was approaching. Tom was looking forward to working full time at Primanti Construction. Ned was home between jobs and finally decided that he and Tom needed to talk.

Gone was the old familiarity, the sense that they were more than just father and son: that they were friends. Instead there was a chilly formality, a stiffness when they encountered one another. They had not spoken much over the years. Ned knew almost nothing about what Tom had been through; this only made Tom despise his father even more. Ned, to him, was a weak man who knew absolutely nothing about 'the real world.' Tom had learned more about life in a few short years than his father ever would. Tom did not realize just how much Vera had lied to protect him, how she had swallowed her fears and put up a good show, making excuses for Tom's absence at night, for his sullenness, for his slouching walk. Ned had been screened off in every way.

They were at dinner when Ned decided to give his speech. Tom was serving himself some meatloaf and the radio was on in the kitchen.

"Son, it's time we talk about your future," Ned said abruptly, or abruptly so it seemed: in truth he had been preparing himself for this moment for months.

"What's to talk about?" Tom said, without looking up.

"What're you planning for your future? School's gonna be over soon."

"I've got a job."

"Construction?"

"Yeah."

Ned nodded. He had anticipated this. He knew that he had messed things up pretty good; but he was bound and determined to get this one thing right.

"I told Mike Neville at the company that you'd come down tomorrow or the next day to talk about a job there."

Tom laughed bitterly.

"Did I say I wanted your help, *Ned?*" he said, pushing his meatloaf around on his plate.

"Tom, don't talk to your father like that," Vera said quickly.

"Why not? It's his name."

"Just go down there and talk to him," Ned said. "Construction is good money, Tom, but just think what'll happen if you hurt your ankle. Or your back. Then you've got a skill but no way to use it. Not to mention the benefits of driving. At the Company we've got health, dental, eyes…"

"*Look,*" Tom snapped, "I told you before and I'll tell you again, I don't need your help. Not now, not *ever.* I got my own life. I'm just waiting until the end of the year and then I'm outta here."

"Driving truck's good, steady money. You can do it after you get too old for construction. I'm trying to tell you—"

"I *know* what you're trying to tell me," Tom said, dropping his fork and staring at his father. "Now listen to me. I don't want your help. I don't want anything more to do with you. You've let me down in every way for years. It's too late. You understand that?"

"Look, your father's right," Vera said. "Just listen to him, baby."

"Listen to *you!*" Tom sneered. "Your father's right! You talk shit about him *all* the time," He pointed a finger at Ned. "This man goes off and fucks around on you all the time, Momma, while you're in church, even, he's off sexin' these ladies—"

Vera's lips began to tremble.

"Now you stop that right now—" Ned growled in a low voice, putting down his fork.

"You be quiet!" Tom commanded. "I'm through taking orders from you! What do you know about anything? You pretend you're some kinda saint, but we all know what you *really* are—"

Ned had a hurt, bewildered look on his face. He didn't know what to say.

Vera did.

"You little snake, you be quiet! How dare you talk to your father like that!"

"I'll talk to him any way I want, Momma!" Tom said. "You should be ashamed to defend him, the way he—"

Vera started to cry.

Ned had very rarely ever seen Vera cry, and the sight of it was more than he could bear. He leapt up from his chair with a noise of outrage. Tom made a horrible face, and grabbing Ned by the shirtfront, dragged him right across the table and dropped him onto the floor. Tom had grown tremendously powerful. He was now twice as strong as his father.

He banged Ned's head off the floor once, twice, three times.

"HOW! DO YOU! LIKE IT!"

Vera took off her shoe and smacked Tom across the face. He leapt back, and shook his head.

Vera crouched by Ned. Ned rolled over, coughing and gurgling, his nose bleeding, his eyes wild with hurt and confusion.

"Your father!" Vera said between her tears. "He's your *father!*"

Tom felt a rush of panic rise up in him as he realized, in all its grim comedy, the cosmic symmetry of this situation.

"Get out of my house, boy," Vera spat. "Get out and don't you *ever* come back, you hear?"

That was many years ago. Since then Tom had come a long way—from laborer to business owner, from thuggish kid to architecture buff, from a tyrant son to a young man deeply apologetic. There was scarcely a day that went by that he didn't think back on that day at the dinner table and flinch. It was two or three years before any of them spoke again. Tom wanted to make it up, but he didn't know how, or really even if he should: yes, he was wrong to have assaulted his father. Of course. But it didn't change the fact that his father was weak and his mother a victim. It didn't change the fact that he had a right to determine his own path. After all, if he'd avoided the fate of Zack Wilson, it was through his own initiative, wasn't it?

Still, looking back over it all, removed now from the tumult of it by many years, he considered that really, his father wasn't a monster. He heard stories of fathers who were wife beaters, rapists, molesters, drunks. Fathers who ran away and never paid a cent to anybody. Fathers who had second families elsewhere.

Ned Johnson was not one of those men. Sure, he'd made some mistakes. He'd proven himself deeply flawed.

But maybe, just maybe, Tom thought, he'd been too harsh. Maybe, in the impetuousness of youth, he'd scourged his father for the ordinary sins of an average man.

Over time they began to speak again. After Tom's infatuation with architecture reached a fever pitch, he started his own remodeling company: not a competitor for Jim Primanti, to be sure, but it allowed him to work with the buildings he loved. How he reveled in arriving at the worksite in the morning and seeing his workers start for the day, going over the plans with the architect, knowing that by his hand he would rescue another of Lewiston's masterpieces.

When Vera and Ned sold their house, Tom helped them move to the boarding house at the House on the Bend. They were tired of worrying about bills, about frozen water pipes and backed up sewers. Enough was enough, they said. It was time to cut losses, to throw in the towel.

Tom guessed that his parents' financial troubles were much more profound than they let on; that little Ranch-style meant everything to them. There was something tragic about saying goodbye to that ugly little house with its beady little windows and artless blonde brickwork: it had been a character in all their lives—living and breathing—for decades. The house seemed sad and dark and lost when they walked around its empty rooms and finally turned out the lights for the last time, shut the door, and said goodbye.

Tom was there for moving day, though it was a strange day of awkward silences, pained expressions and physical discontent between father and son that crackled in the air. As they moved the boxes of old National Geographics and porcelain dolls and heaps of summer dresses, Tom told them that in a year he planned to go to college and start training as an architect. It was never too late, he said.

Never too late.

"That's wonderful, Tom," Vera said stiffly.

"Yes, son." Ned agreed. "You go on. You can do whatever you want."

He installed his parents in the House on the Bend, and met the owner, an attractive white woman named Mary who smiled at him and shook his hand invitingly.

"Your parents will be just fine," she assured him. "We have a good time around here."

Tom nodded and did his best to smile back.

He couldn't help but think that even now, years later, his father still begrudged him everything. No matter what he achieved in life, no matter how successful be became he could be sure.

It would never be the right thing to Ned Johnson.

Today, Tom Johnson lived with his business partner Rashim al-Akbar in an 1860 vintage Victorian on Lewiston's "transitional" East Side. "Transitional" meant that the neighborhood was a strange and uneasy mix of urban hipsters, pioneering yuppies, immigrants and crackheads, all living together in an area of spectacularly historic streets that were slowly shifting away from decay, as murals replaced graffiti and avant-garde boutiques replaced pawn shops.

Their house was a work in progress. They lived in the second floor, in a lofty space with twelve-foot ceilings that they had stripped down to the brickwork, except for the marble fireplaces and the remaining woodwork. With the motley assortment of furniture, posters, discarded clothing, and architectural plans, the placed look like a typical bachelor pad.

Tom's part of the flat was full of books on architecture, photographs he'd taken of Lewiston houses before they got demolished, and lines of beer bottles that he'd collected (some he drank, others he bought at antique shops).

Across the hall in Rashim's room it was a very different world; African music and Reggae blared at all hours, the walls hung with Bob Marley, Malcolm X, and Black Panther posters; on the far wall was a big picture of the Great Mosque in Mecca. Rashim was a scholar of African-American themes; his bookshelves were loaded with Cornel West and Frederick Douglass. Rashim prayed five times a day, dressed in black, and wore a long hennaed beard. He wore Malcolm X-style glasses and a beret. He was an odd match for Tom, who preferred to listen to Bruce Springsteen and liked to watch baseball.

The thing was, Rashim's family had money. Rashim's father was a native Kenyan who had fled the regime in East Africa during the 80s and absconded with some state money; his mother was a professor of Africana studies at Brownsville U. They lived in a nice brick row house near the Brownsville campus, and Rashim's father was often seen on school grounds (where he taught Swahili on a part time basis) in his mumu. Rashim's parents were not Muslims—he had converted while studying at the University of Pittsburgh, where he'd fallen in with the Black Muslim Brotherhood. After six years living there, nurtured by the Brotherhood and its twice-weekly discussions, he came back to Lewiston with the intent of "restructuring the racially-biased economic basis" of the city by wresting power away from the whites and putting it in the hands of black business owners. Soon after, he found that he was having trouble figuring out how to do this: what had seemed so clear at the Muslim community center and in discussion seminars suddenly became muddled.

Enter Tom Johnson. Tom was doing some work on Rashim's family house; they got to talking. Rashim liked Tom's vision; Tom loved the opportunity that Rashim presented.

"We're going to shift the power base towards our people," Rashim insisted vehemently, saying "our people" clearly and with supreme relish.

"We're gonna turn this town into the showcase it deserves to be," Tom said, his eyes dreamy and his heart pounding.

As it turned out, Rashim was a master electrician as well as a scholar with a Masters in Africana studies; paired with Tom's bricklaying, roofing, and devoted team of Mexican workers, they gathered steam quickly.

But still, it wasn't easy, not in a town dominated by the Primanti-Masters alliance.

"Our unholy white oppressors," Rashim intoned. "Masters, Masters, and Primanti form a trinity of racially-biased economic dominance."

Tom rolled his eyes but agreed that somebody had to bring them down. Primanti would just as soon level a Second Empire and build a parking lot if he felt that would be a bit more cost effective.

"We've got to establish a covenant of preservation standards," Tom told Rashim.

"The preservation of Black Dignity," Rashim said. "I couldn't agree more, brother."

With all this going on and eight projects in play around Lewiston, Tom felt caught off guard when Rashim came into his drafting area one evening with the cordless.

"Your mother," Rashim said. "Praise Black Mothers," he said into the phone before handing it over. "You're the strength of our people."

Tom laughed nervously and picked up the phone.

"Hello? Momma?"

"Tom?" Vera said on the other end. "There's a problem over here at the house."

Tom's heart beat harder.

"Is dad okay?" he blurted out.

"Yes, your father's fine," Vera said. "It's nice of you to ask. No. it's the *house. Mary's* house. The county wants to take it away."

Tom furrowed his eyebrows.

He suddenly remembered his conversation with Mary at Wal-Mart.

"How? Why? What do you mean?"

"We need somebody who can do construction," Vera said.

"Momma, I don't understand."

"Here, Mary wants to talk to you."

The phone made a muffled sound as it changed hands.

"Tom?"

"Hey, Mary." He immediately felt nervous in a different, more pleasurable way.

"Masters wants to take my house, and he's using the Safety Department to do it." She sighed like a windstorm into the receiver. "It's complicated. Could you come over so we can talk about it? We need your help, Tom. *I* need your help."

"Yeah," Tom said, running through the endless tasks he had to attend to in the coming days and seeing no convenient breaks or intermissions in sight. "Yeah, sure. I'll come by tomorrow afternoon."

16

Tom spent the next morning at a job site on Risley
Street, overseeing a gut job on a brick two-flat. Rashim
was busy with the new wiring, working with a Ghanaian
named Michael who was training to be a master electrician.
Tom spent the whole time anxiously thinking about his
appointment that afternoon: with his parents, with Mary, with
the looming and mysterious "trouble" that he was supposed
to fix.

After a working lunch and a stop at another project on
Darnell Avenue, Rashim and Tom finally headed out to the
House on the Bend in their Silverado. Rashim played a tape of
Highlife music from Ghana that Michael had given him. The
music was very upbeat and cheerful.

They pulled down the drive and saw Billy walking home,
loping along with his head bowed and a dark look on his face.
Tom slowed down the truck and rolled down the window.

"Billy?" he called. "What's up, buddy?"

Billy saw Tom and smiled weakly.

"Hey, Mr. Johnson."

"I'm going up to your house. You want a ride?"

"Yeah," Billy said with a shrug. "Sure. Thanks."

Billy got in the back of the extended cab with the clutter of dusty tools, boxes of supplies, and scraps of carpet and wood.

"Just clear out a space for yourself," Tom said. "Sorry. Yeah, that's it."

When Billy was comfortably settled in, they started off again.

"So, how's life?" Tom asked. "Haven't seen you in a while."

"Life sucks," Billy answered gloomily.

"Life sucks?" Tom said with a laugh. "Why? What's going on?"

"*School*," Billy said, as if the answer was self-evident.

"What's wrong with school?" Tom needled.

"I hate it."

"How are your classes?" Rashim piped up.

"Okay, I guess. I dunno," Billy said. "I just hate it."

Rashim shook his head.

"You should just count yourself lucky to be on the right side of the racial equation, son," he declared.

"Whatever that's supposed to mean," Tom said with irritation.

"Come on, brother, you know exactly what I mean."

"Black kids *run* our school," Billy said darkly. "They're the loudest, the strongest, the coolest. They get all the girls. They *own* the basketball team. Everybody would *love* to be one of those guys. So I don't quite understand you, Mr. Rashim."

"When you get into the real world, son, then you'll see what I'm talking about."

"High school is the real world, too," Billy said heatedly. "It sucks and it's nothing to laugh about."

Rashim was quiet for a moment. The House appeared through the trees.

"What you have at your High School," Rashim decided, "Is a case of reverse racism and a dangerous tendency towards pigeonholing. You put the Black Man on a pedestal, revering a negative image that glorifies gangster culture and quick ill-gotten gain. It's just another part of the cycle. Black kids buy into it; they put all their love and faith into fulfilling an image White America is busy constructing. The Black Fantasy is part of White Inadequacy; but in the white appetite for the Black Fantasy, the Black child is led astray. Away from learning. Away from ambition. Away from a *true* understanding of Blackness."

"Been following the Pirates this year?" Tom interjected. "I hear they're doing well."

"I don't watch baseball," Billy said as they pulled up in front of the house.

"Right on," Tom said cheerfully. "Who does, these days?" Billy was already getting out. He grabbed his book bag, said a solemn goodbye, and ran inside.

Tom climbed out and squinted in the hot sun.

"Damn, Rashim, can you just *shut up* about your African shit for a *minute?*" he said as Rashim got out.

"I will not rest in my crusade."

"He's fifteen years old."

"That's *exactly* the age group we need to reach. We need to effect change in the white community as well."

"*We?*" Tom held up his hands. "This is not my fight."

"How can you say that?" Rashim demanded as they climbed the front steps. "You are what you are, Tom. This is a war gone underground. But it's still a *war.*"

Tom rang the doorbell.

"I think I'd like to defer this conversation," Tom said. "Indefinitely."

Before Rashim could say anything else, Mary opened the door. She smiled and pushed her hair behind her ears.

"Tom. I'm so glad you could make it. Come in."

They all went into the front hall.

"Mary, you know my partner, Rashim," Tom said, stopping in his tracks when he saw the damage to the house. The hallway was full of holes; from here he could see there were more holes in the dining room wall.

"What in hell…?" he said. "What happened in here?"

"It's a long story," Mary said with a groan. "Mrs. Noonan is just setting out tea. You'll come join us?"

"Yeah. That would be great," Tom said.

They all went out to the side porch, where, as Mary said, Mrs. Noonan had just set out afternoon tea. Mr. Manicotti was there, as were Bert, Ned, and Vera.

Tom smiled a stubborn closed mouth smile and hesitated as Vera stood up and Ned did not. Then Ned clumsily followed suit while Vera stumblingly rounded the table. Mrs. Noonan got in the way and the three of them ended up converging in a mess of abortive handshakes and hugs.

Ned clapped Tom on the shoulder from an awkward distance, so he actually had to lean in a bit to do it.

"Glad you could make it, son," Ned said, knowing that everybody involved would cringe when he said the "s" word.

"Ah, could we all have a seat?" Bert suggested. "Cause Mrs. Noonan won't serve tea until everybody's seated, and I, for one, am *starving*."

The tea in question was Earl Grey; when everyone was seated Mrs. Noonan began to pour it out, and the plates of sandwiches and scones were passed around.

"Where's Sarah?" Tom asked, having trouble keeping his eyes off of Mary, and even more trouble looking at his parents.

"She's at school still. She's taking orchestra this year. The violin."

"That's wonderful," Tom said, nodding encouragingly. "It's good for her to have hobbies. Wish I'd had more hobbies back in the day."

"This is all great," Bert said, "But shouldn't we, you know, get on with it?"

Mary nodded, and sighed.

"Here's the story."

She related to Tom and Rashim the whole sequence of events, from Masters' first visit, to the inspection, to the disastrous attempt to fix the house.

"You know," Bert said, raising a finger, "I still think we could have finished it if we'd had more time."

"Can I see the list?" Tom asked. Mary pulled it out and handed it to him.

"More tea, Mr. Rashim?" Mrs. Noonan said.

"Yes, thank you," Rashim said.

"My husband had a beard very much like yours, sir," Mrs. Noonan remarked, as she poured.

"Was he a Muslim?"

"No, he was a Baptist," Mrs. Noonan said.

"A black Baptist?"

"Oh, no, Mr. Rashim," Mrs. Noonan said, laughing. "My husband was white. No, we didn't marry colored folks in our day."

"No?" Rashim said, unsure how he should react. "Well, that's too bad, I guess."

"Wow," Tom said suddenly, looking up from the list. "They really laid into you."

Everyone turned towards Bert.

Bert froze, his mouth bulging with devilled ham sandwich. "What? What'd I do?"

"How bad is it?" Mary asked with a tremor in her voice.

"Well," Tom said, rubbing the back of his neck, "Here's the thing. Some of this stuff is just to scare you. Underground tank—unless it's registered with the Fire Marshall, and if they haven't seen it, they're just guessing. Same with the lead-based paint. They didn't attach an official report on the paint—so they weren't licensed lead-paint inspectors, which means they've got nothing. More than that, they might even be breaking the law by suggesting that you have lead paint at all."

"We do," Bert said, raising his hand. "Have lead paint, I mean. The coach house is full of cans of it."

"Did they go in there?"

"No."

"Then they've got nothing. It's a bluff,"

"That's good," Mary said.

"*However*," Tom said with apology in his voice, "Other listed problems might very well be legitimate. The roof, for instance. I noticed that coming up the drive. You need to get that fixed immediately. It's dangerous."

Again, everybody looked at Bert.

"How much do you think it'll cost to fix all that?" Mary asked. "And the other problems caused by Bert?"

"*Alan* knocked those holes in the walls," Bert clarified sharply.

"Tell you what," Tom said, putting down the county report. "I'm going to need to take a look around myself before I can give you an estimate."

"Well, off the top of your head, how much do you think it will cost?" Vera asked.

Tom shook his head and pursed his lips.

"I'd say... jeez, probably fifty grand. Repair the roof, fix the walls, hire a lead guy, shore up the foundation, clear out that dry rot... plus, they're calling for updated electrical and plumbing; we'd have to subcontract some of that out. *Then,* there's this part about operating a boarding house. It's gonna require a commercial kitchen: that means a hood and exhaust system. And of course, we'll need permits for all this work. So yeah. I'd say $50,000 and that's minus labor."

He looked at the paper, then back at Mary, and cleared his throat. Mary looked devastated.

"Fifty? Thousand?" she said.

"Yeah, I'd say. Off the top of my head. But like I say, I need to take a look myself to be sure."

Bert whistled.

"Wow. That's... a *lot.*"

"*Thank* you, Bert," Vera snapped.

"Look," Tom said, looking at the report, "The walls, the roof, the porch—we can start with those. I'll do the labor for free, as a favor to you guys." He glanced shyly at his father. "But the fact is those materials are still gonna cost what they're gonna cost."

"You know, the Muslims love tea," Rashim was telling Mrs. Noonan. "Mostly they drink gunpowder tea but in Egypt they drink black tea, with lots of sugar."

"Oh, my, what in heaven's name is *gunpowder* tea?" Mrs. Noonan said with a laugh.

"Green tea, Mrs. Noonan," Rashim explained. "But very concentrated. *Chinese* green tea."

"I don't know where we're gonna find $50,000 dollars," Mary said, folding her arms across her chest and furrowing her brow.

"Well, until you figure it out," Tom said, "Why don't you go and see the judge and tell him that you've got a contractor to do the work. That should buy you another month at least. Tell him I'll need two months, actually. I'll write you an estimate to take in, okay?"

Mary smiled. "Thank you, Tom." She turned to Vera and Ned. "You've got a wonderful son."

Vera nodded mutely and smiled. Ned sniffed and looked down.

"Whatever I can do to help," Tom said, locking eyes with Mary. She felt herself flush, and so that no one could notice, she got up abruptly.

"Before you can write that estimate, you probably need to see the place, huh?" she asked.

"Yeah," Tom said, getting up too quickly and bumping the table. "Yeah, I'd better see the place."

Bert stuffed a scone into his mouth, his eyes wandering around the porch as he thought it over.

Fifty grand.

We can do this.

An hour later Tom and Rashim said goodbye and headed back to the truck.

"You really got on with old Mrs. Noonan," Tom observed as they got in.

"She's a nice old lady."

"But she's *white*, Rashim."

"*Nice* is colorblind, brother," Rashim said. "Now, speaking of *color*—please don't tell me you're agreeing to do this just to nail that white lady."

Tom shot Rashim an angry look and started up the truck.

"*Nice* is colorblind," Tom said, shifting into drive. "My mother and father live here too, remember."

"Come on, Tom," Rashim said. "This is going to be a big job. Am I right? Big?"

"They need our help."

"Whatever, man. We're in this together, so I need to know that you're not doing it for the wrong reason."

"It's not for the wrong reason, Rashim."

They rode in silence for a moment.

"Are you gonna see her again?" Rashim asked.

Tom cleared his throat.

"Well, of course, if I'm working here," he said, looking straight ahead. "And... we agreed to meet for drinks—you know, to talk over the work schedule."

"Damn it, I *knew* it!" Rashim snapped. "What is it about Brothers and *white* women? You're drooling over her like a dog, man. You know how much that demeans the Sisters?"

"It doesn't demean anybody," Tom said quietly. "Could you just imagine, for a moment, that it's not about black and white?"

"Maybe not for *you*," Rashim said, shaking his head. "You ask her if she's ever been with a black man before?"

"That's enough, Rashim."

"Well, did you? I think you should figure out if you're just ethnic cuisine before you go dropping two weeks of labor on this girl."

Tom slammed on the brakes.

"Tell you what, Rashim," Tom said, the motor idling. "Stay out of it. If you're going to run your mouth, I don't want you to have any part in it. *Okay?*"

Rashim raised his eyebrows and stroked his beard.

"Okay, okay, man," he said quietly. "Take it easy. Where you go, I am. That's how it is. I'm just concerned." He gestured ahead. "Come on. Let's drive."

Tom started the truck forward again.

"Besides," Rashim added after a long silence, "I promised I'd show Mrs. Noonan my pictures from Mecca."

17

At dinner that night at the House on the Bend, over a spread of meatloaf and canned corn, the mood started out cautiously upbeat. Tom's agreement to work on the house was a step in the right direction, but it was only one step.

Billy gloomily pushed the meatloaf around his plate; Sarah, seeing this, ate hers as conspicuously as she could, though it was perfectly clear that Mary's mind was not on the dinner. The meatloaf was dry; the corn watery; the mashed potatoes undercooked and yet bone dry.

She was thinking of two things, conflicting and tumbling around like mad in her head.

One: the confident smell and rock hard body of Tom Johnson, who she was going to meet for drinks the following night. The thought of it made her literally tingle. Of course, it was just drinks. Maybe nothing would happen.

God.

She hadn't been with a man since Brian. That was six years ago.

She felt both guilty and thrilled at once. It still seemed like cheating.

Just drinks. Maybe nothing would happen.

Then a second thought would creep around: *$50,000.*

That Tom and Rashim had agreed to do the work for free had bought her a reprieve of an evening from worry; if the judge cooperated, she might have another two months of wiggle room.

But $50,000, even with two months leeway, seemed like an insurmountable task. She'd already taken most of the equity out of the house through reverse mortgages; there might be another ten thousand left, at best.

She could tell that Bert was cooking up something; he wasn't talking. Usually Bert could be counted on to make some inane comment or deliver a lecture on the virtues of laziness, but tonight he just ate and stared at his food. He occasionally nodded and made a "hmm" sound, tapping his fork gently against the side of his plate.

"Mom," Sarah said after she'd swallowed the last bite of her dinner, "Billy told me that we're gonna have to sell the house."

"Billy, don't tell your sister things like that."

"Why not?" Billy said darkly. "It's true, isn't it?"

"It *isn't* true, Billy," Mary said. "Not until there's a for sale sign out front."

"I overheard you guys today," Billy said. "Mr. Johnson said it was gonna cost $50,000 dollars to save the house."

"Mom!" Sarah said with a panicked edge to her voice. "Are we going to be homeless?"

"No, baby, we're not going to be homeless."

"I knew it," Alan said angrily, throwing down his napkin. "I *knew* it! We'll be just like Cain, wandering the earth with no home to return to!"

"Cain killed his brother," Ned said. "This is different."

"I mean the Cain from Kung-Fu," Alan said with a sad shake of the head. "Or the A-Team. Framed for a crime they didn't commit."

"Mommy! Are we going to be like the A-Team?" Sarah asked with rising hysteria.

"Everything's gonna be *fine*, child," Vera said. "Your momma's got it all under control."

"No, she doesn't," Billy said. "We're going to lose the house and go to live in some tiny apartment. I *know* it."

"That's a pickle!" Claude shouted, looking extremely upset by the rising tide of negativity.

Mr. Manicotti lit a cigarette and flicked his ashes onto his plate.

"Mr. Manicotti, no smoking at the dinner table," Mary scolded him. "What are you *thinking*?"

"I don'ta want to go!" Mr. Manicotti said sharply. "I canna go home! I gotta nowhere to go!" Unsteadily, he got up, grabbing for his hat.

"Oh, my," Mrs. Noonan cooed tragically.

"Nobody is going anywhere!" Mary declared. "Mr. Manicotti, *please* put out the cigarette and sit down and finish your dinner. All right? Billy, stop getting everybody worked up! Sarah, stop panicking!" She looked at Bert. "And Bert! Stop plotting!"

Bert snapped to attention.

"Whadya mean?" he said, making big innocent eyes at her. "Plotting?"

"You're up to something," Mary said. "Let me just say *right now*, I would really like you to just sit this one out. I don't want to wake up and find the Oil Company drilling in the back yard."

"The Oil Company." He made a thoughtful face. "Huh. Not a bad idea…"

"Bert!"

"Joking!" Bert raised his hands in surrender. "Joking? Has *anybody* got a sense of humor around here?"

"We are going to figure out *something*," Mary said. "I'm not going to give up this house. It's my home. It's your home. That's not negotiable." She sighed. "We'll figure out something."

Ever since Billy had overheard Tom and his mother talking, he'd been thinking. In truth he'd been a bit more negative at dinner than he actually felt, partly because he was in a nasty mood, and partly because he didn't want anybody to suspect that he had a plan.

The plan was simple, and already proven on a smaller scale. After dinner, while he and Sarah were washing dishes, he decided to bring her in on it.

"Sarah, can you keep a secret?" Billy asked.

"Maybe," Sarah answered. "Depends."

Billy glanced over his shoulder.

"I've got a plan," he muttered. "To save the house."

Sarah's eyes lit up.

"Really?" she squeaked in a crazed whisper.

"Yep," Billy said with a nod. "But you gotta promise not to tell."

"Okay, I promise."

"Swear to God?"

"I swear! I swear!"

"Remember, Dad'll know if you break the promise."

"*OKAY!*"

"Okay. Here's the plan."

Billy loved model railroading. He'd been building a complicated HO scale set in a corner of the basement for several years, a system of interlocking tracks and switches. He wasn't interested, as were some model railroaders, in creating a miniature world of little houses and dogs and people and cars. All he was interested in were the sheer mechanics of the trains and tracks.

At any rate, as any model railroader knows, model railroading is an expensive hobby. Track is expensive, locomotives are expensive. New rolling stock is expensive. With the meager allowance Mary gave him, he couldn't expect to develop his setup very much.

That was when he latched onto the idea of E-bay.

The first item he sold on E-bay was a porcelain unicorn that he was sure no one would miss. He'd found it in a cardboard box full of porcelain unicorns, dragons, and wizards, collected by Brian Shumak's late mother. Surprisingly, the unicorn sold for twenty-five dollars. Not bad. Billy immediately tossed another unicorn on the market. In that way, he had increased his weekly income from fifteen dollars to sixty, allowing him enough money to buy HO railroad accessories and even save a bit on the side for a BB gun.

"But here's the thing," he told Sarah. "The basement is full of old stuff, not just unicorns. I mean, there's paintings, and old clothes, and books and all kinds of crap we can sell. And in the carriage house too. Parts of old cars and tractors and junk."

Sarah was serious and dedicated to the cause immediately. "What can I do to help?"

"Well," Billy said, "There's a ton of stuff down there. I mean, a hundred years worth of stuff. We need to go through all of it and figure out what's junk and what we can sell."

"And what Mommy wants to keep," Sarah reminded him.

"Mom wants to keep the *house*," Billy said. "And so do I. I'm gonna sell all my train stuff, too," he added bravely. "I think I can get a couple hundred dollars out of it."

"Do you think I should sell my Barbies?" Sarah asked. "I don't play with them anymore."

"Nah, keep 'em," Billy told her. "You'll be glad you did one day."

They finished up with the dishes.

"After you get done with your homework," Billy said, "Come downstairs and we'll get started."

18

Sarah got through with her homework as quickly as she could. Being party to a secret was always exciting; being party to a secret of her *brother's* was even better. As soon as she was done with her reading of "To Kill a Mockingbird," she raced down to the basement.

The basement had always been a place of wonder and fear to Sarah. At a very early age she had been terrified to go down there; the furnace was down there, with its metal face and hissing menace; its occasional barking "woolf" as it started up scared her witless. Even after her father had taken her down there and showed it to her, pointed out that not only was it made of metal and thus not alive, but also bolted to the floor, she still feared to tread down there. Sarah imagined that in days past, the vaulted chambers of the basement were used as a dungeon, or slaves' quarters. She knew that ghosts lived in such places.

But then her father died.

For a while she had little notion of what this meant. In the way of small children she could not imagine the permanence of his "being away." It was not her father's death that affected her then; it was that something died in the people around her. Billy sank into a morose sadness from which he had never fully emerged—shocked into an early and devastating lesson in mortality. From then on his thoughts were on death: on twisted limbs, mangled torsos, blood spilled out on the highway like so much paint. Billy was almost her age when Father died: nine years old. Old enough to understand the full import of grief.

For both Mary and Billy, Sarah had been a sunny vessel of hope in the mirthless sea of loss; that she knew nothing of her father's death, or what it meant—that she went on playing and singing and smiling as before—offered both reprieve and solace to the other two. For a while, they relished in keeping Sarah safe from the crushing truth; as long as she was unaware of it, death had yet to fully exert its tyranny.

Still, they knew it wasn't right to keep Sarah in the dark.

Before the funeral, Mary told her as carefully as she could.

Daddy went to heaven a little early.

But remember, Mary said, he was still watching, from very high up, watching and smiling and holding hands with Grandma and Grandpa and Jesus. And whenever she was scared of monsters at night, she just needed to remember that Daddy was right there with her: she couldn't see him, but he was there, guarding her.

Daddy was with Jesus.

This understanding changed things at once. After that, Sarah always had a sense that someone was right behind her, watching as she played with her friends and did her homework and in her private moment as well. She never felt good about a lie; she never had the sense that she could get away with anything. Maybe he couldn't scold her now, but he'd have plenty of time for it later on, when she joined him, with Grandma and Grandpa and Jesus. She was never afraid of

God's scorn, because she knew from Sunday school that God forgave everybody. Daddy, on the other hand, was under no obligation to do so.

She also never felt scared of monsters or ghosts again.

The basement was still the haunt of ghouls and spirits of dead prisoners and old family members locked up for being bad, of babies that had died young and forgotten dogs, but no ghost could hurt her now that she had a ghost on her side. The spirits could watch and make noises, but they couldn't touch her.

And the furnace: well, she'd already gotten to the bottom of that.

She found Billy deep in the bowels of the basement, unloading cardboard boxes of their contents and carefully laying them out on the rough stone floor. So far he'd set aside a good number of curios that he felt might be of value: a metal Rudolph the Red Nosed Reindeer bank; some rubber toy cars from WWII; a pair of Shmoo stuffed toys; a Lone Ranger toy revolver.

Sarah looked over a second pile of stuff.

An officer's cap. A box of pins and medals. An old Marine Corps Zippo lighter.

"Grandpa's stuff," Billy said. "That kind of stuff we should save."

He stood up and put his hands on his hips.

"So, Sarah, I think you kind of get the idea here. Right?"

"The idea?"

"Yeah. What kind of stuff we want to sell, and what we want to keep."

Then he gestured to a third pile of ancient Christmas ornaments, moldy t-shirts, and moth-eaten wool blankets. "And what we should just put back 'cause we can't do *anything* with it."

"What are you going to be doing?" Sarah asked.

Billy took out the digital camera that he'd snuck out of the family room.

"I'm gonna take pictures to help the stuff sell."

He started setting each object under the light, positioning it just so, and snapping a shot. Then he'd review the picture in the image finder and mull it over for a moment.

Meanwhile, Sarah began her journey through the netherworld of storage boxes, a baffling geology of toys, broken appliances, records and fashion accessories.

Sarah had always loved a good treasure hunt. This was like unearthing a museum. To be sure, much of it was no longer of any use: the broken belts, the single beat up sneakers, the Science Fair awards from 1956. The Shumak family never threw anything away. Grandma Shumak loved to hoard everything: tin foil was scrupulously smoothed out, washed, and saved. The house was full of baby food jars, tin cans, and soda pop bottles.

"Never know what you might find a use for later on."

Of course it was rare indeed that any of these items did find a use, but with a basement so large that it was like a private warehouse, it seemed that they would never run out of storage space.

But the Shumaks were more than just junk collectors; they were collectors in every sense. The collection of porcelain figurines had already been discovered; now Sarah was finding the matchbox cars, the Shmoo paraphernalia, the Star Trek lunchboxes and Disney toys. The elder Shumaks had always encouraged hobbies and collections; Sarah had never seen the point. For her the treasure hunt was not fantastic because of the treasure, but for the hunt. She didn't like *having* things, she liked *doing* things.

Three hours passed in a flash and before she knew it, she could hear her mother upstairs, calling for her to get ready for bed. Billy came back from the computer and nodded with approval when he saw the things Sarah had set out.

"We'll net a couple hundred from this stuff. Good job. Better go up now, Sarah. And remember, don't tell Mom."

Sarah was gone, and Billy was alone again, surrounded by the paraphernalia of Shumak history.

It was nice having this project: for whole hours he'd managed to forget how much he hated school.

Two disturbing new developments this year: two popular preps, good looking guys with wily, muscular frames who wore Abercrombie shirts and Ralph Lauren cologne, had decided that he was gay. Tenth grade was only a week old, so the year was young. What was right now limited to a chuckle and a muttered "faggot" was sure to blossom into something clique—and possibly school—wide.

The other development: John Fitzgerald was dating the oval faced girl, who, truth be told, Billy had previously decided that he wanted to go for this year. He showed up at lunch and found them kissing. He looked at Adam Cho and felt like the loneliest person in the world.

The classes lasted forever. The droning of the teachers, the irrelevance of the subjects, the pettiness of the system of detentions and hall passes; by the time the day was finally over he felt as if he'd been in there forever. He stumbled outside, simultaneously joyous that he was free and sickened that it was only for a few hours. Tomorrow was another day.

Another day.

It only got worse from here.

So having this project was a welcome distraction: to be transported to a world where he wasn't despised and ridiculed, where he could forget that he was likely to die a virgin. The people he did business with on E-bay had no idea that he'd been deemed a dork at Lewiston High School. They treated him like any E-bay merchant.

That's what adulthood would be like.

Just three more years.

19

There was no denying that although Bert Wodehouse was unskilled, uneducated, and unprincipled, he was, none-the-less, very lucky.

That Thursday night at the Lewiston Methodist Church, Bert won the second game at Bingo Night. Under the fluorescent lights, in that white cinderblock room full of coughing and half-senile grumbling, Bert let out a whoop and shouted "Bingo!" He jumped up from his chair, his hands raised above his head.

"Behold the champion! Right here!"

Vera shook her head at him, frowning at her bad luck. Statistically it seemed not only improbable but almost impossible: week after week, Bert won at least one game at Bingo, to the extent that there were grumblings that he was somehow in league with the Methodist Church. This, of course, was patently ridiculous: Bert Wodehouse was in league with no one but himself. He leaned back in his chair as the proctor checked his pieces.

"Read 'em and weep!" he said, folding his hands behind his head.

Tonight another hundred dollars would be coming his way. Now he was up to six hundred in his reserves. That was approximately one one-hundredth of the total amount needed to fix the house.

For the past week he had been thinking feverishly about some way to make things better, some way to bridge the financial gap and atone for his two strikes (one more, and he was sure, as a law of nature, that he would be expelled from the house). Whereas before it had seemed doubtful at best that they might undo the dark prognosis of the inspectors, now it was simply a matter of money.

Money, money, money. How Bert hated it! He'd gotten by just fine in life without much of it, but the world of dollar signs and greed had a way of catching a man by the heel.

His first impulse was to go and buy a Lotto ticket. The odds of that working were slim to none, but he considered it nonetheless. Then he thought about going to the Brownsville fertility clinic and donating some sperm. If he did that a few times, *and* got Alan, Claude, and Ned to do the same, they might have a shot. He did the math, and decided against it. Even *if* Claude and Alan could be induced to donate sperm, the process would still not generate enough cash.

That led him to think about his old shell game: no, too small time. What about starting a fake charity? Too slow.

If only Bingo Night was every night.

"I know you up to something," Vera said. "*Nobody* wins that much."

"That's slander, Mrs. Johnson," Bert answered her. "You should be careful about throwing those kinds of accusations around."

"I'll throw whatever I want, whenever I want," Vera said.

"She will. Really," Ned agreed meekly.

"You just can't handle the fact that I'm the luckiest bastard in this room. Never lost a coin toss, either. *Never.*

That's when it hit him, as the proctor in the Bingo hall confirmed his win and a deflated, tragic groan shuddered through the hall, gasps from sallow chests and drooling lips.

Vera said something thorny, but Bert wasn't listening. He was basking in a revelation as bright and plain as the overhead fluorescent lights.

The *casino.*

The idea was simple enough, and it had plenty of delicious irony to it: Bert would go to Master Plays Casino with his six hundred dollars, play a little Blackjack or Poker, and multiply it by one hundred. That would actually leave some for him, a little nest egg to repay him for his trouble. The best part about the idea was that the money would come from Masters himself.

Bert would beat him at his own game.

Bert chuckled to himself all the way back to the house that night, weaving around in the road on his Schwinn, dodging legions of fireflies.

This was just too rich.

Of course, Bert had never been to a casino. Furthermore, he didn't know how to play any games besides the slot machine. But Bert was, if anything, a problem solver. Alan would be his technical advisor. Although he had never been to a casino either, Bert had a hunch that he'd seen something about it on TV.

"What do you know about Casinos?" Bert asked Alan back at the house during the ad break on a rerun of Dr. Quinn, Medicine Woman.

"Well," Alan said, screwing up his face to look thoughtful, "I *have* watched Las Vegas a few times. And a bit of that ill-fated reality show The Casino. I can't pretend to be an expert on gambling, but I do know a thing or two about casino security arrangements."

"Good, yeah, that's good," Bert said, nodding thoughtfully. "Better program your VCR for tomorrow night, buddy. We're going to the riverboat!"

"The... the *what?*" Alan said in horror, realizing suddenly that he'd been duped. "As in... the one in *town?*"

"Yeah, the one in town. What other one is there? The one they're gonna build *here?*"

"Do you mean to say that you plan to win the money for the repairs *gambling?*"

"Trust me," Bert said. "It'll work."

"No. I can't. I'll miss all my shows," Alan stuttered.

Bert cocked up one eyebrow.

"You can tape the shows."

"But... but what if the VCR breaks?"

"You know what *I* think?"

"What do you think, Mr. Wodehouse?"

"I think you're *scared.*"

"Scared? Me? Of the casino?"

"Yes," Bert said. "You haven't left the house in so long, you're afraid to do anything new."

Alan shook his head vehemently. "That's ridiculous. I just don't want to."

"I *need* you, buddy," Bert pleaded. "I need you as my wingman."

"Who'll be *my* wingman?"

Bert saw Claude out in the hall with his broom.

"Claude. Claude will be our good luck charm. As if we need one."

Alan was looking horribly vexed. Dr. Quinn returned.

"Shh! Here it comes!"

Bert grabbed the remote and shut off the TV.

"Mr. Wodehouse!" Alan wailed. "No!"

"Alan, I'm not giving you the remote until you promise you'll come with me tomorrow."

"That's extortion!"

"Suit yourself."

Bert folded his arms. Alan leapt up and hit the "on" switch on the television set. The TV came back on. Bert raised the remote and switched it off again. Alan looked back with frustration and despair.

"Oh, yeah," Bert said. "I can keep this up all night."

"Fine! Fine! I'll go with you! Let me watch my show!"

"That a boy!" Bert cried, tossing the remote to Alan. "Tomorrow at eight. Be ready!"

20

Master Plays Casino was located on a long, 19th century-style riverboat docked on Lewiston's waterfront. For much of the 1980s the waterfront was a wasteland of old warehouses, dilapidated docks, and shacks, a breeding ground for the city's addicts and predators. No longer did barges and riverboats ply these waters; no longer was Lewiston a hub of commerce for Eastern Pennsylvania. With the coming of the Rustbelt, the waterfront lost its purpose.

After ten years of disuse, the entire stretch of riverbank was so polluted and dangerous that plans were in the works to raze the lot of it and build a park. Victor Masters had other ideas. He bought the strip for a song and developed it into a boardwalk, complete with carnival-style attractions, cotton candy vendors, and video arcades full of beeping Frogger and Pac Man machines. It was a huge success—the sagging city latched onto the lights of the boardwalk like a drowning man to a scrap of wood. The music and the laughter of the place was a welcome antidote to the rot and misery of the town beyond.

But Victor Masters was never totally satisfied. Of course, the boardwalk was successful—but how to make it *more* profitable? After flirting with the idea of a haunted house and a roller rink, he hit on the idea of a casino. Gambling was illegal on Pennsylvania *soil*—but not on the water.

Previously, if a Pawnee County native wanted to gamble, he'd need to trek off to an Indian reservation, a trip of many hours. The riverboat made it accessible for all men and women over the age of 21. Victor conceived it as part Showboat, part Casino Royale. The sort of place where Baccarat and Stetsons would be welcome; the sort of place that the hillbillies and the Puerto Ricans and the Italians and the Money from Philly would all feel was cool.

He called it Master Plays.

It *was* cool as far as Lewiston went, cool and fabulously successful. Every night of the week the boat blazed with fortunes won and lost until the early morning hours. Addictions blossomed like mushrooms in dung, and every night a harvest of hundreds of thousands, if not millions, gleamed in the counting rooms of the hold. The casino turned Victor from well-to-do real estate developer to financial royalty the likes of which Pawnee county had never seen, not even in the days of the Captains of Lewiston Industry. Greater than the wheels of progress is the wine of vice.

There were rumors, however, that the casino had begun to attract the wrong kinds of people. This was not in reference to the scatter-toothed trailer-folk or the do-rag and dollar-sign-chain thugsters from 18th Street. These bad men were high rollers, and they were from Philly. They spoke in harsh, tough guy accents and dressed as sharply as the knives they carried in their pockets. They were wolfish, savage men who dressed in ten thousand dollar suits. With the rise of the black gangs and an onslaught of Federal indictments, business was getting hard to do in Philly. Thus, rumor had it, what started as fun weekends in the country for Jimmy and the Wiseguys quickly turned to business. They smelled an opportunity.

So rumor went.

Anyways, Master Plays was exactly the kind of place Bert Wodehouse ordinarily avoided like the plague. He knew that usually, looking like a bum, he was unlikely to be even permitted past the front door. So tonight Bert arrived at Master Plays dressed in one of Ned's suits, a brown corduroy affair with a paisley tie and a handkerchief in the breast pocket.

"You look like a hobo salesman," Alan said as they pulled up to the Casino in Ned's Suburban.

"That's a nice suit," Ned protested. "I still can't believe you roped me into this. As if borrowing my suit wasn't enough..."

"We needed a driver," Bert said. "Who better to ask."

"Well, you *do* have a point there," Ned said with a tip of his head.

"You're easier to play than a slot machine," Alan quipped. "And that suit is loose enough on you to fit Claude in there too, Mr. Wodehouse."

"Baggy's in these days, isn't it?"

"Baggy's been out for years," Alan said with a sad sigh. "And I won't comment on corduroy suits. Suits that are both baggy *and* corduroy are a violation of some law of nature, I believe. You're like Columbo and Pee Wee Herman rolled into one."

"Boy, you're on quite the tear, aren't you?" Bert said, adjusting his tie. "I brought you along to build me up, not bring me down."

"Then you should have listened to me. Black button down, black pants. Real simple like."

"You're wearing a windbreaker, I notice."

"I'm not the one dressing to impress. And now, neither are you."

Ned stopped the truck by the valet station. Claude stumbled as he got out. He was gaping at the cascade of lights, the flurry of neon and hypnotic dazzle. His eyes were lit up like magnifying glasses on a hot day. Ned sniffed and straightened his collar. He was playing Miami Vice tonight: open collar, lots of chest hair showing, khaki pants, white blazer, and of course his battered Mack Truck hat—he'd be a fool to gamble without his good luck charm. He hadn't worn the blazer in a while; it smelled like mothballs and was tight around his waist, but to be honest, it was still better than the damned corduroy suit that Vera had bought him to wear to church. He hated that thing, and he hated the tie even more.

"But just on this one occasion, I'll let you wear it," he'd told Bert.

They climbed the gangway towards a wave of music and laughter. The boat glowed in the night, the letters of "Master Plays" giant and cartoonish in the inky sky overhead. At the door they checked Alan's ID. He was baffled.

"They must be looking for somebody," he told Bert. "I must resemble some thief or other."

"Yeah. That must be it," Bert said, nodding to the doorman.

"Thank you," the bouncer said, handing the ID back to Alan. "And good luck."

They entered the game deck. It had a low ceiling that glowed with a thousand points of light. Right away there were ranks of slot machines, a riot of bright colors and spinning wheels, beeps and whizzes, old women hunched on stools with buckets of quarters, grim and stony faced and beginning to glisten with sweat. Further on were the rows of Pai-Gow tables, the Blackjack tables, the roulette wheel with its sighing crowd, the craps tables. Behind a wall of velvet ropes and red-tuxedoed attendants, in a plush hall of mahogany and gold, was the high stakes salon: Poker, Baccarat, and more Blackjack.

A girl appeared next to Ned holding a tray of drinks.

"Cocktail?"

She was wearing a leotard that glittered and revealed more flesh than it covered; on her head she wore a crown of peacock feathers.

Ned wondered who she was during the day.

Alan thought she looked like she belonged on the credits of Family Guy.

Claude blushed.

"You got ginger ale?" Bert asked.

The girl gave him a funny look.

"Just... ginger ale?'

"Yeah. We'll take a round if you've got it."

"Sure... ginger ale," the girl said, drifting away, looking unsure if she was being kidded.

"So," Bert said as soon as she was gone. "We're inside. Right now Master's cameras are on us like flies on shit. So. Let's split up, try to blend in. If we stay all clumped together it'll just draw attention to us." He went into his breast pocket and pulled out twenty dollars. He gave ten to Alan and ten to Claude. "A little fun money. Don't spend it all in one place." He turned to Ned. "Did Vera give you an allowance?"

"Very funny," Ned said.

"Just asking. Okay." He checked his watch. "Let's meet back here in two hours. Alan, stay close to me—within sight. I might have questions. Or need a distraction."

"You think you can win $50,000 in two hours?" Ned asked. "That's crazy, even for you."

"Hey, you never know," Bert said with a messy grin and a shrug. "All right." He gestured to Alan. "Let's go."

"What about the ginger ale?" Alan wondered.

"Don't worry. She'll find us. That's her job."

First off, Bert went to the slots. As soon as he'd set foot on board he had a feeling that the slots might be where it was at. In fact, one particular machine had drawn his attention: a dollar slot machine with a glowing display overhead proclaiming the accrued pot to be now in excess of $68,000. All around the sign, at the banks of machines, were elderly folk, hungrily punching "play" buttons, watching the wheels spin, watching their dollar vanish forever, and then punching the "play" button again. Each of them operated under the fervent, secret, and almost religious belief that they were special: that tonight was their lucky night.

Someone was going to win that pot. It was a mathematical certainty.

Bert saw that there was one open machine. It was a sign from Lady Luck if he'd ever seen one.

Rubbing his hands together, he approached the machine and fed in a hundred dollar bill.

He had that winning feeling.

"I'm the luckiest man in the world," he said, glancing up at the money display and punching the "play" button."

Cherry.
Apple.
Master Play x 2
Diamond.
Nothing.

Bert felt a momentary sinking feeling, then heartened as he considered that expecting to win on the first try was obviously not realistic.

He hit "play" again.

Heart. Apple. Diamond. Apple.

Nothing.

Bert hit the button five more times before he finally won anything, and when he did it was only three dollars, not even enough to make up what he had lost.

"Maybe you should try something else," Alan suggested. "Something with a bit of skill, maybe."

"Luck *is* my skill," Bert boasted, jabbing his thumb at himself. "That's why the slot machine was such a great idea!"

The man next to him glanced over and gave him a puffy look of remonstration.

"What are you lookin' at? *You* haven't got any skills either, buddy," Bert said to the man, angrily punching the "play" button again.

And again.

And again.

His numbers sank lower and lower. He won five dollars, then lost twenty. After that he won ten, but lost thirty-five.

Soon his one hundred dollars was down to eight.

Bert hit "cash out," unwilling to lose the entire amount.

"That didn't go very well," Alan observed.

"Didn't I say that you should stay at a distance?" Bert said. "Within sight. I think that's what I said."

A glass of something gold and bubbly appeared on top of the slot machine.

"Your ginger ale, mister," said the girl in the leotard. She stayed there, watching him as he took a sip.

"I hope nobody tampered with this drink," Bert said, winking at her; she raised her eyebrows expectantly at him. "What?" he asked finally, before brightening with comprehension. "Oh, right." He took out a dollar and ceremoniously laid it on her tray. "Don't spend it all in one place, doll. Come on, Alan. I hear the blackjack table calling my name."

Bert led Alan through the crowds of Pai-Gow and craps players to the blackjack tables. Here the demographic was much different than at the slot machines. Filling in for the elderly were the obese, the bearded, the red-faced. There were reserved spaces for motorized carts for the infirm. Each person had a cocktail at their right hand on a soaked bar napkin. They wore striped Wrangler button-downs and t-shirts with American Indians and dolphins on them. Bert finally found a table he liked where there was an empty seat.

"Time to let daddy play," he said to Alan with a wink.

"Whatever you say, Mr. Wodehouse," Alan muttered. "I can't believe I'm missing All in the Family for this..."

Bert set down his ginger ale and let himself onto the stool with a dramatic wheeze.

"Hey folks," he said to the table. Then, to the dealer, "Deal me in, Chief."

"There's a ten dollar minimum, sir."

"Yeah, right. I knew that." He got out a crisp hundred-dollar bill and laid it out on the felt.

"So, like I was saying," he repeated, "Deal me in."

Cards were dealt.

"Hit me," said the man to Bert's right.

"Hit me," Bert said too. He realized, suddenly, that he actually didn't know how to play blackjack. Not at all.

There was some key number. Was it 18? 21? 24?

Bert took a sip of his ginger ale.

"Psst," Bert said to Alan, but Alan was too far away to hear. He was standing by the craps table watching the action. Desperate, he looked to the woman at his left, a big dark haired gorgon in a Tasmanian Devil t-shirt.

"What are we trying to do here?" he whispered.

"Win," she grumbled, scowling at her cards. "And it ain't happenin'."

"Please, sir, do not solicit advice from your neighbor," the dealer said.

"All right, fine," Bert declared as the first man mysteriously claimed his winnings. "Could somebody explain to me how this game is played?"

After Bert knew that 21 was the magic number, playing blackjack was much easier. However, as with the slot machines, luck just wasn't with him tonight. He lost relentlessly, watching with aching disappointment and confusion as his stack of chips vanished at an alarmingly steady rate.

Blackjack was not Bingo.

The Tasmanian devil lost even worse and departed the table with a gurgle and a grunt, leaving behind a pungent stink of cheap perfume and stale Dewar's in her wake. Bert managed to slow down his decline for a short while— even to pull ahead slightly, with five wins in a row. The sixth hand, feeling bold, he bet the rest of his chips.

Lady luck was fickle.

"I'm sorry, sir," the dealer said with an apologetic raking motion that claimed the rest of his winnings. Bert was pale and his hands were shaking.

"Well, I guess Blackjack's just not my game," he said at last, getting up from the table unsteadily. The next hand had already begun.

Bert had already lost two hundred dollars. That meant he had four hundred dollars left, give or take. Bert walked through the crowds in a fog of orange lights, garish music, cigarette smoke and bad haircuts. He ended up at the roulette table, soaked in sweat.

"Place your bets!" the dealer cried.

Bert loosened his tie and put a five on number 14.

The wheel spun. The little white ball bounced along innocuously. How friendly and frivolous the roulette ball seemed, not unlike the ball that bounced above music lyrics, or a carefree pinball! Yet how deceptive it was— for no little white ball in the entire world carried with it more heartbreak and sorrow.

The wheel slowed.

The ball bounced in smaller and smaller hops.

Finally, it came to rest.

My lord.

On number fourteen.

"Gentleman wins," the dealer said with vaudevillian enthusiasm, collecting the chips and passing them to Bert. He counted them up.

He'd just made one hundred and seventy-five dollars.

"Place your bets!"

Bert put down two tens this time, one on a red and one on a black. Again the wheel spun.

Again, Bert won.

"Get everybody a drink!" Bert cried to a passing peacock girl. "Beers are on the house!"

The girl narrowed her eyes at him and shook her head.

"Bar's right over there," she said.

"Boy," Bert said, counting his chips compulsively. "Word sure travels fast."

In two games of roulette he'd just won back everything he'd lost and more. He was dizzy with heady success. He began to do feverish math to figure out how often and how much he needed to increase his bets in order to win enough money, but he was too excited to concentrate.

By God, he'd found his game all right.

"Place your bets!"

Bert bet one hundred this time on the even numbers. The wheel spun. The ball bounced.

And slowed.

And came to rest.

Bert let out a whoop and leapt into the air.

"Hot damn! I am on fire!"

Heads turned. People laughed. A ripple of jealous excitement moved through the crowd of onlookers. People were stopping to watch. Whispers passing around like sparks from a campfire.

"Well *done* sir!" the dealer exclaimed.

Bert raked in the chips—one thousand dollars worth.

"I don't think you can keep this up," Alan said suddenly, startling Bert. "You'd better quit while you're ahead."

"Quit while I'm ahead? Are you *crazy*?" Bert cried. "Full speed *ahead*, Alan." He raised his hand for a high five. "Who's the *man*?"

Alan thought for a second.

"Jack Albertson, but I don't understand what he has to do with this."

Bert looked perplexed and his hand dropped slowly; Alan sipped his ginger ale, and shrugged.

"Anyways. I warned you."

"Place your bets!"

This time Bert put it all on even. He had that feeling.

The wheel spun.

Taka taka taka taka.

As the wheel wound down Bert was shaking and sweating like he had Ebola. The crowd held its breath. The ball stopped.

The result was *not* even.

But felt his stomach leak into his feet and his spine slide out onto the floor.

"Well, that's a shame," somebody said nearby.

The crowd began to disperse.

"Sorry, sir," the dealer said, claiming the pot for the house.

"House always wins," Alan said. "First rule of gambling, Mr. Wodehouse. Because the house can play all night, and you can't."

Bert stood dumbly and stared at the wheel as it spun again. He felt dizzy.

He only had two hundred left now.

Two. Hundred.

He should have listened. He wheeled around in his chair. "Well, thanks a *lot,* Alan. I thought you were supposed to be looking out for me!"

"I *told* you to quit, Mr. Wodehouse."

"Well, I guess you weren't very convincing, *were* you?" Bert snapped.

Alan slurped the last bit of soda through his straw. "And you should have tipped that lady better," he added. "Now no one will get me a drink."

Suddenly, Bert felt a hand on his shoulder.

A big hand.

Bert turned around. Standing there were three big men in white suits and sunglasses, with earpieces. The biggest man had a goatee and looked like he could rip off a car door.

"Mr. Wodehouse," he said. "Please come with us."

21

Bert was taken across the gaming floor and up a flight of stairs. Alan had slipped away during the exchange, though Bert wasn't sure if he'd escaped or just drifted off. At any rate, he was alone now, and a little frightened. Bert didn't like arguments, and he really didn't like confrontation.

On the upper deck, the door closed behind them and the festive sounds of the casino were gone. Instead there was faint classical music; the long corridor was decorated with modern art and potted plants. At the end of the hall was a pair of impressive wooden doors. The big man with the goatee punched the red intercom button set into the wall.

"Mr. Masters. Mr. Wodehouse is here."

"Send him in."

Two guards operated the doors imperiously; the third led Bert inside.

The control room where Masters was waiting was a large, round room filled with video monitors, darkly lit, and furnished with a desk and several chairs. On the far wall was a minibar and couch. The result of so few furnishings was that the room looked gigantic, dwarfing its occupants.

The chair behind the desk turned.

It was Masters all right.

Just not the Cadillac Man.

"Leave us," said the fat, short Masters the Greater in a thin nasally voice. "You can wait outside."

Victor Masters rose from this chair as the guards left and quietly shut the doors behind them.

"Bert Wodehouse, I presume," he said, rounding the table and extending his hand. He was wearing several large signet rings that made his hand look fat and unworkable.

"Victor Masters," Bert said. "That's you, right?"

"Yes, that's me," Victor said, putting away his hand when Bert didn't shake it.

"What is it?" Bert asked. "I wasn't cheating. I wasn't stealing. I was *losing*. I won a couple pots but then I lost big. Of course, you probably sent your goons to get me while I was winning. Probably figured I was scamming you somehow, huh?"

"Scamming me?" Victor said with a laugh that distorted his red, fleshy face in an unconvincing imitation of mirth. "Why would I think that? I think it's great that you came here tonight."

"Then... what do you want?"

"I want you to have a drink with me, first of all," Masters said amiably, going to the minibar. "Can I offer you something? I've got beautiful single malt here, and a very rare bourbon that my buyers got me from a family-run distillery in Kentucky. You a Scotch or a Bourbon man, Mr. Wodehouse—or can I call you Bert?"

"I'll take Scotch," Bert said. "With soda. And yeah, Bert's fine."

"With... *soda*." Masters nodded thoughtfully, pouring out two glasses on ice and then adding some Schweppes—with a visible wince—to Bert's. "Here you are."

Bert took the glass and had a sip. It had a musky, heavy smell that he wasn't used to.

"How do you know who I am?" Bert asked.

"My brother has met you and your sister," Victor answered. "And we are in business together, you know. So." He smiled. "I suppose you could say that since you were kind enough to have Collin in your house and offer him drinks, I'd like to do the same."

"Oh," Bert said. "Well, thanks for the drink."

That Victor Masters was from the same gene pool as Collin was quite obvious. Where Collin was pasty, slightly overweight, and a bit younger, Victor was pasty, obese, and oddly shaped, with a paunch and sag that even an expensive suit couldn't remedy. His hair was thin on his head and his legs were short, but his clothes were exquisite and accessorized with diamond studded cufflinks and a platinum lapel pin. He looked even shorter and uglier in person than he did on TV. His wife—who Bert had seen in the society pages of the Lewiston Observer— was by contrast a tall, Slavic beauty, with ice blue eyes and a mane of silky blonde hair.

Money talks. Oh yes, it does.

Bert finished his drink quickly.

"Well, thanks. I think I'll get back to gambling now," he said.

"Have another drink," Victor suggested.

"No, thanks. I'm not much of a drinker, really."

Victor sighed.

"Let's get down to brass tacks," he said at last. "Your sister has something we want."

"Yeah, I know that," Bert said.

"Right. Look." Victor made a sympathetic face. "We know how much that house means to your family. We know that it belonged to your late brother-in-law. I imagine Mary feels that the house is all she has left of him."

Bert didn't like hearing Victor, who he'd never even met before, saying Mary's name and speaking about her tragedy like that.

"Well, she's got kids, too," Bert said. "I think it's got more to do with just not selling out. It's one of those principle things. She'll never sell to you. I'm just laying that out there for you, you know."

Victor took a sip of scotch.

"I know that." He looked at the monitors in reflection for a moment. "Mr. Wodehouse, you care about your sister. And your nephew and niece. Surely, you *must* be able to see how illogical she's being. We're offering a large sum of money for an old house. We're offering security for her and her family. Financial security, forever."

"And I'm telling you, she doesn't want it."

"Mr. Wodehouse," Victor said meditatively, "I did a little research on you. On your employment history, prior residences, things like that. I found out that you've never had a bank account. You've never had a telephone registered in your name. You've never taken out an insurance policy, and you've never paid taxes."

Bert didn't say anything.

"I respect that," Victor went on. "Sure, we're opposites. But it's commendable. Enviable, even, to live free and clear of society like that. I mean, *wow*! It takes real courage to fly in the face of convention. Bravo!"

"Yeah, well, that's how I do it," Bert said cautiously.

"But you're what—forty-four years old now, Mr. Wodehouse? Forty-four. Age is going to catch up with you. Let's face it—if you want to live in security and comfort—and most importantly, remain *free*—you're going to need money. And let's be honest here: you haven't got any."

"Uh-huh."

"I think that we can both agree that in the interests of your niece and nephew, your sister *ought* to sell. Right? Why is she clinging to a bunch of wood and cement? You understand how fleeting and useless that stuff really is. I do too—it's my bread and butter to move it around, tear it down, build it up. It's no more substance to me than it is to you. It's funny, really, that even though we're opposites, we're really not all that different."

"Funny. Yeah."

"My brother—bless his heart—he's all business. He is. He doesn't see the big picture all the time. He doesn't understand that sending inspectors to your house was insensitive and coercive—really, not a great move. I'll admit that. But what's done is done. I can't undo the Safety Department report, much as I'd like to."

Victor poured himself another drink.

"Sure you wouldn't like another?"

"Yeah. I'm sure."

"What I *can* do is offer you a really good deal. Now, I understand that your sister has found a contractor to fix the house. That is going to cost a bundle. $40,000? Fifty? How on earth is she going to pay for that? Is she thinking of her children at all? Bert, as a rational man—a modern philosopher of life—you need to step in. You need to convince her to stop this right away. Maybe she can save the house, but at what cost? She'll listen to you. You're her brother. You can make her see the light.

"I'm offering you $50,000 cash if you talk to her and she sells, Bert. Imagine having $50,000 at your disposal. You wouldn't have to work ever again. That nest egg would carry you through the rough seas of age and beyond. And all you have to do is talk her around. Bricks and mortar are just bricks and mortar. I'm offering financial freedom to you, to her, and to her kids. College educations. A *future*."

Victor paused.

"So, what do you think?

"Well," Bert said after a thoughtful moment, "Ah, first of all, actually, you think I could get that second drink now?"

Prepare to be played, sucker.

"Certainly," Masters said. He quickly made another drink and handed it to Bert.

Bert had a sip and said, "This scotch isn't bad, but you should just keep some Johnny Walker Red." He winked at Masters. "You know, I think I can help you. My sister will basically go along with whatever I tell her; you know, me being the older brother and everything..." He clicked his teeth together and waited for Masters to make the next move.

"Do you want more money?" Victor asked. "We can discuss it."

Bert paused for a long moment, wheels turning. "Look," he said at last, "If you can up that to $100,000, I will personally guarantee that I can make it happen."

Victor's face darkened. He swallowed thickly, his eyes trained on Bert. "You can guarantee it?"

"Yeah. You give me $50,000 now and the other fifty when I bring in the deal." He looked over at the desk. "This is a casino. You *must* have fifty grand in cash around here somewhere."

Masters regarded Bert carefully for a moment, and abruptly smiled. "Well, we deal in markers here. You sign a marker and you walk with fifty thousand." Slowly, he produced a marker from his top desk drawer and laid it out. He took a fancy lacquered fountain pen and filled out the paper, leaving a space for Bert to sign. He looked up, pushed the marker towards Bert, and handed him the pen.

Bert, wanting to take advantage of the situation and walk with the money before the poor sap changed his mind, signed his John Hancock on the dotted line. A flicker of triumph crossed both of their faces at exactly the same time.

Suddenly, the intercom beeped.

"Sir, there's a disturbance on the floor," reported an officious voice. "It's an acquaintance of Mr. Wodehouse. He's deranged or something; we're not sure how to proceed."

"Where is it?"

"Camera 23, sir."

Masters punched up camera 23 and it appeared on the largest overhead monitor. He hit another button and on came the audio feed.

Claude was sitting at a blackjack table, surrounded by a crowd, repeatedly shouting, "That's a pickle!" at the top of his lungs. The dealer was asking him as patiently as he could, "Do you want a card, sir? Sir? Please, calm down, you're disturbing the other players."

"Your friend?" Masters asked in an unpleasant voice.

"Yeah," Bert said, rubbing his eyes.

"I would suggest that you go and calm him down. Then I would ask that you and your other two friends leave my Casino. Immediately." Masters pressed a button on his control panel, and the two guards opened the doors to the office.

"You called, Mr. Masters?" they asked.

"Take him away," Masters said. "Get him and his friends out of here."

"Where's my fifty thousand?" Bert cried as the big men loomed behind him.

Masters narrowed his eyes and grinned. "We'll... hold it for you. Okay?"

Bert was released back onto the floor with two Big Men as escorts. He hurried over to the Blackjack tables, where he found that Claude had already been intercepted by Ned and Alan, who had taken him off to the side and calmed him down.

"What the hell was that?" Bert cried. "Claude, buddy! Jeez!"

"Too much soda," Ned lamented. "I think he had like three ginger ales."

"Oh, so they served Claude," Bert snapped, "But not me."

"Claude was tipping," Alan said.

Claude was back to normal, looking around placidly. The blackjack game had resumed but the players and the dealers were still stealing glances back to see if something else was going to happen.

"I guess he tried to play," Ned said. "And the excitement was just too much."

Ned noticed the big men.

"Who are *they?*"

"Well, guys, I hope you had fun," Bert said. "Because we've been asked to leave."

"Leave?" Ned said. "I was just warming up at the poker tables! I already won two hundred dollars!"

"Better to quit while you're ahead, anyways," Alan observed.

"We agree," said the big men. "Time to go."

Bert turned on his heel and looked up at them.

"I'm not leaving until I get my money," he told them.

"What *money?*" they asked, laughing.

"The money I signed the marker for," Bert explained.

"I think this guy's mixed up," one big man said to the other.

"What did you sign, Bert?" Ned said warily.

"I signed a marker for fifty grand," Bert said.

"You signed a marker for *fifty grand?*" Ned cried. "You *do* realize a marker is an IOU, don't you?"

"Of all the…" Alan muttered.

"Just so you know," one big man said. "Mr. Masters said that he'd like you to pay that back as soon as possible. He don't like to be kept waiting with things like that."

"You shouldn't be so reckless with your money," said the other one. "That's a hell of a lot of money to lose in one night."

"No, you don't understand—" Bert said with rising panic.

The big men started pushing.

"Oh, we *understand,*" they said with a laugh. "We understand *just fine.*"

22

Bert and the gang arrived back home at about 11:30, the headlights of the Suburban sweeping over the hedges and the colonnade of the front porch as it crunched its way up the gravel driveway. Bert was slumped back in his seat, arms folded. He was in a terrible mood. He'd gone in to the casino without a shred of doubt that he would emerge with the money they needed. Instead, he'd nearly lost all of his own money; what's more, it looked as if he owed Masters $50,000.

The others asked Bert again and again about what had transpired between him and Victor Masters. Bert didn't want to talk about it: he was afraid that he'd made things worse yet again. He recalled the look on Masters' face in the moment he'd signed the marker. It was, he thought, the look of a man who had just won a decisive victory. Bert wondered how Masters would try to use the marker against him.

Probably figured he had some kind of leverage now.

Yeah, right. Just *try* and collect it.

They rolled to a stop by the garage and everyone got out with the noise of boots on gravel and thick metal doors slamming.

The light of the verandah was on: Mary must have left it on for them. They started across the driveway, toward the house.

Suddenly they saw a car coming up the drive, with bright halogens lighting up the whole front yard.

"Wonder who that is," Ned remarked.

It got closer. There was a light bar on top and bold lettering on the sides. It was a Crown Vic.

"The cops," Alan said.

A chill ran through Bert like a breeze. He wanted to start running. The foreboding of a thousand bad things buzzed through his head.

"Sit this one out," Mary had told him.

Had he?

Of course not. Idiot.

The squad car stopped by the verandah and two Sheriff's deputies got out, amid the sound of dispatcher chatter and background static.

"Evening." one of the officers said to them. "You folks call in a disturbance?"

"We... just got back," Bert answered cautiously.

"You live here?"

"Yeah. We all live here."

Bert's pulse was as heavy and thick as a jackhammer.

"We got a call that somebody took some shots at the house."

"Took some... *shots*?" Bert managed to choke out. Ned gasped "Vera!" and ran for the house.

"That's what we were told," the second officer said, clicking on his flashlight and stroking its beam over the house.

The screen door banged once as Ned ran inside; then a second time as Mary came out. She was holding Sarah against her.

"Officer!" she said. "I'm the one who called!"

"Yes, ma'am," the first officer said, gallantly, walking cowboy-style toward the porch, gait wide, fingers hooked through his belt loops. He was vaguely handsome; Bert didn't like how he was looking at his sister. "What's the nature of the problem?"

"About twenty minutes ago, somebody shot at the side of the house a bunch of times. They broke four windows."

She didn't sound scared. She had a firmness and strength to her voice that Bert had always admired. Cool as a cucumber. Tougher than he'd ever hope to be.

"Let's see the damage," the officer said. Everyone went around the side of the house, to a side facing the woods. The windows were broken, sure enough, though not shattered. There were small holes surrounded by opaque spider webs of cracked glass.

The Sheriff's deputy nodded as he stuck his finger in one of the holes in the clapboards under the beam of his partner's MagLite.

"BBs," he announced. "You got nailed by BBs."

"*Okay*, so it was a BB gun," Mary said. "So what?"

"Well, ma'am, you made it sound like it was a real gun," the second deputy said.

"It was real enough to break the window," Mary said with a voice that was growing as precise and cutting as a laser. "And lodge itself in my living room wall. What if my daughter was in the way of one of those BBs?"

The deputies glanced at one another. Bert saw it. His blood was boiling. He could imagine Victor Masters having a laugh with them later on.

"Look, ma'am, we'll file a report if you like. But this sort of thing is very common."

"Happens all the time," seconded the other officer.

"Yeah. Kids screwing around."

"They were on my property," Mary said. "This is private property. They damaged my house."

"It looks like it could use some work anyhow," the first deputy said.

"Yeah," said the second. "From what I've heard, a couple BBs aren't your biggest problem."

Mary blinked at them for a moment.

"Excuse... what did you just say to me?" Mary snapped.

"We're just saying that kids do this sort of thing all the time."

"No. What did you say about my house?"

"Nothing," said one of them.

"We could file a report if you want."

"Look," Bert piped up. "We *all* heard you. Give us your badge numbers. And names. *Now.*"

The deputies chuckled.

"All we're saying is that this kind of thing happens all the time. Kids get it in their heads to tag a house with their BB guns."

"And, well, sometimes they just go after that house again and again," seconded the other deputy.

Bert was looking at their badges.

There was no number on it.

There *had* to be a number.

Unless it was a fake.

"Sometimes they do get carried away," the first deputy commented. "But the best thing is not to piss them off. Cause if you do, they might come back with a gasoline bomb."

"Or Daddy's gas powered carbine automatic rifle."

"Yeah, you don't want that."

Mary gently nudged Sarah away from her, towards the front door. "Go inside, baby. Go inside now, you hear?"

Sarah nodded mutely and ran inside.

"Just go, please," Mary said, her head swimming with confusion.

"Yeah, we'll go. Look, best thing to do is to let it ride," the first deputy said.

"Cause if it starts happening more, there really isn't much we can do. They're out there," the second deputy said, motioning towards the woods, "And you know, Ma'am, we just don't have the resources to go chasing kids around in the woods all night."

"Ya'll were thinking of moving anyhow, weren't you?" the first deputy said with a toothy grin. "That's what *I* heard."

"That's a pickle!" Claude shouted. The deputies were startled.

"What? *What'd* he say?"

"Nothing. Nothing at all," Mary said. "Alan, take Claude inside." She looked at the deputies and gritted her teeth.

"Why can't you people leave us alone?" she hissed.

"You *called* us," the deputy said. "We thought you wanted our help. Fine, then. Never mind."

"We'll tell the other deputies that you can handle things on your own," said the second. "You clearly don't want our advice."

"But feel free to call the Sheriff's office," said the first deputy. "We'll keep you on hold for a real long time."

The deputies went back to their car.

"Watch out for those kids," they said as they got in. "They can get real *nasty* sometimes, when they got cruelty on the brain."

They shifted into reverse, and backed the car down the drive. They turned on the floodlight and shined it in Mary's face until they turned, and drove off towards the road.

Bert looked helplessly at Mary.

She was writing the license plate number on the palm of her hand with a Bic pen.

"Shit, Mary," Bert said with dread. "Even the Sheriff."

"Dammit, Bert!" Mary cried. "I refuse to believe that *everybody* is on Masters' side! This isn't the Wild West! Lewiston is not a little town!"

Bert nodded in agreement, hoping she was right.

"He's gone too far," Mary said. "Masters made his biggest mistake tonight. He's crossed the line over to criminal mischief. We're gonna nail him."

"How?" Bert said.

"We'll get the word out," Mary said. "We're gonna shout it out so far and wide that Washington will hear what a slime he is, until the FBI's on him so thick he can't move."

"The newspaper?"

Mary nodded.

"Masters owns the Observer," Bert reminded her.

"I'm thinking bigger than that," Mary said. "Much bigger than that."

They stood in silence for a long moment surrounded by songs of frogs and crickets in the threatening darkness.

"Bert, where did you go tonight?" Mary asked at last, looking at his suit. "*Answer* me."

"We went to the casino," Bert said, too exhausted to lie. "I wanted to win some money."

"To Masters' casino."

"Yes."

"And how much did you win?"

Bert looked away.

"How much did you win, Bert?" Mary repeated.

Bert dug his toe into the ground. "I, uh, lost about four hundred dollars."

"I don't believe it," Mary growled. "You *gave* Masters four hundred dollars that we could have used to repair the house." She took a sharp breath. "What is it going to take, Bert? Why won't you just back off?"

Bert made a face and kicked at the earth.

"I wanted to help," he said quietly.

"*Bert*," Mary snapped, "Do I need to throw you out? Is that what it's going to take?"

"No, Mary, I—"

"Because I will. This is for my children. If it was me, just me, I'd walk away, but this is for Sarah and Billy, and for Mr. Manicotti and Mrs. Noonan and Alan and Claude—where are they going to go, Bert?"

"I know, that... that's why I—"

"You need to understand," Mary said. "You are *not* helping. You have never been responsible enough to help with anything. And guess what: I don't *want* your help. Once, long ago, it would have been nice. But now—really, I'm fine. You're free to go. Don't feel any *obligation*, Bert. You already missed your shot. You can't make up for it now. Not this way. Not *any* way. Do you understand?"

Bert swallowed.

"Yeah," he muttered. "I understand."

Mary stormed past him and up onto the porch. "I've got two kids already," she hissed at him. "I *really* don't need a third."

The door slammed after her, and Bert was left alone. He thought back to the conversation with Masters. Out of spite, he suddenly wished Masters' offer had been real. He would have taken the money—and kept it for himself!

Don't want my help?

Fine.

I don't need you either. You're on your own.

He kicked the dirt, stifling tears, and shook his body in impotent rage.

No. There was no getting around it. He couldn't pretend he didn't care. He wanted redemption. He *craved* it.

And it was too late.

23

As was customary on nights when Victor Masters closed Master Plays, at two in the morning he took a stroll around the gaming floor with Casino Manager Raul Vasquez. Vasquez was a tall, abrupt man with a harsh urban inflection to his voice, a violent intrusion of West Philly vowels that spoke of his capability to be both quickly furious and furiously quick. He walked with a lanky ease that seemed as volatile as a cigarette at a gas station. This was why Victor hired Vasquez in the first place. Vasquez knew how to handle people and he was allergic to bullshit.

After a drink in Masters' office, where they reviewed the numbers, they took a long stroll from aft to bow, through the empty buffet hall where the vacuum cleaners hummed in the hands of the Mexican cleaners, through the shopping concessions, past the doors to the Master Theater now open with the hall lights on high.

All the while Vasquez talked. He told Victor about how much they'd made that night and about some big players who were in town. There was Ron Hormel from Texas, an oilman with a ton of money and a great knack for Blackjack. There was Calvin Armand, a computer giant who was god-awful at gaming and a very sore loser. Vasquez related some amusing tales of things he'd caught on the security monitors: the old woman who had developed a system of communication with her nephew the spotter by tugging at different parts of her pearl necklace, or the man who spent twenty minutes wiping and re-wiping a slot machine before he would finally sit down and play.

Victor nodded and smiled paternally. Few people had ever heard him really laugh—patronizing chuckles didn't count. Victor wasn't a good old boy, and he wasn't interested in small talk; he obliged Vasquez because he liked him and need to be able to trust someone. Furthermore, Victor had found that the key to much of his success was the fact that he hovered over his managers, his sub managers, and his contractors; one never knew if he was about to show up on the job site with a hardhat, or at the accounting offices with his lawyer and a scientific calculator. He didn't do it out of some kind of misbegotten "rolling up the sleeves" leadership building; he did it because he meant business, and everyone knew it. He had few friends but lots of trusted allies. He had a way to him, to his thoughtful, slouching walk, to the frequent pauses when he spoke, to the studious expression of his small eyes that some impolitely compared to a curious pig, but which were full of keen intelligence.

On the gaming floor they saw a few last die-hards remaining at the slots, feeding in a few last desperate quarters in the sweaty, bleary-eyed hope that the night had not been totally in vain. They could hear the piano player in the mostly empty Blue Room at the bow, tinkling away to a slouch-headed smattering of queasy drinks. Victor looked at the empty gaming tables and the bar with its video poker monitors, at the cheesy wallpaper and the stained carpets. It all said one thing to Victor.

Small time.

This was still the small time. Who'd ever heard of tonight's "Big Players?"

Where were the movie stars, the fashionistas, the Wall Street big shots? Where was Danny DeVito? Where was Dennis Rodman or Kenny Rogers?

Small time, this was. Chump change.

Vasquez was still relating the anecdotes of the evening.

"And there was that one guy, the little crazy guy at table 23," he said with a hiss of contempt. "That's a pickle, he kept saying. That's a pickle. What in hell do you think that means?"

"One can only guess," Masters answered, pausing in the doorway to the Blue Room. "Who's this pianist?"

"I'm not sure."

"He's pretty bad. Get another one."

"You got it, sir."

Masters sighed. They looped around the playing floor and began to head aft again, meandering between the poker tables.

"One of Vecchio's boys was in the house tonight," Vasquez said. "We kept an eye on him."

Masters nodded. "Those guys are in here a lot," he said.

"Every night, it seems," Vasquez agreed gloomily. "They're like fruit flies. Impossible to get rid of once they've dug in."

"I've noticed."

"Those boys are bad news, sir," Vasquez said. "I hope you got them under control. Cause if you *don't*, they gotta way of gettin' *nasty* real quick."

"I've got it in hand," Masters said thoughtfully. Vasquez wasn't convinced.

"If need be... we can shake them up a bit. I mean, I got friends... we got ways..."

"They're wiseguys," Masters said. "You can't beat them that way."

"You kidding?" Vasquez snorted. "It's the *only* way to beat them. They only lost control in Philly cause the blacks had more guns. Used to be they'd use a black guy as a shooter or a driver, and if he squealed or started some shit they'd just burn his whole neighborhood down. But now these bangers got Mac-10s, and Tech-9s and all kinds of wicked firepower. So the Italians backed down."

"Tellin' you, Mr. Masters, it's the only way. You gotta hit 'em hard, show them you're all business, or they'll eat you alive."

"Nobody's eating me alive," Masters said, turning to Vasquez. "But thanks for the advice. Why don't you go down to the counting room? I'm going to finish up a few loose ends in my office."

Masters walked back to his office feeling sullen, and poured himself another drink, the fourth or fifth—who was counting? He set the glass—Scotch, neat—on his desk and stared at it for a long time. He took a sniff and had a pensive sip. He liked to think that alcoholics didn't really enjoy drinking, so that as long as he was savoring each sip, he could be fairly sure that he didn't have a problem.

Jimmy Vecchio was the problem, not an extra sip or two of scotch. Jimmy Vecchio on the one side and Mary Shumak on the other. With Jimmy Vecchio leaning on him and Collin, it was going to get harder and harder to prevent something bad from happening.

He rubbed his eyes.

How quickly that relationship went sour.

That was the problem with guys like Vecchio. They seemed so affable, so endearing in their rakish charm, so convincing in their backslapping. Victor had even played pool with Vecchio, against his better judgment. But Collin had insisted; back when nobody else would help them finance the Pirate's Clipper, Vecchio and his boss Bertollucci were willing.

They quickly found out that their help came at a very steep price.

Wiseguys were like houseguests who get drunk and nasty. What started good-natured turned ugly, then offensive, then threatening. Jimmy Vecchio had a way of turning an ordinary conversation into a threat. He was the Christmas guest who got drunk on the eggnog, made raunchy jokes in front of Mother, pinched your wife's ass, and ended up stabbing your dog with the carving knife. An unwieldy metaphor?

Jimmy Vecchio was that bad.

He thought of what Vasquez had said.

"We've got ways."

It was tempting—it really was. But he'd come too far in life, built too much and been too successful, to burn it all down with a hasty act of violence. No, he would *not* have Vasquez deal with Vecchio in "his way." If there was one thing Victor Masters knew, it was that patience and strategy were key to overcoming obstacles. Jimmy Vecchio was an idiot and knew nothing of business. One day, Vecchio would make some crucial mistake, and on that day, Victor Masters would cure the disease of wiseguy interference once and for all.

Until then—he could wait.

24

A week passed after the night of the casino and the BBs. During that time, there was evidence that the nighttime visitations were continuing: trampled flowers in the garden, footprints by the window, and two more instances of petty vandalism—two broken windows on the coach house and a dead bird in the mailbox. Throughout that week, Tom Johnson came by several times to take measurements around the house. He and Mary exchanged quick glances and, if no one was looking, a brief fumbled kiss. Mary had enough money in savings to get him started at least, and it was a good thing, too: the East roof was in imminent danger of collapse, thanks to Bert's "repairs." Fall was fast approaching—and with it windy nights, rainstorms, wood rattling gusts. Tension in the old house ran high. Dinners were eaten in silence; Bert often didn't even come to the table.

The Johnsons were the only ones who seemed *happier* than usual. The night of the BB attack, when Ned had heard about the shooting, he'd run inside at full tilt, like a crazy man, banging doors and thundering up the steps to their room, shouting Vera's name. After seeing her sitting on the bed, safe and sound, Ned threw his arms around her.

"Are you okay, Baby?" he asked. "Are you okay?"

Vera was fine. She'd been spooked by the BB snipers and went up to the room and sat away from the window. Ned's outpouring of emotion, the tightness of his bear hug, the ridiculous drama with which he appeared in their room looking almost chivalrous—well, Vera felt proud of her husband for the first time in many years. She let him "comfort her," and even refrained from telling him that it was just a BB gun and not a real one, just so she could savor that feeling again—the feeling that her husband was someone capable of swift action, the sort of man who could save the day.

"You love me?" Vera asked him as they held each other on the bed.

"Of course I do, baby," Ned answered hotly. "You know I do. God, if anything happened to you—well, it'd be the end for me."

"I know I say some things, Ned," Vera said. "I know I can be hard sometimes."

"Baby, for better or for worse, till death…"

Before they went to bed that night, they were back to bickering: Vera had not approved the casino trip and when she found out that he'd been gambling with their money—even though he'd won—she let him have it.

But that night, and for the rest of the week, they smiled when they argued.

Vera looked at her husband with a twinge of something old and new at the same time.

"I guess there's something to the man after all," she thought to herself, her heart tingling and expanding even as she tried to keep things in proportion.

Nothing's changed, now. Don't be some foolish female. He ain't changed.

That's right. He *ain't* changed.

Maybe, in his way, he's always *been* a good man.

Even after two weeks as lovers, Mary still hadn't told a soul about Tom. The first night, they'd met at Mitch's Bar, supposedly to discuss the details of the renovation. Mitch's was a dim roadhouse a bit outside of Lewiston, the kind of place frequented by washed-up Harley riders and truckers and guys from the hills who wanted a bit of sauce without venturing too far into town. Mary and Tom sat in a booth off to the side, where nobody could see, nervously regarding one another, having trouble talking over the loud hillbilly rock, downing beers and shots like they were going out of style. Finally, after beer number four, Tom reached under the table and put his hand on her leg. Mary smiled and kissed him, hard, thirsty. They each had one more shot of Cuervo at the bar and then went to the nearby motel, where they took off their clothes, turned on the TV, and went at it until nearly dawn, when Mary felt so sore she could barely walk. The bed had badly marked up the wall, and the room smelled like sex. She went home and started breakfast without a wink of sleep.

That first morning she'd felt sickened. There was a stickiness and filthiness to her skin that she couldn't wash off no matter how hot the shower or how hard she scrubbed. Her insides were rubbed raw, and Tom hadn't worn a condom—she hadn't asked him to. The night before she'd plunged in, hoping to forget and move on; this morning, Brian was still there, watching.

She imagined that he'd weep, seeing that.

His wife fucking like some cheap whore.

In the shower, water ran down her face, and she pressed her forehead against the wall.

"Never again," she promised herself. "Never again."

Two days and Tom didn't hear from Mary; then on the third day she called.

"Let's go to the motel again," she said flatly.

"Why don't we go out, first?"

"If you want."

Tom wanted to go somewhere nice—maybe Rocco's or the Roma Café—but Mary wouldn't have it.

"Let's be discreet, okay?" she asked.

Discreet. That meant going to places full of cigarette smoke, red light, and palpable sleaze. Tom hated places like that; he'd already spent enough time in that sort of joint to last a lifetime. On the second date, Tom could see why she wanted to be discreet: she was *ashamed* to be seen with him. Even at Brigadoon's, her eyes were darting around, watching others as they watched them.

She felt angry. Who were they to judge her, to say when and how she should get on with life? Who were they?

A woman has needs.

To hell with them.

If only it were that easy.

The white guys in their flannels looked at her like she was dirt, just another aging broad who'd gone black. They looked at her like she had a disease—like she was somebody to be pitied. The bartender's eyes darted back and forth, back and forth. Black and white, black and white.

And then there were the black guys who looked at her like she was a piece of meat, knowing that she was a girl who liked black men, that if Tom had his back turned, maybe they could get lucky too.

And this was in a roadhouse.

What if they were seen in town? What then? People knew her there. They knew her, and Brian, and her family. They'd look at Tom and think, "Wow, she's really gone to the dogs."

That night, while they grunted and jerked, Brian watched. She had the sense that he watched every night, and every morning she woke up feeling ill at her betrayal of him, of his memory, through this disgustingly thrilling thing she'd done.

Tom was beautiful, there was no doubt; all muscle and bulk, thick and strong and overwhelming. But she had the upsetting sense that while this had started for him as sex, and nothing but sex, that was beginning to change. He watched her while she dressed, and while she brushed her teeth, and while she tied her shoes. He liked to watch her while she slept and sometimes she woke up and saw him looking at her, and then he'd smile and she'd nearly cry, because that was what boyfriends and husbands did.

Mary Shumak was not ready for a boyfriend or a husband. She thought that maybe she'd never be.

She would never be so vulnerable again. She had lost her father, mother, and husband.

Her reserves for grieving were mostly used up.

Tom bought flowers to the house. She smiled thinly and smelled them appreciatively, and then when his back was turned she threw them out. He bought her tickets to a jazz show in Brownsville and she lied, saying she had things to do—but that she could still come over that night. He surprised her with a bubble bath and tea candles at his house one evening when Rashim was out; instead she pulled him over to the couch to avoid the romance of it all; the champagne grew warm and the candles burned out.

Tom became more and more desperate, and the more she pushed him away the more he wanted her. What had begun as a hunger for her breasts and ass and sex had become a fixation on the details of her hair, the look of her fingers, the lines around her mouth. The first night he had been in control; a control he'd given up bit by bit as he grew to love her. Suddenly, it wasn't her legs but her mystery that he daydreamed about, spent whole hours sitting and mulling over, lying on the bed in the motel room long after she was gone wondering why he couldn't get enough and wondering what it was, exactly, that he craved.

He felt he hardly knew her.

To lose a husband was a dreadful thing. He had no idea what that must have been like.

Add to that, Mary was ten years his senior.

These were deep waters indeed.

Tom bought her a necklace; she squeezed his hand shut around it, and in the privacy of their cigarette-smelling roadhouse motel room, she whispered,

"No, Tom. We're not there yet."

"*When?*"

She wrapped her arms around his powerful shoulders, and her legs around his waist.

"I don't know."

Mary Shumak was a mother, and a cook, and a widower.

Such women, she thought, had a responsibility of sacrifice.

Such women had renounced the love of men for the sake of their histories.

Yet she felt that stirring each night and she took Tom into her like a drug, seeking obliteration and abasement as a way to be less and more at the same time, to be desired and a whore, to grieve Brian and to spit in his face, to punish him in Heaven for leaving her with a life she hadn't asked for.

She knew she'd never be able to forget him.

He'd be there as she panted and moaned in the night, as she wept in the blue light of morning, as she shivered and stared at herself in the mirror, at the lines of mascara on her cheeks, as she said *never again* and yet each night crawled back to him, her lover and her pawn. And after it was over, after the night of delicious obscenity was spent, she returned with the dawn to the House, her husband's silent, sad avatar on this earth.

She stopped on the porch, pressed her cheek to the clapboards, groped at peeling paint and splintered wood, wounding fingers that sought atonement.

Oh, Brian.

I'm so sorry.

25

Alan, meanwhile, was busy sinking into a whirlpool of doubt and despair.

The failure of the casino trip and the appearance of the BB vandals were very worrisome to him. He had believed, until recently, that somehow the situation would resolve itself, that it would stay as background noise, as something other people could worry about.

But now it was becoming frighteningly clear: the situation was not good. What if Mrs. Shumak lost the house? Then what? Where would he go? During an ad break on reruns of Space: Above and Beyond, Alan tried to think seriously about his options.

He had little money aside from the small check that his mother sent him each month; that amount didn't even cover his boarding cost, so it was up to his SSI check to cover the rest. He had nowhere to go: his mother was a mess, barely supporting herself as it was on thirty hours a week at Burger King and spending the rest of her time smoking Kools in her moldy efficiency in the Bleeker Street projects. His father wasn't an option at all, still living in his trailer by the junkyard over in Brownsville with his pit bulls and his girlfriend Charlene, waving a sawed-off at people who ventured too close to his property. And Aunt Betty; well, it was safe to say that after the unfortunate death of Fluffy they were no longer on speaking terms.

Alan tried not to think about it.

Life outside of the House on the Bend was worse than The Swan, or Will and Grace. It was so overwhelmingly terrible in its implications and in his inability to deal with it that he beat his eyes with his fists to drive thoughts of it back.

And then, blessedly, Space: Above and Beyond returned.

A few minutes later, as the Space Marines were engaging the Chigs, the front doorbell rang.

There was a long pause. Nobody was answering it.

It rang again.

Alan glanced at the clock.

It was 1:20 in the afternoon. No wonder. Mary was in town, the Johnsons were out for a drive, Bert was in hiding, the old folks were napping, the kids were in school, Claude was off being... Claudish.

A third ring.

Vansen's fighter was hit in a space dogfight. They were fighting an alien ship that was armored against the Marines' guns and had "DIE HUMANS" scrawled on the front—

Knocking, now!

"Fine!" Alan muttered, jumping up from the couch and sprinting to the front door. He flung it open and found a middle aged blonde woman standing on the other side, dressed in a button-down and tan slacks. She had a duffel slung over one shoulder. Behind her was a little Chevy Cavalier, bright turquoise with magenta highlights, the kind of color scheme reserved for rental cars from cheapo agencies.

"Hi," the woman said with a smile that gathered up the skin around her eyes. "I'm Abby Lindeman. Is Mary home?"

"No," Alan said, his pulse pounding as he heard explosions and the sounds of interstellar combat from the TV room. "What do you want?"

Abby looked a bit surprised but kept smiling.

"She invited me here. Do you know when she might be back?"

"No, I don't," Alan said quickly. "If you want you can come in and wait. I think she'll be back in an hour or something."

"Thank you," Abby said. "Maybe Mary mentioned that I—"

Alan was gone already. Abby raised an eyebrow and went in, shutting the front door after her. She set down her bag next to the sideboard and followed the sounds of the television. Finally she found Alan, sitting at the edge of an overstuffed La-Z-Boy, with a yellow notepad in hand. She sat down on the couch next to him.

"What're you watching?"

"Space: Above and Beyond," Alan answered quickly. "I'd be happy to talk during the advertising break, but I need to concentrate right now, okay?"

"Yeah, okay..." Abby nodded awkwardly at the young man in the old windbreaker, and sat quietly, looking around the room—there were big holes in several walls, as if somebody had taken a hammer to them; exposed were the joists and wiring underneath. Above the defunct fireplace was a "sofa sized" painting, most likely of the "starving artist" variety: paint by numbers. In the corner were a couple of old Barbies and some bulging cardboard boxes. There was a fancy molding on the ceiling from which, long ago, a chandelier once hung.

The promised ad break came.

"So," Abby said. "What's your name?"

"Alan," came the distracted answer. After making a few last notes, he looked up with a patient smile. "What can I do for you?"

"Mary invited me. We were old friends in Pittsburgh. We went to school together."

"Oh." Alan blinked at her in a clear deficit of interest.

"I'm a reporter."

"Okay."

"Are you her son?"

"Mrs. Shumak's son?" Alan laughed nervously, realizing suddenly how nice that would be. "No. Not me. I just live here."

"Is it nice here?"

"Yes. It's great. I can watch a lot of TV."

"You seemed really into your show. Is that your favorite program?"

"My favorite?" Alan scrunched up his face as he considered this delicate question. "No, not my favorite. It's pretty good, though. Have *you* ever watched Space: Above and Beyond?"

Abby smiled.

"I don't watch a lot of TV."

"Well, you're missing out with this one. It's Sci-Fi, and that turns some people off. But it's way better than Star Trek, or Battlestar Galactica, or Stargate SG-1. I'd even say it trumps Farscape and Babylon 5. You know why?"

"No," Abby said with a laugh, tying her hair into an efficient ponytail. "Why?"

"Because of sheer storytelling power. Here was a show that took risks every episode. It focuses on a tightly knit band of Marines in a war with a superior alien race. It's a losing war and they know it from Episode one. Every week they lose ground; if they win for once, it's only because they got lucky or cheated."

"Wow, that's grim."

"It's life. It's a show where the alien planets seem alien, where they need space suits and the whole terrain looks different. That's what I always hated about Star Trek: the Next Generation—nothing ever seemed alien. How can they breathe on all those planets? Why does everybody look like us? *Space* depicted a universe where we're alone, and up against aliens who are smarter, stronger, and faster."

"Who would want to watch something so depressing?"

"Nobody," Alan said. "It got cancelled after one season."

The show came back. Suddenly, Alan was all ears again. He resumed his note taking.

There were footsteps on the front porch. The door opened and Mary came in with some bags of groceries. Abby jumped up and ran to meet her.

"Oh my God!" Mary cried, putting down the groceries and hugging Abby. "I saw the car out there and figured it was you!"

"No doubt, that car's got my name written all over it," Abby said, laughing. "Jeez, Mary, wow—it's been so *long*."

"I know. You got here *early*!"

"Yeah, I came as quick as I could."

"So, what do you think about what I said?" Mary asked.

"I think we're gonna nail them to the wall, girl," Abby said with a grin, "Wow, my *God*. I can't get over how *good* you look."

"Thanks. You look good too."

"You don't need to lie, Mary," Abby said. "I look like a grandma and you look like you did in college—and that's *after* two kids."

"Come on," Mary laughed. "You do *not* look like a grandma." She shook her head. "Where are my manners? You want a cup of coffee? Tea? A beer?"

"I'll take a beer. Got any Yuengling?"

"Rolling Rock okay?"

"I'll drink Rolling Rock."

They walked down the hall, past the TV room, where Alan was watching his show.

"Alan let you in?" Mary asked.

"Yeah," Abby said. Then, in a whisper, "He's a strange boy."

"He's had it hard," Mary whispered back. "He likes his TV."

"He's smart, though,"

"I know," Mary said as they reached the kitchen and she put the groceries on the counter. "He's a TV trivia genius. He could write a book." She went into the big metal refrigerator and got out a pair of Rolling Rocks.

Abby toasted with Mary and took a long pull. She looked at a photo of Sarah and Billy on the fridge. "Your kids?"

"Yeah. My babies," Mary said. "How's Barry?"

Abby smiled at the band that had replaced her wedding ring.

"Oh, he's gone. Twelve years of hell, over at last. I'm seeing somebody else now. His name's Tim. We've been together for three years. No plans to marry." She glanced at the photo again. "So."

Mary pursed her lips, nodding.

"So," she said after a pause, "How's Pittsburgh?"

"Same old place," Abby said. "A little better some places, a little worse in others."

Mary put a hand on the counter, had a slug of beer, and asked,

"Your editor. What did he say?"

"He said run with it. I've got three days," Abby said. "We'll see how it goes. I mean, I'm not the Post-Gazette's ace reporter,

Mary. Never was. I usually cover city government meetings and stuff like that. I'm no Lois Lane. Plus, remember, the day they're planning on running a piece on page one—which we're not guaranteed—there could be a terrorist bombing or a hurricane, and boom, we're page four. It happens."

"But he's planning to publish it."

"It'll be in there."

Mary smiled.

"Can you do it in three days?"

"It's part of the job, Mary, weaving a sweater out of an inch of string. I already set an interview with Victor Masters."

"*Really?*" Mary said. "You *did?*"

"Yeah," Abby laughed. "I told him that the Post-Gazette was interested in the new casino and he jumped like a spawning salmon. He thinks he's in for a PR puff piece." Abby smirked. "Heh. Wait until they get a load of me."

"That's *fantastic.*"

"But, before that, I need more information. I need to know everything. Show me the report, the house damage, everything you've got."

"Abby, I *really, really* can't thank you enough."

Abby snorted and polished off her beer.

"Honey, we're gonna nail this sucker."

26

When Abby Lindeman told Mary that she wasn't an ace reporter, she was not being modest: if anything, it was understatement. Abby's journalistic edge had been declining ever since her divorce, and as her writing got sloppier and her instincts grew duller, she was yanked from her front page work on national news and dumped into the nether regions of Metro. Once, she'd covered gubernatorial elections and serial killings and exposed human trafficking rings. Now, she was lucky to cover a hearing at city hall instead of a school board meeting. At one time, her career, while not meteoric, was at least modestly promising; today it was in the trashcan.

This was something Abby didn't really feel like sharing with Mary. Mary had written her out of the blue; they hadn't spoken in years. Then suddenly here was Mary, begging Abby to help, using her "powers of investigative reportage." Somebody was committing a terrible injustice; somebody was trying to steal her house. Mary still believed in the redemptive powers of the media, in just the same reckless, fresh way she did way back when. Abby could hardly remember how it felt to be that young.

And now, just look at the woman: tight butt, perky breasts, skinny as she was at twenty. Damn her. Abby felt like a melting wax sculpture when she looked at herself in the mirror: what had been on top was dripping bottomside, collecting in odd places, and then refusing to budge.

Mary still believed in her, and she didn't want to dissuade her from that belief. The truth was that this was personal time, not a paid assignment; and that there was no certainty of publication at all. What this was, for Abby, was a chance to shoot back up onto the front page with a scandal filled, Geraldo Rivera-style muckraking comeback piece. Abby Lindeman's name would be heard in the halls of the Post-Gazette offices again; the feature in the Sunday paper would spawn a longer, more literary version in the New Yorker. Maybe then a book, a top ten New York Times Best Seller: Homeowner vs. Rapacious Big Business—fight! The movie adaptation would follow. Move over, Hunter S. Thompson. Outta the way, Susan Orlean!

Well, Abby thought, we've all got to have dreams.

Might as well aim as high as we can.

She and Mary were on the back porch, looking at the county report. Abby was making a list of Master's crimes.

The fake cops.

The telephone calls.

The BB gun attack.

The belligerent inspectors.

God, Mary, Abby thought. Look at us.

I'm a nobody reporter and you're a single mom.

Just what we promised ourselves we'd never be.

Neither Abby nor Mary were nostalgic people, so this afternoon they did very little reminiscing, though they had plenty to reminisce about. At one time they had been best friends, two college girls from blue-collar families who believed in something greater than the nine to five and the tyranny of the dollar. Abby was from Homewood in Pittsburgh, back when it was still half white or so; her steel worker father had stubbornly stayed put after the Homewood Steelworks closed its doors and the neighborhood began its abrupt, nasty decline. Pittsburgh, in many ways, was the story of Lewiston played out on an epic scale. When Abby and Mary were in school it was a time of a great darkness: the crack epidemic, the AIDS epidemic, the gang wars.

The University was in Oakland, a place populated by college students, devout Italian families, and frequented by bangers from East Liberty. It was also full of cafes featuring poetry slams, open mike nights, house bands and underground art. Mary was from an artless, dying industrial town; Abby grew up rough in an anti-communist, anti-fag, anti-Jew neighborhood. The two girls took like fish to water in a place where the life of the mind was given some breathing room.

Abby was always the wilder of the two; Mary was prettier but Abby always had the boyfriends, and Abby was the one who smoked up most nights and could drink just about anybody, male or female, under the table. She was a tough girl and Mary loved it; and Mary was sweet and quirky and passionate, which Abby adored.

All through the second two years of college they were inseparable. They partied in Oakland, dropping acid and hanging out in rooms thick with incense and patchouli, listening to the Grateful Dead and Jimi Hendrix while a shirtless Jim Morrison look-alike gave them backrubs and tried to convince them that ménage-a-trois' were where the action was at. Abby wrote furious, righteous articles for the school paper; Mary hung photos in the cafes around town and gave intimate guitar concerts, close gatherings on snowy nights lit softly and full of cigarette smoke and good vibes.

Summer nights, they lay side by side in the park and stared at the moon; Abby thought it was corny but saw how much Mary loved it, so she went along with it, lying on her back in the grass under a sky sapped of stars by the city lights. On occasions such as this they had conversations of DPM—Deep Philosophical Meaning—about the true nature of man, or the subjectivity of morality. Mostly it was Mary who talked and Abby who listened, the philosopher quoting Mill, Machiavelli, Derrida, Heidegger, and Aristotle.

"All I know is," Abby would say after a hissing drag on a fat joint, "Everything's bullshit."

Mary hated that simplistic view; so the argument would start again.

Later, talk would wind on to the future, to the women they were going to be. In years to come they would both look back on those summer nights and remember the plans and the promises they'd made; that they'd be friends forever, that they'd never let a man control them or dictate terms, that they'd uncompromisingly follow their loftiest dreams, even unto death, rather than live a minute more in the dank rot of Blue Collar America. Mary would join the Peace Corps and help in Africa, eventually going on to champion the rights of the Tibetans and the Burmese; meanwhile, Abby would root out male-dominated corruption in Pittsburgh, and then, one day, join forces with Mary in a kind of dynamic duo of reformative power. Neither would marry—they would use men for sex and money, nothing more. Men were painfully simple and pathetically juvenile in their cruelty. One minute they beat a woman; the next they were weeping and groveling at her feet. Men were the problem in the world; they were the Junta, the Party, the Reich, the Viet Cong. They were the Nixons and the Kissingers and the Husseins and the Pinochets. For every Gandhi or King, the male species produced ten Stalins.

Did women build the atom bombs, or chemical weapons, or death camps?

Well, Mary would point out, there were the Amazons of the Ashanti. They were the most feared, savage, and technologically advanced crack troops in 19th century Africa.

Okay, Abby rejoined. Got any more? Didn't think so.

Women like Mary and Abby were going to be the future. Women who had rejected the male/consumerist/Christian/pro-war model of society.

It was heady stuff.

Graduation came, and Mary was getting her Peace Corps application in order when her father fell ill. She and Abby parted after graduation with the promise that no matter what happened, they'd never take their eye off the prize, and they'd never forget one another.

At the Greyhound station, Abby kissed Mary on the lips, and they hugged tightly.

"Be strong, Mary," Abby whispered hotly. "*Never* let them win."

Through their first year apart they wrote with some frequency; every week at first, then every two weeks, then once a month. Abby wrote finally that she'd met someone: a really amazing, liberated guy who built guideboats and wrote short stories so beautiful, "they could barely even exist in this world," whatever that meant. After that the letters came every two months, then bi-annually, then just on Christmas. By the time Billy was born, the letters had stopped.

Abby looked at Mary's beautiful face, lined gently around her eyes and mouth—if anything, she was *more* beautiful at 42—and thought back over the past fifteen years of her own life. They had no more substance than a handful of sand, a web of infidelities, lies, separate sides of the bed, and a deepening anger and resentment that split her marriage like a yawning gulf; resentment that she was barren, that he was chronically depressed, that she was a compulsive cheater, that he secretly liked young men. In the end it tore itself apart with startling suddenness: Barry up and left with the car, a trunk- load of clothes, and the dog. Abby came home to an eviscerated house and a long, partially incoherent rant scrawled on butcher paper in angry, blunt pencil.

Twelve years, gone like so much sand.

Abby looked at Mary sadly, with a deepening sense of what they'd both lost. The Mary talking to her now *looked* the same, but she was not the same. A fire had gone out, what had been so essential and fabulous about Mary Wodehouse, something that had burned in her eyes like the North Star, cold and unknowable but casting a glow over a nighttime landscape— well, it was gone now. Mary's eyes were dull, workaday, her mouth full of words about kids and mortgages and real estate. Anyone could tell that Mary was no longer a dreamer.

Abby put down her pen next to her notepad, and looked around the porch, listened to the crickets in the bushes, the crows barking their early autumn lamentations. She sighed.

"So really, Mary," she said in her non-reporter voice, achingly aware that between them now was none of the feeling of before, that it was dead air, as if a phone line had been cut. "How are you?"

"What do you mean?" Mary said with a sad smile.

"You know. In the DPM of the question."

Mary grinned at that.

"I'm getting by."

"That's so sad," Abby said. "That we all just 'get by'." She rested her chin in the palm of her hand. "It's sad that we were exactly like everybody else and just didn't know it yet."

"That's the great thing about being young," Mary said. "Believing."

"When did it happen?" Abby said. "When did we give up?"

"Give up? Mary said. "Who gave up? I didn't."

Abby smirked. "I notice that you're not in Tibet right now. Or is that still coming down the pike?"

Mary smiled a tight-lipped smile, and gazed across the lawn. "We get older and the battles change. Part of being a grown up is realizing you'll probably never change the world, Abby—but that everybody's got a battle to win *right here*. Every life doesn't need to be an epic." She looked at Abby, and some of that old twinkle came back. "It's not giving up to recognize the beauty and worth of small dreams."

Abby stared at her for a moment, and then burst into a grin.

"Mary Wodehouse," she said, "It's good to see you again."

27

Abby's welcome dinner at the House on the Bend was an improvised affair. Mary had not been expecting her for another couple days, so dinner for the night was pot roast and instant scalloped potatoes. To juice it up a bit, particularly in light of Abby's love of drink, she sent Ned to the liquor store to buy some bottles of wine; at a quarter to six, Ned came back with some jugs of Carlo Rossi, the Merlot and the White Zinfandel. Mary tucked them away, under the sink.

Billy and Sarah were on hand, as always, to help make dinner. Sarah prepared the potatoes; Billy sautéed the vegetable medley (canned vegetables were originally on the menu, but this, too, was changed at the last minute). Abby was in the living room interviewing Mrs. Noonan and Mr. Manicotti, though in truth it was mostly Mrs. Noonan who did the talking; it took her very little prompting to open the floodgates of recollections both profound and mundane. In that hour before dinner, Mrs. Noonan's flights of memory ranged from an early recollection of drawing on her great uncle's starched shirt front, to a trip to Cuba in 1947, back when the mafia still ran the place and

Havana was a glowing carnival of sin, vice, and untold ill-gotten gain.

Here, Mr. Manicotti, between drags on a Pall Mall, laughed.

"I was a-there the same year," he said. "Maybe we see each other."

Mrs. Noonan said she'd visited Cuba on a trip from Galveston with her father; when Abby asked Mr. Manicotti what he was doing in Havana in 1947, he just crinkled up his eyes and said, "Business."

Bert watched the whole thing from the couch. He'd said hello to Abby and not much else. He didn't like having this interloper here. He was aware that she was an old friend of Mary's, but he was also aware that they had not spoken in many years. Reporters were snakes. So Abby *said* she was covering the story to the benefit of the House and everybody in it. *Right.*

That's what she said.

But who was to say that she wouldn't turn around and come up with some kind of scathing satire about a bunch of half-crazed country folk, taking all their comments out of context and weaving them into a kind of half-fiction, half-truth monster, one that would depict them as buck toothed, inbred lunatics, menaces to society or else a curiosity to be laughed at by the good folk of faraway Pittsburgh, PA. He didn't like the "sincere" way she spoke with Mrs. Noonan—come on, who could be *that* interested in the old bat's ramblings? How much did we really need to hear about Beaumont?

Bert didn't like it one bit, but he was so fed up with the whole situation and so afraid that he would screw things up further that he tried to just watch TV with Alan.

He'd already packed his bag, actually—the same old leather duffel he'd carried on his sordid, footloose travels from the Hudson Bay to San Salvador, from Quebec to San Diego. It was one of the blessings of his situation in life that he could leave at any time he chose. He'd packed his t-shirts, underwear, a pair of old jeans, and a couple pairs of tube socks. He'd taken the two hundred dollars he had left and put it in his wallet. The only thing he hadn't packed was his toothbrush—because once it was stowed, there was no going back.

He'd given a bit of thought to where to go: Savannah was nice this time of year, and not so far—he could do a little street hustle and restore his money easily once he got there. Savannah was, like New Orleans, one of those fabulous Southern fantasias where bloated, slow Midwestern folk came, waving their handicams around and talking loudly and ruffling through their fanny packs, sweating and arguing with Francine or Mabel while the street artists licked their chops and put on their running shoes. There could be no easier pickings. Then he might coast down to Key West, or maybe even Puerto Rico—he'd never been there before...

All he had to do was pack that toothbrush.

The bag had been sitting next to his bed for three days.

Now that this Abby character was here, he knew he'd have to stick around for at least three days more. There was no way he was letting some media vulture take advantage of the situation.

Over his dead body.

"Aren't you going to ask me *my* back story?" he piped up suddenly, making Alan wince and cup his ear so as to better hear the antics of Bill Huxtable.

Abby looked at Bert with a quizzical smile

"Sure, Bert," she said. "I love a good story."

"I'll bet you do," Bert said. "That's what you reporters do, right? You go fishing for sad stories, and then you sell them to the highest bidder?"

"If we didn't sell them, we wouldn't be able to make a living," Abby said patiently. "I don't know about you, but I have bills to pay."

"Oh, right," Bert said, smirking unpleasantly. "I see. So you've done your research. Hey, Mrs. Noonan, you might as well save your breath, cause she already knows about your father's Studebaker!"

"Mr. Wodehouse, *please!*" Alan cried. "I can't hear!"

"My… research?" Abby asked. "What are you talking about?"

"You're only the second person this month to turn up the fact that I've never had a bank account," Bert said angrily. "I know how it works. Our whole lives are on the Internet. As *if* you even need to ask us questions." He looked over his shoulder to see if Mary was nearby, then leaned in and jabbed a finger at Abby. "Here's the scoop, sister. I'm like a *bloodhound* when it comes to scumbags who go around exploiting people, because I happen to be one—as, no doubt, you've turned up on the Internet. So as long as you're here, I'm gonna be watching. I'm gonna watch you like a *hawk*, lady. Think you can *worm* your way in here—well, think again." Bert stood up defiantly, jamming his thumb into his chest. "If you're a worm, then I'm the robin that's going to drag you out into the light of day!"

"Robin?" Alan said, stifling a laugh. "You're the *robin?*"

"What? What's wrong with that?"

"Well… besides being a little tiny bird, it's also the name of a superhero *boy* who wore green *tighties.*"

"Fine, I'm not a robin. I'm a *hawk!*"

"You already said you're *watching* her like a hawk," Ned commented from the doorway. Bert gritted his teeth, blinking away flopsweat.

"Yeah. How about a loon?" Alan suggested. "Or an albatross?"

"Those birds don't eat worms," Ned chided.

"Well, then, what does, smart guy?"

"*Vultures.* They *must* eat worms; they eat *everything*," Ned said.

"We had so many vultures in Beaumont," Mrs. Noonan reminisced.

"Yeah, Mr. Wodehouse, vultures are much more threatening than robins," Alan said. "Go with vulture."

"But *I'm* not the vulture," Bert seethed. "*She* is!"

"Well, what eats vultures?" Ned wondered, clearly frustrated at this new development.

"Just—just *forget* it. Forget I said anything!" Bert said. He jabbed his finger at Abby again. "You'd just better watch it!" he snarled, and before Abby could answer, he stormed out of the room.

"Hey Bert!" Ned called after him. "Dinner's starting soon!"

"I'm going to go find some road kill!" Bert called back. "I'm a vulture, remember? Thanks, pal!"

"*Wow*," Abby said, raising her eyebrows. "If I wanted a story, I guess I got one."

"Bert's a character," Ned agreed.

"He was a homeless person," Alan added.

"Lots of *nice* people are homeless," Abby said.

"We're going to be homeless, too," Alan went on. "I'm trying to get in as much TV as I can, while the getting's good." He turned back to his program. "So if you *please*."

Abby smiled at Alan, and turned to Mrs. Noonan.

"Never a dull moment around here, is there?"

"Oh, no dear," Mrs. Noonan said. "It's always *something*."

Ned cleared his throat.

"I'm here to tell you that dinner is ready," he said.

"FINE!" Alan cried, shutting off the TV. "I give up!"

"Dinnner's ready *now*, you say?" Bert asked from outside the window.

"Well, look who's sniffing around," Alan said. "He's not a man, he's a hyena. A scavenger with funny teeth and bad posture."

"At least I'm not a little blinking mole," Bert shot back.

Mr. Manicotti yawned, and lurched to his feet.

"I'm-a hungry as a bear," he said. "Lets-a stop a-talking and eat, *capisce?*"

28

The dinner table was set with candles, flowers, and a white tablecloth—rarely had it looked so stately. Abby took the seat reserved for her in the middle with Claude on one side and Billy on the other. Wine was already poured into small, robust glasses, and the pot roast and potatoes and stuffing steamed enticingly.

After everyone was seated, Mary tapped her fork on her glass and raised her hand to make an announcement.

"Before we eat, I'd just like to thank Abby one more time for agreeing to come here and help us out."

Abby smiled uneasily.

"I don't want to oversell myself here," she said. "It's not like I'm a Pulitzer Prize winner. And even if I were—well, it usually takes more than a single article in a single paper—from a different city no less—to stop somebody like Masters."

Mary gave Abby a perplexed half-smile.

"You weren't talking like that *before.*"

"Well, you know," Abby said slowly, "With everybody here, I just want to be forthright about what I can do and what I *can't*."

"Yeah, *this* I want to hear," Bert said, already shoveling potatoes on to his plate. "What *can* you do?"

Abby fixed her caustic gaze on Bert, and hoping to change the subject, said in a loud voice, "So, Bert, I heard that you already started repairs on the house."

Vera snorted. "Can you believe that Mr. Knucklehead here had Mr. Manicotti up on the roof?

Bert rolled his eyes. "Don't start *that* again. I told you, I would've gone up there myself, except I've got heightraphobia."

Abby stifled a laugh. "*What* do you have?"

"Heightraphobia. You know, a fear of heights. I'm surprised you didn't know about that, college girl," Bert said smugly.

Abby gave Bert a little smile. "Bert, I think you mean *acrophobia. That's* a fear of heights."

Bert glared at her. He wasn't used to being challenged at the dinner table. He glanced around and saw that the others were watching. His reputation was on the line.

"Acrophobia? Are you kidding?" Bert said confidently. "That's something totally different."

"Really," Abby said, leaning forward and narrowing her eyes at him. "What is it, then? Why don't you tell us all about it?"

Bert hesitated, and licked his lips.

"Okay... acrophobia...for your information, it's... a... fear of *acrobats*." He brightened up and nodded affirmatively.

Abby made a funny noise but tried to watch him seriously.

"That's very interesting," she said. "I guess you learn something new every day. And why would people be afraid of acrobats?"

Bert glanced around again. Even his staunchest supporters—Ned, Alan, and Billy—looked a little uneasy, fumbling with their forks. Claude had gone blank. Vera flashed him a big smile that said *gotcha!*

He couldn't let Abby win. Abby *or* Vera. Not on his home turf.

"Look," he said desperately, "When the circus came to town, the acrobats got all the attention, what with all the flipping and jumping and trapeze acts. They got to thinking they were better than the other performers, like the Bearded Lady, the Clown Brigade, the Tall Man, whatever. The Acrobats got real big heads and started shooting off their mouths. Problem was, they were so quick and so strong that if you ever tried to slug one you'd end up in a world of pain. So all the other performers ended up resentful and scared of the acrobats—so, anyhow, that's how it started."

Ned nodded thoughtfully.

"Yeah, I could see that."

Vera frowned indecisively.

"You have *got* to be kidding," Abby said.

Bert waved her off, and breathed an inward sigh of relief.

"Look, I ain't got time to explain *everything* to you. It's exhausting, knowing so much. You give and give and give."

"Bert's like an encyclopedia," Ned observed.

"More like Ripley's Believe it or Not," Abby deadpanned.

Mary cleared her throat.

"Abby," she said pointedly. "You were in the middle of telling us what you could do to help us stop Masters."

Abby stiffened, and the table fell quiet. Bert cleared his throat loudly.

"Okay, well, I can bring out the truth," Abby said. "Put it on public record. Package it in such a way that people sit up and take notice. The truth will be heard."

"Well, then, somebody's got to do something about it," Vera reasoned.

"Why?" Bert said. "How often does *that* happen? Nobody cares about anything anymore."

"But," Abby protested, "What about Michael Moore's work? Bowling for Columbine? In response, K-Mart stopped selling ammunition! Or what about Super Size Me? Fast Food Nation? The Jungle?"

"What side of this argument are you on, anyway?" Bert snapped.

"I'm not arguing a side," Abby said. "What I'm doing..." she looked to her right and saw Claude giving her an unnerving, impassive stare. "Ah... is being realistic."

"When you tell a story," Bert said with his mouth full, "You throw your realism out the window."

"That's not what I mean."

"What *do* you mean?" Vera asked impatiently.

"Well," Abby said, "I'm getting to it, if certain people would let me." She shot an angry glare at Bert, then glanced at Claude again with an uneasy smile. "The media has its influence. That's not being debated here. People will read about your situation and they'll get angry. They'll be passing around Masters' name like a dirty diaper. But is it going to make the government leap into action? Eventually, maybe. I *think* you're underestimating how *long* things take. The wheels of justice move very, very slowly. "Go on, everybody," Mary said dourly. "Eat up." She looked at Abby. "You didn't say this before."

"Didn't say *what?*"

"You said, 'we're going to nail the bastard.' That's what you said."

"We are. Everyone will know what he did."

"But you're saying that might not be enough."

Abby made an exasperated face.

"I'm saying that maybe it won't happen right away. The cavalry isn't going to ride in the day after the article goes out, you know. If it was that easy, then Richard Gere would have freed the Tibetans years ago!"

"Honey, take more vegetables," Mary said to Sarah.

"Mary?"

"*Yes*," Mary said, folding her arms. "I'm *listening*."

"It's going to take a *long* time. You need to petition the county government and the state government. You need to take *action*. You can use the media to popularize a problem, but it won't *fix* the problem. You can't just sit here, in this house, and hope that the answer will fall into your lap. Because it *won't*. You've got to take the fight up yourself. You do that and you'll inspire others to join in. When you stand tall, others will stand with you. *That's* where I can help. But an article in the Post-Gazette isn't a silver bullet. It's a bridge."

"*Mary*," Bert said. "You told us she had the silver bullet!"

"Be *quiet*," Mary said, sighing. "I just…" she gazed sadly at the hunk of pot roast on her plate. "I just don't know *how*, Abby."

Abby took a bit of meat.

"Well," she said, "Have you thought about hiring a lawyer? Masters has broken the law. Repeatedly. He's tried to intimidate you. He's harassed you. He's threatened your family. And while you can't connect the two conclusively, the county has broken a few laws, too. They've made accusations they can't support. The lead paint, the mold, the storage tanks—the entire notion that the house is a menace to *anybody* is a lie. There are thousands of houses in Pawnee County in much worse shape than this one. Have they been inspected? Have they been threatened with condemnation?"

"Probably not," Mary said. "But I don't really know."

Abby tapped the table top with her hand.

"Get a lawyer, Mary. You can at least *delay* the process until you've got the allies and the ammunition to *end* it once and for all."

"How can I afford that?" Mary demanded.

"You said the repairs were going to run 50,000 dollars?"

"Yeah."

"A lawyer won't cost 50,000 dollars."

"I've only got a couple thousand, Abby. We've got so *little*," Mary pleaded. "And anyways, I'm not sure we've got a case. Who are we going to go after? The government? Masters? He's covered his tracks, Abby." She made a frustrated face. "The fact is, we don't have enough money or evidence to hire a lawyer. We just *don't*."

"Well…" Billy said suddenly, "Actually, we've got a little more money than you think."

The conversation stopped dead in its tracks. Billy stared at his plate and blushed.

"I wasn't going to tell you yet, but… Sarah and me, we've been selling stuff we found in the basement. To raise money for the repairs."

"Selling *what* stuff?" Mary asked.

"Well, you know… junk. We didn't sell any of grandpa's medals or anything. Just stuff that nobody was ever going to touch again."

"Could you provide some *specifics*, William?" Mary said.

"Like grandma's crazy old porcelain collection. And some toys, and lunchboxes."

"Billy sold most of his train set, too," Sarah announced.

"You *did*?" Mary asked, making a pained face. "Honey, this isn't your responsibility. I didn't want you to sell your *toys*. It's not your *problem* to need to deal with…"

"I live here, don't I?" Billy said. "We need money, don't we? So, I thought I'd do what I can."

"How much did you... get from all that?" Mary asked after a moment's guilty hesitation.

"Twelve hundred dollars," Billy said.

"And thirty five," Sarah added.

Mary looked like she might either laugh or burst into tears.

"That's wonderful. I love you two so much," she said with a hitch in her voice.

"You can keep the thirty-five, baby."

"Mom, *please*, don't call me baby, okay?" Billy said.

Sarah gritted her teeth and folded her arms in deepening frustration as she saw that credit would not be given where credit was due.

"And we sold the old Jeep frame in the carriage house. We haven't been paid yet. The guy's coming on Friday to pick it up, when you go shopping."

"Don't you need to be in school?" Vera asked.

Billy shrugged.

"I don't think they'll miss me."

"Don't talk like that, Billy," Mary pleaded. "Why all the secrecy? Why not just tell me?" She pointed at Bert. "Between you and *him*, there's an awful lot of sneaking around going on here... who else's got something up their sleeve? Mr. Manicotti? Claude?"

"*Mom*," Billy said. "I wanted it to be a nice surprise. And I knew that you like to... keep stuff longer than you need to, and so you might not agree to let me sell it."

Abby made a "there we go" swipe with her hand. "So there's your lawyer. Twelve hundred will get him started. Stop this thing in its tracks."

"You couldn't hire Denny Crane for twelve hundred," Alan pointed out.

"Maybe for five minutes," Ned suggested.

"You could hire Ally McBeal for twelve hundred G's but it wouldn't be to practice law," Bert said.

Alan made a face at him.

"Please, Mr. Wodehouse, let's try to keep it tasteful. There are women and children at the table."

Sarah was now in a deep sulk. She could see that she'd seriously miscalculated in helping Billy. It was just like him to go on and grab all the attention and all the thanks. The fact that *she* had spent countless hours pouring through the old boxes of the Shumak family seemed to mean nothing. For that she'd get a "you did a nice job too, honey," and a pat on the head. To hell with that. If Billy was going to reap all the rewards, he could do all the work. She was *out*, permanently.

Billy, for his part, didn't like the attention. He hadn't done it to be the star of the family; he'd done it to get some distraction from each humiliating, crushing day at school. He didn't want to be the center of attention, here or there. He wanted to be left alone, driving down highway 41, under a big sky. It really wasn't much to ask.

Abby watched the buzz and clatter of dinner and saw the paragraphs in her head, streaming through, so much she could fill a whole book if she wanted to. She glanced at Claude and smiled. Stiffly, Claude's face tightened up into something resembling acknowledgement. She looked across the table at Vera and Ned, arguing because Ned didn't want to eat carrots and Vera insisted that he must. She glanced at Bert, who was in turn gazing at Billy with jealousy; what a petty man. She looked at Mary, smiling at her children with the commonplace beauty of commonplace pride.

Hell, she thought. I'd better be able to pitch this story.

Abby hated a lie, and she could feel herself getting neck deep in one.

29

After the dishes were cleared, the house filled with the aroma of brewing coffee as everybody eagerly retired to the living room to share their stories with Abby. She'd announced during dessert that she wanted to do more interviews afterwards: she wanted everybody's story.

Only Claude and Alan were not interested.

Claude took his broom from the front closet and began to sweep the hall; Alan turned on the TV and sat in the La-Z-boy erect and angled forward, so that he could hear over the self-indulgent chatter.

Abby had always felt that people were most eloquent when telling their own stories: just listen to homeless men, abused children, and minimum wagers, and you'd be treated to free-verse poetry of sharp clarity and rare beauty. Everyone had a story worth telling; most people just didn't realize that the world would be interested. So Abby scrawled her notes as fast as she could, knowing that there was enough overflow to fill a dozen short stories after the muckraking was done. She ran a recorder too, but there was something about the immediacy of taking notes that she liked; the excited scratching of her pen drew the truth out of people like the march of the pied piper.

Mrs. Noonan could have gone on all night with her reminiscences of Beaumont, but interesting as Abby found all that, she wanted a chat with Mr. and Mrs. Johnson. Vera did most of the talking; Ned agreed now and then or offered a detail or enhancement that Vera swatted down like an irritating fly. These two were the perfect foil to the Masters' Old Money opulence. From her research she knew that Victor Masters lived in a French-style palace; Collin lived in a Spanish-style villa. Combined, their residences were worth well over ten million dollars, an astonishing amount for the Rustbelt.

Who better to use in skewering the rapacious developers than an old working class couple, betrayed by the company to which they'd devoted their lives, pensions dried up, benefits gone, house sold during foreclosure, devoutly moral and religious, and best of all, black. Their story was utterly typical and for that very reason it would sell; the people of Pittsburgh were all too familiar with companies bleeding out and packing up. With the crash of Homewood Steel's slamming gates still ringing in their ears, this cautionary tale of bottom dollar-loving, pro-Chinese, anti-Blue Collar Big Business would hit a nerve for sure. She could see it now: "First they did it in small town PA—are you next?"

Oh, yeah. They'd eat this stuff up with a spoon. It's all about the hook.

Oldest rule in the journalism playbook. No hook, no story.

Taking a break from her interview with the Johnsons, Abby went into the kitchen to help Mary bring in the coffee. Bert studied her from across the room.

What's she up to, he wondered.

Tried to make a fool of me in front of everybody.

I *hate* her.

While Bert stewed and the others waited anxiously for Abby to come back so they could talk some more about themselves, Alan was busy watching a quiz show.

On a colored set, behind a pair of podiums, stood four contestants on two teams.

"I'll take 60s for 300," said one man.

The question appeared on the screen and was read with authority by host Tad Langley.

"Gomer Pyle, USMC, starring Jim Nabors as Private Pyle, was a spin off of...."

"What is 'The Andy Griffith Show,'" Alan said quietly.

"...what show?"

"Ah... the... ah..." The contestant made a frustrated face. The opposing lectern lit up red.

"The Andy Griffith Show," said one of the two men at that lectern.

"That's right!" Langley said with a blinding grin as the dollar total on the winning lectern went up with a cheerful beep. The studio audience clapped.

After the women came back from the kitchen and passed out the coffees, Abby sat down next to Alan.

"What are you watching?" she asked.

"A TV quiz show," Alan said. "It's called TV Wonderland."

"70s for 400," the winning team said after giving each other a high five.

"They win every week," Alan said with a sigh. "They've been on for two months. It gets old after a while, seeing them win, again and again,"

Host Tad Langley was reading the next question.

"What did Felix Unger, played by Tony Randall, do for a living on TVs 'The Odd Couple'?"

"What is photographer," Alan said.

"He was a photographer," answered the incumbent winner a moment later. Studio clapping, cheerful buzzing, dollar total going up, while Langley cried "That's correct!" and the opponents, a balding man and his red haired, frail brother, mopped sweat off their brows and gazed bleakly at the question board, then at their alarming negative score in red, then back at the board.

"That was an easy one," Alan said with a shrug. "I watch sometimes because once in a great while they stump me. It's a nice test of my television proficiency."

"90s for 400."

"I'll bet you could clean up on there," Abby said.

Alan shrugged.

"I guess so."

"On 'Felicity,' what condiment did Ben's roommate Sean invent?"

"What is Smoothaise," Alan said with a yawn. "Felicity: there's a show that overstayed its welcome."

From the TV contestants: silence.

A buzzer went off and a portly Asian man appeared from behind a curtain, dressed like Oddjob.

"You have fay-elled!" he shouted to the striking of a gong. The crowd laughed and the contestants made uncomfortable faces.

"The correct answer is: Smoothaise!" Langley shouted. A deep, amplified voice echoed "Smoothaise!" a moment later. Four hundred dollars were deducted from the winning team's grand total.

"I wonder how you get on there?" Mary wondered quietly.

"Why?" Alan asked cautiously.

"Come on, Alan, you just got one that nobody could answer!" Abby said. "I'll bet you could give those guys a real run for their money!"

"So what?" Alan said with some irritation. "I like watching. I don't want to play."

"But you'd win for sure!"

"I don't want to win!" Alan cried. "Please, Mrs. Lindeman, I don't like games! I just want to watch my show!"

Alan suddenly realized that the room was silent, except for Mrs. Noonan's quiet, oblivious ramblings. All eyes were on him.

"Name the character played by a young James Brolin on Marcus Welby, M.D.," Langley declared.

"Who is Dr. Steven Kiley?" Alan muttered, unable to help himself.

"Is it... Dr. Steven Kiley?" the winning team said after a long silence.

"That is.... CORRECT!" Langley enthused.

Thunderous applause. Beeping. Lights.

High fives between the winners, after which they each ran a hand over their slicked back hair and winced to show how hot they were.

"And that brings us to the end of round 1!" Langley said. "Stay with us! We'll be *right* back after these messages!"

Alan abruptly changed the channel to CSI: Miami.

"Alan, you know you really should go on there," Ned said. "You could win enough money to fix the house."

"They shoot that in Pittsburgh," Abby said. "At Massive Studios."

"I'm *not* going on there!" Alan said with hysteria in his voice. "Please! Just *leave me alone*! Go back to your storytelling!"

Everyone made disappointed faces.

"We just thought it was cool how you knew all the answers, Alan," Mary said. "That's all."

"Waiting list to go on there is a mile long," Abby said. "Anyways."

"See?" Alan said, folding his arms and trying to look like he was concentrating on CSI. "So there we go."

"But I do know a producer who works on the show," Abby went on, giving Alan a wink that he didn't see; he'd already trained his attention back on the screen.

Bert, pretending to adjust the curtains, took in everything.

Soon Vera was talking again, and Abby went on taking notes. Alan was alone, like he'd asked to be.

"Find somebody else to save the day," he snorted, jumping between the stations. He didn't know what to watch, and suddenly wasn't interested in anything in particular.

Suddenly he recoiled in horror and threw down the remote: he was behaving like a *flipper*. On Iron Chef America, Bobby Flay (what a made up name!) was taking on Emerill.

He wanted to just watch TV and forget.

But now, he realized, that was impossible.

He had a power.

He *could* save the day... if he wanted to.

30

Nine o'clock in the morning and Victor Masters was waiting at Filter, the coolest coffee shop in Brownsville. As a rule, Lewiston had diners and Brownsville had cafes; while the diners in Lewiston were the haunts of burned-out factory workers, street cleaners, and assorted vagabonds, Brownsville's cafes thronged with bright-eyed students and hipsters from the college. While the diners were all fluorescent light, red vinyl seats, smoker waitresses and country on the radio, the cafes had eclectic rock soundtracks, cool student art, and girl baristas with horn-rimmed glasses and pixie-haircuts.

Masters liked giving interviews at cafes, as opposed to the office, for the simple reason that he could get up and leave at any time that he wanted to. Any pretense would do; a forgotten appointment, an urgent phone call, bad stomach ache, whatever. At the same time, cafes put people at ease; there was none of the uptight formality of offices. This was important when projecting the progressive image of Master Developments; that it was hip and young, fresh and fun. They must never appear as the big man on the hill, the Boss Hoggs of Pawnee County, so to speak. The last thing they wanted to be were Willy Wonkas locked up behind high walls and presiding over their empire by video conference and e-mail, descending on a storm cloud to inspect the troops once in a blue moon.

Victor knew that his usual no nonsense approach was fine for handling contractors and architects, but when you were dealing with the press, with financiers, with politicians, the name of the game was *branding*.

He always showed up at an interview half an hour early; this morning he arrived at Filter at 8:30. He saw the extra time as a tactical advantage, like a general scouting out the terrain before a battle. This gave him time to decide on a seat where the lighting would flatter him, in the midst of the bustle but not too close to the hissing and distraction of the coffee bar; then to settle in and establish himself in the space, to inhabit it, to make it his own.

When meeting with a politician or a banker, the key was to outclass them. Better cologne, nicer cufflinks, slimmer suit, more expensive watch. With "power men" it was important to immediately establish what Victor liked to think of as the Benevolent Alpha Male Posture; that is, to demonstrate that he was stronger and more confident, but also he was a really nice guy. A firm handshake *and* a casual clap on the arm set the tone at once.

"Please, have a seat. Look at how impeccably dressed I am. Bet you wish you had worn a nicer suit, huh? Bet you wish you had a watch like this. But it's okay. I'm not hung up on myself. I'm impeccably put together, but I'm cool with you being a protoplasm in a JC Penny suit."

Take the high ground.

That's the key.

On the other hand, with journalists, like this Post-Gazette reporter, it was important to project an image of ease and lightness. No tie; open collar. He ordered a latte instead of a double espresso. He claimed the couch by the fireplace, so that they could sit next to one another. He put a copy of Esquire on the coffee table—he carried the men's magazine around for occasions such as this. Reporters picked up on details like that, and details like that invariably ended up in articles.

When I meet Victor Masters he's reading a copy of Esquire at his favorite coffee shop. He's dressed business casual, a kind of latter-day Telly Savalas. He takes a sip of his streamed non-fat latte and we chat about the Steelers and Caravaggio, about Fair Trade Coffee and the new Modest Mouse album, before we get down to business.

Or something like that.

Nine o'clock came. Victor looked around the café, at the vintage shabby-chic couches, the vintage vinyl swivel chairs, the vintage café tables, Formica and wood and plastic, no two the same. The walls were exposed brick, the floor unfinished concrete. Overhead was track lighting and exposed ductwork. Giant framed paintings hung on the walls.

Anybody who was hip knew that hipness was the product of a little intuition and a lot of calculation.

He was a little heavier on the calculation, that was all.

At 9:03 a blonde woman came in the front door dressed in a white button down blouse and an unflattering black pleated skirt. Her haircut was functional and cheap, with bangs and a ratty back that she had tied in a ponytail. She was carrying a cheap black satchel, and on coming in she paused and looked around the room for one, two, three seconds.

Victor raised his hand and smiled. The woman saw it and picked her way across the room between the tables, between open newspapers and backpacks. Breathing hard, Masters hauled himself to his feet.

"Abby Lindeman?" he panted with a forced smile.

"Victor Masters?" she answered with a smile that matched his. They shook. She was thin, he observed, but in all the wrong ways: bony hands, skeletal arms, sallow face; but with menopausal chunk around her waist. The K-Mart cut of the skirt—waistline above the belly button—certainly didn't help.

"Have you been here long?" Abby asked.

"No, not long," Masters said, gesturing to the couch. "I come here every morning anyways—to relax before hitting the office. You know." They sat down so their knees were almost touching. Masters studied her face as she put down her satchel and got out her notes. It was attractive, but yellow and blotchy with light brown spots that she'd crudely tried to cover up with makeup. There were spots on her hands too.

"Can I get you a coffee?" Victor asked, flashing her another puffy smile. "They make a lovely cappuccino here."

"I'm fine, actually," Abby said politely, pushing her tinder dry hair behind her ears.

"You sure?"

"Definitely."

Victor nodded.

"So, Pittsburgh Post-Gazette," he said with a whistle. "The big city. We get reporters from Philly from time to time, but Pittsburgh—wow—that's clear across the state! Pirates are doing well this year, aren't they?"

"I don't watch baseball," Abby said, clicking her pen. "I might be the only person in Pittsburgh who doesn't."

"You know, I went to school at the University of Pittsburgh," Masters said, looking dreamy. "I was a huge Panthers fan. Did you go to Pitt? No, wait, I'll bet you went to Duquesne. Right? Duquesne? Have I got it?"

"Nope," Abby said. "Pitt, just like you."

"Wow, imagine that," Masters sighed. "Takes me back. What a town, huh? Loved Pittsburgh, I really did. But hey, my roots are here, you know? I like the Burg, but deep down I always was a small town boy. And I guess I always will be."

Abby wrote that in her notes.

"Before we go any further, Mr. Masters—"

"Call me Victor, please. Can I call you Abby?"

"If you like, Victor. Can I use a recorder?"

"Go ahead," Victor said with an indulgent wave of the hand. "Hell, put me on camera if you want." He laughed at that and let his eye twinkle while Abby dug out her digital recorder, hit record, and put it on the table.

"So, where were we?" Abby said.

"Did you ever go to Nick's Fat City?' he asked. "They get some great bands there."

"I went there once or twice. It closed a few years ago"

"You know, Mercury got their start there. Used to play there from time to time."

Abby cleared her throat.

"I don't want to take up too much of your time Mr. Masters—Victor, sorry—so I'd like to ask you a couple questions about the new casino development."

"Oh, right," Masters said. "I'm in no hurry here, but sure, fire away." He folded his fat hands and pursed his lips expectantly.

"There's been a great deal of buzz surrounding Bluebeard's Pirate Clipper, the second Master Developments Casino. People are saying that it's going to be one of the most ambitious casinos outside of Vegas. Would you agree with that?"

"*Outside* of Vegas?" Masters said. "Well, obviously I take issue with that. See, the thrilling thing about Pirate's Clipper is that it is just as ambitious—and just as exciting—as anything in Vegas. Sure, it isn't as big as Caesar's Palace or Barbary Coast—but it's not the size of the ship, if you know what I mean." He winked at Abby. "In terms of amenities, restaurants—in terms of how damned *cool* it's going to be—this is going to lead the pack by *miles*." He raised an eyebrow at Abby. "Feel free to quote me on that."

"Oh, sure,' Abby said, nodding.

"We're talking the *best* odds, the most tables. We're talking cutting edge dining, live shows, music, a whole experience."

"Wow."

"Yeah. The casino's going to be amazing. Have you ever been to Master Plays?"

"No, I have not."

"We'll go there tonight, if you want. I'll give you the royal treatment." Masters winked at her again, eying her flat breasts with what he hoped appeared to be surreptitious interest. "You'll see that Master Plays is major league. Yet Pirate's Clipper will blow it out of the water."

"Will that be very profitable, for Master Developments to have *two* casinos in town?"

"Well, Master Plays caters to a certain kind of clientele, and we expect that die-hards won't jump ship so easily. But, eventually, we do plan to close down Master Plays and concentrate on Pirate's Clipper."

"Wouldn't it be *more* profitable to keep Master Plays where it is, and then just build Pirate's Clipper in some other part of the state?"

Masters nodded patiently, as if he heard this question all the time. "Abby, we have a commitment to this community. I guess I should make that clear. We're not going to cut and run. We're here for the long haul. Besides, we feel that Lewiston, situated right off the Turnpike, is uniquely positioned to attract business from both ends of the state—and beyond."

"We've already been getting press releases about the development," Abby said. "You're clearly trying to generate a lot of buzz."

"That's right, Abby. We're excited—and we want to share that excitement. That's why I wanted you to meet with me—and *not* my publicist. We don't want to hide behind PR guys and spin-doctors. We're right out there." He raised a finger in rising excitement. "And Abby, we're not the only ones who are excited. *Lewiston* is excited. Lewiston *needs* this. The tourism revenue this will generate will be like a breath of fresh air to that great town. Let's face it: Lewiston needs jobs. Lewiston needs opportunities. Lewiston needs a *future*." He paused for dramatic effect. "Pirate's Clipper—and Master Developments—*is* that future."

"You care deeply about the community," Abby suggested.

"Abby, Brownsville and Lewiston are my heart." He pounded a fist against his chest. "I grew up here when times were tough. I can see how much potential there is. Somebody else might have gone to Philly. Or Pittsburgh. Or New York. That's what a lot of people would do. But my brother and I—well, we're not like a lot of people. You know why, Abby?'

"Why, Victor?"

"Because: we *believe* in Lewiston."

Abby paused for a moment while she jotted down a few notes. Victor mentally patted himself on the back, and reclined comfortably. With a grunt he crossed his legs. Depeche Mode was playing.

"Sure you wouldn't like a coffee or something?" he asked indulgently.

"Yeah," Abby said. "I'm sure. Okay, *now*." She looked up, and stared Masters in the eye. "Lots of press, lots of buzz. How far along is Pirate's Clipper? When can we expect a finished product?"

"We're shooting for an opening in one year. We'd like it to coincide with the tenth anniversary of Master Plays."

"When did you break ground?"

Masters smiled warmly.

"We haven't yet."

"You haven't even broken ground?"

"No, not yet."

"Where is the site located?

"At a bend in the Pawnee River, about three miles outside of Lewiston. It's a lovely spot we've chosen, very natural. It's far enough from Lewiston that it will benefit from the open space and natural beauty of the countryside, but close enough to provide ease of access to hotels, gas stations, and the turnpike."

Abby nodded. "That's great. When do you plan to begin construction?'

"In the spring, probably. There are a few final details to sort out. But as soon as the ground thaws in the spring, we should be ready to go. We're shooting for groundbreaking in April."

"What kinds of details?"

Abby was studying Masters closely. *Boy*, she thought. *He is one cool customer.* His face was as serene and collected as ever.

"Zoning, mostly," Masters said. "There are some land use issues to be sorted out."

Land use issues. That's cute.

"I understand that you haven't actually purchased the property yet," Abby said carefully. "Is that true?"

A slight shadow fell in Masters' eyes.

"Well... the sale is late in negotiation."

"County tax records say that the property is in the possession of a certain Mary Shumak..." Abby flipped a couple pages back in her notes, and nodded affirmatively. "I did a title check and there's been an unbroken line of ownership of that house by the Shumak family since 1854. Is that right?"

"I'm not sure about that," Masters said, still smiling, but with a chill in his voice.

"But they're willing to sell?"

"I'd say the sale is assured."

"But you're not totally sure?'

"Well, Abby, nothing is ever one-hundred percent."

"Why isn't it one hundred percent? And, aren't you concerned, given the high stakes riding on a timely construction and opening of Pirate's Clipper?"

"No, I'm not concerned. Everything will be fine. Everything is moving smoothly and on schedule. If you'd like, I can show you some artist's renderings of the casino—" he suggested, reaching for his attaché case.

"I'd love that," Abby said. "But first I'd like to clarify a few questions that I have. So, plainly, Mr. Masters, speaking *plainly* please—do the Shumaks *want* to sell their property, or don't they?"

Victor pursed his lips, and then grinned at her.

"Yes, Abby, they do. It's just lawyer stuff at this point. They're very… interesting people, and they have a number of contingencies that we need to work out."

Immediately, Victor knew he shouldn't have lied.

It was just so easy.

But if there was one thing he'd learned, it was that while distortions make the world go round, outright lies *always* catch up with you in the end.

This one didn't take long.

Abby's eyes twinkled and he knew he'd been had.

"That's interesting," Abby said. "Because I recently spoke to Mrs. Shumak, and she tells me that not only is she not interested in selling, but that you've been intimidating her and trying some… well, frankly *alarming* tactics to force her to leave her house."

Victor forced a tight, upturned line of a smile.

"Well, Abby… look, I told you that she is a somewhat difficult person. She wants some unreasonable things in return for the sale, things we're not prepared to give her—and frankly, that I'm not prepared to discuss." He sighed, and closed his eyes for a moment. "She's not a terribly reliable source of information, let me assure you."

"So you deny that you've tried to coerce her into selling."

"Yes. I deny that. That's a preposterous accusation."

"She told me that your brother paid her a visit in person, when he threatened to 'make her life difficult.'"

"No."

"No, he didn't threaten her, or no, he didn't visit in person?"

"No—he *did* visit in person. We thought we'd do her that courtesy, a courtesy she obviously hasn't repaid—instead she's feeding you a pack of wild accusations that are *totally* baseless."

"She also said that two inspectors from the County Safety Department visited her the day after your brother's visit and wrote a very harsh report about her house—a report that led to the issuance of a county condemnation order."

"Yes? So?"

"Do you know about that?"

"I am… aware that the Safety Department issued a condemnation order. Yes."

Abby nodded. "But you didn't have anything to do with it."

"No, of course not," Masters said with a laugh. "I don't control the Safety Department, Abby."

"Despite the fact that they came the *day after* your brother's visit."

"A coincidence."

Abby smiled.

"That's interesting." She took out a second Dictaphone, and put it on the table. "Apparently, your brother called the House soon after the departure of the inspectors, and left a message. Mary—Mrs. Shumak—had foresight. She saved the tape from her answering machine—which she'd previously thrown across her yard in her anger. Fortunately for her, the tape survived. Would you like to listen to it?"

Masters looked blankly at the Dictaphone. Abby waited for a moment, and getting no answer, she hit play.

Mrs. Shumak, this is Collin Masters. I hope you're well. I'm still interested in your house, but I'm afraid that I will have to offer you fifteen percent less than I did last time; I've learned that there are some building violations that I didn't know about. It's still a good offer. Don't pass it up. Remember, we'll get the house one way or another. My patience is waning, Mrs. Shumak. I know you're there—"

"What do you have to say about that?" Abby asked.

"I... that is..." Victor said, looking shocked, then intense, then trying to appear pleasantly surprised, then giving that up and licking his lips.

"You do realize that even *if* she sold the house to you, she could have the contract voided, don't you? Clearly, this is coercion. This is a state of duress."

"Look," Victor said, trying to muster his forces. "Her house is a menace to those within. It is a dangerous structure. It is beset with structural and environmental problems. It's full of health hazards and fire hazards. The Safety Department was doing their job. And I was doing mine."

"*Was* the safety department doing its job?" Abby asked, pulling out a Xerox of the report sent by the county. She watched with pleasure as Masters blanched. "I notice on this report that mention is made of lead paint, groundwater contamination, and asbestos. Yet I checked county records, and neither of the inspectors who issued this report are licensed lead or asbestos abatement professionals."

She paused, waiting for a reaction.

"I'm sorry," Masters said finally, "What's the significance?"

"Being a developer, I'm surprised that it isn't obvious to you. Conducting a lead paint or asbestos inspection with out proper licensure is a misdemeanor under Pennsylvania law. This entire report is invalid."

One. Two. Three beads of sweat appeared on Masters' forehead.

"Now, what I find interesting is that this report was approved by the Safety Department and ruled on by a judge. That's a lot of desks it had to cross. I mean, if *I* could spot this, how is it that that Pawnee County Department of Safety *and* a judge of the Circuit Court missed it?" She smiled. "Unless they *didn't* miss it."

"Your implications are bordering on slanderous," Masters growled. "I'd watch what you say."

"I'm more interested in watching what *you* say, actually, Victor. You told me, just minutes ago, that Mrs. Shumak wanted to sell her house. That's what you told me, but that is completely untrue. If she were completely unwilling to sell, yet you had announced publicly that groundbreaking would begin in April... well, I don't want to insinuate too much, but I think you can see how the reading public might interpret the whole thing."

"Honestly, I expect much more of the Pittsburgh Post-Gazette," Masters snapped.

"Be that as it may, Mr. Masters," Abby said with an impassive smile. "I am writing this piece. It will be in the papers. So, I would suggest that you tell me your side. It's in your interest."

"Well... I mean..." Masters fumbled, gritting his teeth. "This is the first I have heard of this Safety Department matter. I was certainly unaware of any wrongdoing on their part. I apologize if I seemed... aggressive in my offers to purchase the house."

"So now you admit that Mrs. Shumak had no interest in selling her house."

"I am *unsure* of the situation—my lawyers are handling the matter—"

"Your brother is on her answering machine. Threatening her. *On tape.*"

Masters closed his eyes. His jowls settled. He opened his eyes again.

"If you run a piece that in any way suggests criminal or ethical wrongdoing on my part or the part of Master Developments," he said evenly, "You will be hearing from my lawyers."

"Thanks for the warning," Abby said. "Now, would you like to show me those artistic renderings?"

31

The meeting with Victor Masters ended abruptly, with Masters lurching up, excusing himself, and blowing out of the café like a cold wind. Abby knew that she had very little time to execute the next part of her plan.

Leaving the café, she got in her turquoise rental Cavalier and drove east through the narrow belt of orchards and dairy farms that separated Brownsville from Lewiston, through woods that were just beginning to burnish yellow and red. Pennsylvania was especially beautiful in the fall—within three or four weeks the whole place would be a riot of color, crimson trees bright against ancient barns, narrow lanes vaulted by Technicolor silver maples, where the Amish carriages went their leisurely way, deep into the glades and hollows of the back country.

Then she was back in the city again, driving along crab-grass avenues of tumble-down aluminum siding houses with plastic tarps in the windows, and then suddenly there was the Lewiston Common, surrounded by the castles and cathedrals of industrial fancy. The prisoners from Brocton Penitentiary, in their orange jumpsuits, were picking up trash around the white gazebo where on summer nights the Big Bands played to legions of seniors, where on winter days children pelted each other with snowballs, where in the fall young dreamers liked to come and listen to their I-Pods and watch the derelicts congregate by the Walter F. Riesman fountain with their shopping carts, where they fed the birds and discussed the things only other derelicts could relate to. Just off the common was City Hall in all its greystone neo-gothic glory; there was Hilliard's Department Store where Halloween decorations were already up; there was Murphy's Soda Fountain; and there was the County Building, solid and red brick—built, it seemed, to resist a violent siege by a foreign army. Sheriff cruisers were parked outside, and Department of Safety cars as well.

Abby parked at a metered space by Plunkett Furniture (advertising a Grand Re-Opening Sale) and fed in a couple quarters. She checked her watch. She'd parted company with Victor Masters exactly twenty-two minutes before. She slung her satchel over her shoulder and jogged up the steps, between twin stone guardian lions, and up to the metal detectors, where they gave her a security pass.

At the front desk she determined that the offices of the Department of Safety were on the fourth floor. The elevator was slow in coming, so she jogged up the stairs.

As it happened, Abby nearly collided with bald Inspector Vallone in the hallway leading to the department offices as she came out of the stairwell. He was carrying two Venti cups of Mongoose Coffee, with a copy of the Lewiston Observer tucked under one arm.

"Mr. Vallone?" she asked, eying his security nametag.

"Yes?" he answered in a sonorous baritone.

"I'm Abby Lindeman, reporter with the Pittsburgh Post-Gazette. Do you think I could have a few moments of your time?'

"Well, Ms. Lindeman, I've got to be honest, I'm pretty busy this morning—"

"Five minutes, Mr. Vallone?" Abby said with a sweet smile. "Please?"

Vallone smiled too.

"Yeah, okay. Five minutes." He jerked his head towards the office. "Come on."

They went in and passed the secretary's desk, and down a corridor of glass partitions looking into several individual offices. Vallone popped into Henderson's office, where his partner was buried under tons of deskwork. Vallone set down the coffee.

"Venti Double Skim latte," Vallone said.

"Thanks, bud,"

Vallone continued to his office, a neat place hung with photographs of sailboats. He sat down behind his desk, and had a sip of his coffee. He glanced at his blinking answering machine.

"Five minutes, Mrs. Lindeman. Shoot."

Abby opened her satchel and took out her recorder.

"May I?"

Vallone looked uneasily at the recorder.

"Sure. I guess."

Abby turned it on and put it on the desk. "Right. I'll get to the point. The House on the Bend. What's the situation there?'

Vallone squinted at her and pursed his lips.

"I'm not quite sure what you mean."

"What I mean is, you and your associate have written a report that condemns the House on the Bend. Is that true?"

"Ms. Lindeman," Vallone said uneasily, "We write lots of reports all the time. I can't remember all the details. That's why we keep careful records."

"Uh-huh. I may be from out of town, Mr. Vallone, but I do know that the the House on the Bend is pretty famous around here. It seems strange that you wouldn't remember."

"Well… well. So *what?*" Vallone said with irritation. "What's your point?"

"I just came from an interview with Victor Masters, the developer. You do remember who *he* is, don't you?"

"Yes."

"Did he ask you to inspect that house?"

Vallone snorted.

"No."

"Because your inspection seems to be working hand in hand with the new casino development. Do you know Mr. Masters well?"

Vallone smiled unpleasantly. "No, it had nothing to do with the development, and *no*, I don't know Victor Masters well. He's a public figure. I deal with him from time to time. That's the extent of our relationship." He paused, and wagged a finger at Abby. "But I see what's going on here. I've got it. Interview's *over.*"

Abby pulled out the Xeroxed report.

"You realize, Mr. Vallone, that issuing an abatement order for lead and asbestos without a license can constitute a criminal offense?"

"*Out.*"

"Do you wish to comment?"

"No comment. Get *out* before I call security."

Vallone's intercom beeped.

"Mr. Vallone," the secretary said. "Victor Masters called twice while you were out. He wants you to call him back. He says it's *urgent.*"

Abby watched as Vallone's face blanched.

"Sir?'

"Yes. Thank you, Emelia," Vallone said, turning off the intercom.

"Making plans for the weekend?" Abby asked. "Or is it business?"

"I'm not answering any more questions," said a perspiring Vallone. "Leave my office. And turn that damned thing *off*."

Abby picked up the Dictaphone but didn't turn it off yet. She got to her feet.

"Look, Mr. Vallone, I know you're not the boss here. You do what you're told." She looked at the family portrait next to his inbox. "Masters is the circus master in this town. He's got everyone jumping through his hoops." She smiled, and handed Vallone her card. "The dust is going to settle on this, and everyone is going to know what happened. Right now, the truth isn't written yet. You can give me your side, if you want." She gave him a meaningful stare. "I'm giving you a chance to save your own ass, Mr. Vallone."

Vallone took the card, and slipped it in his breast pocket.

Not, Abby noticed, in the trash.

"Goodbye, Ms. Lindeman," he said icily. "I think you know the way out."

32

A bby spent the balance of the day going to visit various people involved in the Pirate's Clipper construction; some, like the Mayor and the Director of the Department of Safety, would not even meet with her; others, like Jim Primanti, had apparently not been alerted or forewarned—he talked amiably about the construction and the plans, saying that he was unsure about the phase of land acquisition, but that he was sure that it was coming along nicely. Primanti showed her around his offices, a big open-plan space in an old factory, now converted to high-end commercial lofts of steel and finished concrete, exposed brick, and high-grade brass fixtures. He let her see the model of the ship, the schematics, some artist's renderings, and some new promotional materials.

"This is the most exciting thing I've worked on, like, maybe *ever*," he said brightly, leaning on a filing cabinet amid the buzz of the draftsman and contractors. "I'm telling you, this is *just* what Lewiston needs." He smiled at her in a way that, uncomfortably, seemed sincere. "We hit some rough patches, but I'm tellin' you, we're on the way up now. My company is

turning out high end condos like their goin' out of style—
and once this casino is open we're gonna see new hotels, new
restaurants, more *jobs*—the biggest thing since Wal-Mart hit
town."

Driving back to the House on the Bend, Abby watched the
flicker of autumn light through the tall elms that stood along the
river's edge, and thought about what Jim Primanti had said. The
heartbreaking thing about it was that, despite how despicable
Masters and his cronies were, Lewiston *needed* them, and it
needed the casino. Those boulevards of boarded-up mansions,
those abandoned lots, those castaway washing machines and
burned out minivans reminded her uncomfortably of her own
neighborhood. She knew the prison of hopelessness; she also
knew that for all their unscrupulousness, it was people like
Victor Masters who drove society. You could talk all day long
about the evils of capitalism and greed and money lust, but
the sad fact was that in America the game was played by those
rules. Without Masters, Lewiston would be a dead city. When
everyone else had abandoned the place—the car factory, the
steel mills, the fabricators—Masters stayed.

"I believe in Lewiston," Victor said.

Well, that was true. He *did* believe in Lewiston.

He believed that in a commercial vacuum he could make a
fortune. And he was right.

That was the tricky thing.

Still, Abby wasn't going to write something fair and balanced.
She didn't have that luxury. In this dog eat dog world, she had
one shot to make her comeback. She needed to rain fire and
brimstone. She needed screaming headlines. This was no time
for subtlety and nuance. This was no time for shades of grey.

When you write a story, you throw truth out the window,
Bert had said.

Well, so be it.

Abby got back to the House at four in the afternoon, and parked the Cavalier alongside the house. Claude was sweeping the side walkway, Ned Johnson was helping his son Tom unload roofing materials from a truck; above, from the attic, came sounds of hammering and sawing, the buzz of radial saws.

She went onto the back porch and set out her notes on the card table, and lit a cigarette as she organized them and tried to work up a hook.

No hook, no story.

"So, back from the wars, huh?"

Bert was leaning in the doorway, his hands in his pockets.

"Bert," Abby said, raising her eyebrows. "I'm actually trying to work, so I really don't feel like sparring…"

"I don't want to argue either," Bert said, coming over to the table and sitting in one of the folding chairs. "I want to hear how it went with Masters. Which one did you meet with?"

"Victor. The older one."

"You stick it to 'im?"

"Oh, yeah," Abby said with a hoarse laugh. "Nailed him. Nailed the inspector who came over here, too."

Bert grinned, all crooked teeth.

"Which inspector? What'd he look like?"

"Bald guy."

Bert rubbed his hands together. "I hope you get him fired. That guy is a major asshole."

Abby nodded, and went back to sorting notes. Bert grabbed a pile of papers and started leafing through them. They were labeled at the top, in the header margin, for the interviewee— Mrs. Noonan, Mrs. Noonan, Vera Johnson, Mr. Manicotti, Ned Johnson, Mrs. Noonan again.

"Feel free, Bert," Abby said without looking up. "Look at whatever you want, if it'll put you at ease. I'm on your side. I hope you understand that now."

Bert noticed that there was nothing about him in there. Of course there wasn't—he hadn't given an interview.

"You gonna put me in the article?" Bert said finally.

"I'll put your name in there," Abby said. "What else should I say? That you're suspicious of me? That you've made a big scene ever since I came here?"

"Well, come on, look at it from *my* point of view."

Abby glanced up.

"I know you want to protect your sister. I like that about you, Bert." She smiled. "You're a very loyal person. You just go about expressing your loyalty in strange ways."

"You know, I've lived a very interesting life," Bert said.

"I'm sure you have."

Bert licked his lips.

"Okay, look," he said abruptly, "I've been thinking, and I'll admit it, I was a *bit* out of line when you first got here. It's just—you know, Mary, she's...."

"Trusting."

"Yeah." Bert smiled and rubbed the back of his neck. "You know, she's been through a lot, a lot of hurt and trouble, and *still* she *believes* in the world. You know, I never believed in anything, so... well, I like *seeing* it even if I can't feel it. You know?"

"I know *exactly* what you mean, Bert," Abby said, locking eyes with him and putting down her pen. "Mary's an idealist. It's like... I always felt like being around her, I could at least *taste* what that was like. To be about something. To be something other than cynical."

"Yeah!" Bert said, clapping and pointing a finger at her. "Damn. That's it. Well, that's why you're the writer." He leaned back and put his hands behind his head. "So, anyhew, like I was sayin'... I think that I kinda jumped the gun. Point is, what

I mean is…" He drew in his breath. "I really, really want to be in your story."

Abby laughed.

"You do?"

"Yes!" Bert cried, pounding his fist on the table. "I mean, if anybody's been tryin' to fix this mess since the word go, it's me! Oh, sure, I might have messed up a couple things—but I've been trying. And besides, Vera, Mrs. Noonan, all them—you know, I'm more interesting than all of them combined. Somebody should write a *novel* about me, Abby. Really. They should."

"First thing's first."

"Well, right. That's okay. I just feel like all of them, they're just sitting around—but not me! I tried to fix the house, I tried to raise money. I tried to scare off the inspectors. You write your story without *me*, you've only got half the story."

"*Okay…*" Abby said, folding her hands. "So you want to be interviewed. Is that it?"

"Yes. I want to be interviewed."

"I'm leaving tomorrow, you know."

"Okay, then—after dinner?"

"After dinner it is."

"Great!" Bert clapped his hands together. "You get all your stuff in order. You just get ready, cause I'm gonna drop the best story on you that you ever heard."

33

The fact was, Bert was still suspicious. Looking through the notes, he'd seen nothing amiss, but then again, he'd only seen a small part of her paperwork. He'd spent the morning at the library, Googling Abby Lindeman and trying to get a feeling for her work. She hadn't written much in a long time—her last big article was written five years ago. Somehow, he wasn't surprised that she was a has-been.

That just made her more dangerous.

She *seemed* to be pro-little guy, but then again, she was desperate for a by-line. Time was running out. If he was going to get to the bottom of this, he was going to need to work quickly.

Fortunately, he had a secret weapon—he'd stolen the two jugs of Carlo Rossi from under the sink and added to that a dusty bottle of schnapps. These he put in his backpack, along with a couple plastic cups.

Abby loved a drink.

Woman, loose thy tongue!

Dinner that night was roast chicken, green beans, and brown rice. Sarah talked about a test she'd taken in Social Studies and then talk shifted to the repairs Tom Johnson had made to the roof—it was going to be another week but things had gotten off to a good start. Then Mary talked about the lawyers she'd called that day; everybody had told her to forget it except for Rupert P. Burmeister, Attorney at Law, a glad-handing crocodile with a face plastered on billboards all over the Pawnee County area—he'd promised to take a look.

"I don't wanna promise anything, now, little lady," he'd said over the phone. "But Rupert P. Burmeister loves a challenge, oh yes he does,"

"He actually referred to himself in the third person?" Billy asked.

"Oh, yes, he did," Mary said with a laugh.

"Oh boy," Sarah groaned.

"It might just take one slime to beat another slime," Vera said.

It might take one parasite to catch another, Bert thought, as he stole glances at Abby.

"Abby," Mary said, "You've been awfully quiet tonight. How did the interviews go?"

"Fine," Abby said with a smile. "Just fine."

"You met with Victor Masters."

"Sure did."

"*And?*"

"Well… he said some things that he'll probably regret." Abby glanced at Bert. "Anyhow, I'd rather not talk too much about it right now."

"Do you have what you need?" Vera asked.

"You know, to nail him to the wall?" Ned added.

"Did you blow the lid off the whole thing?" Mary cried.

"Did you expose him in the manner of Jessica Fletcher?"

Alan said.

"That's a pickle!" Claude shouted.

Abby closed her eyes serenely, and held up her hands to silence them. "Guys, guys, *please.* It's been a long day. I got some really good stuff. Let me write my article. I'll send you a copy as soon as it's done."

"We'd just like to know how things are going, dear," Vera said.

Abby smiled inscrutably.

"And I told you. They're going well." She sighed. "It's been a long day. I need some time to think."

Mary nodded slowly, and, Bert thought with relish, a bit suspiciously.

"Right. You heard her. Give her time to think."

After dinner, Bert winked at Abby and pulled her aside.

"So, where do you want to do it?" Abby asked, tying her hair in a dull yellow ponytail.

"I set up a little studio out in the carriage house," Bert said. "Come on."

Down the side steps and across the yard they went, the sky still glowing with the memory of dusk and the air getting a slight chill to it. Behind them, the house was warm and bright, lights slicing across the receding gloom of the yard, the air busy with post-dinner chatter, the blare of the TV, Vera's yelling. On the second floor, a light came on, followed a moment later by the faint warbling of Ella Fitzgerald on well-loved vinyl. Billy was in the basement; Sarah's violin began to shriek.

Bert opened the doors to the carriage house and let Abby inside, around the hulk of the jeep that still remained, around the buckets of lead paint under the dirty tarp, around cardboard boxes full of rotting board games, and up the creaking wooden steps to the second floor. Up there it was dim, lit with kerosene lamps and candles that Bert had lit around an old corduroy couch. On the coffee table was the minibar. Bert had even lit some incense.

"Wow," Abby said with an embarrassed smile. "This is... nice." She glanced at Bert. "Very... romantic, actually."

Bert turned to her and wagged a finger.

"Hey, now," he said with a sly smile. "Don't be getting any ideas." He gestured at the couch. "Shall we?"

They sat down. Abby looked at the jugs of Carlo Rossi.

"Wow," she said, laughing. "Breaking out the good stuff, huh?"

"Only the best for *you*," Bert said, pouring out the wine into two plastic cups.

Abby took the cup and looked at it for a moment.

She thought of Tim, back in Pittsburgh. He wasn't perfect but he was good to her. Then she looked at Bert, ugly Bert, with his sloping shoulders and messed up face.

Abby shook her head, and took a gulp of wine despite herself. Bert watched her drain the first cup, then refilled it.

Out came the notes and the Dictaphone.

"So, Mr. Wodehouse," Abby said. "You promised the best story I ever heard." She took a greedy sip of wine. "Can I record it?"

"Sure," Bert said, cracking his knuckles. "Here's the deal, Abby. I'll tell you my story. But then, I want to hear yours."

"You want to hear *mine*?" she said incredulously. "Why?"

"I just do. You get other people's stories all the time, and you never give anything back. Just take take take."

Abby made a face.

"Never thought about it like that."

"Well, philosophizing runs in the family," Bert said. "That's *me. Outside* the box. *Off* the grid. *Off* the hook."

"Yeah. Okay," Abby said, laughing.

"You wanna hear how I ate for a month on two dollars?"

"How?" Abby asked, drinking her wine and staining her teeth red.

"Cozumel, Mexico. Two dollars in the market I bought an old Nikon camera. Old thing, busted to shit. So. I needed to get to Amarillo, Texas—for reasons I'll go into another time. Problem was, a Mexican pimp stole all my stuff—I had nothing but the clothes on my back. I mean, not even my shoes. He took those too, the bastard."

"Wow."

"Yeah. Bad times. So you're probably wondering—why would the foolish gringo go out and blow his last two dollars an a camera?"

"Why, Bert?"

"I'll tell you why. Took me a month, but I hitched and walked all the way to Amarillo. Now, here's the thing about Mexico—people love to get married. They get married all the damn time, Abby—here, have some more wine—because they screw like crazy and they love God, so they need to make all that screwing legitimate. Whatever. Point is, every little Podunk town I'd come across, there was a wedding going on. I'd show up with this old Nikon with my hair combed really nice and my shirt tucked in and I'd get Pappa Juan over and put it to him like this: I was a traveling Americano photographer and would be happy to photograph his daughter's wedding for *free*—I'd even develop the pictures when I got back to the States, and then send them back to the bride and groom. All they had to do to get a *free* photographer for their special, special day was let me chow down on the barbacoa and mole, a couple cervezas, a few shots."

"And they went for it?"

"What do you think? Hook, line and sinker! Oh, man, their eyes lit up like shiny pennies. Mind you, cameras are a bit of a rarity in rural Mexico. To be able to catch those memories forever was everybody's dream. I was welcomed with open arms. The band played. The beer flowed. The tortillas steamed. There I was, surrounded by the senoritas and the mariachis, shooting pictures like they were going out of style. Not a day went by, Abby, that I didn't go to bed full and happy. I'd be sent off the next morning, on to the next town and the next wedding, with pats on the back and flowers in my hair."

"Where did you get all that film?" Abby asked.

"Film?" Bert said with a reckless grin. "What film?"

"That's terrible, Bert," Abby said.

"Is it?" Bert said, filling up Abby's cup again. "You ride into town, offer a glimmer of hope to some people who didn't have it before? They felt good at the time, right? And I got what I needed, too." He nodded slowly at Abby. "I think you see what I mean."

Abby lit a cigarette.

"You mind?" she said, exhaling.

"No, go ahead."

"You said you've never had a job," Abby said. "You seem proud of it."

"I *am* proud of it," Bert said. "I may not have much, but I've really *enjoyed* my life, Abby. Damn, it's been a wild ride—and best thing is, it's only half over. I got a lot of life left to live." Bert smiled and took a small sip of wine. "Not that alternative income is all easy street. I remember one thing I did in San Francisco. There were these Chinese guys I got to know—real shady Chinamen. Well, they had a brother or something back in Hong Kong who made watches at a watch factory. But Abby, these weren't just any watches. They looked damned good, these watches did. They were heavy, too, all steel construction. Real classy looking. They had this Greek letter on them—an Epsilon. Here's the rub—they only cost brother Hu a dollar-fifty a watch. After shipping we had these watches for two fifty."

"What are you getting at?"

"Patience, Abby, patience. The Hu brothers and the Wang brothers and me, we all pooled our money and put an ad in Maxim. In the ad we printed a suggested retail price of four hundred dollars. I took those watches and that Maxim and drove around in the Wang brothers' black Lexus. We drove to the suburbs and crawled around strip malls. We offered the watches for a hundred dollars. Showed them the Maxim advertisement. 'Well,' they said, 'If it's in Maxim.' Best thing was, when the cops stopped us there wasn't a thing they could do, because it wasn't fake and it wasn't stolen. The whole thing was perfectly legal."

"But unethical."

"Who *says* what's ethical?"

"Well, *we* do."

"Exactly. See, that's why you're the writer. You've got *all* the answers."

Abby took a drag of her cigarette.

"So, basically, your whole life is a sequence of ethically challenged vignettes."

Bert thought about it for a minute.

"Yeah, I guess so." Bert sat forward. "What about you? Tit for tat. Quid pro quo."

"*My life,*" Abby said, her eyes starting to glaze over on glass number four. "Oh, Bert, *my life* is not amusing or funny or even interesting. It *is* ethically challenged, however. It *is* messed up. Just so *messed* up, Bert. Damn. I've screwed everything up."

She laughed bitterly.

"Quid pro quo, huh?" she said. "Okay." She stubbed out her cigarette. "Little girl gets born to alcoholic, abusive father. Gets slapped around. Grows up really fast. Gets pregnant at age fifteen with math teacher. The abortion messed me up bad, Bert. No babies after that. I killed off the only one I ever might have had."

"What about the math teacher?"

"I didn't want my dad to hear about it. He would have killed Mr. Parsell. *Killed* him. My dad was that kind of guy. Fifth of Jack before four in the afternoon. He loved to get together with his buddies and go 'pound some blackies,' as he liked to put it. Saw himself as some kind of Charles Bronson, saving the neighborhood. Anyways, I was scared for Mr. Parsell. And for myself. Maybe he wouldn't *mean* to kill me… oh, dammit." She sighed, and collected herself. "I remember how the neighborhood got worse and worse. Our car got stolen, and then we never had a car again. Some kid trying to steal our TV broke our window. Some nights there'd be guys sitting on our steps. Cops took an hour to come around. Dad, he wouldn't move. He said it was home." She made a pained face. "God, I hated him. My house was an embarrassment. The place was a sty. Food all over the place, dishes in the sink. Beer bottles lined up on every table. Cigarettes piled sky high. I promised myself I'd never be like him."

"That's a good thing."

"Yeah, except then I turned around and became somebody even worse."

"Worse how?'

"I became my mother."

"You lived with her too?"

"No. They got divorced because she kept fucking other guys. She'd get drunk and she couldn't help herself. She'd wander in at two in the morning, half-naked. My dad would fly into a rage. He'd beat the crap out of her, but she'd do it again. I'd hear him crying in the TV room at one in the morning on a Saturday, him knowing that she was on her back somewhere in the neighborhood. She moved to Latrobe, with her sister. She died two years ago. Alcohol poisoning."

Bert nodded.

"You're right. That's not a very funny story."

"I thought in college that I'd be able to leave it all behind. Then I ended up with Barry, and we couldn't have kids because of that stupid abortion. I started doing pills. I started drinking. My writing sucked. I got yanked off important assignments. I started staying out all night. I started acting like my mother. Come home, find Barry asleep on the couch, with some flowers he'd bought for me, in the early light, my body still hurting from the drugs and rough sex of the night before. I was so *sorry*, Bert, but do you understand what *compulsion* is? To do things you hate? To be drawn there like a moth to a flame?"

"Well... I was really, really hooked on Gummy Bears for a while..."

"Then one time I was on our computer, and I found Barry's collection of child porn. It wasn't of girls, either—as if being heterosexual would make it better. By then we were hardly speaking—two strangers tied at the hip by a mortgage, a car, and a mountain of debt. I was *glad* to find that shit, Bert. I felt like suddenly I was justified to do what I'd done. I ran out and bought a plastic jug of cheap vodka and had a time. Wound up naked in a house I didn't recognize, surrounded by passed out people, all my shit stolen." She took Bert's hand in hers. "Then I sort of knew that it was *bad. Really* bad."

Bert nodded sagely.

"Okay," he said. "My turn again. I was in New York, where I drew daily specials signs for this trendy restaurant. Anyhow, every night there was this guy who came in, dressed in a yellow suit, and he carried a briefcase with him. He always came in right before closing, and ordered the pumpkin ravioli. Now, at this point, that guy—we called him Colonel Mustard—he was the only guy in the place. He'd sit there and eat his ravioli, and sometimes he'd take a little peek inside his briefcase. Just—just a little peek. He'd glance in there, look around, and laugh. Well, so, you can imagine, we all wanted to know what was in that case. This went on for months. A bunch of us placed bets. The Chef thought it was Colonel Mustard's money; the hostess thought it was a dirty magazine. I thought it was empty. Well, one day, one of the waiters comes running up. 'Bert!' he says. 'I was walking by Colonel Mustard's table when he opened his case—and I saw what was inside!' 'What is it?' I ask him."

Bert paused. Abby started laughing, "Well?" she asked. "What was it?"

"Get this," Bert said, leaning in. "A stuffed monkey."

"*What?*" Abby said, laughing. "A real one or a toy?"

"A toy. An old stuffed monkey toy."

Abby lit another cigarette.

"So Bert, what are you trying to tell me?"

"Nothing," Bert said. "I'm just telling a funny story to lighten the mood."

Abby looked at him with a look of exquisite affection, and then lunged forward and kissed him.

"Whoa! Whoa!" he said, his heart pounding. "What's that?"

Abby kissed him again, harder.

"Don't you like it?" Abby breathed into his ear.

"Well, yeah, ah, sure—" Bert said, now swimmingly dizzy.

"When was the last time you were with a woman?"

"You mean, like—a *real* one?"

"*Yes,* silly."

"Well, let's see… I *think* sometime in the last five years…"

Abby crawled across the couch. Bert tried to get away but she straddled him.

"What's… ah…." Bert stammered. "What are you doing?"

Abby undid her blouse. Bert's face lit up like Coronado finally finding El Dorado. She laughed hoarsely.

"Just... lightening the mood."

The night passed in a thick blur of sweat, slapping skin, rug burned knees and backs, and spilled Carlo Rossi. Bert woke up when the morning light started to come through the slats in the barn in piercing shafts—he found himself naked, on the floor, face down in a puddle of drool. He dragged himself to his knees, which hurt—in fact, everything hurt. He felt like he'd run a marathon.

There was Abby lying spread-legged on the couch, also naked, all skinny legs and stretch marks.

Their clothes were strewn everywhere.

The place smelled wet and musty.

Oh my God.

Bert's eyes went wide.

I had sex last night!

He looked at Abby again. Her eyes opened.

"Oh! Hey! You're awake!" Bert choked out, flushing as he realized that he was standing there naked in the unflattering morning light. If she didn't look good naked, he could only imagine how bad he looked. "Ah... well, that is... I'm just looking for... my clothes..."

He put his underwear on backwards, then tripped as he tried to put on his pants. Abby slipped her skirt back on.

"Shit," she said. "I've got a headache." She checked her watch. "*And* I need to be at the airport in an hour."

"*Wait!*" Bert said, sitting next to her and grabbing her hands. "Wait. So... what happened last night?"

"What does it look like?" Abby asked, her makeup smeared and her hair a brambly mess.

"I mean, did you *like* it? Cause I had a great time. I mean, you know—"

Stop stammering, man! Stop sweating! Stop shaking!

He was quaking like a leaf. His tongue seemed to be getting fatter and more immobile by the second.

"Yeah, I liked it," Abby said. "You're *okay*, Bert. And, let's face it," she added with a conspiratorial glance at his crotch, "God blessed you enough for *two* guys."

"*And?* Now what?" Bert said desperately as Abby pulled away and put her shirt on. "When can I see you again?"

"I don't know," Abby said. "I'll see you when I see you, okay? I really need to go."

"No! Please! Don't go!" Bert cried, following her around the room as she got her things in order. "Stay a couple more days!"

"Bert, calm down," Abby said, grabbing his shoulders. "It's just sex. People have sex. It happens all the time. It's no big deal."

"But Abby! I think we *had* something!"

"I gotta go," Abby said, kissing Bert on the forehead. "I'll see you." With that, she ran down the steps.

Bert sat down hard on the couch, and sighed.

He realized, suddenly, that he'd been played at his own game.

He'd failed to extract any important information at all.

He was no closer to getting to the bottom of things than he was before, but it really didn't seem to matter any more.

Bert smiled and felt himself melt into the couch, basking in the light of morning.

"Wow!" he said, out loud "What a *woman!*"

34

I t was late Wednesday afternoon when Mary came up the
drive in the Caprice, the fan belt squeaking, the air limpid
and full of the noise of autumn crickets. Wearily, she pulled
the car around the side of the house, onto the grass, where
she shut off the engine and then sat, in silence, listening to
the bang of Tom and Rashim's hammers in the back annex.
Letting out a deep sigh, she rested her head on the steering
wheel and rolled it back and forth a couple of times with a low
moan of frustration.

Today was not a good day.

Slamming the car door, Mary marched across the side lawn
and up the steps to the porch, where Mrs. Noonan was clearing
away the last remnants of afternoon tea.

"Got any lemonade left, Mrs. Noonan?" Mary asked with
a tired smile, sitting down at the table and absently pushing
around some crumbs of scone.

"A few dribs left, dear," Mrs. Noonan answered, putting
down her tray to pour Mary a glass of watery Countrytime. It
was cold from all the melted ice and tasted oddly medicinal.

Mary greedily drank down half of it, and then gazed absently out at the lawn, at the brambles and weeds and crab grass basking in the gentle late afternoon light.

Heavy boot steps on the stairs and the screen door yawned open as Tom came up, his jeans and muscular arms covered in sawdust.

"Hey, Tom," Mary said, trying her best to brighten up a little. "Want a sip of my lemonade?"

"Already had some, thanks," Tom said. "Mrs. Noonan brought us each a glass while we were working." He turned, and grinned at Mrs. Noonan, who was in the process of her lengthy return journey to the kitchen, the lemonade pitcher and porcelain teapot rattling on the tray. "Thanks again."

Tom's smile faded as he turned back to Mary, and saw that a shadow had fallen over her face. After a quick glance in all directions, he tipped up her chin with an outstretched finger, and tenderly brushed back a stray hair.

"Hey," he said in a gentle, low voice. "What's going on?'

Mary puffed out her cheeks, and shrugged.

"Went to the bank today," she said in a strange, high voice. "I told them that I wanted to refinance the house again, you know, pull out some home equity." She pressed her lips together in a thin line.

"What did they say?" Tom asked cautiously, leaning forward and resting his elbows on his knees.

Mary slapped the flats of her hands on her legs and said, "They turned me down, Tom. What else? Of course they did. Turned me down *flat*—and then they *actually* suggested that maybe I'd be better off selling."

"Selling, huh?" Tom said with an apologetic face.

"Yeah. They recommended a real estate agent and everything."

"What did you say?" Tom asked tensely.

"What do you think?" Mary said, looking at him with raised eyebrows. "I threw the card in the trash and marched out of there." She grimaced right after she'd said this, and gazed at Tom. "But *now* what? How am I going to go on *paying* you?"

Tom reached out and patted her hand.

"You've got some money yet," Tom said in a low voice. "Let's cross that bridge when we come to it, okay?"

Mary nodded miserably.

"Okay… it's just… you and Rashim are so *kind* to be doing all this work, and doing it all for so little *money*…"

Tom put his finger to Mary's lips.

"What're you, trying to talk me *out* of it?"

From the driveway came the sound of an engine as a big red Ford F-150 came roaring up the drive; it pulled around to the front, and parked right next to Tom's Silverado.

"Oh, Jesus, *now* what?" Mary muttered. "Lately, every time a car pulls up here we end up in more trouble."

Out of the F-150 climbed a tall, barrel-chested man, dressed entirely in denim, with a shiny brass belt buckle and a pair of tan Cat boots on his feet. He was wearing a pair of silver reflective aviator sunglasses that he pulled off, folded up, and slipped into his breast pocket so he could better squint at the House with naked disdain and pity.

"Jim Primanti," Tom muttered, getting to his feet. "What in hell is *he* doing over here?" He touched Mary lightly on the shoulder, and said, "I'm going to see what he wants."

Primanti's face broadened into a ruddy good-old-boy grin as the screen door slapped shut and he saw Tom Johnson striding across the lawn to meet him.

"Mr. Primanti," Tom said with a cautious smile. "What's up?"

"Tommy boy," Primanti said with much greater familiarity than was actually appropriate. "Every time I call over to your office they tell me you're here, so I finally thought I'd just come out to have a word with you in person."

The two men shook hands, and then Tom took a step back and folded his brawny arms.

"Have a word? About *what*?"

Primanti winked at Tom, and said in a low, conspiratorial voice, "Everybody's talkin' about you, buddy."

"*What*?" Tom said with an incredulous laugh. "What are you *talking* about? *Who's* talking about me?"

"Everybody. All the contractors in town. Everybody's talking about how you're turnin' down jobs so you can put in more hours out here."

"Yeah? So?" Tom said. "It's my business what jobs I take and what ones I don't."

"Look, son," Primanti said, wrinkling his brow. "*Tom.* I always knew you'd make it. I remember back when you worked my bricklaying crew. You were sharp. *Damn*, you were sharp, kid. Can't say I was thrilled to lose such a skilled pair of hands, but I always *knew* you'd make it. I knew it from the start."

"That's very kind of you, Jim," Tom said with a nod.

"So it… I don't know, in some *weird way* it *bothers* me to see you out here, squandering the hot season on this… this *project*. Look, I know—your Mom and Dad live here. But I've got a bunch of new condos on the East Side." He jabbed a thumb back at Lewiston. "I could set 'em up in one of those. Real high end shit, all Brazilian cherry and tile, washer dryer in-unit, first floor so they don't gotta climb no stairs."

"They're really happy here," Tom said. "I don't think they want to move again."

Primanti nodded, digging a steel toe of his Cat boots into the dirt.

"I got a *lot* of work I could throw your way, Tom. A *lot*. More than my guys can handle. I know you do good work—I can't refer these jobs to just *any*one, you know."

"I appreciate it, Jim. I really do," Tom said solidly. "It's a huge compliment, coming from you. But the thing is—I *want* to work on this house. Of course, when it's *done*, I'd love to have any spillover you've got. I sure would."

Primanti looked up again.

The smile on his face had faded noticeably.

"Well… I guess all I can say is, *think* it over, Tom. Look, I got nothing against this Shumak lady. More power to her, trying to hold onto this old heap. But here's the thing—the forces she's up against… well, one way or another, this house is going *down*. I just hate to see you wastin' your time." He smiled tightly. "You know?"

Tom set his jaw, and nodded once. "Thanks for your concern, Jim."

Primanti took a step back, then clapped Tom on the shoulder. "Hey, Tommy. Nice seein' you again. You should come down to McGuffy's some time. I'll buy you a beer."

As Primanti's truck pulled back down the drive, Tom came back up onto the porch, and sat down next to Mary.

"What was that all about?" she asked, looking a bit unsettled.

Tom shrugged.

"He's my old boss. We haven't spoken in a while."

"*And?*"

"*And* he said he just hoped I was doing the right thing. You know, making the right choices in my career."

"He came out here to tell you *that?*" Mary said.

"Yeah, he did," Tom said with a little laugh.

"And what did you say?" Mary asked in a small voice.

Tom wrinkled his brow, looked Mary in the eye, and broke out a dazzling grin.

"I said I already was."

By the end of the week, Rupert P. Burmeister had good news for Mary Shumak.

"Well," he said over the phone. "I guess I should actually say I have good news *and* bad news. Tell you what—why don't you just come on down to the office and we'll have a chat about it."

Rupert B. Burmeister was one of these ubiquitous "face lawyers" that can be found in just about every town and city in America, the sort of lawyer whose name evokes the catchy, maddening jingle that plays every hour of the day on every local radio station.

"Hi, I'm Rupert P. Burmeister," this particular ad went, Burmeister standing in front of a scholarly looking wall of law books in a blue blazer and a bright yellow power tie. "Have you or someone you love been hurt in an accident? Has somebody tried to play games with you, your family, or your money? Well, I'm *not* playing games. It's time to strike back: BURMEISTER STYLE!"

Work Injuries!

Bankruptcies!

Messy Divorces!

Wrongful Death Lawsuits!

Malpractice!

"Let's throw the book at them!'

Burmeister's face was on billboards, bus benches, shopping carts, newspaper ads, TV ads, radio ads, sides of buildings, tops of taxis, sides of buses, and jerseys of the little league team. And it worked: ask anybody in Lewiston to name a lawyer, and eight out of ten, without hesitation, would name none other than Rupert P. Burmeister.

Mary went over to his Main Street office in late morning: she waited for twenty minutes while Burmeister finished up with a consultation; at the end of the twenty minutes, a panting fat man in a neck brace emerged from the office and shuffled with difficulty towards the hallway door.

"Thanks again!" Burmeister said, coming to the door. He immediately laid eyes on Mary, and his manic face seemed, improbably, to grow even more manic.

"Mary Shumak! You're a vision! Come right in!" he said, standing theatrically to the side to let her into the office. The place was curiously decorated with posters of bronzed babes posing on Ferraris, blind statues of justice, and assorted artifacts of erudition: a phrenology head, a brass ship's compass, an old farmer's almanac.

"Have a seat, please," he said, closing the door after him. "Can I get you something to drink? Water? Tea? Gin martini?"

"Just the update would be fine, Mr. Burmeister," Mary said with a tired smile.

"Right," the lawyer said, sitting down behind his desk. "But first, I hope you don't mind if I tell you that you look absolutely *fantastic* today, Mrs. Shumak. Really. Just the *picture* of feminine grace."

"Great. What've you got for me?'

"All right. Straight to business. I like that in a woman. No nonsense. We're not so different, you and I. *Okay.*" He laid his hands flat on the desk blotter. "Look. I'll start with the bad news. In the words of my father, the late, great Alfred Burmeister esq., bad news spoils like rotten fruit, but good news ages like wine."

"That's an odd saying."

"He was a wise man, Alfred Burmeister. He also taught Rupert P. Burmeister everything he knows. He taught me that good news travels on the wings of angels, but bad news flies on the arrows of devils—that is, much faster than good news."

"Please, could we get *on* with this?"

"Feisty. Knows what she wants. Rupert P. Burmeister likes that in a woman. Oh, yes he does." He rubbed his dry, ring-decked hands, and laid them on the blotter again. "Not unlike me. Get right to the heart of the matter. Lay all the bullshit on the line. BAM! Right out there! Drag all the pestilence out in to the light of day! Justice may be blind, but I'm hawk eyed, Mary. Nothing escapes the eagle-eyed glare of Rupert P. Burmeister!"

"Should I… should I come back another time?" Mary asked. "Leave you and Rupert P. Burmeister alone for a while?"

"*No.* No, don't go away. Like I said, I'm gonna lay it on the line for you, Mary. No bull, no beating around the bush. No siree. Just straight shooting from the hip. BAM! Here's the bad news, Mary: they won't invalidate the report from the Safety Department. They won't rescind the condemnation order, either. And they've ordered a new lead and asbestos inspection, set for next week, by real mitigation inspectors."

Mary raised her eyebrows.

"So… what am I paying you for?"

"There's still good news, Mary."

"How could they *not* invalidate the report? *How?*"

"They said that they'd investigate the inspectors. They said that the rest of the report was sound, though they'd reevaluate it during the next inspection."

Mary shut her eyes to steady herself.

"So… what's the good news, Rupert P. Burmeister?

Burmeister's eyes lit up.

"I got you an extension—no action by the county until a formal investigation of the inspectors has been completed."

"How long is that?"

"Well, it depends how long it drags on. I'd say *minimum* that buys you two months. Sometimes these things take a year. Or they get lost in the shuffle and *never* happen."

"What if they get it done next *week?* They want my *house,* Rupert."

"I know they do. That's why I also filed for a periodic reevaluation of your house, based on the fact that you already submitted the work order from your contractor."

"What does that mean?'

"That means, that *after* the investigation is finished, you will have an opportunity to delay the final condemnation and revocation of your license as long as you can demonstrate that work is continuing on the house, to bring it up to spec. The only exception is the lead paint thing—if they find you have lead paint next week, you'll have ninety days to get rid of it. And *that* can be costly."

"What about all the harassment? What about *Masters?*"

"I'm still working on that," Burmeister said quietly, looking around as if Masters could be listening. "I don't have a lot to work with. Proof, I mean."

"You *have* him on *tape.*"

"Well, but, he's not really doing anything *illegal.* Just unethical. And they don't award damages for unethical behavior." He held up a declaratory finger. "*But.* Give me time. Once wrongdoing of the Department of Safety has been determined, I'll initiate a suit of defamation and distress against the county."

Mary's brow furrowed with discontent.

"So that's it."

"For *now,*" Burmeister said, flashing her a cheesy smile. "But never, and I mean *never,* count Rupert P. Burmeister out of the game. So," he added, leaning in close, "What're my chances of scoring dinner with you tonight? Little surf and turf? Little champagne? Oh, yeah, Rupert P. Burmeister knows how to treat a lady."

"No doubt about it," Mary said with a wry smile, "You're a charmer." She pointed sternly at the lawyer as she got up. "Get me results, Burmeister. If you find a way to blow Masters out of the water, then—maybe—I'll think about dinner. Until then—you'd better burn the midnight oil."

Burmeister smiled and winked.

"You bet, doll. Just pay my secretary on the way out, 'kay?"

35

Bert was playing chess with Ned on the porch while Mary went into town to talk with the lawyer, go shopping, and pick up Sarah from school. Vera was in town also—today was her lady's bridge club at the Baptist Church.

Ned was a good chess player. Back when he drove truck, he took a set with him, and whenever he met other drivers at coffee shops along the way, he'd shoehorn them into playing a game with him. He was steady and methodical and patient. He sometimes tried to read the chess section in the paper, but he couldn't wrap his head around the complicated numbers and letters; anyhow, he never understood how studying what Kasparov or Karpov did would help in a real game. After all, the same game would never be played twice. Chess was about strategy and intuition and logic all rolled into one. It was an opportunity to escape to a world where he was competent and excellent. It was highly appropriate that chess was, for him, forever associated with his truck.

Bert was also quite good at chess, and for this reason they loved to play together when they got the chance. If Ned was reserved and built up layer after layer of defense, Bert loved to go for quick, dramatic kills, sweeping in with his queen and sending his knights on mad forays. Bert was of the opinion that the best defense was a good offense. He was not a careful player, but he had an excellent facility for understanding the game. Usually he lost; he loved flashy checkmates and in his eagerness to arrive at an explosive denouement, he sacrificed pieces and position. Then, finally, with a deep sigh, Ned would slowly—ever so slowly—take Bert's queen and add it to the knight and two bishops he'd already taken.

And then Bert would know that it was over.

"Can I quit now?" Bert asked after surveying his newly hopeless position. Ned's fortress of pawns and crossfire of bishops and rooks were impregnable—his king, exposed and vulnerable just moments ago, was now, once again, untouchable behind his wall of defenders.

"No quitting," Ned said. "You got yourself into this, now get yourself *out.*"

"I can't get myself out," Bert said. "That's why I want to quit."

Ned looked at him placidly. "You can stop playing when I checkmate you."

There were footsteps in the hall, and Rashim came out onto the porch.

"Mr. Wodehouse," he said, stroking his sawdust-flecked beard. "We need to pull a truck next to the house to cart away some pieces of the old roof. Okay?"

Bert was scowling at the board.

"Yeah," he said with a wave of his hand. "Sure."

"Just checking. Because the grass might get a little bit tore up."

"Sure."

Rashim looked at the board.

"Ah, chess, the great Muslim game," he said.

"The Russians invented chess," Bert said. "Everybody knows that."

"No, Bert, the Russians didn't invent chess," Rashim said with heat. "The Persians did."

"Oh, really?" Bert scoffed. "Then why is every chess champion a Spassky or Kasparov?"

"Or at least a Fischer?" Ned suggested.

"Yeah. How come there's no Assad or Aladdin or Karim?"

"The game was hijacked by the White Man," Rashim said. "Same as everything else. You think the White Man could have invented a game like Chess? Absolutely not! No more than Jesus could have been white!"

"Wait a minute," Ned said. "Aren't Persians white?"

It was too late—Rashim wasn't listening.

"Rock 'n Roll. Jazz. Hip Hop. Impressionist Art. Elvis, Dave Brubeck, and Modigliani all stole from the African soul."

"Yeah… but the Persians aren't black," Ned said again.

"Muslims are one people," Rashim explained.

"Aren't there a few white Muslims?" Bert asked.

"Islam is colorblind," Rashim told him.

"That's funny, coming from you, Rashim," Bert snorted.

"There are white Muslims, but no White Man is a Muslim."

"So it's not enough to make Jesus black," Bert moaned. "But now you have to take Muslimism from us, too?"

The phone began to ring in the next room.

"Here—do your Persian brothers proud," Bert said. "Finish this game up for me. I gotta answer the phone."

Ned was already protesting, but it was too late—Bert slipped inside, to the front hall, and yanked the receiver off the cradle.

"Hello?"

"Bert?"

It was Abby.

Bert's pulse was pounding at once. Palms, sweating. Epiglottis, frozen.

"Uh… hey!" Bert stammered. "How're you *doing*?"

For a week he'd thought of little else. Her skin, her breath, the feel of her body against his. The sweet sound of her voice, rough as sandpaper and ravaged by smoking. Her laugh, like a 1947 Ford pickup struggling to turn over.

It wasn't the only thing he'd been thinking of, though. That night in the TV room—the night when Alan was watching TV Wonderland—had started his wheels turning. Abby had mentioned that 25th Anniversary Extravaganza and he hadn't been able to get it out of his head. Now, his raging lust and his burning ambition wrestled at the tip of his tongue like thirst and hunger in the desert.

"I'm *fine*, Bert," came that adorable Swamp-Thing voice. "Is Mary there?"

"No. No, she's not here. She's en absentia. 'Fraid so."

"When's she gonna be back? Do you know?"

"I have no idea. No idea at all. I am available to answer your questions, however," he offered.

"I'll just wait until Mary comes back."

"It might be a while. So in the meantime," he said decisively, "I have a question for *you*. Remember that one night we were all in the TV room, and Alan was watching TV Wonderland?"

"No, not really."

"*You know*. The TV quiz show, where Alan could answer every question perfectly? It's the quiz show in Pittsburgh. Next week is their 25th Anniversary Extravaganza? Remember now?"

"Yeah. Right. The show at Massive Studios."

"That's the one. Abby, they just announced the prize money: *fifty thousand dollars*. See, I *know* Alan and me could grab this thing. You said you know that producer from the show. Do you think there's some way—*any* way—we could get on there?"

Abby exhaled thoughtfully into the receiver.

"Maybe," she said. "I'll have to make a couple calls. I'll see what I can do, though honestly, I don't know why I'm agreeing to help you, after what you did."

Bert screwed up his face.

"What do you mean by *that?*"

"You know exactly what I mean. Bert, do you think I wouldn't figure it out eventually?"

"Abby," Bert said darkly, "What are you *talking* about?"

"The fifty grand you owe Masters? Or maybe you've forgotten already. That wouldn't surprise me, actually."

Bert groaned.

"I don't owe Masters a damned thing. He tricked me into signing a marker. I guess he wanted something to hold over my head. But it's bull. That's for sure."

"Well, whether it's a trick or not—"

The front door slammed. The slap of a backpack hitting the floor. The thud thud thud thud of Sarah running up the stairs to her room.

Keys hitting the change tray on the sideboard in the foyer.

"Who's on the phone?" asked Mary as she came into the hall.

"But what about *us?*" Bert blurted out, knowing he was out of time. "I've been thinking about you all *week!* Have you been thinking about *me?* Why didn't you call earlier?"

Mary planted her fist on her hips.

"Is that Abby?"

"Is that Mary?" Abby asked.

"Talk to me, baby! Talk to me!"

"Give me the phone, Bert."

"I'll be talking to you," Bert said. "Work your magic fast, Abby—the thing's in a week!"

Mary finally grabbed the phone away from Bert.

"Abby. What's going on?"

"Mary. I've got news. It's about the article."

Mary's heart leapt into her mouth.

"Yes? And?"

"My editor is publishing it. It's hitting the Sunday Features section next week."

"Well, that's great!" Mary cried.

"Yeah, except for one thing."

"What? What is it?"

"James Murdoch. He's a big-shot reporter here at the Post-Gazette. The same day I submitted the article to my editor, he submitted one too."

Mary swallowed and licked her lips.

"Look," Abby was saying, "I... I don't even know how it's possible, but somehow Murdoch has put together another article. It tells the story from a different angle. It's very... persuasive."

She told Mary that in Murdoch's persuasive article, there were photographs of Bert at the casino and mention of the $50,000 he owed Masters. There were clinical descriptions of Claude and Alan. Mary Shumak and her brother were portrayed as predators running an unscrupulous boarding house operation that preyed ruthlessly on the mentally deficient, and then blew their government checks on gambling rather than fixing up the dangerously run-down house. She didn't mention that Murdoch, besides being a star, was a tremendous writer. Better than her.

It wasn't difficult to imagine where he'd gotten all that information.

The Masters brothers had put James Murdoch on the payroll, and James Murdoch was more than enough of a match for Abby Lindeman.

It was a miracle that Abby's article had been published at all; fortunately, her editor had needed to fill some pages and decided to run a point/counterpoint format debate.

"But basically… it's a wash," Abby concluded.

Dead air.

"Mary?"

A heavy sigh.

"So, I'm back to square one."

"Look, I'm *sorry*, Mary. I'll send you a copy of my article. It's good. It really is."

"It's just not good *enough*."

"I wish I could say it was."

"Yeah. Shit. Story of my life," Mary hissed. "It is just so goddamned obvious how Masters is screwing us. Right? Isn't it?"

"Yes, Mary. It is obvious."

Mary shut her eyes.

"So, why can't I *stop* him?"

Silence.

"Well…" Abby ventured gamely, "What about the lawyer?"

"He got me an extension. But that's only good for as long as I have money to pay Tom to make repairs. I'm running out of *money*, Abby. *Fast.* Look, I understand that you came here *purely* to give your career a boost. I get that."

"Mary, that's not fair."

Mary sighed.

"I'm grateful that you came here at all. That was great." She swallowed her anger down. "Just… I just hope that you got what you needed out of the whole thing. Because frankly, I *didn't*."

"Mary…"

"I just needed to count on somebody, Abby. I guess I really can't. I guess you were right. I need to fight this thing all by myself."

Abby was angry now, too. Angry because she *had* tried. And angry also because if she was honest with herself, she'd admit that she really didn't give a damn about anything any more at all.

Mary stared at the wall, listening to Abby's breathing on the other end.

"But I really do appreciate your trying. Okay?"

"Okay," Abby said quietly.

"I'll call you," Mary said at last, "Goodbye, Abby."

The phone hit the receiver and a moment later, Mary was in the TV room, towering over Bert. She was shaking with rage, her hands on her hips, then balled up into fists, then covering her eyes as she tried to stop herself from leaping on her brother and pummeling him.

"You... owe... Masters... HOW MUCH?"

Bert cleared his throat.

"I see. So, Abby told you about the little matter of the fifty G's."

"The *little matter*?" Mary screamed. "This is the last straw, Bert! The *last one*!"

Bert held up his hands to shield himself. "Listen, Mary! I can explain!"

Mary squeezed her eyes shut, then breathed deeply and counted to ten in her head.

"Explain away, Bert. This had better be good."

"Look," he said quietly. "Like I said before, when we went to the casino, I was trying to win enough money to fix the house."

"You thought you were going to win $50,000?"

"Well, it's *possible*, isn't it? So, I didn't win any money. I lost money. But I only lost those four hundred dollars I told you about, not fifty thousand. Masters tricked me into signing a marker for fifty grand. It's just crap, Abby. He'll never get a dime of it out of me. He knows that I know that it's all a scam."

"Well, it might *be* a scam, but it's a scam that just cost us every bit of ground we'd taken with Abby's article."

Bert looked puzzled.

"I don't..."

"Please, Bert, just *stop* trying to help. Even the four hundred dollars you lost at the casino—like I was saying before, that's four hundred dollars that we could have spent on nails, and wood, and termite spray, and whatever else. Now it's in Masters' pocket. You *gave* that son of a bitch four hundred dollars."

Bert hung his head.

"I'm not going to ask you again, Bert," Mary said, her voice a trembling growl. "This is *my* house and you're only allowed here because I say so. If you can't do what I ask you to do—then I'm going to need to ask you to leave."

Bert nodded quietly.

"Do you understand, Bert?"

"Yes."

"Promise me you'll stop meddling. Promise me now."

Bert crossed his fingers on the hand he'd tucked under his right leg.

"I promise. *I promise,*" he said.

Mary glared at him for a moment longer, and then stormed out.

Bert allowed himself a little smile.

"On to Plan B."

36

That night, after dinner, Bert bolted into the TV room ahead of Alan and commandeered the remote. Alan followed a moment later with his notepad and pen, ready for an entertaining evening beginning with Millennium and followed by the X-Files; instead he found Bert flipping channels.

"Mr. Wodehouse," Alan said, standing uneasily by the couch. "What… are you doing?"

"What does it look like I'm doing, little buddy? Watching TV!"

"Yes…" Alan said. "I can see that. Don't you have some manner of mischief to get into? Why don't you go listen to Mr. Manicotti's records, or help Billy sort through boxes in the basement?"

Bert turned slightly, and looked at Alan with amusement.

"No, tonight, I think *I'm* going to watch TV."

"But Mr. Wodehouse," Alan complained, "There's no rhyme or reason to what you watch. You're equally happy watching Cheers or the Brady Bunch, Melrose Place or the Equalizer!"

"Not tonight, Alan."

"Oh? What are we watching tonight, then?" Alan pouted, slumping onto the couch and folding his arms petulantly.

Bert finally found the channel he was looking for.

"70s for four hundred."

"Who played the original landlord, Mr. Roper, on Three's Company?"

Alan shook his head.

"Who is Norman Fell?" he said.

"Is it… Norman Fell?" asked one of the slickster winner incumbents, now in his third month of straight wins.

"Yes, it is!" the announcer enthused to much cheerful applause.

"Of *course* it's Norman Fell," Alan muttered. "Mr. Wodehouse, we watched this show last week."

"I know," Bert said. "And I enjoyed it so much, that I'd like to watch it again."

"But you weren't even watching it before. Only I was. Everybody was carrying on with that annoying reporter."

"First of all, Abby is *not* annoying. And secondly, people are allowed to watch the same show two episodes in a row."

"Well, when watching 24 or V, that's certainly advisable," Alan concurred. "But TV Wonderland is the same thing every week. It never gets any harder or more interesting. Look, those same guys are still on there."

"Burgess Meredith played which Batman villain on the 60s TV show?"

"Who is the Penguin?" Alan said. "I mean, what a snoozefest. Why don't we watch Who Wants to Be a Millionaire or something?"

"Nope," Bert said, folding his arms too. "I want to watch TV Wonderland. It's only a half hour. Then you can watch whatever you want."

"Great," Alan said darkly. "The second half of Millennium. That'll make loads of sense."

"News flash, Alan," Bert announced. "You don't own the TV! Now quit your whining, and start answering questions!"

Tad Langley fired off the questions, one after another.

"On the Dick Van Dyke Show, what high school did Sally Rogers attend?"

"What class of starship is Captain Kirk's Enterprise?"

"On Beverly Hills, 90210, what fraternity does Steve join?'

Alan batted back, not wanting to play along with Bert but unable to resist answering such obvious questions.

"Herbert Hoover High."

"Constitution Class."

"KEG."

Slickster incumbent Mick Marley matched him one for one, though he fumbled a bit on the Enterprise question and needed back-up from his partner and brother, Nick Marley. The challengers, a sad pair of pasty couch potatoes from, ironically, Boise, Idaho, were getting annihilated. Nobody seemed surprised. Alan certainly wasn't.

"The problem," Alan said, "Is that nobody has universal knowledge of TV. Most people watch every sitcom, or every crime drama, or every sci-fi series. Very few people have the wherewithal or the discipline to watch *everything*."

"It isn't enough to just watch a *lot* of TV," Bert suggested.

"Right. You need to watch lots of the right kinds of TV." He pointed at the screen. "That's why Mick and Nick clean up. They've watched everything. And nobody else has."

Bert pointed to Alan's yellow pad.

"*Nobody?*"

"I'm not sure what you're suggesting," Alan said. "But it reeks of one of your long-shot schemes. Do you have any idea how hard it is to get on that show?"

"No. Do *you?*"

"Well…" Alan said, clearing his throat. "No, not *exactly*, but you can be sure that it's pretty darned hard."

By the final round there was no contest involved. The "challengers" were in the double digits and the Marley brothers were well into the thousands. Now the challengers again had a chance: but only if Mick and Nick bet and lost it all.

"And the question *is…*"

Drum roll, dimmed lights.

"Name three minions who lived inside Decepticon Soundwave on the 80s television show The Transformers."

Digital sound effects, accompanied by snippets of the Transformers' theme song. Heads bent diligently over pen and paper. Bert turned to Alan.

Alan shrugged.

"What? Am I supposed to know this?"

"Well, do you?"

Alan sighed. "Who are Rumble, Laserbeak, and Ravage."

A loud beep.

"Answers, please!"

On the challenger's screen was scrawled: "We Surrender."

The studio burst into laughter.

"That is *in*correct!" the host declared. A booming explosion sound effect dropped their sixty dollars to zero.

"Mick and Nick Marley!" the host cried. "Your answer, please?"

"Ravage, Ratbat, Laserbeak," was written neatly on their answer board.

"That is *ab*solutely *correct!*"

Bert turned to Alan, shocked.

"Alan. You got it *wrong.*"

"No, I didn't," Alan said, condescendingly. "Rumble was season one. Ratbat appeared in season three as a sort of replacement for Laserbeak—as if Laserbeak *needed* a replacement. Just an excuse to sell more toys, really. They asked us to name *three*, not *all* of his minions."

"That's all for today, folks!" shouted Tad Langley. "But tune in next week for our 25th anniversary ExtravaGANZA, when the winning team from this week's qualifiers will challenge our reigning champions, the Marley Brothers. As if that weren't enough excitement, we're sweetening the pot with a cash prize of $50,000 to add to your final winnings! That's right! If you think you've got what it takes, come on down to Massive Studios in sunny Pittsburgh, PA, and join the lightning qualifier's tournament. Do *you* have what it takes?"

"Why, no I don't," Bert said to the TV. "But egad! I know somebody who does!" He turned dramatically to Alan.

"Are you suggesting what I *think* you're suggesting?"

"If by *that* you mean I'm suggesting that you go on that show and win the money we need to save this house, then yes, that is what I'm suggesting," Bert said.

"I thought I already answered that question with a resounding *no*," Alan said, reaching for the remote. "Now, let me watch my show."

"Alan, c'mon," Bert said, holding the remote out of Alan's reach. "*Think*. We're really running out of options. If you and me go on there, I *know* we'll clean up. Can't you see it? We'll go down in history, Alan! We'll be famous!"

"I don't *want* to be famous," Alan said. "Can you grasp that? And, by the way, you twisted my arm once using the old 'hide the remote' trick. It won't work twice. I'll wait you out."

"Oh yeah? I can play all night."

"I can too," Alan said, sniffing resolutely, folding his arms, and staring forward.

Bert watched the TV for a moment longer, clutching the remote, then shifted gears. He had to be careful not to be too aggressive in pushing the plan. If upset too much, Alan had a tendency to freeze up and not speak for hours. It looked like they were heading down that slippery slope right now.

Gotta play nice, Bert told himself.

"Alan, buddy," he begged. "Think about it. It's not just for me. It's not just for Mary. Even if you don't care about Mr. Manicotti, and Mrs. Noonan, and Claude and the rest—which, by the way, I hope you do—you've gotta wonder where the *hell* you're going to go if we lose this place." He threw up his hands. "Me? I'll be fine. Always have been. I'm at home anywhere I lay my head at the end of the night. Mary? Oh, she'll manage. She's tough. But you, Alan. What are *you* gonna do? Start an Internet company? Go be a consultant with Accenture?"

"Don't mock me."

"Well, have you considered it?'

"Yes, as a matter of fact, I have."

"And what conclusion did you arrive at?"

Alan's eyes were troubled and stormy.

"That you're right," he said quietly. "I have nowhere to go."

"*Exactly!*" Bert hissed, crawling across the couch to Alan. "*Help* us. *Save* yourself! You can *kick* their *asses*, man! *You* know it, *I* know it."

Bert hovered there, expectantly, watching Alan's features dance the chasm between abject terror, stalwart courage, and a healthy dose of bravado.

"Okay," Alan whispered. "Let's do it."

At eight o'clock, the X-Files began, and Alan, previously too agitated to sit quietly and enjoy Frank Black's exploits on Millennium, now settled down, with a serious look on his face, and prepared to tackle another hour of Mulder and Scully.

At eight ten, the phone rang again. Bert bounded over to it and picked it up at the second ring.

"Hello, this is the Wodehouse residence," he said.

"Bert?'

"My love. What's up?"

"All right…" she said. "Here's the scoop. I made a couple calls over to Massive Studios and I called in a couple favors."

"And?"

"Well, if you can get here by Monday, and if Alan qualifies, he'll be in the round table freeze-out. There's gonna be ten teams chosen from all the qualifiers: I told them about Alan's… colorful personality, and his history, and they agreed that he'd be an asset to have on the show. So. That leaves just one question: who's gonna accompany him on there? These are two-person teams."

Bert laughed.

"You kidding? *I'm* going on there, of course. Who do you think taught Alan everything he knows? Who better than me to be his second?'

"Well… *whatever*. Be here on *Monday*."

"We'll be there. I owe you one, Abby," Bert said. "See, I know there's something between us. A spark, baby. A *fire*."

"I'm trying to *help*, that's all," Abby said. "Look—you can stay at my house, but you need to promise to behave yourself in front of Tim."

"Who's Tim?"

"He's my boyfriend, Bert. The man I *live* with. Do you understand?"

Bert felt a dawning of comprehension: of why Abby was so aloof, and what he needed to do about it.

"Bert?'

"Oh, I understand," he said. "One hundred percent."

"So… Alan's fine to go on?'

"He's into it. And besides, with me up there with him— we're gonna be unstoppable." He laughed. "Just you wait. TV Wonderland'll never know what hit it."

37

Saturday night and the atmosphere was tense at Gilliam's Steakhouse. To the casual diner, perhaps, nothing seemed amiss; the live jazz played as it did every Saturday night, filling the place with soul and heat, and the kitchen turned out beautifully cooked and trimmed steaks the same as always.

But to the waiters and the regulars it was evident that all was not well. All eyes in the know stole futive glances toward the Masters table. Waiters rigidly looked on, afraid to draw near to refill water glasses or sweep up breadcrumbs. Collin Masters was there, dressed immaculately as always; that was nothing new. It was the company he kept that set the restaurant on edge: six men of rugged and ill-repute, foremost among them Jimmy Vecchio, with his perpetually snarling mouth and oversized signet rings, his wide collars and glossy black hair. His friends had been seen at the casino on occasion; they had the look of well-groomed hyenas. Tonight they were all smoking, three on one side of Masters and three on the other. They had a bottle of Vodka at the table along with the customary bottle of

Lafitte Rothschild. They wore razor thin ties and wingtip shoes. Two of them had prominent scars on their faces.

One of them, a thin man with a sharp widow's peak and a cruel mouth, snapped his fingers.

"Yo! More water over here!" he shouted to the Mexican busboy.

That was why Gilliam's was on edge. Under normal circumstances, Mr. Gilliam would have come over and discreetly informed the man that such behavior was not appropriate in this establishment, but tonight was different, and Collin Masters himself had already come to Mr. Gilliam before dinner and apologized in advance, slipping Gilliam five hundred dollars by way of this apology.

"For your guys," Masters said, "For dealing with *my* guys."

Now, Gilliam thought, Masters looked ever-so-slightly nervous. This was not customary; in fact, it was the first time that Gilliam had ever seen the younger Masters ill at ease.

Vecchio was shaking his head.

"I don't like it," he said. "I don't like it *one bit.*"

"We aren't out of options," Masters assured him. "We just need to be patient."

"I'm *done* bein' patient," Vecchio said. "And so is Mr. Bertolucci. We have ways of dealing with this, Masters."

"I *think*," said Vecchio's cruel mouthed compatriot, "That what Jimmy is trying to say is that we're *done* bein' *patient*,"

"And," said a second associate, "That we have our own ways of dealin' with this."

"Let me… let me see if I got this *straight*," Vecchio said. "You're tellin' me that we're lookin' at another three months, give or take, before we can do *anything*. And *then*, this piece of shit lawyer might sue you and sue the *county*?"

"We are *done* with delays, Masters."

"And *now* I hear that this shit is in the papers," Vecchio carried on.

"Yes, but it's handled," Masters said quickly. "Totally handled. I got the editor of the paper who ran that piece to run a counterpoint piece. One negates the other."

"One negates the other," parroted Vecchio. "What the fuck is *negates*? What are you, a fuckin' mathematician?" He looked to his boys. "Do you remember Masters being a mathematician?'

"No, boss," said one of the scarfaces. "He ain't a fuckin' mathematician."

"So *why* is he tryin' to talk all this fancy shit to me? You know what you *shoulda* done?" Vecchio said, pointing a finger at Masters. "Let me tell you. Bobby here—" he said, indicating a thin-faced guy with a lazy eye, "He's real good with *accidents*. You know, car problems, slipping and falling in the tub, suicides. That kinda thing. What you *shoulda* done is called Bobby, and he'd've arranged accidents for that fucking lawyer and that goddamned reporter. You understand what I'm sayin'?"

Masters took a sip of his wine and held Vecchio's stare. He hated being talked to like this. It was intolerable. Even if nobody else in the place could hear what was being said, they could see: Collin Masters was being browbeaten.

"*Now*," Vecchio said, "Well, *now* this thing is totally fucked. You said you'd *handle* it, but you ain't handled shit. You know what you've done, Masters?"

"No, Jimmy. What have I done?"

"You dropped the fucking ball. You dropped it, and now we gotta pick it up. You understand what I'm sayin'? I'm sayin' that we're gonna have to handle this our way."

"*No*. I *told* you—"

"You been busy *negating* shit," Bobby hissed. "That's why we're in this mess."

"Mr. Bertolucci told me to handle this," Vecchio said. "And I will. That's why I invited my friends, Masters."

"We wanted to see the fucking fall colors," said another scarface, causing the others to burst into ugly laughter.

"This week," Vecchio explained, "We're goin' over there. We're gonna have a *sit down* with ol' Mary Shumak. We're gonna talk some goddamned sense into that broad."

"And if that don't work," a hoarse voiced hyena said, "There'll probably be some kinda *conflagration* at the house sometime next week."

"Whoa, Vinny, *English*," Vecchio said. "First, Masters is turning all mathematician on us, an' now Vinny's a fuckin' *novelist*."

"A *fire*, Vecchio," Vinny said with irritation. "A *conflagration* is a *fire*."

"*No,*" Masters said, feeling his power over the situation run through his fingers like so much sand. "*No.*"

"Now, let's say she *still* don't wanna sell?" Vecchio prompted.

Bobby laughed.

"Well, then there's always those sweet *kids*'a hers."

"*Exactly,*" Vecchio said. He turned back to Masters. "And *that*, my friend, is how business gets done."

"I won't allow it," Masters said.

"Oh, you'll *allow* it," Vecchio said. "And you'll *like* it. Unless you'd like to lose a leg in a car accident. I hear those Escalades have some serious problems with the *brakes*."

They stared at one another.

Masters wanted to leap over the table.

And meanwhile, Victor was at home.

This was *not* a fair arrangement.

"So," Vecchio said, lighting a Pall Mall. "Here's what you're gonna do. *Nothin'*. Just sit on your pretty ass and smile. Smile and look surprised when *bad shit* starts happenin' over at that goddamned house. We are *through* waiting, Masters. First you tell us one month, now it's three. What's next? A year? Three years?" He banged his fist on the table, making Masters flinch. "By the end of the fuckin' *week*, one way or another—it's gonna be *over.*"

38

On Sunday morning, everyone came to the breakfast table as usual. Sundays were waffles and sausage links; after that Vera and Ned usually went to the Baptist church, and Mary took Sarah and Billy to the Unitarian church. On occasion, Mr. Manicotti and Mrs. Noonan went to the Eagle Street Catholic mass, at a church of now-much diminished congregation that opened its doors just once a week.

That left Alan, Bert, and Claude at home. After breakfast was over, the dishes cleared and church-bound cars pulled down the drive, the house was empty but for these three.

After the last car was out of earshot, Bert ran into the TV room where Alan and Claude were watching a telethon featuring Pat Robinson. "Get your bags!" he instructed. "Let's move!"

The timing would need to be just about perfect. The Greyhound bus for Pittsburgh was leaving at 10:30: that was in just forty-five minutes. Bert had already bought three tickets the day before: one for himself, one for Alan and one for Claude, who would keep Alan busy while he carried out his plan to woo Abby.

Bert had two more things to do. First, he ran up to his room, where he'd stashed Ned's corduroy suit; this he threw on quickly, taking more time to tie the tie just so, and arrange the handkerchief in his pocket. After a quick once-over in the full body mirror in the hall, he thundered down the grand staircase and grabbed the yellow notepad that was by the phone.

In dull pencil he wrote,

> DEAR MARY,
> WENT TO VISIT ABBY IN PITTSBURGH. I AM MADLY IN LOVE WITH HER. I TOOK ALONG ALAN AND CLAUDE FOR COMPANY, AND BECAUSE THEY HAVE NEVER BEEN TO PITTSBURGH. WE WILL BE BACK ON TUESDAY NIGHT.
>   BERT

He knew that under no circumstances could he have gotten away with leaving had he delivered this message in person: Mary was far too suspicious of him now to believe anything he said. How all that would change, when, as instructed, Ned led the whole family over to the TV set on Tuesday evening to watch the 25th Anniversary of TV Wonderland, and saw, to their incredible surprise and delight, who else but Alan and Bert *on TV* winning all that prize money. Just a few hours later, they'd be back in town and hailed as heroes. And meanwhile, Bert would have Abby as his own, after a night of torrid passion in which she swooned and exclaimed that she could no longer live without him. Bert might tease her boyfriend, or he might not—he hadn't decided yet. He'd have to play that one by ear.

Alan, for his part, was terrified. Besides the trip to Master Plays, he hadn't left the House on the Bend since he'd arrived five and a half years before; not only that, but he'd never in his entire life left Pawnee County. He'd never ridden a bus and he'd never been on the thruway.

And he'd never been on a TV show.

It was sort of strange, having watched thousands of hours of TV, to be finally on the other end of it. And, like watching a gunfight on TV, or a car chase, or a love scene, he knew that the depiction he saw on a small, flickering screen would never prepare him for the reality.

Reality.

He had never been happier than he'd been in the past five years and change at the House on the Bend. Why? Because that time had been strikingly reality-free. There had been no piss-smelling couches, no dark closets, no feces in his bed, no Aunt Betty and no Dad. At the House on the Bend there was none of the hard edges, the harsh light, or the bad odors of the Real World. Out There the world was cruel and unpredictable and suffocating. In Here the world was just and good, where his most pressing concern was whether he should watch MacGyver or Stargate SG-1 in pursuit of his Richard Dean Anderson fix. The people at the House—Bert included—were kind people, sort of like TV people. Here was a world that he'd previously thought existed only on sitcoms: only in the Tanner House, the Banks House, the Taylor House. A place where people were nice and had dinner together and didn't swear. A place where there was *love*.

But reality had a way of breaking down everything nice and good about the world; all the kittens and rainbows and teddy bears were constantly under siege by rot and grey skies and men who only laughed when they were hurting somebody. And reality was coming for the House on the Bend. It was hammering on the door and beating on the windows. It wanted in.

And now it turned out, unsurprisingly, that the only way to keep the fangs of reality away for a bit longer was to plunge into its icy pool and stick a knife into its heart.

Life had a tendency to be ironic and symmetrical, like that.

So he packed a shopping bag the previous evening, during the 4:30 time slot before dinner when Moesha seemed to be the best thing on TV. He packed a couple button down shirts and a pair of corduroys. He packed his toothbrush and his notepad and pen. Bert told him that they'd be staying at Abby's house, and surely she had TV. The thing that concerned him was that he had no idea what the schedule was for Pittsburgh Sunday and Monday night TV. Somehow he'd need to get a hold of their TV Guide.

At 10:10 Ned's suburban came roaring up the driveway, and slid to a stop outside the front door. Ned climbed out in his Sunday best: a navy blue blazer with a red and green striped tie and a yellow shirt. He stood there in the settling dust around the truck and honked the horn three times. After the third blast, Bert, Alan, and Claude came out, clutching their bags.

"Where *were* you?" Bert asked as they jumped in.

"You ever been to my church, Bert?" Ned asked. "It's not *easy* to break away from that much Jesus love! I had to tell Vera that I forgot my wallet: we can't be the only folks to skimp on the offering plate. So she sent me home to get money. Thank the Lord she was too busy praisin' to really lay into me."

"That's great," Bert said. "We now have twenty minutes before our bus leaves. Punch it!"

"You won't miss your bus," Ned grumbled. "But if I'm gone too long, Vera'll know something's up."

"Well," Bert said, checking his hair in the mirror, "Whatever you do, don't tell anybody what we're up to. Just like I said: at seven tomorrow night, bring everybody into the TV room. We'll do the rest, right buddy?" He clapped Alan on the shoulder. Alan winced and smiled weakly.

"Right."

Ned roared down Riverbend Road at sixty, all the way to the left turn onto Oxtail Road—then a mile north to the Greyhound station. They got there with minutes to spare.

Soon they were in line to board the bus; Bert watched his bag disappear into the hold while Alan examined their fellow riders; a fat bald man with a ratty ponytail; a couple black girls with gold weaves and hoop earrings; a student with a goatee and a black trench coat; and two white guys in Carhartts and camo army caps, who spat their chaw juice onto the floor of the terminal.

Ned shook Bert's hand.

"Good luck." Then he turned to Alan. "I'd wish *you* good luck but you don't need it. You'll *own* that show for sure." He checked his watch and blanched. "Ohmygod. I've been gone for twenty-five minutes. She's gonna *kill* me. I gotta go."

"Just remember—" Bert called after him. "*Keep* your trap *shut.*"

"You know me!" Ned yelled back as he shuffle-jogged across the terminal. "I'm a vault."

"Seinfeld," Alan groaned. "Geez. Can't anybody say anything original anymore?"

The bus engine started up.

"That's a pickle!" Claude blurted out.

The driver, a big fat grape of a man, climbed down from the bus, huffing and puffing with the exertion of his descent.

"Tickets, please!"

Along the turnpike, the ride from Lewiston to Pittsburgh was five hours by car. Greyhound did not take the turnpike, of course: rather, it wound its way along the old, narrow routes of Pennsylvania's backcountry, between small farming villages, dying mining towns, and aging river depots with names like Vincentville, Freemont, and Fort James.

Bert, Alan, and Claude sat near the back of the bus, a habit left over from years before, when Bert and his friends always made sure they sat at the far rear of the school bus; here, they'd be free to light fires, smoke cigarettes, show off switchblades, and read porno mags without arousing the ire of the driver. It was odd how such habits trickled into adulthood: the two Carhartt men sat in the very last row, next to the greasy fat man. Bert and company sat one row farther up. The two black girls sat one further up still. Up towards the front sat the student, some nuns, a Mexican woman with her three children, and a couple Chinese college kids. The bus was in poor shape– the greasy windows were smudged with fingertips and hair oil and crumbs and gum were stuck in between the seats. The armrest between Alan and Claude was missing—only its sharp metal support remained. Claude sat by the window, open-mouthed, staring at the passing patchwork of cow pastures, silos and barns, and horses in fields. He smiled as the bus raced a slow-moving freight train. He touched his hand to the window as the road snaked though dense pine forest and deer could be seen, soft and brown, in the dense green.

"I'm a dee-jay," the greasy fat man told the two chaw-spitters. "I've got more CDs than you ever seen," he boasted.

"How many CDs you got?" one of the Carhartt men asked.

"Oh, thousands. Tens of thousands. And my equipment's worth more'n m'house."

"Yeah? Where you live?"

"Silvercreek," Fat Man said.

"Hey, George, don't *we* live in Silvercreek?"

At Mission Bend a grizzled black guy in a green army jacket got on with bulging pockets and a pink plastic flashlight. He ambled up and down the aisle for a while, then went into the bathroom. Soon the cabin began to smell like something dank and green.

"I got a pistol in my bag," the fat man said a few minutes later.

"What kahnd?" one of the Carhartt men asked.

".22" Fat Man said. "Carry it with me everywhere I go."

"Yeah? You like guns?" said the chaw-clogged voice.

"Not me," said his friend. "See, I like a nice baseball bat. Nice, aluminum baseball bat. Like so. Now *that* takes care o' business *real* quick."

Alan stared straight ahead, listening to the conversations that spun through the air like leaves in the fall air. To say that he was bored, hot, tired, and uncomfortable would have been an understatement. He was all those things but he was also, for the first time in a long while, left alone with his thoughts. Bert was busy writing love poems to Abby; Claude was persona non grata. That left him in between, staring at the stained seat ahead, queasy with carsickness and flooded with the shadows of bad times past.

At Silvercreek the three back row squatters got off and the two Carhartt men followed the fat man out of the terminal; a Deerfield, plainclothes police boarded the bus and kicked in the bathroom door, dragging the army coat man away in cuffs; by the seventh hour of the trip, the two girls in front of them were asking them if they were all brothers, giggling when all they got in return from Alan and Claude were blank stares. Somewhere between nowheresville and nothingstown, the bus pulled over suddenly and the driver could be seen in the late afternoon light, asking the gas station attendant for directions.

"Sorry about the delay," the driver said as they started off again. "We'll just be a couple hours late getting into Pittsburgh."

At the dinner stop, everybody stumbled out at a Burger King and Bert got on the phone and called Abby.

"We'll be getting in soon,' he said. "I can't wait to see you."

"You need to behave yourself."

"*I* will if *you* can."

"See you soon." He promptly went into the Get N' Go and bought a plastic wrapped bouquet of flowers, a card and envelope, a small box of Cadbury chocolates, and a pack of condoms.

"Big night, huh?" asked the Nigerian behind the counter.

"For my future wife," Bert said with a sloppy grin, counting out his change with some difficulty: his hands had been shaking since they'd passed Forestvillle.

39

After the Sunday service at the Unitarian Church, Mary liked to take the kids out to eat at Sandy's Diner, where Mary had worked for a while as a waitress years before. Sarah loved it: she got to eat without cooking anything or clearing any dishes, and she got to eat whatever she wanted. Usually she liked to get the hot dog on a toasted bun, waffle fries, and then an ice cream sundae afterwards.

But if it was a nice event for Sarah, it was agony for Billy. He tried to minimize any public appearance, and public appearances with his mother and sister were especially excruciating. During Sunday lunch at Sandy's it was almost assured that he would encounter one or another of his classmates. One girl, Amy Lawrence, worked as a hostess there and each Sunday regarded him with a look of polite disdain. Today, as he hunched over his orange juice, he spied two other fellow Lewiston High classmates: Brian Lunt, a meathead with a varsity jacket who stared at him without comprehension for a full fifteen seconds before brightening up and waving a meaty paw; and Julie Lundeen, a pretty redhead who seemed straight out of Blondie, complete with bobbed hair and pneumatic tits, eating an ice cream sundae with her equally hot sister and little brother. Billy managed to get through his soup before she spotted him and flashed him a shy smile.

Oh, they weren't uncivil about it, but that only made it more infuriating. In school, in the midst of their steamy teen jungle of alliances and double-crosses, they were required by the law of descent to be mean to him, to curl up their lips, to flip their hair in disgust and laugh at the misfortune of his second hand clothes, his bad haircut, his tragic stature in the hierarchy. Outside of school, taken each by him or herself, they were polite; they smiled, they called him by his first name rather than some cruel moniker; in short, they treated him like an equal.

Which he *was.*

This was precisely the reason why he hated school as much as he did. The students of Lewiston High were not really bad, and he was not really a dork. It was the *entity* of Lewiston High that by some dreadful alchemy turned Brian Lunt's cheerful wave into a shove into a locker, turned Julie Lundeen's shy smile into a snarl. School, like some sort of sadistic university psychology experiment, brought out the worst in everyone. Sometimes he wished that the House *would* be sold, and then they'd move to a new town. He'd show up to his first day at the new school as the person he'd always wanted to be: a loud-talker, grinning ear to ear, shoulders thrown back, every girl in the place staring at him, wondering who he was, where he was from, what he was all about. He'd choose the best of them and they'd have sex in his new car. Hey, it was a fantasy: why not?

But seriously, the unfairness of it was almost comical: Billy knew that he was good looking, and smart, and tall. He didn't wear glasses, and he didn't snort when he laughed. He had a regular-sized penis that didn't attract attention in gym class.

He dressed in t-shirts and jeans, nothing strange or gay-looking or oddly fitting, nothing his mom had made and nothing obviously from Goodwill.

Richard "Dick" Winkley, with slicked over hair and square coke bottle glasses: pure nerd. Jon Fozzerelli, with his Star Wars t-shirts and transition lenses and dirty little mustache, *he* was a dork. Harvey Prell, with his stick-thin arms and pastel shirts and overly eager laugh and constant chatter about Warhammer—now, *there* was a loser.

There was no disputing that.

"I've been mislabeled," Billy thought, staring at Julie's gorgeous legs when she wasn't looking. "I'm like a spider that got put in the beetle collection. I should be able to get a girl like that."

She looked over again, and caught him staring.

She smiled and blushed.

Damn! It! Dammit!

Billy could feel himself trembling with anger that he'd allowed himself to be caught. He'd catch hell for this tomorrow from Kyle Brunswick and Fred Ashton and their crew. He looked at his mom and sister, playing tic-tac-toe on the paper placemats with crayons.

"You wanna play, honey?" Mary asked.

"*No,*" Billy said. "I do *not* want to play."

Billy looked back at Julie again. She and her sister—a Freshman—were both looking at him. He felt himself flush this time. He got dizzy. They were *still* looking, for God's sake. Now they were laughing and talking secretively.

Billy was a bug caught under a magnifying glass.

He was heating up under their blazing gaze.

The food arrived suddenly: chicken fried steak for Mary, hot dog for Sarah, and cheeseburger for Billy. He stared intensely at his burger, carefully putting on ketchup and mustard. He ate a couple fries, and finally, he forced himself to look back at the girls again.

Oh, no.

They were gone.

Their empty ice cream cup was all that remained.

Suddenly, there was a flash of color by the table.

"Hi, Billy," said Julie Lundeen, on her way out.

"Hi," said her sister, grinning and waving frantically. Little bro stuck out his tongue. They fluttered out the door, all giggles and look-backs. Billy could still smell their perfume.

He stared at his burger, and then looked at Mary.

She was grinning.

"Wow. Mr. Popularity, huh?"

Sarah made kissing faces at him.

Billy darkened.

"It's not what you think," he said dourly.

"Well," Mary said, "I know what it *looks* like."

"It's *not*," Billy assured her.

But still, he thought with a swell in his chest:

I guess you never know.

After lunch, Mary, Billy and Sarah headed home. Billy and Sarah had homework to do and Mary planned to vacuum the first floor.

Coming in the front door, Mary saw Bert's note waiting for her on the phone stand in the front hall. She picked it up, gave it a once-over, and felt a dark feeling well up in the pit of her stomach. She ran upstairs, to Bert's room, and threw open his closet. Most of his clothes were still on their hangers; his sneakers were still by the bed. She went down the hall to Alan's room. It was bare except for his filing cases full of yellow pages of notes; in the closet were a few pairs of jeans and t-shirts. Claude's room: ditto. Claude's room was completely empty: he had no personal effects of any kind except for the single hard shell suitcase that he'd arrived with, half full of button-down shirts.

Mary wasn't sure what she was looking for, exactly; perhaps a clue, some indication of what he was up to. One thing was for sure: if Bert really *was* interested in visiting Abby, then he certainly wouldn't have brought Alan and Claude with him. It occurred to Mary, as she shut Claude's door, that since Bert didn't drive, and since Alan and Claude had gone with him, that he would have needed help getting to Pittsburgh. He must have taken the bus; but even so he'd need a ride to the bus station.

Who drove him?

It was a short list.

There was one man alone in the house who commiserated with Bert, who was always there helping him in his schemes, driving him around when a Schwinn simply wouldn't cut it.

Ned Johnson.

But Ned and Vera were not back yet. This was odd, since usually they returned by one or two. Mary went down to the verandah and sat in a wicker rocker. She rocked fiercely for a half hour and watched the driveway. At two o'clock, a black '83 Cadillac came rumbling up the drive at a crawl: the Manicottimobile. Mrs. Noonan, dressed in her Sunday finest, sat happily in the passenger's seat. Manicotti pulled the car up to the front, and eased himself out: then he crept around to the other side over the course of a minute and a half and opened the passenger side door for Mrs. Noonan. She got out, all taffeta and flower print, with a southern sun hat nesting on her ball of white hair.

"Oh, my. What a *lovely* Sunday drive!" she said as she bustled up the front steps and Mr. Manicotti pulled the car around to the barn where he parked it.

Mary loved seeing Mrs. Noonan on Sundays. Mr. Manicotti was a perfect gentleman, holding doors, coats, and hats for the morning, then taking the old bird on a twenty-mile-an-hour drive around town, down by the river, and eventually, back to the house with hardly a glance in the rearview at the honking snarl of traffic kissing their bumper. Mrs. Noonan was a Baptist, so really she ought to have gone with the Johnsons; but it was Manicotti she felt best with. Sundays were the days when her eyes shed their autumnal nostalgia and seemed well and truly in the present.

Nice as it was to see Mrs. Noonan in her Sunday bliss, Mary was getting anxious to speak with Ned. He and Vera were now well overdue.

Where on earth were they?

Another twenty minutes went by and they didn't show; finally Mary gave up waiting and began to fitfully vacuum the first floor, banging the old Hoover into table legs; every minute that went by was another minute of damage to be done by Bert. The sun began to drop low in the sky: soon it was tea time, a very quiet tea time with Mary nervously sipping her tea, Mr. Manicotti smoking his Pall Malls and Mrs. Noonan, hands folded on her lap, whistling a nonsensical tune.

The crickets began to chirp.

The trees were bought into sharp relief by the setting sun.

Mary made dinner for five: spaghetti and meatballs. Sarah prepared the salad, Billy stirred the pot of sauce, feeling the clammy unease that came along on a Sunday evening at five-fifteen, the malignant in-betweenness of it, the impending week of school lurking nearby, the house smelling of Sunday cooking and filled with late Sunday light, bringing with it a sense of finality and inevitability, a regret for the missed chances of a weekend slipped past before he could even blink.

The Johnsons returned while the kids were clearing the table after dinner. Ned and Vera came bustling in, with arms full of Amish bric-a-brac—a loaf of kerosene-tasting Amish bread, a quart of Amish butter, an Amish Quilt, an Amish riding crop and an Amish hat.

"Get that butter in the fridge before it spoils!" Vera commanded, laying out her trophies on the dining room table. "Lordy, my dogs are barkin'!"

Mary poked her head out of the kitchen.

"Visited Apple Hollow, did you?"

"Did we ever," Vera said with a robust laugh. "Walked about ten damned miles to see all them little barns and such."

"We had a ride in a carriage and saw them make butter," Ned said cheerfully. "And I bought some."

"You know that's not pasteurized," Sarah told him. "That butter's got all kindsa bacteria in it."

Ned looked askance at the butter, and back at Vera. She was too busy putting her expensive little Amish jams in a row to notice.

"So…" Mary said, fully emerging from the kitchen and wiping her red hands on a dishrag. "Ned. I've been meaning to ask you."

"Yes?" Ned said obliviously.

"You'll notice the TV isn't on. That's because Bert took Alan and Claude on a little trip today." She smiled tightly at him. "I don't suppose you'd know anything about that, would you?"

Ned stiffened up. He blew out his cheeks and shrugged.

"Ah, *no*, can't say I would. We went to Church this morning, Mary, *you* know that."

Vera stopped arranging jams and reared up.

"But you *left* church, Ned," she said. "For a *very* long time."

"I…uh…" Ned swallowed, eyes darting from one woman to the other as they circled him like sharks. "Forgot my wallet. I told you, Vera. I had trouble finding it…"

"Well, that's what you *said*," Vera said, cocking her head. "But now I'm hearing somethin' *different*."

"Because, well," Mary said, "Bert doesn't drive. And his bike is still in the barn. So *that* means that somebody gave him, Alan, and Claude a ride to the bus station."

Ned shook his head.

"It's a mystery, isn't it?"

"Ned, Johnson, you are the *worst* liar I've ever *seen*!" Vera bellowed. "Out with it! Did you take them to the bus station? Don't make me take my shoe off!"

Ned cringed.

"Okay, okay!" he said. "I took them! I'm sorry! Bert asked me so nicely!" He shot a dirty look at Vera. "And since I'm not *used* to that, I'm a sucker for a kind word…"

"Now, Ned, nobody's getting *angry* with you," Mary said.

"*I* am!" Vera thundered. "You lied to me, Ned! You cut church and you *lied* about it! Shame shame shame! *Shame on you*!"

"Well, *I'm* not angry with you," Mary said. "Bert can be charming. He's very persuasive. I understand." She put her hands on Ned's big shoulders. "So, now, just *tell* me… *why* was he going to Pittsburgh?"

"*Oh*," Ned whined, looking away. "I promised not to *tell*."

"Ned," Mary said, raising her eyebrows knowledgably, "I'm *going* to find out sooner or later."

"Well, that's the point: you're not supposed to find out until Tuesday."

"Tuesday? What's on Tuesday?" Mary said, trying her best not to snap.

Ned scrunched up his face, cast a wary eye at Vera, and suddenly blurted it out.

"They're gonna play on that TV trivia show, TV Wonderland."

"Who is? Alan?"

"Alan *and* Bert," Ned said. "It's a team thing. The prize is $50,000, on top of whatever they win. It's some sort of anniversary special."

Mary took a step back.

"Oh… my… they're actually doing it," she muttered. "Bert convinced Alan to *actually* leave the house and go on there." She grinned at Ned. "My God, he could really win, couldn't he?"

"*Alan* could," Vera said with a thick slathering of sass. "Can't say for that *fool* brother of yours."

As quickly as Mary's expression went all smile, it blackened.

"Oh my God. You're *right*," she gasped. "Bert's gonna screw the whole thing up!"

"But—" Ned protested, "It was his idea in the first place!"

"Right," Mary seethed. "But he needs to hog all the glory for himself. That's how he is."

"And by doing *that*—" Vera added.

"He'll lose the money!" Mary cried. She stamped her foot on the ground. "Dammit! Damn! Damn!"

Vera tried to console her but Mary shook her off, and grabbed Ned's shirtfront.

"Think, Ned! When is the show taping?"

"Tomorrow morning," Ned said in a small voice. "*Early.*"

"Then there's still time!" Mary shouted. "Pull the car around! We're going to Pittsburgh!"

40

When the bus finally pulled into Pittsburgh's greyhound terminal, it was 9:45 at night. The bus disgorged its bleary passengers and reunited them with their baggage. The station was staffed by a full compliment of ornery, overweight black women who treated the entire notion of passengers and customers as a serious irritation; they screamed at passengers to get in the right lines—no, not *that* line—and tossed the bags from the bus hold to the ground with violent contempt.

Alan felt dizzy and ill after the eleven-hour rip; Claude seemed as fascinated by the bustle of the station as he'd been with the passage of the Pennsylvania countryside. Bert was in a lather of nervous expectation; he clutched the bouquet of flowers like a torch in a cave; the chocolates bulged in his breast pocket.

"Alan! Bert!" came Abby's voice through the crowd.

Bert looked over his shoulder.

There she is.

Abby was wearing a light jacket and khaki slacks; her hair was tied back in a ponytail. Bert felt blood rush into his head and his groin. He thrust the flowers at her.

She took them with a look of nervous embarrassment.

"Oh, *thank* you," she said, looking to the man at her right; he was tall man, a slight stoop and silver hair. "Everybody, this is *Tim*." She cast a significant glance at Bert. "Tim, this is Bert, this is Alan, the TV wiz, and… well, here's…" she trailed off as she came to Claude.

"That's *Claude*," Alan said.

"Claude," Tim said, extending a hand. "Pleased to meet you."

Claude stared at his outreached hand. Bert shook it instead.

"Claude's a special case," Bert said. "I'm Bert Wodehouse."

"Yes, I've heard a lot about you," Tim said coldly. "I hear you're a special case as well."

"I'm hungry," Alan complained. "Think we could get some grub?"

They went to the sandwich shop in the station, where Alan and Bert got burgers and Claude got a soda.

"So it's all set for tomorrow," Abby said as Bert loudly smacked his lips. The flowers sat by the napkins. Tim sat back with his arms folded. "We'll take you over tomorrow morning. They'll give you guys a test—a questionnaire of TV trivia—and then you'll be fast-tracked to the lightning round."

"What time?"

"They want you there by eight."

"By *eight*," Bert said, his mouth full of burger. "That's mighty early."

Tim cleared his throat significantly.

"What's up, buddy?" Bert asked sharply.

Tim looked quizzically at him. "*Excuse* me?"

"You cleared your throat."

"I had something caught in it."

"No," Bert said, putting down his burger. "You made a face. About what I said. About the eight o'clock thing."

Tim rolled his eyes. "It's nothing, okay?"

"You just did it *again*," Bert said. "I *saw* it. Alan, did you see it?"

"I'm staying out of this."

"I'm here backin' you up, now back *me* up!"

"I'm not getting involved in lover's spats," Alan said.

"*Lover's* spats?" Tim said, looking at Abby, and then at Bert. "What's *that* supposed to mean?"

Abby was rubbing her eyes. "It's nothing, honey."

"So, Tim," Bert said loudly, "What is it you do for a living?"

"I'm an accountant," Tim said.

"That sounds *thrilling*."

"What do *you* do?" Tim shot back acidly. "I hear you don't do *anything*, Bert. How's *that* working out for you?"

"Actually, it's working out *great*," Bert snapped. "Better than being some blowhard trapped behind a dumb desk all day, that's for damned sure!"

"Boys, *please*," Abby said. "Can we just behave?" She got up, and said. "I'm going to the bathroom. When I get back, I expect this argument, and those burgers, to be finished. We should get you guys to bed. You've got a long day ahead."

As soon as she was gone, Tim jabbed a finger at Bert.

"Look, the flowers, the outfit, it's all real cute," he said. "But I gotta be honest—I feel like you're kinda stepping on my toes, and I don't appreciate it. I'm letting you stay in my house, but my patience is not *infinite*. You better *watch it*, okay bub?"

"What, do you think you *own* her?" Bert cried. "She's a free woman! She can do whatever she wants! This ain't Saudi Arabia, buddy!"

Tim laughed bitterly.

"This is incredible. Really. Look, *Bert*, I'm only tolerating this because Abby *warned* me that you're a little kooky, and that you had a weird fixation on her."

"*First* of all," Bert shouted, "There's nothing weird about having a fixation on Abby! She's a beautiful woman! Second, uh, news flash: I'm not a *kook*. I could've gone to MIT if I'd wanted to."

"I agree, Tim," Alan said, "There's nothing great about Abby. She's just a normal, everyday woman. I have absolutely no idea *why* Bert is so fixated on her, but he is."

"Now, hold on here," Tim said, clearing his throat.

"Abby and me," Bert declared. "We've got a connection that you can't understand. You can't stop fate, baby!"

"What do you think you have to offer her anyways?" Tim asked. "I mean, *look* at you! What, you take that suit off a *dead* guy? No *job*, no *car*, no *money*—yeah, you're a real catch all right."

Abby, who'd been eavesdropping from the soda fountain nearby, suddenly reappeared. "Okay, boys, that's *enough*. I think everybody's just a bit cranky after all that bus riding. Greyhound will do that to *anybody*." She patted Tim on the back. "Let's all go home, okay?"

Bert caught her eye and winked.

"Look—Abby this is ridiculous," Tim cried.

Abby knelt down and whispered to Tim, "Remember, he's deranged. Don't pay any attention to him."

They got the car from the lot and drove through downtown, which looked deserted at night except for homeless men on the street corners, then through the urban wasteland of the Hill District, and finally to the peaceful Jewish neighborhood of Squirrel Hill where Tim and Abby lived. They had a small red bungalow there with a well-trimmed lawn on a street of pretty little bungalows with well-trimmed lawns. Tim pulled the Dodge Caravan up the drive and put it in park.

"I'm gonna have a drink," he said as they unlocked the front door and tramped inside. In the claustrophobic living room, it was all shag carpet and brown furniture; the striped wallpaper was discolored with tobacco smoke. There was a painting of dogs playing poker over the mantle; a series of collector plates featuring the All-Stars of the Pittsburgh Penguins were on display over the couch. "Anybody else want one? Abby, you want one, right?"

"Rum and coke," Abby said, stooping so as not to bang her head into the low-hung chandelier. "We're out of Carlo Rossi, Bert. How about a G&T?"

Bert noticed, suddenly, that his flowers had been left on the table back at the bus station. He narrowed his eyes in spite.

"No, I'm fine. I think I'll just turn in."

While Tim made nightcaps for Abby and himself, Abby showed Alan and Claude into the guest room where the old NordicTrack was stored. Once they were settled in, she took Bert to the small back pantry where they'd set up a folding cot for him. The house was very cramped, even for two people: all the hallways seemed half as wide as they ought to have been, the shelves overflowing with books and trinkets and trophies from two overlapping lives.

"Here you go," she said, clicking on the light. Bert would sleep surrounded by Progresso and Campbell's soup, wall to wall. The house had an odd musty smell of vegetarian food and mothballs.

Bert felt his disappointment lift as he realized that this was his moment—and possibly the only one he was going to get.

"*Look*," he said in a low voice. "I was hoping to do a bunch of romantic stuff for you, but I can see that *Tim* is going to be hanging around, so…" He fished in his pocket and pulled out the chocolates.

"Here." Then, out of his side pocket, the poems he'd written on the bus. "And

here."

Abby took them with an embarrassed smile.

"Look Bert, I…"

"I *know*," Bert said with a groan. "I know. You've got your life here. You've got a home, and a car, and the rest of it. All I'm *saying* is… give *love* a *chance*!"

He got on one knee. "I may not have money like Tim, and I might not have a job like him, and I might not have any of the things he can do for you, but whatever I *do* have, it's *all* yours!"

Abby's face softened.

"Bert, come on," she said. "Come on, get to your feet. *Please*."

"Not until you say you'll give it a try."

"*How*, Bert? How am I supposed to do that? What should I do, just up and leave my home, my job, all of it, to come live with you at your sister's house? Is that it?"

"Well, yes!"

"Abby!" Tim called from the living room. "Your drink is *ready*!"

"*Coming*!" Abby called back. "Look, Bert, I heard what you said about me at the station, to Tim. It was… really *sweet*. You're a sweet man. But it's *just* not going to happen." She touched Bert's cheek. "*Okay?*"

Bert took her hand and kissed it.

"No. It's not okay. I'll never give up. *Never*. Not until you're *mine*."

Abby looked over her shoulder and then kissed Bert on the lips. He felt angels sing as their lips brushed together.

"You're impossible," she whispered, and putting her finger to her lips, she walked out.

Hope springs eternal.

Bert was sleeping soundly that night until a noise startled him. He woke up, dizzy with fatigue. In the darkness of the pantry, he could see a looming figure.

"Dad?" he asked, confused.

"Shhh!"

Soft skin, against him.

She smelled of booze.

"Abby?"

"Shhh," she said again, unbuttoning Bert's pants. "You'll wake Tim."

"He's right down the hall," Bert rasped, scared stiff.

"I know," she slurred. She was drunk out of her mind. "I want you to *have* me, right now, while he's down there. Do anything you *want*, Bert."

She was naked, crammed onto the narrow, squeaking cot with him.

A bigger man, Bert reflected, would say, "No, Abby, you're drunk, and this isn't the way I want it to be. Go back to bed."

Yeah, that's what a bigger man would do.

Fortunately, Bert didn't have that problem. He reached for the condoms in his pants pocket.

"Do you love me?" Bert asked.

"Sure I do, baby," Abby said, her voice sounding like somebody else's, heavy with rum and too many cigarettes. "Sure I do."

41

Morning came suddenly. Bert woke up to a hammering on the door of the pantry. Still reeling from the night before and the two hours of sleep he'd gotten, he shot straight up in bed, feeling around him in the dark. Abby was not there. He felt one used condom on the pillow next to him; he stepped on a second one as he got out of bed and accidentally slipped on a third as he groped around for the light switch.

"Mr. Wodehouse!" It was Alan. "Mr.Wodehouse! Hurry up! It's already seven-thirty!"

Bert found the light switch at last and flipped it on. He threw on the suit from the day before and opened the door. The house smelled like coffee.

"Come on," Alan said, adjusting his glasses. He was white with terror. "Let's get some pop tarts."

In the tiny eat-in kitchen, Tim was reading the paper at Formica Island, dressed in suspenders and a tie. He glanced up and regarded Bert with a laugh.

"So… you're going on TV today?" he asked. "Maybe you'd like to borrow some clothes. You look like a *clown*."

Yeah, well, I boned your girlfriend for three hours last night.

"You look nice too, buddy," Bert said with a tight smile, slapping Tim on the back. "Where's Abby?'

"She's still in the shower," he said.

Claude came out of the front hall with a broom, and started sweeping the kitchen.

"He's been sweeping the house since five this morning," Tim said.

"Yeah, he does that," Bert said.

"He must have been woken up by a *loud noise*," Alan said, yawning. "Or a *series* of loud noises."

Bert elbowed him in the ribs. "So, what kinda grub you got round here?

"Look," Tim said, casting a glance towards the bathroom. "I'm not running a charity here. I've got toaster strudels and cereal. There's orange juice in the fridge. Gimme a five-spot and you can have whatever you want."

Bert laughed. "You want five dollars?"

"I let you stay here for free, didn't I?" Tim said. "Well, didn't I?"

"I'm *hungry*," Alan complained.

"How about three dollars," Bert suggested. "A buck per person."

"*Five*," Tim insisted.

The bathroom door slammed.

"Tim," Abby barked. "Give them breakfast. *For free.*"

Tim made a face, and tossed the box of toaster strudels onto the counter. "Whatever. Freeloaders. Have whatever you want. See if I care. I gotta get to *work*."

He tossed on his sport jacket, grabbed his attaché case from beside the door, and tried to give Abby a kiss goodbye. She looked exhausted and wasted this morning, her eyes puffy with hangover toxin. She reluctantly presented her cheek.

As soon as Tim was gone she poured herself a glass of vodka, dumped orange juice on top, and then spiked it with a dash of vanilla extract.

"I feel like I got hit by a truck," she croaked, gulping down her screwdriver and lighting a Marlboro Menthol.

"You did," Bert said. "*Repeatedly.*"

Alan groaned.

"I really don't need to hear this."

"Hear what?" Abby asked, popping a couple Advils and washing it down with a final slug straight out of the jug of Mr. Boston. She winced, and caught the three of them staring at her with disbelief.

"What are you looking at?" she asked, taking a drag of her cigarette. "Some people like coffee. This is *my* way of starting the day. So what?" She glanced at the Mickey Mouse wall clock. "We'd better get a move on."

"But I'm still *hungry*," Alan whined.

"I'm sure they'll have food there," Abby said. "Come on. We don't want to be late."

The day outside was overcast and in the mid-fifties, with a promised high for the day in the low sixties. Autumn had arrived in Pittsburgh. Abby drove them in her Honda Civic down to Massive Studios in Oakland. It was a big square white building on a side street, surrounded by messy frame houses given over to college students. The street glittered with broken glass.

On a normal weekday the streets around the studio would have been quiet but for the comings and goings of the paperboy, the staff of the studio and the old ladies of the surrounding neighborhood ambling out on errands. But today was not a normal weekday. The streets were packed with fans of TV Wonderland, thousands of them, pressing against the studio gates, milling around on the sidewalks, camped out with metal folding chairs and newspapers and thermos' of coffee. Overhead, spanning the street, were hung banners reading, "TV Wonderland: 25th Anniversary!" The energy out there was so high that it fairly crackled in the air. The guards were letting small groups of people in through the side gate.

Abby pulled slowly through the crowd, leaning on her horn, until she reached the service gate. She flashed her press credentials to the security guard.

"I'm with the Post-Gazette," she said. "I'm meeting with Paul D'Angelo."

The guard opened the gate and let her car pass—they slammed it shut against a mob of TV Wonderland fans trying to rush the opening.

"This is *crazy*," Alan said, looking out the back window as the guards struggled to close the gate. "What is this, the fall of *Saigon*?"

"I had no idea that people loved this show so much," Abby said.

"I'll tell you what they love," Bert said, adjusting his tie. "They love the idea of fifty thousand dollars cash."

Alan, Claude, Bert, and Abby met the producer, Paul D'Angelo, in the crowded lobby. He was a bald man with a scruffy adolescent-looking beard, dressed in a hip vintage tee, and had a pair of headphones hanging around his neck.

"Hey, babe!" he said, giving Abby a squeeze. "Great to see you! How've you been? Fantastic? Wow! Big day! Big big big! So, is this Alan?" he said, patting Claude on the shoulder.

"*I'm* Alan," said the real Alan Berman.

"And I'm his associate, Bert Wodehouse," Bert announced, not to be left out.

"Great. Wow. So *you're* the orphaned, obsessive-compulsive wunderkind!"

"I'm not obsessive-compulsive," Alan said. "And my mom and dad are still alive."

"Well, whatever," Paul said, slapping Alan on the back. "If they ask you about your folks, just say they're dead." Then he looked at Bert. "*Wow. Abby.* All I can say is, holy crap, where'd you get *this* guy?"

"What's *that* supposed to mean?" Bert snapped, smoothing back his hair and feeling his cowlick stick straight up despite his best efforts.

"The *suit*, the hair—the *flower* in the lapel… you work in the circus or something?"

"Well, yes, *once*… but I don't see—"

"*Really*, Abby. You outdid yourself. Awesome. All right, fellas." He handed them a test and a pair of pencils. "Just answer this. If you get ninety percent or better, you're *in*. Once you finish, just hand it to my assistant Jenny over there—" He indicated a skinny, short haired brunette girl talking to a mass of people, "And she'll give you badges to go on the show. Okay? Buffet is in the next room; after you get your badges, dig in. We start taping in an hour." He gave Alan and Bert an encouraging back slap, and put on his headphones.

"Yeah. Yeah. Right. I'll be right there."

Alan looked at the test and wrote both of their names on top.

"I'm starving," he said, rapidly answering each fill-in-the-blank question. "Let's get this *over* with." He was done with the test twenty seconds later and went to Jenny the assistant.

"Paul sent us," Bert said.

Jenny scored the test.

"Perfect hundred!" she said, handing Bert and Alan VIP badges and then guest passes for Claude and Abby. "Well done and good luck!"

Through a pair of doors at the end of the hall was a staging area for the studio. In there, five other teams had assembled around the buffet table, where to Alan's delight, they found a range of donuts, danishes, and sliced fruit. The place was a swirl of activity: grips, light men, sound guys, make up. Everybody was in a fit of excitement, milling around the breakfast table, grabbing food, taking a bite, and finding they were too nervous to eat any more.

Bert gave the other contestants a once-over, sizing up the competition as he crammed a cheese danish into his mouth. There were a pair of red faced Midwestern women in matching Dale Jarrett sweatshirts; a military buzz-cut Kurt Russell type with his wiry, Army Jr. son in tow; two pear shaped men in v-neck sweaters and thigh-hugging jeans who were looked to be *castrati*; and two black guys in suits, one purple, one orange.

"Look at these jokers," Bert aid to Alan. "*Please*. As *if* they have a chance."

"*Excuse* me?" said the man standing next to Bert. "What did you say?"

Bert turned his head, and saw none other than the slick-haired incumbent himself, Mick Marley.

"Well, well," Bert said with a smarmy grin. "Look who it is. The great champion. Where's tweedle-dum?"

"Who the *hell* are you?" Mick asked looking at Bert, then Alan, then Claude.

"We're the guys who're going to knock you off your pedestal, Mickey Mouse," Bert said. "*This guy*," he said, pulling Alan forward, "knows so much about TV, he might as well be God."

Alan looked vexed and tried to escape, but Bert pulled him back.

"Yeah, yeah," Mick said. "Heard it all before. You and everybody else thinks they've got what it takes. *Three months,* buddy. Nick and I've been on here longer than anybody in TV Wonderland *history*. So far we've answered 98% of the questions right."

"Oh *yeah?*" Bert said. "Well, Alan's gotten 100% when we watch at home."

"It's a lot different live than it is at home, you know," Mick said to Alan. "You're not in the comfort of your living room. You're under the lights. In front of the cameras and a live studio audience." He smiled as he saw Alan begin to squirm. "All those folks out there, all that pressure... well, it's enough to make *some* people *crack*."

"Well, Alan *won't* crack," Bert said. "And neither will I. Course, we might just go and snap you over our knee like twigs."

Nick showed up and put his hand on Mick's shoulder.

"Are they troubling you, brother?" Nick asked.

"Not at all," Mick said, laughing a high-pitched laugh. "Just a pair of jesters heading for LOSERville."

The two pear shaped men had drawn near.

"Good luck to all of you," said the first one in a wispy, pear-soft voice. "I hope that we'll all win in our own way."

"I hate to break it to you," Bert said, "But there's only one way to win—and that's to come in *first*.'

"I'm doing this for my mother," the pear said. "She's dying of cancer."

"And I'll stand by Ferdinand in all he does," said his partner.

"Ain't that sweet," Bert said. "Ain't that sweet, Alan?"

"I think *my* mom might be dying of AIDS," Alan said. "But she lives in a room in the projects and she doesn't have a TV. They probably cut off her electricity long ago, actually."

"My mommy told me, you go on there and win that for me. You win it for *me,* sonny," Ferdinand said.

"Hate to break it to you, fat boy," Mick said. "But if you even make it up against me and Nick, your Mamma's gonna have to watch you get pounded. Maybe you should quit now, to save her the pain of seeing you lose."

"This is getting nasty," Abby said to Bert.

"Mick and Nick!" called out the two Dale Jarrett fanatics in unison from across the table. "We're gonna run you off the *road*!"

"Prepare to be shocked and awed!" cried the military dad.

"Yeah!" shouted his son. "Fire in the hole!"

Mick and Nick drew in back to back.

"Methinks we should retreat to our inner sanctum and await the call to battle," Nick said.

"I concur, brother. Let us make haste, before these ravenous commoners tear us limb from limb in their jealous fits of passion."

"That's it, white boy!" shouted the man in the purple suit. "You run your ass outta here!"

"Just wait until the battle is joined!" Mick cried. "Then you shall see all your proud words come to naught!"

Suddenly, the masses parted and applause began to rise from the crowd. The host, Tad Langley, appeared at the buffet table, a white towel around his neck, his hair combed and parted and his makeup artists buzzing around him like wasps around honey.

"Is everybody pumped?" he said. "The excitement's high, I can feel it. Can you feel it, everybody? That 25th Anniversary Extravaganza FEVER?"

"I can feel it, Tad!" shouted the brother in the yellow suit.

"It's the spirit of the Lord Jeeezus!" cried a sweating man in a gray suit, newly arrived with his vampiric wife. They had badges identifying them as TEAM 6. "He is moving through the crowd, moving through, separating the blessed from the damned, the winners from the losers, the living from the *dead*!"

"Give us an *Amen!*" the wife cried.

"I feel him… I feel him setting *upon* me. I feel him… bestowing victory *upon* me… oh, thank you, Lord, *thank* you for your blessings. I will wear you as my shield and *wield* you as my sword—"

"My mother is dying!" Ferdinand cried. "Jesus wants the victory to go to me!"

"I might have to go live with my father who hates me," Alan piped up. "But maybe Jesus doesn't care about that."

"Sure he does, child," the lady vampire cooed. "Just not as much as he does about us, his devoted preachers, his walkers through sin and death."

Tad Langley raised his hand and cleared his throat as he swallowed a bit of croissant.

"Excuse me! Hello! I have a request! Could we please tone down the exhortations to Christ? Please?"

Jenny the assistant raised a megaphone to her lips.

"All teams are chosen! Shooting in ten!"

"You heard the lady!" Tad said. "So, like civilized people, if you could all make your way into the studio and take your spots at the lectern bearing your team number and names—we'll get this show on the road! See you in ten!"

He raised twin peace signs above his head and jogged back to his dressing room with costumers and make-up in tow.

"Wow, this is pretty intense," Abby said. "It's like some kind of cult around here.'

"They don't have a chance," Bert said, starting to walk towards the studio. "Not with me and Alan on the job."

Suddenly, through the press of people, a production assistant appeared.

"Excuse me," he said, blinking his small eyes at them. "Is one of you Bert Wodehouse?"

"Yeah," Bert said. "That's *me.*"

"Your sister is here. She has an important message to give you."

"My... my *sister?*" Bert said, feeling the bottom drop out of his stomach. He looked at Abby in confusion. "Did you tell her?"

Abby raised her hands.

"Wasn't *me,* Bert."

"Then... then *how...*"

"Eight minutes to taping! All teams, please take your places!" cried Jenny the assistant.

"Bert!" *Vera.*

"Bert! Stop right there!" *Mary.*

"I'm sorry, Bert! I can explain!" *Ned.*

"You can't—hey! You're not allowed—" an assistant was saying as the three of them pushed their way through the crowd of team members and production staff.

Mary was out of breath from running from the parking lot, arguing with the doorman, then faking him out and sprinting for the studio. She grabbed Bert by the arm.

"Do *not* go on that show!"

Bert blanched.

"What... how did you...?" Bert stammered.

"Ned spilled the beans," Vera said.

"*Ned,*" Bert snapped. "I *told* you—"

"I *tried,*" Ned said. "But there were *two* of them and just one of *me.*"

"We drove all night," Vera said.

"I'm tired, and cranky, and I am *not* letting you on there," Mary said. "I know all about your scheme. I am not going to let you mess this up, Bert. I won't. This could be our last chance."

"But it was *my* idea in the first place!" Bert protested.

"Great. Good idea. Now just step aside and let Alan go on there by himself."

"He *can't*, Mary," Abby said. "It's a team show."

"Look," Mary said, rubbing her eyes. "All I know is that if you go on there, you'll screw it up. You'll try to answer questions you don't actually know the answer to. You'll start a fight. You'll create whatever mayhem you can. And we won't get the money. We *need* the money, Bert. I *need* you to step aside."

Bert folded his arms. "No can do, Mary. This was *my* idea. I get to go on there with Alan."

Mary jabbed her finger into Bert's chest, making him wince.

"Listen to me, Bert," she said through gritted teeth, "If you go out there, I swear to God, you are never setting foot in my house again. Do you understand me?"

"Five minutes!" shouted the assistant.

"Do you?"

Bert lowered his eyes.

"Fine. Have it your way. But if *I* don't go on there, who will?"

Mary threw her arms up.

"I have no idea! Alan doesn't need any help. He'll win the thing all by himself. All we need is somebody who'll just stand there and keep their trap shut!"

Everybody looked at Claude.

"Four minutes! Everybody on set!

"Claude," Mary said. "I think you're our man."

42

On Monday morning, Billy and Sarah walked down the drive to Riverbend Road and caught the school bus as it passed going towards Lewiston at 7:25. Billy walked out that day with a certain sense of confidence—whether he was going to be beaten by Julie Lundeen's boyfriend or not, at least now he could be certain that *something* was going to happen. It was good to know that he would not be faceless; he would not be nobody.

This morning the house was ominously silent. A modest buffet of cereal, coffee and orange juice had been laid out by the children for the two ancients who still remained in the house. Mrs. Noonan and Mr. Manicotti ambled downstairs at eight and engaged in a largely silent repast of slurping milk and hummed nonsense, after which Mr. Manicotti lit a cigarette and went for his morning stroll around the grounds, and Mrs. Noonan retired to the sitting room, where she sat on the couch, folded her hands in her lap, and stared at the window. She could have turned on the television, but nowadays the effort to grasp the meaning of all that noise and confusion made the proposition hardly worthwhile. And she could have read a book, yes, true, but in all honesty she had never been one for books, that being more the realm of her erudite sister Patricia, "the smart one." Sally Noonan was more one for tennis, bridge, and dancing. She'd always been mad about dancing, and was once very good at it, too. Her Johnny was never fond of dancing, though, and that was one of the little ironies of her life, that she had spent 46 years of it with a man who could neither dance the Charleston nor swing a tennis racquet, but who would much rather read the works of Dickens and James. So, books, being both boring and something of a reminder of her Johnny, were out as well. That left dancing and sports, and honestly, she was a bit too old for all that business now, wasn't she? Not to say that she couldn't dance the Charleston, even at age 77—but who to dance with? And why?

The only times of the day that had significance to her any longer were the meals, and of course teatime, which was a tradition that she hung onto fiercely because she felt that, if that final thing were to go, she'd probably slip away without even knowing it. At her age, she reflected, there was nothing so important as *routine*. It was a life raft one clung to in the dark sea of impending forgetfulness, a bulwark against a world grown so vast and confusing and *fast* that even if she were to live another hundred years, she could never hope to catch up with it now.

So, instead, she spent these in-between times in quiet reflection, thinking back over all those years past—about Johnny, about Beaumont, about her father—and about her son, who went to Vietnam in 1967 and did not come back. There were so many things to remember, some happy, some sad, one thing leading to another in a kind of Jacob's Ladder, a free association madcap dash from the Great Depression to the Kennedy Assassination to the day that her Johnny died and her life ended.

After that, you're just biding time.

At 9:30, Tom and Rashim showed up. The new roof was finished, and now they were busy shoring up the foundation. They parked their van outside and came trudging in, the two contractors and their three Mexican workers. Tom went downstairs with the Mexicans in tow; Rashim dallied around by the stairs until they were gone.

He came back into the living room and grinned at Mrs. Noonan.

"Hello, dear," she said, seeing him standing there.

"Hey, Mrs. Noonan," he said, coming and sitting next to her. "How's it been?"

"Oh, just fine. Giuseppe and I had a lovely drive yesterday. Really, just lovely."

"That's good." He reached into his pocket and took out some tapes. "I brought some music for you. Do you like music?"

"Oh, *yes*," Mrs. Noonan said with a toothy grin.

"Well, I brought you something you might like... this one is a mix tape of my favorite Algerian Rai bands; and here's a recording of the call to prayer in Istanbul."

He looked at the tapes in his hands, feeling a bit foolish, and then presented them to Mrs. Noonan. "Something... different. You know."

"When Mary comes home," she said, "I'll ask her to play these for me."

Rashim smiled anxiously, and got up from the couch. "Okay... good. Well, have fun... sitting here."

"It's not s'bad," Mrs. Noonan said gently. "Now go on. I expect you have work to do."

On Riverbend Road two black Cadillacs pulled in slow by the turnoff to the House on the Bend. The front passenger window of the lead car rolled down with a purr; Jimmy Vecchio was sitting shotgun. He had Collin Masters on the phone.

"So that's the place? 321 Riverbend? Big white house?"

"Yeah," came the tense answer. "I should call the cops on you."

"You do and there'll be some dead bodies. Maybe some dead cops. Certainly some dead kids. I know you don't want that."

"Keep it friendly."

"Tell you what," Vecchio said, putting on his sunglasses. "Hows about you just shut the fuck up and mind your own business, and let me and my boys do our job. Capisce?"

Masters hung up without another word. Vecchio chuckled and rolled up the window. He turned to Bobby, who was driving.

"Let's head in and pay the little lady a visit."

The two caddies pulled up the drive ominously, their big-rim tires crunching the gravel as they came through the trees and up by the house. They parked alongside Tom's van, and leisurely emerged from their cars, eight guys in black suits with sunglasses, Vinny with his baseball bat and Bobby with his guitar case, inside of which he stashed his sawed-off, his piano wire, and his duct tape: he liked to come prepared.

Vecchio signaled to the four guys from the second car to hang back and look tough; meanwhile he and his three top boys climbed the front steps and rang the doorbell.

Nobody came. Vecchio, who'd been pretty pumped, cleared his throat and rang it again. For the second time, he sniffed, straightened up, and widened his stance.

Still, no answer.

"Maybe nobody's home," Vinny said.

"She's home," Vecchio assured him. He pointed to the Caprice by the barn. "That's her car. She's here. She just don't want to open up."

He opened the screen door and hammered so hard it made the knocker jump.

"Hey!" he shouted. "Hey, open up! We need to talk!"

There were footsteps from behind the door, slow and shuffling, and finally the door opened. Standing there was a very old woman, blinking and smiling without comprehension at the four stern-looking gentlemen with slicked hair and scowls so sharp they could cut glass.

"Why, hello," she said. "Can I help you?"

The boys looked at one another hesitantly, before Vecchio, clearing his throat again, said in his most intimidating growl, "This *your* house?"

Mrs. Noonan smiled breezily at him.

"Why, no, dear. I just live here."

"You're *not* Mrs. Shumak?" Vecchio asked.

"No. I'm Sally Noonan."

Vecchio peered inside, past Mrs. Noonan.

"Is Mrs. Shumak home?"

"No, dear. She left suddenly last night. She was going someplace, but I can't remember where. Oh, my, my memory is not s'good as it once was."

"Mind if I have a look *inside?*" he said, swinging the door all the way open and pushing past her.

Mrs. Noonan's smile began to falter.

"Well, no, please, I can't—"

"Just shut up and don't move," Vinny said, twirling his bat in a circle as he stepped over the threshold. "And you won't get hurt. Got it?"

Mrs. Noonan did not get it, not really. This was very strange. She certainly had the feeling that these men ought not to be here, but try as she might, she simply couldn't put two and two together. And why did that man have a baseball bat indoors?

Now they were all inside the house. Vecchio walked down the main hall, into the kitchen. He peered onto the porch, out the back windows, and then finally opened the fridge.

"I don't think she's in *there*, boss," said Bobby.

"You *think*?" Vecchio said, pulling out a beer and opening it on the countertop. "Bobby, upstairs. Vinny, Joey, downstairs. I'll stay here. *Bring* her to me."

They did as they were told, trudging over the old floorboards noisily and disappearing into the nether regions of the house. Mrs. Noonan was left standing in the kitchen with Vecchio. He took a slug of Honey Brown and winced.

"Fuck is this shit?" he said, looking at the bottle. "Fucking frou-frou beer." He looked at Mrs. Noonan. "What, you want one? Huh?"

"No, I—"

"Well then stop looking at me. You hear? I said *stop fucking staring* at me. Go into the other room and sit your old ass down!"

Mrs. Noonan's face dropped, as she finally understood what this man was, and what he was about. He was not a friend. There were bad people in the house.

Footsteps in the hallway. Into the living room came Joey and Vinny with Tom, Rashim, and the Mexicans. Joey was casually waving around a .44 Desert Eagle. The workers looked terrified.

"No broad downstairs," Joey said. "Just some wetbacks and a couple o' niggers."

"You're pathetic," Rashim said. "You Philly gangsters. I know *all* about you. You guys have to come out here because the brothers in Philly were too much for you to handle," he said with a laugh. "Fucked you white boys up."

Joey made a face.

"You believe this guy?" he said. "Boss. Let me fuck up his jaw. Please. At least let me tear out that stupid fuckin' beard of his."

"This is a social visit," Vecchio said, lighting a smoke and tossing the match on the floor. "Nothin' serious right now. Justa few words amongst friends. Why don't we let those guys go." He flicked his hand towards the front door. "You heard me. *Go.* Get the fuck outta here. And don't call the cops, or we'll hunt down you and your family."

The Mexicans ran out as fast as they could; Tom and Rashim didn't budge.

Tom folded his brawny arms.

"I'm not leaving until you do," he said.

"Me either," Rashim said, shaking like a leaf but managing to fold his arms as well.

"*Please*, boss," begged Joey. "Let me fuck these guys up. Just a little."

Vecchio leaned on the counter and looked at Mrs. Noonan, who was on the verge of tears.

"Well…" Vecchio said, considering it. "Alright. Just try not to leave too many marks, okay?"

Joey grinned at Rashim and Tom and pulled a pair of brass knuckles out of his pocket. "Just a *little*, boss. I promise."

Suddenly, there were footsteps on the stairs.

Bobby came into the kitchen, white as a ghost.

Vecchio held up his hand to stop Joey.

"Whoa! Hold on a second." Then, to Bobby. "*Well?* Where is she?"

"I… ah, didn't find *her*," Bobby said weakly.

"Oh? Bobby, what the fuck is wrong with you? You look like you've seen a ghost."

"Not a ghost," said a little old man who ambled into the kitchen, calmly smoking an unfiltered Pall Mall, clutching a chromed .22 in his right hand. He stopped in the middle of the room and stared at Vecchio.

Vecchio narrowed his eyes.

"And who the hell are *you* supposed to be?'

"Giuseppe Manicotti is-a my name," the old Italian said. "And I want-a you to leave or *else.*"

"Or else *what?*" barked Joey. "What's this old guy gonna do? Huh?"

"I'm a-warning you," Mr. Manicotti said coolly.

Vecchio smirked at him and waved him off.

"Ah, you ain't gonna do nothin'. Hand over your gun and shut up."

"No."

Vecchio laughed horribly, and quickly reached into his coat.

Manicotti didn't even flinch.

His gun went off.

43

Mick Marley was right, Alan thought.

Watching TV is no preparation for being on it.

One minute to taping, the other contestants all at their stations, and Claude and Alan stepped behind their brightly colored podium. There was a microphone and two glasses of water. In the darkness beyond the hot lights of the stage was the studio audience, a seething mass of heads and bodies coughing, laughing, talking, and scrutinizing. All eyes were on them. Alan looked to Claude. Ah, to be Claude. To do nothing, to say nothing, to be nothing, and to pass through the world as safely as he had managed to do. His quiet compatriot stood there, a head shorter than Alan, staring benignly at the audience.

Paul D'Angelo was explaining the rules, pacing back and forth with his sleeves rolled up and a pair of puffy director's headphones on his head.

"You'll each have one chance to answer the questions put to you. If you get it wrong, you're out and the question goes to the next team. If half the remaining teams get the question wrong, we disregard the question. Now, try to be good sports about it; remember, everybody gets a $100 dollar gift certificate to Wal-Mart just for participating. Remember, you don't get to choose which decade the question is from. There are *no* buzzers. Once you're disqualified, there'll be a little light show and then the spotlight over your podium will go out. Just quietly and calmly walk towards the right side of the studio, over by that big X on a sign. Everybody see it? Okay! We're taping in ten! Any questions? No? Let's roll! Good luck, everybody!"

He gave a high hand signal to Jenny the assistant, and ran back behind the cameras. The back-lights went down, the applause signs lit up, and the place erupted into applause as, on cue with music and cameras swinging by on booms, Tad Langley came jogging out on stage, waving to the audience, stopping, and blowing a couple kisses.

"Hello, and welcome to TV Wonderland's 25th Extravaganza hour-long special," he said after the place had quieted down. "We've come a long ways in those years—four hosts, ten time slots, two changes of sponsorship. They tried to cancel us five times, people. But in the end, you guys—*the fans*—wouldn't allow that. You raised your voices and opened your hearts, and twenty-five years on we've got the highest ratings we've *ever had.*" Deafening applause. Tad grinned and finally waved his hand to quiet them down.

"So, to say thank you on this special day, we're trying something new. Going up against our reigning champions of three months, Mick and Nick Marley, are ten teams chosen from qualifiers who showed up here this morning as early as two o'clock. That's right—*none of them* knew that they'd be on this show when they woke up this morning; how's *that* for democracy?"

More loud applause.

"This is *instant death,*" Tad said. "Round Robin style. Only one will survive to challenge the Marley brothers, for a chance at TV Wonderland *glory!*"

Bert, Abby, Ned and Vera were sitting in the third row, watching. They were all bolt upright at the edge of their seats. Alan and Claude looked so small.

"First," Tad said going to Podium One, "Let's introduce our teams." He thrust the mic towards Ferdinand and Charlie.

"I'm Ferdinand Grundy," the pear said, squinting his beady eyes in the studio lights. "And I'm here to win this for my mother. She's *dying.*"

"Oh, that's terrible to hear," Tad said, looking at the audience. A foghorn sounded. "And *you* are?"

"I'm Charlie Madsen," the second pear rasped. "And I'm Ferdinand's life partner. His mother is *dying.* Of *cancer.*"

"And what do you do? Both of you?"

"I copy illuminated manuscripts," Charlie said.

"I'm a florist's assistant," Ferdinand sighed. "God help my mother, my poor, poor—"

His mic was cut and Tad went onto the next podium.

"And who do we have here?'

"I'm Marcy, this is my sis Candy, we're from Erie, Pennsylvania and *we love Dale!*" They started screaming and jumping up and down, grabbing at the Dale Jarrett likenesses on their sweatshirts.

"Dale, get on down here," Tad said. "You'll get lucky *tonight!* And next, we have?"

"Moe Sherman."

"And Al Sherman."

"And we from Homewood. We wanna give a shout out to Dee, Snog, and Diki-G, yo, and to Hormel, Latawnda, and Clarence, and all them folks what can't be with us."

"Blessed be the dead."

"Holla!"

An enthusiastic whooping could be heard from here and there in the studio audience.

"*Next* up," Tad said, "Who do we have here?"

"Alan."

"What's your trade, Alan?"

"I watch TV."

The studio laughed.

"Wish we were all so lucky. And *you* are?"

Silence. Claude stood there, looking perplexedly at the microphone. The studio was quiet as a tomb.

A loud buzzer went off and the studio laughed as instructed.

"He doesn't talk much," Alan said. "He mostly just stands there."

"Interesting choice for a teammate." Cue the "boing" sound effect.

"Where you from, Claude and Alan?'

"Lewiston—well, actually, I'm from Brownsville. And to be honest, I don't know *where* Claude is from, but now—"

"*Lewiston.* Wow! So there *is* a town over there! And here I thought that was just a smudge on my map!"

The audience burst into laugher, except for the four people sitting in the third row.

"Not funny," Vera said. "Not funny at all."

"Don't be angry, honey," Ned said. "They're big city people. They don't know any better."

"Poor Alan," Mary said. "He looks so nervous."

"Shoulda let *me* on there," Bert grumbled, slumped way down in his seat. "Should be *me* up there, doing the talking. Waited my whole life for that, and now Claude's up there instead."

"—and then the Lord Jeeezus spoke to me, and he said, 'John, John my son, you must go forth to the sinful places, go *forth* into the world and win TV Wonderland!' And I *have* accepted Jesus Christ as my personal savior! Have *you*, Tad?"

"As my *personal* savior?" Tad asked. "I have intimacy problems. I prefer doing the business through St. Augustine or the Virgin."

John "The Baptist" Hammerstein of Scranton, Ohio, was still talking, now angrily, but his mic had been cut. "And last but not least, who do we have here?"

"Gravely McAdams," said a big thick man with a snake tattooed on his arm that reappeared on his neck. "And this here's my wife Mary-Anne. I been in jail for 25 years, so's I got lotsa time to watch the tee-vee. An' Mary Anne, she don' fuck with nobody, she just stays at home an' watches the ol' tee-vee, too! I *love* you, Mary Anne!"

"Gravely, you damn fool, you can't say the 'f' word on TV!" The studio laughed and a loud censor "beep" sounded.

"That's why we tape first, show later," Tad said. "We'll just edit you out. When'd you get out of prison, Gravely?"

"Oh, last week," he said. "I'm a *new* man. I ain't gonna kill nobody ever again if I win this show!" Tad winked at the audience and the soundman fired off a Fay Wray blood-curdling scream.

The last three teams were introduced: two Chinese students, a Navajo couple, and a pair of video game testers from Chicago.

"Okaaay!" Tad said, walking to the middle of the stage. "Stay with us for Instant Death Action! Back after these messages!"

The lights went down for a moment. Make-up ran out to Tad and dabbed him as he took a swig of San Pellegrino proffered by an intern. Paul D'Amato clapped his hands.

"We're back in 10! 9! 8!"

Tad straightened his tie and his minions fled the stage.

"3! 2!"

"And, *welcome* back! Ten teams! This is a round robin freeze-out. The rules are simple: each team will be asked a question. If they answer correctly, then we move onto the next team and a new question. If they answer *in*correctly, they'll be eliminated—and it'll be asked of the next team, until somebody answers correctly. In the end, only *one* will prevail and go on to challenge our champs, Mick and Nick Marley! Are you ready!"

"Yes," came the answer.

"I said ARE YOU READY!"

"YES!"

"Here we go!"

The big screen flashed a series of decades rapidly, like a slot machine. It slowed down and stopped on the 90s.

"Team One! What was the name of the Banks family butler on the Fresh Prince of Bel Air?" Tad cried. "You have five seconds to answer!"

Ferdinand and Charlie conferred.

"It's Geoffrey," Ferdinand declared.

"That's right, Geoffrey, the Banks Family butler!"

There was a cheerful chiming sound, and the spotlight moved to team two.

"Team Two!" Tad cried as the big screen flashed. "On Hill Street Blues, actor Dennis Franz played two different characters. Name them *both*!"

"Sal Benedetto," said one Dale Jarrett groupie.

"Norman Buntz," said the other.

"Correct. Team three!"

"These are really hard," whispered Vera to Mary.

"Think *you* could answer these?" Mary asked Bert.

"You kidding? Piece of cake," he said, making a face at her.

"Team Three," Tad Langley was saying, "On the Bullwinkle Show, where did Rocky and Bullwinkle live?"

"*Damn*, ain't you got something better than *that*, son?" Moe Sherman said.

"That's Frostbite *Falls*, dog." Al Sherman hollered into his mic.

"*Correct!*" Tad declared.

Moe and Al let out a two-tone howl and bobbed their heads to the Bullwinkle Show theme song.

The spotlight roved on to Alan's podium. Mary grabbed onto her armrests.

"Team Four! On Jake and the Fatman, what was the name of the Fatman's bulldog?"

"Who is Max?" Alan said immediately.

"This ain't jeopardy, kid. You don't answer a question with a question."

Alan blushed.

"Oh. Sorry."

"But Max is *correct!*"

On the spotlight went to team five.

"On Get Smart, Maxwell Smart worked for CONTROL. What was the name of the evil agency he worked to defeat?"

The Colonel, without missing a beat, leaned forward into the microphone and fired it off: "Tad, it's KAOS."

"It most certainly is, Colonel. It most certainly *is*. And that brings us to team Six!"

As the Hammersteins answered a question about Survivor, Mary watched Alan mouth the answer, casually, as if it were a foregone conclusion. She felt an unfamiliar swell of hope, and tried to tamp it down.

Don't *jinx* yourself, she thought.

On to Team Seven.

Gravely the convict was grinning big and squeezing his wife's hand.

"On All in the Family, what was Meathead's relationship to Archie Bunker?"

Gravely snorted and laughed, and looked at his wife.

"Go ahead, baby doll," she said.

"No, you."

"No, *you*."

"Guys, we need an answer *today*," Tad said cheerfully.

Gravely stared down at the microphone, barked, "SON! IN! LAW!" and then looked around, quickly, for approval.

"Yes! Meathead was Archie Bunker's *son-in-law*!"

"YEAH!" Gravely bellowed, throwing his arms in the air. "THAT'S *RIGHT*!"

For six more rounds this went on, with only three eliminations—first the Chicagoans, then the Navajo and next the Chinese students. During the intermission, Tad could be seen tugging at his tie and drinking his sparkling water while Paul D'Amato conferred with his production staff.

They were getting impatient.

They wanted to speed this thing along.

Round four and the spotlight returned to Ferdinand and Charlie.

"Okay, boys," Tad said as the big screen flashed and the question appeared. "Here's a good one for you. Question: *what famous TV detective had a recurring fat problem?*"

Charlie and Ferdinand looked at each other without saying anything for a moment as if unsure if they were being insulted; then they began to hastily confer.

Finally, with only a second to spare, Ferdinand squeaked into the microphone, "Frank... Cannon?"

A deep BOOM resonated in the studio.

"Oh, I'm *sorry*, but that is *not* correct."

Ferdinand and Charlie burst into tears as the light over their podium shut off abruptly. The spotlight came on over Team Two's podium as two production assistants pulled and pushed the sobbing pears off stage right.

Tad read the question again.

The Dale Jarrett Sisters regarded each other with saucer eyes as they shook their heads, exchanged some panicked whispers, and desperately bleated, "Jake and the Fat Man?"

"Well," Tad said, shaking his head sadly, "That's pretty much the same thing as Frank Cannon, isn't it?"

The BOOM resonated a second time.

Team Two was plunged into shadow.

By the time Team Three got the spotlight, Moe and Al Sherman looked positively terrified. They said something, clapped their hands, and Moe leaned into the mic.

"It's *Kojak*, man."

"I'm sorry, boys—" Tad lamented.

"Damn, son, I *knew* it wasn't Kojak!" Al cried. "He's *bald*, he ain't *fat*!"

Light: *off*.

Team Four.

Vera leaned forward and took Ned's hand in hers.

"Come on, Alan," she whispered. "Come on, son."

Again, Tad read the question. Alan blinked in response and remained quiet for several seconds, tilting his head this way and that in thought. Then suddenly, his eyes brightened, he cleared his throat, and he leaned confidently into the mic.

"Steve *McGarrett*."

A sigh of disappointment swept the crowd.

"Steve McGarrett," whispered somebody in the second row, "He's not fat *at all*."

Silence reigned—then Paul D'Amato flashed the verdict on the prompter:

CORRECT!

"YES!" Tad Langley cried. "Steve McGarrett had a big problem with recurring villain Wo Fat." Alan nodded affirmatively. Tad raised a declaratory finger. "For those of you wondering—Frank Cannon didn't have a *recurring* fat problem because he was *always* fat. Well played, Alan!"

By round five only three teams remained: Col. Jeb Sackett and his son, Lance, Jon "The Baptist" and his wife Magdalene, and Alan and Claude, each lit by a spotlight against a dark stage.

"Team Four! On I Love Lucy, when was Baby Ricky born?"

Alan leaned into his microphone without hesitation.

"January 19, 1953."

"This kid's on fire!" Tad said. "Team Five! On the classic TV show The Honeymooners, what was the name of the lodge that Ralph and Ed belonged to?"

Nobody answered.

The Colonel looked at his son in disbelief.

"Two seconds!" cried Tad.

The boy cradled his head in his hands.

The detonation of failure filled the room

"Dammit, son, The Honeymooners fell under your area of responsibility! You have *failed* us, boy. You have *disgraced* this—" His mic got cut.

"I didn't want to come on this stupid—" So did Jr's.

Their light shut off.

"Down to the final two!" cried Tad.

Team Nine picked up the ball. "The answer, Tad, is The Racoons."

Questions volleyed back and forth; neck and neck for eight questions straight.

"Team 9! On the TV show Ferris Bueller, who played the part of Jeannie Bueller?"

"The Lord is with me, Tad. He whispers the answer to me. It was… it was Jennifer Aniston, Tad!"

"*Yes!* Jennifer Aniston! Pass some of that Jesus magic *my* way, John!"

"I *will,* if only you'll accept—"

"It's really down to the wire! Team Four! What TV character was famous for saying 'kiss my grits'?"

Alan yawned.

"Flo."

Ted looked at his crew, then back at Alan. "I'm sorry, I need a full name. You have three seconds."

Mary covered her mouth with her hands.

"Then you should have *said* so," Alan said. "*Florence* Jean Castleberry. There. Are you happy?"

"*Ab*solutely correct. Ball's back in your court, Team Nine! On Thundercats, what gives the Sword of Omens its special powers?"

John and Magdalene exchanged panicked glances.

"That—that's a show of devil worship!" John protested, slick with flop sweat. "*Jeeezus, punish* these—"

"I'm sorry, that is *in*correct!" Tad shouted, drowning out their curses with a double dose of explosion sound effects. "Team Four—*you are our winners!* Would you like to answer the question for a bonus two hundred dollar gift certificate at Wal-Mart?"

"Tad, it's the Eye of Thundera," Alan said, taking a sip of water.

"Yes! Yes!" Tad enthused as Team Four's light strobed yellow, red, green, and back to white. "You are correct! Congratulations! Coming up, you will go head to head against our reigning champions Mick and Nick Marley for the grand prize of FIFTY THOUSAND DOLLARS! Right after these messages!"

"And *cut*," the producer cried.

The lights came back up.

Bert, Mary, and the Johnsons leapt out of their seats.

"He did it!" Ned cried.

"I knew he would," Mary said as they ran down the steps.

Mick and Nick came out of the wings and joined Alan and Claude at their podium.

"Well done," Mick said, shaking Alan's hand for the cameras. Then, in a low voice, "We're gonna make you squeal."

"Prepare to be creamed—*Marley* style," Nick added.

"You shaking yet?" Mick taunted. "Cause you should be. *Losers*. They turned to Bert, Mary and the Johnsons with a smile. "Good luck, everybody!"

Alan looked at Bert, at the studio audience, then back at Mick and Nick, retreating to their isolation area.

He thought about the House, about his Aunt Betty, about his Dad at home in his trailer.

He looked into Mary's smiling face.

His heart thundered in his chest.

"Take fifteen everybody!" shouted D'Amato.

When will this be over? Alan thought feverishly.

Please, let it be over.

Just don't lose.

44

The kitchen was in chaos. Vecchio was on the floor, balled up by the sink, moaning and swearing, clutching his leg in the bloody spot where the .22 bullet had hit him. Joey, Vinny, and Bobby drew their guns and had them pointed at Mr. Manicotti.

"Boss! You okay?" Bobby shouted.

"Jimmy, let me kill the sonofabitch!" Vinny screamed, holding the muzzle of his gun just inches from Mr. Manicotti's head. "Just let me *pop* him!"

"No! Leave him alone!" Tom cried out desperately.

"*Shut the fuck up*," Joey cried, swinging his gun around, and pointing it recklessly at Tom's chest. "Shut *up* if you know what's good for you."

Mr. Manicotti looked completely unconcerned; his .22 was still trained on Vecchio. He didn't seem to notice, or mind, the pistol being thrust into his face.

"I said, a-get out," he repeated in the same voice he'd used before. Vince's gun was shaking; Mr. Manicotti's was not. He held it so he could shoot off the hip.

Vecchio was sweating profusely and his face had gone a deathly white. "Oh, fuck," he said weakly, "I think I'm gonna… I'm gonna…" His chest heaved and he lost his lunch on the linoleum floor. Vince and Bobby made faces and tried not to look.

"I need… gimme—what the *fuck* are you clowns standin' around for?" he said. "Gimme a towel or something! Jesus Christ, you fucking *morons*, ain't you ever watched a war movie before? I'm fuckin' *hit*. I need to apply *pressure*."

"O-okay, boss," Vince said, going to the counter, careful to sidestep the pile of vomit, and reaching for a dishrag. He tossed it down to Vecchio, who folded it into a square and pressed it to his leg. He winced, drew in his breath sharply, and blinked the sweat out of his eyes. "Shit, boys, it's gettin' real dark in here."

"Vecchio's *dyin'!*" screamed Joey, pointing his pistol this way and that. "And I'm sendin' *all* you motherfuckers with him!"

"We should get him to a hospital!" Bobby cried, putting away his pistol.

"We should call an ambulance," Vinny said.

"*No* hospital, *no* ambulance," Vecchio said. "And I *ain't* dying." The square of dishrag was soaked with dark purple blood. He tossed it aside. "I'm in goddamned shock. I can't see a goddamned thing, now. Fuck. Get me out of here. Drive me back to the hotel."

"Boss," Vinny said doubtfully, "You want to let this clown get away with this?" He looked at Mr. Manicotti.

"I didn't think he'd shoot," Vecchio grumbled. "I can't *believe* he shot me."

"I'm-a *old*," Mr. Manicotti said with a shrug.

"He's fuckin' *crazy*, is what he is," Joey said. "I'd shoot 'im, but I don't think he'd even *notice*."

"Don't do *nothin'*," Vecchio demanded, gesturing in Joey's direction. "You hear me? Nothin'."

"But *boss*—"

"But *nothin'*. You got wax in your ears, kid? Do what I said and don't talk back. Now, GET ME OUT OF HERE!"

"Here," Bobby said, lifting up Vecchio's feet. "Ey! Vinny! Joey! Little help!"

"*Easy!*" Vecchio shouted, groaning in pain. "Take it *easy!*"

Haltingly, they hoisted Vecchio up, his arms swinging back and forth. Vecchio's gun fell out of his pocket and hit the floor. Vinny and Bobby paused, shifting Vecchio this way and that, trying to get a free hand so they could pick up the gun without dropping their boss.

"Hey," Bobby said, looking at Mrs. Noonan, "Think you could... you know, grab that for me?"

Mrs. Noonan looked about to get up, but Mr. Manicotti put a hand on her shoulder, and shook his head. "You-a get it yourself. Leave her *alone.*"

"Anyways," Rashim said, "He got hit with a .22. It wasn't a gut shot or anything. This is *pathetic.*"

Joey swung his head around as they awkwardly retreated down the hall, leaving drops of blood along the way.

"You are *lucky,*" he hissed. "All'ya. I'd love to come back here with a fuckin' Uzi. I really would. Teach you a fuckin—"

"Hey, Joey, watch out for the door," Bobby was saying. "*Watch* it, I said."

After much stomping and grunting, the screen door slapped shut. Clomp clomp clomp down the front steps. The car door slammed. A moment later Bobby came running back in and grabbed Vecchio's Glock off of the floor. He looked at Manicotti, and smiled despite himself.

"I ain't ever seen anything like that before. You got *balls*; I'll give you that. Either *balls* the size a' fuckin' watermelons, or you're just plain senile." He shook his head. "Shit. All we wanted to *do* was *talk.*"

Mr. Manicotti didn't say a word to him. He motioned to the door with his chromed pistol.

Bobby chuckled uneasily, put Vecchio's pistol into his side pocket, and walked out as casually as he could.

Tom, Rashim, and Mrs. Noonan all looked at Mr. Manicotti, who put away his .22 and lit another Pall Mall.

"Now *there*," Tom said at last, "Is something you don't see every day."

"It's-a mess in here," Mr. Manicotti observed, motioning at the vomit and dark pools of blood. "Some-a-body ought to clean it up."

"Who would have *thought*," Rashim said, still wide eyed with disbelief.

Mr. Manicotti let the smoke trail out of his nose. He shrugged, and smiled at Mrs. Noonan. "I don't-a like boys with *guns.* "

In the Cadillac they'd put down some plastic on the back seat so that Vecchio wouldn't bleed all over the leather; he was holding another dishrag to his leg, and that one was almost soaked through also.

"How you feelin', boss?" Vinny asked from the front seat.

"How you *think* I feel, jackass?" Vecchio groaned. "Like I got shot in the leg, that's how I feel. Somebody get Masters on the phone. *Now.*"

Bobby pulled out his cell phone, dialed the number, and handed it back. After two rings, Victor Masters picked up.

"Yes?" he asked on the other end.

"Masters," Vecchio breathed into the phone, "I got *shot* in the *fucking* leg."

A brief silence.

"*What?* Where?"

"At the House on the Bend."

"They *shot* you? Who was it? Who?"

"Some *old* guy. *Ancient.* He pulled a .22 and nailed me in the leg."

"Are you okay?"

"Why do people keep *asking* me that? No! I'm not! It hurts like a bitch! I'm going back to my hotel. Send over a doctor."

"Go to Lewiston General," Masters said. "It could get infected."

"I ain't going to Lewiston General," Vecchio said. "You crazy? You want them askin' all kindsa questions?"

"Just tell them what happened!"

"And *then* what? Explain what the fuck I'm doin' over there? Explain why me and my boys were waving guns in their faces in the first place?"

"Well, that *was* a stupid thing to do, don't you think?"

"*Look,*" Vecchio said, coughing. "Just get the doctor over to our hotel. Okay? Stop trying to give me advice. *I* give the advice, not you."

"Right, Jimmy. *You* give the advice." Masters paused for a moment. "So... I guess this means that you didn't get them to sell."

"That Shumak broad wasn't even there," Vecchio said. "Look, this is totally fucked up now. Mr. Bertolucci told me, *no undue attention.* You understand what that means?"

"I do have some idea what that means, yes," Masters said.

"It means that we already got the Feds on us like flies on shit. It means that if I bring any more heat on the family, Bertolucci'll have my fuckin' *head* on a platter." He sighed, and cleared his throat. "We're done with this. You figure it out *somehow.* We can't be involved like this no more. Not without the whole thing blowing up. And then what? No casino, no money for nobody."

"You're preaching to the choir, Vecchio," Masters said. "Look, I said it from day one. We don't need you guys blundering around. I'll handle it. They'll run out of money soon, and when they can't afford to bring the place up to code, I'll swipe the place out from under them. It's only a matter of time. By spring, it'll be all over."

"Right."

"*Patience,* Vecchio. Patience is a virtue."

"Just get it done, Masters."

"Oh, it'll get done. Listen, I'll send over that surgeon. After you're patched up, just take your boss' advice. Leave it to me.

"I'll *get* that house."

45

"Okay! We're back in twenty!"

Mary sat next to Abby. They'd said almost nothing to one another this morning, but now Mary took Abby's hand and squeezed it. Bert watched that with envy, as he sat at the end of the row, by himself. Alan looked especially mole-like under the lights, still dressed in his blue windbreaker. Claude, appearing miniature, stood by him. Bert could imagine himself down there, basking in the attentions of the studio audience, this peak moment of fame; and what was Claude doing in his place? *Nothing.*

Bert glanced back at Mary, then at Abby, and caught her eye. She smiled briefly, and then squeezed Mary's hand. Mary's face was tight, her body rigid. Her eyes grew large as the cameras swung around and the intro music blasted.

"3...2..."

"And here's our host, Tad! LANGLEY!"

Tad jogged out onstage to wild applause. Midway he stopped and raised his hands over his head.

"Thank you, and welcome back! In our round robin event, we narrowed the field of competition to one team: Claude Perrywether and Alan Berman, from Lewiston, PA!" Tad strolled to their podium and leaned on it, thrusting his mic into Alan's face.

"How does it feel to have a chance at the title, Alan?"

Alan blinked at Tad, then at the audience.

"It's a little hot."

"Hot?"

"Yes. Under the lights. Or maybe I'm just nervous. I dunno."

The studio laughed.

"Ever been on TV before Alan?" Tad asked.

"Once," he said. "There was a shooting at the housing project where I used to live and I was on the news."

Tad wrinkled his eyebrows and a police siren sounded.

"You didn't have a chance to win 50,000 dollars on the 6:00 news, did you?" Tad asked with a sly wink.

"No, Tad," Alan said with irritation.

"And what about your buddy here? How do you know him? "

Alan hesitated. "He lives in my building. He likes sweeping."

Claude smiled.

"I noticed you've answered most of the questions—in fact, you've answered *all* of them, Alan. Is Claude your good luck charm?"

"No."

Tad licked his lips, and glanced at the audience.

"So...what's your favorite show?" Tad asked. "Claude, feel free to jump right in if you like."

"Claude doesn't really watch TV," Alan explained. "And I don't have a favorite show."

"You *don't?*"

"Well... I *do*, but I like so many, and if I said my favorite out loud... well, it wouldn't be fair to the other shows."

The audience burst into unprompted laughter at that.

"Wow. That's an interesting... philosophy," Tad said with a cheesy grin.

Alan looked annoyed. "What's *your* favorite, Tad?"

"*My* favorite?"

"Fair's fair. You ask me, I ask you."

"Fair's fair, right folks?" Tad asked the audience. "That's an easy one, Alan: my all time favorite is Married with Children."

Tad held the mic to Alan, expecting a response, but Alan just stared ahead blankly.

"Okaaay! Let's hear it for Alan Berman and Silent Claude!"

The audience clapped to the tune of "Love and Marriage" as Tad crossed the stage over to the Marley brothers.

"And in this corner, we've got our three month champions, Mick and Nick Marley, from Cincinnati, Ohio! Mick and Nick have had the longest winning streak in TV Wonderland history! Are you pumped, Mick and Nick?"

"We are *pumped*, Tad," "Nick said into the proffered mic. "We are ready to conquer all."

"Looks like some stiff competition you've got from the Lewiston boys."

"We're not concerned," Mick said. "We're steamrollers, Tad. Better clear out or get flattened."

The Marleys gave each other high fives.

"Fair's fair," Tad said. "What's your favorite show, boys?"

"The Shield," said Mick.

"Growing Pains," said Nick.

"Very diverse," Tad observed.

"The yin and the yang of television, Tad," Nick said, pointing at Alan and pantomiming a gun. "Two halves of an unstoppable, TV Trivia *machine.*"

"*Yeah,*" Mick shouted.

Nick: "Prepare yourself for the agony of defeat."

Mick: "Resistance… is futile."

Alan loudly cleared his throat.

Bert rubbed his eyes and leaned in to Mary.

"He's a real charmer, isn't he?" he whispered. "Bet *now* you wish I was up there."

"Charm doesn't win the game," Mary said as Tad, to a roar of cheers and applause, retreated to his master podium, the TV Wonderland theme blared, and the lights dimmed.

The big screen came on, displaying the rows of decades, ordered by hundreds of dollars.

"By popular demand!" Tad cried. "Let's get this show on the road! Mick and Nick, as the reigning champions, round one starts with you!"

"Round One," declared a deep, booming voice, followed by a dazzling explosion of laser light.

"80s for 200, Tad," said Mick.

The question appeared in giant letters.

"What is the name of the organization that MacGyver worked for?" Tad declared.

Alan leaned forward and said something unintelligible into his microphone.

The Marley podium lit up.

"The Phoenix foundation," Nick said, biting his lip and nodding at Mick in triumph.

"That is *correct!*" Tad said as two hundred dollars appeared on the Marley's podium screen. "The champions open strong!"

"70s for 400," Mick said.

With a beep the question appeared.

"Name both spin-offs from MASH," Tad announced.

Again Alan said something into his mic that did not register.

Nick hit the buzzer and said, "After MASH and Trapper John, MD."

Mary grabbed Bert's arm.

"What's happening?"

"He's not hitting the buzzer," Bert groaned, slapping his forehead. "Good God." He stood up, and shouted at the top of his lungs, "HIT YOUR BUZZER, ALAN!" Paul D'Amato made a horrible face at him and ran a finger against his throat. Alan's face brightened with comprehension.

"Just to clarify," Tad Langley said, "In order to answer, contestants need to punch the big red button on their podiums *first*."

The studio laughed and Alan blushed fiercely. He shot an angry look at the Marleys as they folded their arms across their chests. Mick cleared his throat.

"This Decade for 300," he said.

The question appeared.

"On 'Malcolm in the Middle,' what is Malcolm's IQ?"

BEEP. BEEP. BEEP. BEEEP.

"One sixty-five," Alan said hotly.

"That is correct, Mr. Berman," Tad cried. "But pressing your button once *is* sufficient."

600 to 300, and Alan now had the ball.

"90s for 300," Alan said.

"In the 1991 season of Knot's Landing," Tad narrated, "Who played young Debbie—"

BEEP!

"—Porter?"

"Halle Berry," Alan said.

"Correct," Tad declared. "Look at this, folks, the challengers from Lewiston are now *tied* with the Marley boys! Oh, the suspense!"

Psycho violin shrieks.

The Marleys looked at each other with a flicker of concern.

"90s for 400, Tad," Alan said impatiently.

The question appeared.

"On Homicide: Life on the Street, how many times was Detective John Munch Married?"

The Marley buzzer sounded.

"*Three* times, Tad," Mick said.

The Marleys climbed back into the lead.

"60's for 300."

"What was the name–

BEEP!

"—of the—"

"BEEP!

"—OF THE Robinson's spaceship on Lost in Space? And please, Mr. Berman, wait until I have finished *reading* the question."

"Fine, fine," Alan said. "The *answer* is the Jupiter II."

"Right you are, for a total of nine hundred dollars!"

In the stands, Bert started biting his nails. The Marleys were actually giving Alan a run for his money; not surprising, since there were two of them and only one of him.

"Name the two actors who played Lionel on 'The Jeffersons,'" Tad read.

"Mike Evans," Mick said.

"Damon Evans," Nick added.

A cheerful beep took the Marleys into a five hundred dollar lead. Mick looked over at Alan and smirked. "80s for *Five Hundred*, Tad."

"Breaking out the heavy firepower," Tad narrated, "The Marleys seem intent on widening their lead. Here we go! On the sitcom 'The Golden Girls,' what town did Rose Nyland hail from?"

BEEP.

"St. Olaf, Minnesota," said Alan. There were complimentary murmurs from the audience. Alan smirked back at Mick as their scores tied again.

"60s for 300," he said.

"On Gilligan's Island, what was Mary Anne's last name?"

"Summers," Alan answered immediately. "Give me 70s for 400."

"What was the name of the receptionist at the Blue Moon Detective Agecny?"

Mick and Nick were whispering frantically. Alan considered it for a moment, and hit his buzzer.

"Agnes Dipesto."

"*Absolutely* correct!" Tad shouted. "Mr. Berman's lead is *growing!*"

"70s for 300," Alan belted out. He glanced over at the Marleys, who were glistening with sweat, their fingers on their buttons.

"Which 1973 TV movie introduced everyone's favorite bald detective, Kojak?" Tad narrated.

The Marley buzzer sounded instantly.

Nick fumbled.

"Is it... uh... um..."

"Out of time!" Tad cried as an explosion sound effect brought the Marleys crashing down by 300.

"Alan Berman, do you care to answer?"

"Yes, Tad," Alan said easily, "The answer is The Marcus-Nelson Murders."

Alan's score jumped to 2100. The audience applauded fiercely. Mary was hopping in her seat, her hands fluttering in the air. Mick was shouting at Nick for punching their buzzer without knowing the answer; Nick, his face bunching up, started to cry.

The studio burst out laughing.

"60s for 500!" Alan shouted over the commotion.

The question appeared on the screen overhead and Tad whistled.

"What was the name of Vito Scotti's character on the Flying Nun?"

Silence from both teams. Mick's forehead contracted until it looked like it would break; Nick looked hopeless. Alan pursed his lips and shook his head. Suddenly, with a nod, he yelled, "Police Captain Gaspar Formento!"

"Yes, that is *correct!*"

Mick bared his teeth like a vicious dog and screamed, "What the *hell!*"

Next: 80s for five hundred.

"Another tough one, boys! On Miami Vice, what was the name of Crockett's pet alligator?"

Alan punched his buzzer.

"*Easy* one, Tad. The alligator was named *Elvis.*"

"Impossible!" Mick shouted furiously. "This is completely unfair, a total—"

"60s for 500," Alan said over Mick.

"On Mister Ed, who did the voice of Mister Ed?"

"Allen Lane," said Alan. "Do you have anything for *six* hundred?"

"This kid is on fire!" Tad cried to the audience.

D'Amato pointed at the flashing teleprompters which blinked ALAN. He pumped his fist in the air. The audience began to chant his name. Mick, his mic cut and his voice drowned out, slapped his crying brother on the back of the head and screamed until his face was red.

Alan pounded his fist on the podium.

"Quiet, please!" he demanded, flushed with pleasure, his name ringing in his ears. "90s for 200."

The questions rolled as fast as Alan could ask for them.

Tad: "What was the name of the short-lived spin-off of Melrose Place?"

Alan: "Models Inc."

Tad: On Magnum, PI, what was Higgins's middle name?"

Alan: "Quayle."

Tad: "In which city did Ted Baxter claim to have gotten his start in broadcasting?"

Alan: "Fresno."

Tad: "In early episodes of Happy Days, Ritchie Cunningham had an older brother. What was his name?"

Alan: "Chuck."

The crowd was on their feet as Alan's score soared from 3000, to 5000, to 8000 dollars. A new board of questions appeared to replace the one he'd answered too quickly. The Marleys were in a disarray. Nick was flustered and had locked up like an overheated engine; Mick knew half the answers but was weak on certain genres. Every time Nick missed, Mick got angrier. Nick slumped down behind the podium while Mick, his neck popping with veins and tendons, punched his console with an angry fist each time Alan answered before he could, and then browbeat his melted-down brother.

The second board dwindled. They were down to the last question: 50s for 500.

"In the 1980, Stacey Keach starred as Mike Hammer: Private Eye. Who starred in the 1950s version?"

Alan grinned at Mick and hit his buzzer.

"Darren McGavin, Tad."

"Alan, that is correct!" Tad shouted. Alan's total hit 14,000. A montage of cathedral bells, sirens, and whistling fireworks filled the studio. "Alan Berman, you are now the single highest winning contestant in this show's history!"

Mary and Vera were jumping up and down in place; Bert grabbed Abby and kissed her on the lips. Ned pumped his fist in the air. The studio was shaking with the convulsions of the studio audience.

"Alan Berman!" Tad said as the big screen flashed off and Tad jogged to Alan's podium. He grabbed Alan's wrist and thrust it in the air. "You are our WINNER!"

Fifty thousand dollars jumped onto Alan's screen.

The new total: $64,000.

Mick broke away from his podium with a rabid yell and made for Alan's podium at full speed. Security leapt out from behind the cameras and knocked him down halfway there in a tangle of arms and legs. Two others came out from behind the curtains and hauled sobbing, broken Nick Marley to his feet.

As they wrestled him, Mick was cursing Alan in every way he could think of, but Alan had gone glassy eyed, staring at Claude, then Tad, then the audience, which was in an uproar: for *him*.

Tad was saying something.

Despite the roar in his ears, Alan tried to tune in.

"...in honor of this special day and these *very* special contestants we have an incredible, one time opportunity! Mr. Berman, Mr. Perryweather, you have done well today. You've won a king's ransom *and* the fifty thousand dollar jackpot. But *now* we are offering you a last, *daring* choice: keep your money and walk—or bet it *all, double or nothing*, on one final question: Category, 60's TV shows!"

The audience gasped.

DOUBLE OR NOTHING appeared on the big screen.

Bert, Mary, and Vera were on their feet, waving frantically at Alan, mouthing "No" as expressively as they could. Mary swiped her arms back and forth like a ref; Bert held out his hands flat like he was trying to stop a speeding truck.

Alan didn't see them. The blood was thick in his head. The crowd was screaming his name.

"I'll go for it, Tad!" he cried with a crazy glare at the host. "Double or nothing!"

The audience went wilder still.

Tad jogged back to center stage.

"You heard the man, ladies and gentlemen! Stay tuned: we'll be right back with the $128,000 question, right after these messages!"

46

Paul D'Amato swung his arm.

"And CUT!"

As soon as the lights came up, Mary, Bert and the others burst out of the stands and joined Alan and Claude at their podium. Alan waved off security and beamed at Mary and Bert.

"See? I *did* it! I really *did* it!" he cried breathlessly.

"You did," Mary said with tears in her voice. "But *why* did you have to go for the double or nothing, Alan? You just made $64,000! *More* than what we needed!"

"What are you now," Bert complained, "Some kinda big-time gambler?" He shook his head sadly. "Like I'm *always* telling you, quit while you're ahead."

Alan didn't seem to be listening. He had a sip of water, and looked at Ned.

"I was great! Wasn't I, Mr. Johnson? Wasn't I great?"

"Yeah, Alan. You were really great."

"Four minutes!" D'Amato shouted.

"I just hope they don't ask you something you don't know," Vera said. "I mean, double or nothin', they ain't gonna ask you no powder puff question. They gonna come up with the meanest, nastiest, *hardest* question they can—"

"Vera, come on now," Ned said, peering back at the audience. "Don't load the kid up with all kind of negativity, now."

"I'm just sayin', theys gonna try'an win *back* all that money, any way they can."

"*Yes*, Vera, we understand that," Bert said.

Ned looked back at the audience again.

"Wow," he said. "It's real scary up here. All them folks out there…"

"*Three minutes*," D'Amato cried.

"I'm not worried, Mr. Wodehouse," Alan said. "There's nothing I can't answer. Unless they ask me about The Biggest Loser, which I refused to watch out of principle."

"Which they can't," Mary said. "Because the topic is TV shows of the 60s."

"Exactly," Bert said.

"Right. Quit while you're ahead?" Alan snorted. "That's for *losers*, Mr. Wodehouse. Do I look like a loser to you?"

"Right now, Alan?" Bert flashed a messy smile, and patted Alan on the arm. "Definitely *not*." He jabbed Mary in the ribs. "Aren't you glad *I* came up with this idea, Mary? Aren't you?"

"When we've got the money, I'll be glad," Mary said.

"Let's just let Alan have his moment," Abby suggested quietly. "How 'bout it?"

"Two minutes! All extras, clear the set!"

From behind the curtains, near Alan's podium, came a dry scuffling sound, grunts, heels squeaking on the polished floor, and suddenly the curtain was flung open as Mick Marley sprung out, his shirt torn and security right behind him.

"You!" he screamed, pointing a finger at Alan as a bald security man leapt out and wrestled him into a headlock.

"The whole thing is rigged!" Mick shrieked to the audience, who looked on aghast, unsure whether to laugh or recoil in horror. "They wanted me off the show! They can't handle a big winner!"

"Come on!" security growled, trying to pull him off the stage. Mick stamped on Security's foot, and wriggled out of his grip. The audience gasped.

"I mean, how can somebody get *every* question right?" Mick cried imploringly to the studio. He spun around and pointed an accusatory finger at Alan. "You *cheated*! A dirty rotten—"

Two security men grabbed hold of him this time and carried him back to the curtains.

"You hear me, *Berman?*" Mick shrieked. "I'm onto you! You're a cheater! A no good, rotten, lying, cheating— I'm gonna *kill* ya!"

And he was gone.

Alan was beet red.

Paul D'Amato sprinted up.

"I'm really sorry about that," he said. "*Really*. You okay? Great. Fantastic. What a kid. Let's do this, people! Two minutes, and *please*, people, let's clear the stage!" He gently tugged on Abby's arm and then ran back to his control area.

Alan folded his arms across his chest, and stared off into space.

Mary noticed it at once.

"Uh, Alan? *Alan?*"

"I'm not continuing," Alan said in a small voice, "Until he *apologizes.*"

"Alan," Bert said with a nervous laugh. "You're joking, right?"

"I am *not* joking," Alan said bitterly. "This is the one thing I do well. I did not cheat. I did not lie. I *earned* it. *Me*. It was all *me*."

"We know that," Mary said desperately. "We're all *so* proud of you."

"*They* don't know that," Alan said, jerking his head towards the audience.

"*One minute!* Off the set! NOW!"

"And until he apologizes, I'm not saying another *word*." Alan nodded affirmatively, and pressed his lips together.

"*Alan*," Bert moaned. "He *ain't* gonna apologize! He *wants* you to lose!"

"Alan, *think* about it—" Mary cried.

"Please, baby, don't be a fool—" Vera shouted.

"You can't listen to that guy, kiddo—" Ned lamented.

"Do this for *us*, Alan—" Bert begged.

Their voices ran together into a loud tangle. Alan looked up at the lights in the rafters and shook his head.

Two production assistants appeared next to the podium.

"Guys," said Jenny the assistant, "We're rolling in thirty seconds. We need you to take your seats."

"But—but—" Mary stammered.

"*Now*."

They were pushed back towards their seats as the lights in the audience went down, the TV Wonderland theme blasted, and the applause signs lit up.

"3—2—1—and here we go!"

Paul D'Amato ran back and forth like a clown, throwing his arms in the air to stir up a riot of excitement, as Tad Langley appeared on stage and the laser show kicked off. He jogged to Alan's podium, and with a cheesy grin, he raised the microphone to his lips.

"This is the moment we've all been waiting for, folks. Alan Berman, you've chosen to bet your *entire* winnings—sixty-four *thousand* dollars—on one final question." The audience burst into applause. Tad nodded and held up a hand for quiet. "I would like to say, speaking not only for myself, but also for the studio audience and folks back home, that we *certainly* admire your courage…"

Alan continued to stare up at an indefinite point in the rafters. Claude gazed blankly at Tad. There was a booming and a thundering from the audience.

A drum roll sounded.

The lights dropped low, save for the spotlights over Alan's podium, and Tad's and the glare of the big screen.

Mary covered her mouth.

"Okay! For *all* the money, here goes!" Tad cried. "The category is 60's, double or nothing. You'll have thirty seconds to respond."

A hush fell over the studio audience.

The crash of a cymbal and the question appeared overhead.

"On the Andy Griffith Show, Aunt Bee's best friend was Miss Clara Edwards," Tad intoned. "What *contest* did Miss Clara Edwards win at the County fair for *twelve* years in a row?"

A deep boom resonated in the studio.

Tad breathed into his microphone, low and raspy, "You have thirty seconds."

The TV Wonderland "tune of decision" began, low and tinkling, just beginning to build, as a big clock on the screen ticked off the seconds.

Expectantly, Tad held out his microphone to Alan.

At that moment, the host noticed that Alan was not looking at the question board.

Or at him.

His lips were still pressed tightly together.

"Twenty-five seconds," a computerized voice announced

"Oh my God," Mary moaned, burying her face in her hands.

Tad looked at Claude, then at Alan.

"Twenty seconds, Mr. Berman. We need an answer. *Please.* Anything."

Claude began to fidget, his eyes darting around wildly, at Tad, at the audience, at Alan, at the clock, the agony of all that tension pressing at his head like a vise.

Fifteen seconds.

"Please," Tad begged, sweat trickling down his forehead. This was not the ending he had hoped for. "Say anything. You're gonna lose *everything.*"

He swung the mic back and forth, between Claude and Alan, as the ticking from the clock grew louder still.

The computer voice read off the final seconds.

"Ten."

"Nine."

"You've *got* to be *kidding* me," Bert whispered.

"Seven."

"Six."

"Oh *God,* Alan, *please,*" Mary moaned quietly. She was starting to feel faint.

"Four."

"Three."

Bert jumped out of his seat, and in the deadened studio, shouted "Say *anything*! Dammit!"

So he said it.

They were the only three words he could say.

The only three words he had *ever* said.

Try as he might, he couldn't help himself.

"THAT'S A PICKLE!" Claude blurted out, clapping his hands over his mouth a moment too late.

The clock stopped at *one*.

The studio was silent as a tomb.

Tad raised his eyebrows and looked to the prompter.

It read CORRECT.

Reaching across the podium, Tad grabbed Claude's wrist and thrust it in the air.

"Thaaat's *right*!" Tad cried at the top of his lungs. "You are *ab*solutely correct! Miss Clara Edwards repeatedly won a *pickle* contest!"

The house lights came up and the audience was on their feet screaming as Claude sweated and looked at the podium, Alan continued to stare at the ceiling, and $128,000 flashed on the podium's display board and on the overhead screen.

Mary had just dramatically fainted and her face was planted against the seat ahead of her. Abby and Bert hauled her back into the fourth row and sat her on the floor.

"Give her air! Give her space!" Bert shouted.

Mary moaned and rubbed her face, blood rising in the line where she'd cut it on the chair.

"Oh my God... what *happened?*"

"We won, we *won*!" Bert cried. "*Claude* saved the day!"

"*Claude?*" Mary asked.

"Yeah, Claude. That's why I brought him." Bert grinned and puffed out his chest. "Damn, I'm a genius!"

"You did it," she mumbled to Bert, tears in her eyes. "You really came through." Staggering to her feet, she looked at Bert, then at Abby, and threw her arms around both of them. Vera and Ned, not to be left out, joined on from the outside.

"Yeah, I know," Bert said with a messy grin, planting a kiss on Abby's forehead. "I guess this would be a good time for 'I told you so'?"

Tad Langley was in the middle of the stage, doing a lively jig. When the noise had died down a bit, he raised up his microphone.

"What a show, folks! History has been made here on TV Wonderland's 25th Anniversary! Thanks again for a *fantastic* 25 years, and here's to another stupendous quarter century! Thank you, and *good night!*"

47

In the days that followed the game show win on TV Wonderland, there began a series of phone calls that set off a domino effect of sorts. First, Mary called Rupert P. Burmeister to tell him about the win and the influx of money. Burmeister in turn called Victor Masters' lawyer, to tell him in no uncertain terms that the work would be done on time. Masters could see the writing was on the wall. After a few minutes of dark contemplation, he placed two calls: one, to Jim Primanti, to tell him that they were going to need to quickly shift to plan B; the second, to his PR advisor. He wanted to call a press conference *immediately*, to head off any speculation or bad press thrown up by the crafty Shumak woman. He'd barely contained the last piece in the Post-Gazette, and he could only imagine what she'd be capable of now that she was on her feet again, no doubt with vengeance on her mind.

Masters knew that with Mary Shumak's sudden fortune, the repairs on the house would be done right away. Not to mention: he'd already seen Alan Berman on the six o'clock news, with Claude and Mary, arm in arm. This Alan Berman was suddenly a minor national sensation and would no doubt become a major local sensation. After Vecchio's screw up, and Abby Lindeman's article already threatening to blow the situation wide open, he couldn't afford any more bad press. Mary Shumak and company were now celebrities of a sort. It would be difficult to play hardball with celebrities, no matter how minor league they were. That could only mean one thing.

Pirate's Clipper was moving.

What he hadn't mentioned to anyone was that he had a second option that Master Developments had drawn up, a smaller, more modest version of the Clipper that could be floated at another bend in the river, slightly downstream from the House on the Bend. This development would be farther away from Lewiston and smaller in scale, but it was better than nothing. The PR packet would have to be modified but not substantially. It was a blow, but it could be managed—if it was handled *at once*.

Of course, Victor mused as he gazed out his window and squeezed a rubber stress ball, he couldn't let Mary Shumak get away with this.

No way. She'd cost time, money, and reputation. And what's more, she'd *won*.

Correction, he thought with a grim smile: she'd won the *battle*.

Let her have her moment.

But.

This is *war*.

After getting back to Lewiston, one of the first things Mary did was to go down to Best Buy and choose out the biggest flat screen high definition plasma TV, and a digital cable service that would bring over six hundred channels into the house. The Best Buy delivery men brought it early the next morning while

Alan was eating breakfast and carried it up the stairs, amid the screaming of buzz saws and stomping of construction workers, to his room. They mounted it on the wall, hooked up the cable box beneath, and then the amp and surround sound system, with two column speakers on either side of the TV and small ones hung on brackets all the way around the room.

When Alan came upstairs to see what all the commotion was about, he looked shocked and horrified at first to see all these invaders in his room, tromping around in such close proximity to his files. But once he saw just what it was they were doing, he realized what this meant: it was the dawning of a new era of TV watching. No one would ever be able to take the remote from him again.

Alan moved his bed off to the side, by the window, and pushed his filing cabinets towards the closet. In the cleared floor space he put his new leather La-Z-Boy, shipped direct from the showroom on Monroe Avenue in Lewiston. It was plush and overstuffed, sheathed in soft calf-skin, and smelled lush and new, the smell of wealth. After that he could close the door, shut the blinds, and turn on his system; and lo and behold, Charles in Charge or Lost in Space would appear wall-sized, crisper and cleaner than he'd ever imagined it could look, the air throbbing with 500 megahertz of THX-quality sound. It was as if he'd never really watched TV before; the first hour or two with his new system and he just stared, slack jawed, at this world that had been there all the while without his knowing. Then he settled in, kicked back, and set his yellow notepad on his extra-wide armrest. To be perfectly honest, he was too distracted and too awed, to take many notes that first day.

The new TV, the massive construction being done on the house, the new paint, all of it: everyone knew it was thanks, in the end, to Claude. Yet if Claude understood that he'd done anything special, he certainly didn't show it. When they'd run up to him after the game show win and hugged him, he just stared at them benignly; he'd looked distractedly out the window of the Suburban on the ride home; and on arriving back at the House on the Bend he ambled inside, went straight to the front hall closet, and grabbed his broom. With all the contractors stomping to and fro, the place was a mess.

There was sweeping to do.

Mary wanted, more than anything, to somehow thank Claude. He'd done nothing more than get worked up and yell his old tagline at a very fortuitous moment—she realized that as well as anyone. Still, it seemed only appropriate to reward him in some way for being the bit of blind luck they'd been missing all along. Yet if Claude was their angel of mercy, their lucky turn of the wheel, Mary knew nothing about his likes or preferences. He had no favorite food, no favorite animal, no favorite color. Claude had no preferences at all. It was impossible to prepare a feast in his honor, when Brussels sprouts were eaten with the same air of distraction as pizza or roast duck. Claude did not collect anything, enjoy anything, or want anything. He accepted what he was given, and did not ask for more. If there was no one to feed him, Mary was sure, he would uncomplainingly waste away to nothing.

How to reward the man who wants nothing?

Was he aware that he had saved the day?

If he were aware, did he care?

It was perhaps merely symbolic, but Mary went ahead and bought Claude a new broom. The old broom was a pink plastic thing with plastic bristles that collected dirt in fuzzy strings by the action of static cling; the new broom had a lacquered wood handle and straw bristles, handcrafted by the Pennsylvania Dutch of Livingston County. At night, after Claude had retired she quietly opened the front hall closet door and put the new broom next to the old one.

She hoped he would understand what she meant.

*

After their dramatic win on TV Wonderland, Alan and Claude were told by the producers that, since they'd been the victors, they were expected to return the next week for the following episode. In the intervening week the show would pay for their hotel and given them a food stipend; not that it was so much of a problem to afford a week of hotel bills when they'd just won over $100,000 in cash.

"No," Alan said.

"No *what?*" asked Paul D'Amato, crowded all around by assistant producers and reporters.

"No, I don't want to play any more," Alan said, blinking in the harsh lights. "No. I don't want to come back."

D'Amato couldn't seem to understand this.

"But…" he mumbled, "But you're our *champion.*"

"Somebody else can be your champion next week. I'm *retiring.*"

This immediately set off a media storm. After all, no one had even heard of Alan Berman before, or Claude Perryweather. Alan had answered nearly every question put to him instantly and correctly, except for the last one, which, for what—a sense of theatrics?—he'd reserved for his silent partner. He'd risen from nowhere, broken records and stolen hearts, and now *wanted to retire.* Nothing whets the public's appetite like somebody who quits while he's ahead. To simply *bow out* when the sky was the limit—when the show's questions were as playthings to him—was unconscionable. Alan Berman had just become the latest in a line of celebrity quit-while-you're-aheader's.

"Well, what are you going to do with all that money?" a reporter asked.

"I'm going to watch TV," Alan said, with a shrug, causing a storm of laughter. "Just like before."

For the weeks afterwards the headlines ran "Who IS Alan Berman?" and "The Bobby Fischer of TV Wonderland!" and "Was it Rigged? Mick Marley Speaks," but nobody had the whole story—the *real* story—because Alan refused to do interviews. Only after much prompting by Mary was Alan persuaded to allow Abby an exclusive, which she got. Front page of the Sunday Arts & Entertainment section read: *Alan Berman: Portrait of a Genius.*

Alan got his fifteen minutes of fame; Abby rode that to hers. In the new article, she tied Alan and Claude's win to the David and Goliath-style fight to save the Shumak boarding house. The new angle worked—the public loved it. Letters and e-mails poured in, from lawyers offering their assistance to TV producers hoping to make a prime time special about the whole, bizarre drama. Abby Lindeman was suddenly fielding dozens of important calls a day.

Bert Wodehouse was not happy.

"I mean, it was *my* idea," he told anybody who would listen. "He'd've never gone on there unless I convinced him to. *Never.* It was all me, I tell ya'. Taught the kid everything he knows. Believe you *me.* The *real* brains behind the operation? That's right. Yours truly."

But try as he might to insinuate himself into the situation, the best he could manage was to be quoted as a close friend of Alan Berman. Credit was not given. Quotes regarding his true involvement invariably did not make it into the news. He had actually managed to pull off a scheme, at long last—but where were the bragging rights?

"I should be glad that I did something nice," Bert told himself. "I wanted to help Mary, and I've done that. That should be reward enough."

It wasn't enough, of course. Sure, Alan had been generous enough to give Bert ten thousand dollars of the winnings, but it wasn't about the money. Bert wanted to see his name in lights; he wanted to be on the 6 o'clock news, on the front page of the newspaper, on the Yahoo! News headlines. Bert had never craved riches, or power, or material things. But he *had* always wanted fame. He wanted people to say: there goes Bert Wodehouse, the slickest operator there is.

Well, not today.

At the end of that day in Pittsburgh, Mary pulled him aside at the Italian restaurant where they went to celebrate.

"Bert, " she said. "I do want to thank you."

Bert smirked at her.

"*And?*" he said.

"And what?"

"And aren't you going to apologize for yelling at me all those times?"

"For some of those things you needed to be yelled at," Mary said with a laugh. "But I *am* glad you never gave up."

"Well," Bert said, rubbing the back of his neck, "I figured something had to work—sooner or later. You don't get results unless you take risks. I take risks."

"*Yes,* you do."

"The ends seem to justify the means, wouldn't you say, sis?"

"You did good, I'll give you that," she said with a grin, and pulled Bert in for a hug.

As she wrapped her arms around him, Bert felt something well up inside.

No fame or fortune today.

But it was all right.

There are more important things in life.

48

That first night that they were back, after the kids were in bed, Mary drove over to Tom's with a six-pack of beer. They made fierce love while the beer chilled in the freezer—afterwards, Tom ventured out in his underwear into the kitchen, nodding sternly to Rashim, and brought the beer back, longnecks sticking out of a bucket of ice.

"To the future," Tom said as they toasted. He hoped she would see all that he meant when he said that.

"Yeah," Mary said distantly, having a sip of her beer. Tom sat on the bed and gathered her in next to him.

"What is it?" he asked, already sick of asking that but unsure of what else to say.

"I dunno," Mary sighed. "I just feel like... like I *failed*, Tom."

Tom laughed uneasily.

"Mary," he said, kissing her on the head. "You saved your house. Your kids can go to college. You *won.* I mean, I don't see how you failed. In *any* way."

"Alan and Claude saved the house, Tom," Mary said. "And it was Bert's idea in the first place. Abby helped them make the whole thing happen."

"Let's not forget about Mr. Manicotti," Tom reminded her. "He was amazing. Talk about brass balls."

"I told you," Mary said, rubbing her eyes, "I never want that... *incident* mentioned again. So whatever you do, *don't* tell anyone. I still can't believe that somebody actually got shot in my kitchen. If we're lucky, Mr. Manicotti and Mrs. Noonan will just... forget about the whole thing." She shook her head. "But seriously, Tom, how did I do anything? What part did I play? What did I do except sit on my hands and *worry*?"

Tom licked his lips.

"You did what you do best—you held everybody together."

"*Bert* held everybody together—behind my back," Mary breathed. "God, he makes me angry—but he never gave up."

"And neither did you."

"I was a lamb going to slaughter," she whispered. "I had no idea what to do. What was my best idea? Invite a reporter. Great. Abby was right. Waiting for somebody to save the day wasn't going to do anything. But that's what I did. I waited. And if it hadn't been for Bert and you and the others, Masters would already have my house." She pursed her lips. "No, Tom, I failed my family. I failed everybody. We saved the house, yes. But it was no thanks to me."

Tom started kissing her neck, but Mary pulled away.

"I've got to be more than just a mother and a cook, Tom. I need to be. I was once, and I want to be again."

Tom felt his eyes stinging.

"You *are*," he hissed. "You're amazing. Absolutely—"

"Tom, Tom, *please*," she said. She put a hand on his chest. "Okay?" She breathed deeply, and took a swig of her beer.

"I never want to be that powerless again. I won't allow it. *I won't.*"

Tom pulled away a bit, and propped his head up with his hand. He watched her, this beautiful stranger in his bed, stormy eyes staring at the architectural drawings on the wall.

"Mary," he said. "When can we tell people? About us?"

She looked at him, at his wounded face. She didn't want him to be wounded. She needed him to be a force of nature, something wild and strong as steel, ferocious and single-minded in his lust for her, like he'd been those searing first few weeks.

That's what she wanted. What she expected.

But instead, he'd turned out to be just a man.

"We'll take it one day at a time, okay?" she said, kissing him on the head.

She hoped he would understand what she meant.

49

Bert had money in his pocket, the House was safe, and Mary was happy. His feet were itching.

He'd saved the day.

Now it was time for an adventure.

He'd have stayed in Pittsburgh if only Abby had let him. But the night of the win, everybody checked into a hotel and Abby went home. There would be no midnight tryst, no romp in the early morning hours. At one o'clock, alone in his hotel room with Skinemax on TV, he dialed her up.

She got on the phone, her voice heavy with sleep.

"Bert, you realize what time it is, don't you?"

"Come to my hotel," he said. "I'll give you some more of what you like."

"I can't, Bert."

"Why *not?*"

"Because I *can't.*"

"You did before."

"And I shouldn't have. It was a terrible mistake."

"What's a terrible mistake," Bert said heatedly, "Is staying with that idiot Tim. I'm crazy about you. I love you. He doesn't care; he's a scumbag. Come on, it's as plain as day."

"Bert," she said. "I'm *sorry*. Really." She sighed. "I've got to go."

Bert blinked away the stinging in his eyes.

"You don't need to be sorry," he said. "I never felt like this before, not in my whole life. And don't say good bye, 'cause you'll be seeing me again. It's fate, baby. You can't run from it."

"In another life, Bert," Abby said sadly, her voice sounding hollow and deep, "it could have been something."

More than anything, Bert really just felt sad for her. Sad that she'd closed all the doors and windows of her life, sad that she'd accepted a black and white world when she could have full color. She'd accepted a world of possibilities in dreary miniature. That was the real tragedy of life, Bert thought: we come into the world so full of hope, and we lose that hope day by day, we shade in the bright open spaces and forget the expansiveness of a horizon that stretches on forever.

To stand at the edge of a boundless sea.

That's how life should feel.

Until his dying day, Bert promised himself, he'd be standing at the edge of that sea.

He would not give in.

He would not accept.

He would not say, "That's just how it is."

Never.

That last day at the House on the Bend, Bert stood on the porch after breakfast with Mr. Manicotti while the old Sicilian smoked, and watched the mist rise off the river in the autumn chill, the trees a riot of red, gold, and orange. He listened to the calls of the crows in the branches, troubadours of winter.

The work crews had not yet arrived for the day. Billy and Sarah had left for school.

He wrote Mary a note, left it on his bed in his room, and slung his duffel—packed the night before—over his shoulder. He'd packed pants, shorts, and swim trunks. He'd packed his Spanish phrasebook. Now he went to the bathroom and brushed his teeth; after a moment's hesitation, he slipped the toothbrush inside his bag and zipped it up.

There was no going back.

He stopped at Ned's room and knocked, pushing the door open a small ways.

"What's up?" Ned asked, sitting by the window and peering at the newspaper with difficulty.

"Where's Vera?"

Ned shrugged. "I ain't her keeper."

Bert looked out into the hall, and whispered,

"I'm heading out."

"Heading *where?*" Ned asked, putting down the paper.

Bert grinned at him gleefully. "I'm not sure yet."

Ned sat up, looking vexed.

"When are you coming back?"

"Don't know," Bert said. "But I'll be back—*someday*. I just wanted to say, catch you later, buddy."

"Oh, wow. Okay. You want a ride somewhere?"

"Nah. I'll take my bike. You know."

"Okay." Ned nodded a bit sadly. "It'll sure be lonely around here without you. You're just about my only friend, you know."

"I know," Bert said, with a wink. "But there's a world out there to be discovered, man. Can't sit around here all my life."

They shook hands and Bert went down the stairs and slipped out the side door. He ran across the dewy grass, to the carriage house, and pedaled out on his Schwinn. The tires crunched along the gravel drive, the duffel was slung over his shoulder. The House loomed behind, the world yawned open ahead.

Beyond lay Ankorage and Death Valley, the Amazon and Patagonia.

Beyond lay the open door of possibility.

The Ocean.

Life.